THE BOXING
BARONESS

Also by Minerva Spencer

Dangerous
Barbarous
Scandalous
Notorious
Outrageous
Infamous

And read more Minerva Spencer in

The Arrangement

THE BOXING BARONESS

MINERVA SPENCER

KENSINGTON
PUBLISHING CORP.

www.kensingtonbooks.com

This is for history's forgotten women

Acknowledgments

First and foremost, I'd like to give a giant thanks to Meg, who is the Women's, Gender & LGBTQ+ Studies Librarian at the Library of Congress. Thank you *so* much for the oodles of good stuff you sent me on the subject of women in warfare and munitions as well as primary research on women in traditionally male occupations, not to mention about a dozen other subjects!

Thanks so much to Alicia Condon, who lets me explore all the crazy ideas I come up with and is always so supportive.

A huge thanks to the Kensington art department for this fantastic cover. I love it!

Thanks also to Pam Hopkins for getting excited about my stories.

A great big thanks to George, who calmly talks me down whenever I write myself into a corner.

To Brantly, who still loves me even though I always go a bit crazy around deadline.

And my biggest thanks of all goes to *you,* dear reader. If this is the first book of mine you've opened, then welcome to my world! If you've read my stories before and have come back for more, then thank you, thank you, thank you!

Chapter 1

Whitechapel, London
Farnham's Fantastical Female Fayre
1815

The first punch in the one-two combination slammed into Marianne's stomach, quickly followed by an uppercut to the jaw that sent her staggering backward into the ropes.

Predictably, the bloodthirsty, all-male crowd went wild, their cheering and jeering reminding Marianne that she should be paying attention to the woman across from her, rather than gawking at a distracting stranger out in the crowd. She stumbled but recovered her footing, hastily bringing up her guard.

Unfortunately, finding her breath was not nearly so easy.

After boxing for two years, Marianne knew to ignore the all-too-familiar sensation of having the wind knocked from her lungs. But knowing it and doing it were two separate things. It took all the strength she possessed to remain upright and moving while her lungs fought to resume their natural rhythm. Her vision blurred and incipient hysteria, rather than air, expanded her chest.

Marianne shook the spangles from her head and struggled for breath again and again and again before a thin, miserly stream of air trickled into her lungs. It wasn't much, but it was enough to clear her vision in time to evade the poorly conceived cross from Lizzy Lowry's large—but generally sluggish—fist.

Marianne had never lost to Lizzy before, and that had made her complacent, which led to her lowering her guard—both literally and figuratively. And why would she do such a stupid thing?

To steal a glance at the startling sight of the Duke of Staunton standing in the front row of her uncle's theater.

The gorgeous but notoriously starchy peer stood out like a beacon amid the throng of screaming men, his very stillness setting him apart.

Not that his stillness was the only thing different about Staunton.

There was his height—he was taller than most of his fellows—and his shockingly pale ash-blond hair. He was garbed austerely in evening blacks but something had glittered when he'd crossed his arms over his chest. A ring, and the stone must be prodigious if Marianne could see the sparkle from such a distance. The ring was on the little finger of his left hand, which meant it was a signet, not a statement of fashion.

Although it was the glimmering stone that had caught her eye, it was his intense gaze that had seized her attention as masterfully as a highwayman commandeering a carriage. The cold, almost aggressive set of his handsome features stripped her bare, and not in the same way the other men in the crowd were doing.

Jack's voice rang in her head: *Take yer mind in 'and or you'll be facedown on the floor.*

The sound advice came none too soon as Lizzy threw a flailing roundhouse. It was a poor decision and one she was notorious for making when she began to lose her wind. Marianne dodged the graceless punch, came up under Lizzy's sloppy guard and delivered a proper muzzler that sent Lizzy flailing backward, her stout torso slamming against the thick ropes before sliding bonelessly to the floor.

Lizzy's knee man—who was also her husband and trainer—rushed to her aid, but the other woman wasn't getting up again anytime soon.

Marianne's uncle Barnabas, the proprietor of Farnham's Fantastical Female Fayre, climbed over the velvet ropes, grabbed her wrist, and raised her arm in victory. The screaming crowd sounded less like men and more like the mad cacophony of gulls down at the London docks.

When Marianne glanced toward the spot where the stern-faced peer had been standing—front and center in what used to be the theater pit—the Duke of Staunton was gone.

Backstage was hectic as men and women scurried to change the props for the next act, and it took a few minutes for her to push through the crush of bodies and get to the dressing room.

Cecile Tremblay, who was up next, was the only other person in the cramped, cluttered dressing room when Marianne entered.

The beautiful brunette was applying the heavy face paint Barnabas required all his female entertainers to wear when they worked.

Cecile wasn't just another of her uncle's employees, she was also Marianne's closest friend and housemate. The Frenchwoman had moved into a spare room in her uncle's house at the same time she'd taken the job in the Fayre. Marianne had immediately liked the outspoken older woman and they'd become as close as sisters over the past three years.

"I saw you looking at him," Cecile said in her charming French-accented English, her eyes not moving from her reflection as she smoothed a glossy carmine color on her generous lips. "That's twice the Duke of Flawless has come to see you."

Marianne smiled at Staunton's nickname—or one of them; there was also Lord Flawless, His Grace of Flawless, and just plain Flawless—and held out her wrists so Cecile could untie the tapes that held on her mufflers, the wool-stuffed mittens that Barnabas insisted all his boxers wear.

"Yes, I saw him," she admitted.

"I know you did; I *saw* you seeing him. I think you have a new admirer."

"He's come to your shows, too, hasn't he?"

Cecile gave a very Gallic shrug, as if to say *what man didn't come to her shows?* "Just once—last Tuesday."

Tuesdays were the only nights Marianne fought. Her uncle would have liked her to work two nights a week, but even he knew that was too much for any boxer. One night was already difficult enough.

"He doesn't come to see Nora or Lucy," Cecile added.

Nora and Lucy were the other female boxers her uncle employed.

Farnham's Fantastical Female Fayre was open six nights a week. In addition to boxing, there was Cecile's shooting, Josephine Brown's knife throwing, Cordelia Black's Players, Francine Gordon's magic act, tumblers, and jugglers—all female.

Cecile's slender fingers worked on the knotted string of Marianne's second muffler. "The duke is much more handsome than the cartoon I saw in Mr. Humphrey's window a few weeks ago."

She meant Humphrey's Print Shop, where crowds gathered outside the small shop to gawk at the cartoons and satires the savvy printer posted in his window every day.

"Has Staunton tried to talk to you?" Cecile asked.

"No," Marianne lied. Actually, her answer wasn't really a lie because she had no idea what the Duke of Staunton's message had said. She'd thrown it away without reading it.

Cecile finished her task and sat back in her chair. "Has he sent flowers? Anything that sparkles?"

"No, thankfully." Marianne stripped off the gloves.

Cecile muttered something that sounded like *English oaf* before turning back to the mirror to touch up one of her eyebrows with charcoal.

"The duke is said to be great friends with the Marquess of Carlisle," she said, not looking away from her reflection, her cheeks tinting a delicate shade of pink. "Has the marquess been to any of your fights?"

"Not that I've noticed," Marianne admitted.

"I think you would notice if *that* one came to watch you." Cecile gave a vaguely disgruntled snort that made Marianne smile.

Cecile was an avid consumer of gossip columns and made sure

to pass by Humphrey's Print Shop to look at the satirical cartoons in his window at least twice a week. She left copies of various gazettes lying all over the house she shared with Marianne and her Uncle Barnabas and even collected some of the newspapers. Marianne had often wondered if Cecile hadn't developed a bit of a fixation on some of the men who filled the gossip columns, like the Marquess of Carlisle, who was one of the most sought-after marital prospects in England and a staple of the society pages.

If she weren't so exhausted just then, she might have teased Cecile a little.

Instead, she dropped onto the stool in front of the other dressing table and used a cloth to clean the paint from her face, hissing when she accidentally touched the underside of her jaw.

"Did Lizzy hurt you badly?" Cecile asked.

"Nothing too serious," Marianne lied, her head still ringing. In truth, the uppercut had been close to a leveler—boxing cant for a powerful hit that was enough to put a fighter down.

"You need to find some other manner of work. You have—been remarkably lucky to keep your looks—and all your teeth—this long." Cecile's gaze lingered on the bridge of Marianne's narrow nose, which had been broken twice. Thankfully, Jack—Marianne's trainer—had quickly reset her nose both times, so the bump was barely visible.

The bouts that Marianne, Nora, and Lucy fought were not fixed, nor were they choreographed for the punters' entertainment. They were real fights, which meant real injuries. Marianne was usually just beginning to feel pain-free when it was time for her next fight.

"If you keep going, you are likely to look like Jack one day," Cecile added.

Jack had been a career fighter in his twenties. Now, at five-and-forty, his face showed his history as clearly as a road map. She loved Jack, but she certainly didn't want to look like him.

Marianne knew Cecile was right: She risked serious injury the longer she did this work. The only reason she looked as well as she did after almost two years fighting was because anyone who boxed at Farnham's had to wear padded mufflers. The rich punters who flocked to the Fayre paid well to watch any female in the ring, but they paid even more if the woman was attractive. It wasn't that Marianne was a beauty, but she was prettier than many of the rather desperate women who found themselves reduced to pugilism to earn a living.

Once she'd cleaned off the heavy face paint, she unbuttoned the gown she wore for her fights. Barnabas would have liked to dress her up like Cecile—in a tight, low-cut satin gown that displayed her wares—but Jack had refused to train her if she fought in a garment that hindered her movement. The costume Jack eventually approved was loose enough that she could move, not constricting to her breathing, and not made t of heavy fabric that would bind her legs. As for stays, the ones she wore were the barest nod to propriety and didn't interfere with her ability to breathe.

Barnabas being Barnabas—which was to say a consummate showman—he had the costumer use the thinnest muslin available and Marianne's gowns were spritzed with water before each fight, ensuring she looked all but naked when she went out on stage.

Marianne quickly stripped down to a chemise and men's drawers—which she'd started wearing after having most of her dress and petticoat torn off in a fight—and poured some tepid water into the basin, sponging off her arms and legs. She would have a proper bath when she got home tonight.

She was just slipping into the worn brocade robe she kept in the dressing room when the door opened and Jack popped his head in. "'Ay there, ducks!"

Marianne caught him in a fierce embrace. "Happy to see your ugly mug."

Jack gave her a rib-crushing squeeze before releasing her and turning to Cecile. "And 'ow are you, princess?" he asked, bowing low over the Frenchwoman's hand.

Cecile yanked his head down and kissed him on both cheeks, making his homely face flush. "It is good to see you, Jack."

"It's good to be 'ome." He shoved aside the tangle of costumes and clothing that covered the dressing room settee and lowered his six-foot-three frame. "It was a long trip." His good humor drained away when he saw Marianne's swollen jaw. "Criminy, Annie—what's that I saw out there tonight? 'Ow often 'ave I told you about keepin' yer mind in the game?"

"I know, Jack. I was distracted and I was punished for it."

He grunted, his expression telling her she'd not heard the end of it.

"Marianne needs another line of work," Cecile said. She stood up and gave a firm downward tug on her black satin bodice, pulling it low enough that her nipples couldn't be far below the top.

Even Jack, long accustomed to being around half-dressed women, swallowed hard as he gazed at Cecile. Cecile was a beauty, and the black satin complemented her lustrous inky hair, which was a dramatic contrast to her porcelain skin and dark brown almond-shaped eyes. She looked wicked and sensual. And when she slung the custom-tooled leather pistol holster around her waist and buckled it low on her generous hips, she looked like danger in female form.

"Don't you think, Jack?" Cecile asked.

Jack pulled his eyes away from Cecile's décolletage with visible effort. "Er, what?"

"Marianne—she needs to stop fighting."

"Oh. Aye, I've told 'er that. I told 'er that before she even started." Jack began to warm up to one of his favorite subjects. "A pretty, smart girl like you should—"

The dressing room door flew open hard enough to bang against the wall and Uncle Barnabas's angry red face appeared in the doorway. He jabbed a finger at Cecile. "*There* you are! Get your arse out there, missy, you're bloody late and the lads are getting restless."

Cecile, who responded to orders as well as a cat, suddenly decided it was time to examine her cuticles.

Barnabas made a strangled noise of frustration but prudently forbore nagging.

Instead, he turned his attention to Marianne. "And *you*," he said, cutting Jack a quick look. "I want her in tip-top shape before we go on tour. Quit fobbing her off on your mate Andy to train; she needs *you*."

"What she *needs* is anovver job, Barney."

Barnabas scowled, either at Jack's advice, the unwanted nickname, or both. "I want her training with you three days a week until we leave."

Jack rolled his eyes, but Marianne nodded. "Yes, Uncle."

"Oh, and I almost forgot," Barnabas said. "The Duke of Staunton wants to talk to you."

Marianne almost laughed out loud at the notion of her uncle *almost forgetting* to relay a message from a duke.

"No."

"Marianne, don't be foolish. This is the second—"

"*No.*"

He managed to look annoyed and aggrieved at the same time. "The man just wants to speak to you. You can invite him next door to the house—receive him in our book room and—"

"No."

Barnabas growled. "Stubborn."

Somebody walked behind her uncle, and Barnabas—infamous for having eyes in the back of his head—whipped around. "You!" he shouted at the unfortunate victim to have caught his attention. "Get those bags tied tighter." He left the door hanging open as he continued his harangue. "I felt bloody sand on my head while I was—" His voice faded as he strode after his target.

Marianne couldn't believe that he'd had the gall to nag her about Staunton. Again.

Cecile jerked her chin in the direction where Barnabas had been standing. "Want me to shoot him for you, *chérie*?"

It was an old jest, but it always made Marianne chuckle. "It's a tempting offer."

"Talk some sense into her, Jack." Cecile tossed the words over her shoulder as she sauntered from the room, closing the door behind her.

"She's right, you know—about quittin'," Jack said.

"I know she's right, Jack. Don't you think I'm aware that every fight is just another injury waiting to happen?"

"I never should 'ave taught you."

"Barnabas would have found somebody else—somebody not as good as you."

"'E should 'ave chosen somebody other than 'is own bloody niece!"

"He did; Nora and Lucy aren't his nieces, Jack."

"They're different—they *needed* to be tough growin' up in St. Giles."

"Are you saying I'm not tough, Jack?"

He ignored her teasing. "You're different, and you know it."

"I'm no better than they—you're just biased." In fact, Marianne's reputation—if you could call it that—was a great deal worse than Nora's or Lucy's.

"And whose fault is that? Farnham's!" he answered. "You're 'is bleedin' niece. 'E shoulda done better by you."

"He took me in when he had damned little himself, Jack. I owe him. Besides," she added when he looked unconvinced, "I get paid extremely well. I earn more than any governess or companion. Not that I could get either of those positions. With my reputation, I'd be fortunate to get a job as a charwoman."

Jack growled. "That bastard did you wrong, Annie. What 'appened wasn't your fault."

By *bastard* he meant Baron Dominic Strickland, Marianne's former lover, and the reason she was known all over Britain as the Boxing Baroness.

"Unfortunately, the rest of England believes otherwise, Jack."

"Everyone'll forget all about what Strickland done to you if you get away for a few years," he said. "You could stay on the Continent after this tour is over—you speak French as good as any Frenchy."

"What in the world would I do? I have no skill other than fighting."

Jack opened his mouth, doubtless to argue.

"Please, Jack—not now?"

He sighed heavily. "Fine, then. So, 'ow long 'as that uppity arsehole been comin' to yer fights?"

Marianne laughed at the description of the Duke of Staunton. "Just the last two fights—while you were out of town."

The door to the dressing room opened a crack and young Neddy poked his head in. "Er, this is for you, Miss Marianne." He held out a piece of parchment that had been folded and sealed with a blob of red wax.

Marianne recognized the seal and looked hard at her uncle's youngest employee. "You know what will happen if Barnabas hears that you delivered this."

Neddy's face crumpled. "Please don't tell him, Miss Marianne. The toff offered so much meg I couldn't say no and—"

"Bloody 'ell! You runnin' messages for punters now, bantling?" Jack demanded.

Neddy trembled under the big boxer's glare.

"Run along, Neddy," Marianne told him. "But no more messages—from anyone. Understood?"

"Yes, miss." He sniffed piteously and closed the door without making a sound.

Marianne turned the expensive rectangle around in her hands.

"Is that from Staunton?" Jack asked.

"Yes." The wax was a dark red that was almost black.

"You gonna open it?"

Marianne tore the letter in half, and then tore those pieces in half.

Jack sucked in a breath. "Annie!"

"What?" She opened the small stove and tossed the letter inside.

"You ain't gonna read it?"

"Why should I?"

"Er . . . well, 'e is a duke, after all."

"Listen to you. I thought you believed all men were equal."

"I do. But that don't mean some ain't more equal than others."
She laughed.

"It's unwise to make enemies of that sort, Annie. Besides," he
added, "you don't know what 'e wants."

"He's a man. I have a fair idea of what he wants."

Oddly, Marianne was disappointed by the thought. Everything
she'd read about the Duke of Staunton indicated the man was upstanding, moral, and decent—a noble bulwark against the profligate
excesses of mankind—especially the men of his class. Yet here he
was, sneaking messages to a female pugilist.

"Maybe you're wrong, luv. Maybe 'e don't want *that*."

"If not sex, then what? What else would a man like that want
from a woman like me?"

"You ain't curious?"

"Not in the least."

Jack clucked his tongue. "Well, the man must be touched in the
upper works."

"Because he's pursuing me?" she teased.

"Don't be daft. I just mean that 'e's got some nerve after what he
said about the Fayre and women pugs."

Jack was referring to the Duke of Staunton's diatribe the year
before—in Parliament, no less—after a female pugilist was killed
during a bare-knuckle fight. The duke had linked the decline of
morals to females boxing, among other tawdry activities. Although
he'd not singled out her uncle's circus, he had lumped the Fayre in
with operations that had rat pits, bear baiting, cock fighting, as well
as cruel and revolting dog and children fights.

Barnabas had been livid about Staunton's speech. Something he
seemed to have quickly forgotten now that he was a messenger boy
for the duke.

Marianne yawned and stood up, stretching. "Staunton's a preachy
sort, but you have to admit his crusading has done a great deal to
eradicate child labor and the virgin trade."

"That don't mean the 'igh and mighty Duke o' Staunton don't
fancy run goods 'imself."

Virgins, or *run goods* in the vulgar cant, were an expensive commodity which usually only the wealthy could afford.

"I've never heard any rumors of Staunton fancying children." Indeed, his name was conspicuously absent in the scandal sheets that Cecile left scattered all over their house. Nothing she'd read about him suggested that he engaged in any of the self-indulgent behavior most aristocratic males believed was their right and privilege. Or maybe the duke was just better at concealing his debauchery.

Jack gave an irritable shrug. "I doubt 'e's up to any good lurkin' about and eyeballing you."

"Maybe he's lurking about to gather evidence to shut us down on the grounds of moral turpitude." The Duke of Staunton wouldn't be the only one to come after Farnham's. There were numerous women's groups who'd made closing her uncle's circus their goal in life.

Fortunately, the Fayre would be leaving on tour at the beginning of March, and Marianne would be gone almost a year. She hoped their extended absence would force London busybodies to find another target for reform.

Certainly, the Duke of Staunton would have lost interest in her long before then.

Chapter 2

Marianne tossed a coin to the bleary-eyed stable lad before taking Reginald's reins and mounting the gelding without the aid of a block—something she wouldn't be able to do if she were dressed in a constricting riding habit rather than boots and breeches.

Once she was comfortably astride, she urged the gray gelding out of the livery stable's small courtyard. Jack would have preferred that she run behind a horse, rather than ride one, but she despised running and couldn't bear doing it every day; in her opinion, taking a jaunt in the park was a good compromise.

Her uncle had refused to buy her a decent mount, insisting that any old hack would do, so Marianne had purchased Reggie herself. She'd paid more than she should for the gelding, but he was exceedingly well-trained and comfortable with both regular and side-saddles.

By the time they reached the entrance to Hyde Park, Reggie's body was tense with anticipation and Marianne had finally woken up.

"Are you ready for a run, Reggie?"

His sensitive ears flickered, and he snorted as if he knew what she was asking.

"Let's go!"

Reggie's powerful body surged forward, and he channeled his awesome strength with breathtaking grace.

It really was like flying, and she couldn't help her joyous laughter as they soared through the cool morning air, just her and Reggie, the only two creatures alive in—

Marianne yelped as a horse and rider thundered past so close that their knees almost brushed.

Reggie's stride stuttered and he veered off to the right, but he quickly recovered.

She eyed the duo's departure with an angry glare. "Go get them, Reg."

Although the wind whipped away her words, Reggie read the determination in her body and threw his heart into the race, hurtling ahead. Just as they began to nip at their competitor's heels, the pair abruptly pulled up.

Marianne blinked to clear the blurry chill from her eyes and abruptly reined in, so caught up in the race that she'd not realized they'd reached the end of the Row. By the time they'd slowed to a trot, the other rider had guided his mount to the edge of the wide path and was walking the big gray stallion back and forth.

Marianne's plan to guide Reggie in the opposite direction, and thereby avoid a meeting, was foiled when the man called out, "Good morning, Miss Simpson."

She jolted at the sound of the deep, cultured voice and reluctantly turned her mount.

A fair-haired, pale-eyed, glorious god stared down at her from his horse, which was a good hand-and-a-half taller than Reggie.

His aristocratic, sculpted features were fixed in a haughty expression she imagined was his resting face. His eyes, the color of which she'd not been able to see from the boxing ring, were a pale green that looked as chilly as a killing frost on a new blade of grass. Right now, they glinted with an icy hostility that was enough to make her shiver.

He nudged his mount forward. "You *are* Miss Marianne Simpson, if I am not mistaken."

"You know I am," she retorted. "And you are the Duke of Staunton."

His pale gaze slid over her body slowly, insolently. It was a look she had endured countless times, even before her notorious ex-lover had publicly cast her aside. The nostrils of Staunton's fine nose quivered and pinched—as if he were smelling something foul.

Instead of wilting beneath his harsh glare, Marianne conducted her own inspection. She was unsurprised by the classical perfection of his face and figure. He was, after all, Lord Flawless: flawless in both person and deportment.

It irked her to admit that the word suited him—at least when it came to his face and body. He wasn't just handsome; he was flawlessly beautiful in an entirely masculine way.

"You are a difficult woman to speak to, Miss Simpson."

She shifted in her saddle. "Oh?"

"As I'm sure you know, I was at your uncle's establishment last night and asked to see you."

"Unfortunately, I am not receptive to men mooning outside the theater door."

The fair skin over his high cheekbones darkened at her insulting words. "I also sent you two written messages, Miss Simpson, over the past week."

"I received them."

His blond eyebrows lowered. "I received no answer."

"I threw them away without reading them."

His eyebrows rose again, disappearing beneath an attractive sheaf of ash-blond hair. "Why would you do such a thing?"

"There is no law that says I need to explain my actions to you."

"There is no law," he agreed. "But there is common courtesy."

Marianne burned at his cool, accusing words. She was not, in general, a discourteous person. Unless she was faced with an aristocratic man. And she had never met a man quite as aristocratic as this one.

Still, it shamed her to behave like an ignorant shrew and confirm his impression of her. "I can see you will not stop hounding me until you get what you want. What did your message say?"

"That I wish to speak to you."

She gave an exasperated sigh. "Clearly I don't wish to speak to you, Your Grace."

Once again, it was his body that betrayed him, rather than any voluntary reaction. The color seemed to leach out of his eyes as his pupils shrank to specks, his irises like pale green glass that had been washed by the sea.

"You are not curious to know what I have to say?"

"No."

Although he gave no sign of it, she suspected he was furious. A duke would be accustomed to command and would expect obedience from a woman like Marianne. She surmised that not very many people dismissed His Grace of Staunton.

Marianne's face heated under his brooding stare, which—annoyingly—prodded her to speak. "I can guess your reason for wanting to speak to me, Your Grace."

"Indeed? And what would that be?"

"Men of your kind only bribe my uncle's employees for one reason."

"My kind." He repeated the words softly and the corner of his mouth lifted just enough to expose a flash of white.

Marianne would not have called the expression a smile.

"You may rest assured it is not my habit to importune circus entertainers to warm my bed, Miss Simpson."

Marianne's face scalded in the cool morning air. She had believed herself immune to aristocratic derision. Apparently, she had been wrong.

Rather than shut her mouth and retreat, she pressed forward. "Ah, that is correct—you are Lord Flawless, are you not?" she taunted. "Peerless among men and without any base urges." She sneered at his narrowing eyes. "Although I suspect that even you do not entirely *go without*. No, you are a man like any other. You just choose your whores from a more elevated class of women."

An expression of vindication settled on his handsome, austere features, as if her crude words had confirmed his opinion of her as the uncouth ex-strumpet of Baron Strickland, the man all England had called the Rake of Rakes.

As she stared into his forbidding green gaze a wave of hopelessness swamped her. Why shouldn't this man think she was a trollop after what he'd likely heard about her? Thanks to Dominic, she was a target of offensive offers and subject to mockery from men of all orders, but especially wealthy, powerful men, who seemed to find her equal parts fascinating and repellant.

"What do you want, Your Grace?" she asked wearily.

"I want to speak to you."

"We *are* speaking."

"There is something I would like to show you, and I prefer to do so in private."

She almost laughed. "This *thing* you wish to show me—is it at the ducal residence? No," she said before he could respond, "that would not be your way at all. It will be in a more *private* location. Perhaps a small pied-à-terre. Someplace . . . discreet."

Marianne had not believed his eyes could grow any colder.

"You have my word as a gentleman that I have no designs on your person." His gaze raked over her as brutally as a knife scraping the bristles off a hog. His lips thinned with disgust. "I am willing to speak to you at your place of business—hence my presence at your uncle's theater—or anywhere else you deem appropriate, just so long as we are not in the middle of a public thoroughfare." The determined, dogged set to his face told her that he would not be denied.

"Fine. I will call on you. Where and when?"

He did not appear startled by her sudden capitulation, as if her submission had never been in any doubt. "I am at number five, Grosvenor Square. It is not far. Why not now?"

"I am hardly dressed to pay morning calls."

He shrugged, the gesture drawing her attention to his powerful shoulders, which were sheathed in an exquisitely tailored black overcoat. "There is nothing unusual in a gentleman calling on another gentleman wearing his leathers after a morning ride."

She studied his haughty, beautiful face. What could such a man want with her? And want it badly enough that he should persist so? Well, whatever he wanted, she admitted it didn't appear sexual. After all, he would hardly invite her to his home at seven in the morning—in broad daylight—for an amorous tryst.

Marianne nodded. "Very well. Lead on, Your Grace."

Chapter 3

St. John Powell, the seventh Duke of Staunton, seethed silently, not bothering to make pleasant conversation with the hostile female pugilist riding beside him.

He kept reliving their brief conversation, snatching glances at her person, and trying to reconcile his idea of her with the reality of her.

The woman was nothing like he had expected.

Her directness—no, her *combativeness*—had left him raw and off-center. Not since he'd been a boy had he bickered so childishly with another person—nor tolerated such impudence. In the five minutes he'd spent with Miss Simpson, he had suffered more insults—and behaved more rudely, himself—than in all the rest of his years combined.

The worst part was that he was largely to blame.

St. John had gone to the park that morning furious that this—*this* circus-performing harlot, a woman who had brazenly shared Strickland's bed—had repeatedly refused to speak to him as if he were some sort of encroaching cit.

He desperately wanted to tell her to go to the devil, but—and this ate at him worst of all—he was reliant on Dominic Strickland's ex-whore if he wanted a chance to rescue his brother.

And so, because of that resentment, St. John had made almost no effort to mask his dislike and disgust of Marianne Simpson. She—being no fool—had seen through the tissue-thin veneer of civility immediately.

He was angrier with himself than he was with her. It was not like him to behave discourteously to anyone—no matter their station—or to display his feelings so openly. It was crass, mortifying behavior. He had behaved like a cad, and she had taken him to task for it.

He could not blame her, but that did not mean he had to like her rude reaction—or her. This was no game to him; his brother's life hung in the balance, and this woman was somehow the key to bringing Benjamin home.

St. John glanced at her as they joined the flow of traffic outside the park. She looked remarkably like a man in her coat and breeches and hat, and it wasn't just because of her exceptionally short hair.

She also sat her horse like a man—a very skilled equestrian—and the black-leather-clad hand that loosely held the reins was broader across the back than any lady's hand.

Her shoulders, although fine-boned, were surprisingly broad and her tailored coat displayed noticeable biceps before tapering to a narrow waist and trim hips. Her muscular thighs flexed beneath tight buckskins and her top boots were snug over well-formed calves.

She was the very image of a wasp-waisted young buck, a shape that so many dandies padded and cinched their bodies to achieve. Her figure, he guessed, was not the product of corsets or buckram wadding, but the result of demanding physical exertion.

She held herself with a coiled awareness and emanated an almost masculine vitality. He supposed her physicality should not have surprised him. She was, after all, a boxer. He had assumed the fights her uncle arranged were more in the nature of an acrobatic display than real pugilism, but she obviously kept her body trim and fit to play the part convincingly.

When they turned onto his street the sun struck her face, illuminating her features more clearly beneath the brim of her hat. An ugly bruise discolored her jaw and a faint, inch-long scar ran from her lower lip down her chin.

So, perhaps her fights were more than just theatrical presentations, after all.

Her jaw was well-formed and firm, and her oval face surprisingly soft and feminine. Traces of dimples marked her cheeks and smile lines bracketed her mouth. He placed her in her early twenties, although her confident bearing was that of a more mature woman.

Her heavy-lidded eyes were an unremarkable hazel, her nose slender with a slight hook, the bridge bearing a bump that told him it had been broken at least once.

The only feature that was in any way unusual was her mouth. Not only was her top lip a perfect Cupid's bow, but the bottom had a distinct divot, as well. The effect was piquant and made her resting expression appear as if she were pouting.

Her only true claim to beauty was her pale-as-porcelain skin, which glowed with the luster of a pearl—at least the part that wasn't swollen and bruised.

She exuded a quiet dignity and reserve that he never would have expected from a circus performer, nor from the ex-mistress of Dominic Strickland, an unrepentant hedonist who was infamous for depravity and sensual excess.

By the time of his alleged death, Strickland's behavior had put him well beyond the pale. And the woman riding beside St. John had shared Dominic's bed when he had been at his very worst, when he had shocked even jaded society—one time wagering that he could find a man who would eat a live cat. A wager he had made good on, according to reputable sources.

St. John frowned at the distasteful tumble of thoughts. Dominic's relationship to this woman was neither here nor there. What was of critical importance was convincing Simpson that it was her moral duty to help him save his brother's life—a life that had been jeopardized by her treasonous ex-lover.

If she did not assist him willingly . . .

Well, he did not want to think about that just now.

★ ★ ★

Marianne had expected a duke's London residence to be sumptuous, but her imagination paled in comparison to reality.

It was the biggest house on a square that held some of London's most magnificent residences. An astounding six-story mansion fronted with elegant Portland stone, it loomed over the grand square with a tangible air of smug superiority. Much like its owner.

Two grooms materialized as they approached, relieving them of their mounts. A man dressed in the somber clothing of a butler opened the massive front door before they reached it, bowing to his master and reaching for his coat and hat while a second, lesser flunky in gold-laced, blue velvet livery, assisted Marianne.

If either servant noticed the tension crackling between her and their employer, they did not show it by so much as the flicker of an eyelid.

The duke turned to her once he'd been divested of his outerwear, his bottle-green claw-hammer coat bringing out an almost verdigris hue in his unusual eyes. "Mr. Simpson will be joining me for breakfast. See that his mount is—"

"Please, no breakfast. I would rather have done with this quickly, Your Grace." Marianne felt, rather than saw, the shock of the two men who hovered nearby. Clearly *nobody* ever interrupted the duke.

"Very well," the duke said after a slight pause. "Excuse me a moment."

Marianne inclined her head.

He stepped away and exchanged a few quiet words with his butler.

The servant nodded. "Right away, Your Grace."

The duke returned to Marianne. "This way, please." He gestured to a magnificent marble staircase.

The first-floor corridor was as wide as an avenue, the burnished wood floor covered with an ancient, elegant runner. Waist-high wainscoting was topped by silk-covered walls on which hung the artistic wealth of nations. Marianne was no expert on paintings, but even she could recognize a Titian when confronted with one.

Never in her life had she been surrounded by such opulence; she felt . . . oppressed by the weight of it, her senses overwhelmed. What must it be like to grow up in such a place? And to know that one day it would all be yours? No wonder he behaved like a god and believed himself to be above other human beings.

The grandeur that surrounded her was crushing, and she was struck by a mad impulse to run from this house that made her feel so insignificant and gauche. Only by sheer force of will did she ignore her impulse.

Two more footmen flanked a double set of doors. One of the men opened a door as they approached. Staunton was so accustomed to being served hand and foot that he didn't appear to notice the men or the courtesy, but Marianne nodded her thanks, even though the footman did not make eye contact.

The door closed behind them, and Marianne found herself in a library so grand that it was all she could do to keep from gaping like a hayseed.

"Please, have a seat, Miss Simpson." Staunton gestured to one of the oxblood leather wing chairs that sat across from a desk fit for a king. Or a duke, she supposed.

As she lowered her body onto butter-soft leather, Marianne became aware of how clenched and rigid her posture had become since entering this cathedral to wealth and power.

Anger pulsed through her veins and her stomach muscles tightened the way they did when she fought. Why was she allowing this man and his possessions to intimidate her? He was no god. He was only a man; a man who'd become rich off the labor and sacrifice of others.

Rather than sit tensely like a quivering boy awaiting discipline from his schoolmaster, Marianne lounged back in her chair, allowing her thighs to fall open in a relaxed, comfortable sprawl, just the way she'd seen countless men sit: as if they owned the room around them.

The duke's pale gaze flickered over her body and his dark blond eyebrows rose slightly, his eyes lingering at the level of her hips. He had the full lips and generous mouth of a sensualist, but his stern, uncompromising mien reminded her of a painting she'd once seen of Cromwell.

Was he really as pure and noble as he appeared? Did he repress his own sensual desires? Or was he only interested in repressing those of others?

Marianne couldn't help being amused by the faint red stain that spread over his cheekbones and the slight flexing of his jaw muscles as his gaze lingered on her buckskins and the body they covered. A virtuous woman would be offended by his bold examination. But then a virtuous woman wouldn't wear breeches to begin with.

Marianne had given up any claim to being virtuous after Dominic made a shambles of her life.

If not for the duke's treacherous skin betraying him, she would have had no clue that her body made him uncomfortable. Even so, she couldn't tell if it was disgust, arousal, curiosity, or some other emotion that caused the subtle flush.

His eyes slowly rose to hers and a hot spike of physical awareness shot straight to her core at his darkened gaze.

A sudden image assaulted her—the duke looming over her, his hard, beautiful face tight with another emotion, his pale skin flushing for a different reason, his breathing strained, his—

Marianne blinked away the erotic image. *Good Lord. Where had that come from?*

"What is this all about?" she asked more sharply than she'd intended.

"I recently received a letter from your lover, Baron Strickland."

Of all the possible topics of conversation he might have raised, Dominic Strickland would have been her last guess.

But Marianne earned her bread and butter responding to unexpected jabs, so she quickly found her footing. "Have you been visiting spiritualists and communing with ghosts, Your Grace? Or are you the only person in Britain who did not hear about the baron's death almost a year ago?"

"It appears reports of his demise might have been premature."

He extracted a small cluster of keys from a coat pocket and unlocked a drawer in the middle of his desk.

When his piercing gaze lowered to the drawer, Marianne briefly closed her eyes and inhaled a shaky breath. *Dom is alive? Impossible!* She felt feverish and dizzy, her heart thrashing as if it were trying to beat its way out of her chest.

Take hold of yourself. Or would you like to appear a fool in front of this man?

Marianne forced her eyes open just as the duke slid a letter across the desk with his pale, long-fingered hand, the monstrous sapphire in his signet glittering in the low light of the library.

Against her will, she leaned forward to look at the letter.

Her stomach pitched as if she were on the deck of a ship, and she lifted a hand to her mouth at the familiar, distinctive script. Dominic was a sinister who'd been beaten as a child when he'd refused to use his right hand. Instead of hiding his left-handedness, he had enjoyed emphasizing the odd slant by employing the most flowery script Marianne had ever seen. The S in the word Staunton was so ornate, it reminded her of a medieval illumination.

If it was not Dominic Strickland's handwriting, then the letter was written by somebody who'd made an excellent forgery. Marianne worried her lower lip, unable to look away from the letter.

Dom is alive.

Her pulse quickened just thinking his name. Fear, dread, shame, and hate swirled in her fluttering belly. She swallowed several times, but the lump in her throat remained. "Why would you believe this might interest me?" she finally asked.

"Because he mentions you in his letter."

She wrenched her eyes away from the missive and met Staunton's opaque stare. "What does he say?"

"You may read it."

Marianne's eyes lowered, as if pulled by some invisible force, and she stared at the letter with all the caution she'd show a live viper. Her hands were heavy, as though gloved in lead, and they refused to move to take the seemingly harmless piece of paper.

What could Dominic possibly have to say that would interest her? *I'm sorry I asked you to marry me when I was already married? I'm sorry I staged a fake wedding ceremony in order to bed you?*

Humiliation flooded her at the memory of the last time she'd seen him. Although it hadn't been even a year ago, she had been so heartbreakingly naïve. In a span of only a few days Dominic had stripped Marianne of both her innocence and her ability to ever trust another man. At least no aristocratic man.

Bile rose in her throat as her memories—which she'd so carefully buried—unearthed themselves, rising like specters from their graves.

Marianne clenched her teeth, horrified that she might cast up her accounts right here on the duke's luxurious carpets.

No. No. She would not shame herself again for Dominic.

She sat back in her chair and looked up. "I don't wish to read it."

Some emotion flickered across his face. Disbelief? Anger? Disappointment?

"I don't care what he has to say, Your Grace," she said, although he hadn't asked. "Perhaps you should bring this letter to his wife, the *real* baroness. Does she know that her husband is alive?"

"I have not shared the information with her. The financial position Strickland left her in forced her to remarry quickly."

Marianne should feel satisfaction at the thought of what a mess Dominic's resurrection would mean for the baroness. After all, Caroline Strickland had treated Marianne as if she were lower than dirt the one time they'd had the misfortune to meet.

But she could not work up any genuine pleasure in contemplating the other woman's incipient misery. Indeed, she felt nothing but pity for anyone who'd been ensnared by Dominic Strickland.

A new thought pushed its way through the chaos swirling in her head, and she narrowed her eyes at the duke. "Why is the baron writing to *you*, Your Grace?"

"He claims to have knowledge of my younger brother, Benjamin, who was reported killed in early 1814." He stared at her, his gaze like a raptor's. "He was an Exploring Officer."

Marianne had heard of those men, high-born officers who scouted for information to use against the French. They were no better than spies, of course, although they proudly—and rather foolishly, in her opinion—wore their uniforms as they gathered intelligence for Wellington.

"Strickland claims your brother is alive?"

"He sent my brother's ring, accompanied by a letter in what appears to be Ben's handwriting."

"And you accept this as ample proof of his claim?"

"The army never found Ben's body, so it is possible Strickland is telling the truth."

Marianne took a deep breath and held it while she considered what she was about to say. "I sincerely hope your brother is alive, Your Grace." Marianne didn't wish death on anyone, not even Dominic. "And I appreciate your thinking I might want to know that the baron is alive." That was a lie; it actually annoyed her that Staunton believed she would care to hear from a man who'd humiliated her in front of all and sundry. Marianne would have been happy if she never had to think of Dominic again.

"But?" he prodded.

"But, in my experience, Baron Strickland is a manipulative, scheming liar."

The duke did not look surprised.

She continued, "He is entirely motivated by self-interest. If he claims your brother is alive, then there is most certainly something in the situation for him. Knowing the baron, it will be money."

"I agree, Miss Simpson. And you are correct—in part, at least. He is asking me for money for his help recovering my brother."

She gave a bitter bark of laughter.

"I apologize, Your Grace," she said when he frowned at her. "I am not laughing at your situation. I am laughing because *that* is the man I knew: a person who is always willing to profit from somebody else's misery."

Marianne pushed up from her chair. "I wish you the best of luck with your brother, sir, but I don't want anything from Dominic

Strickland, not even a few words on a piece of paper." She inclined her head. "You needn't ring for a servant. I can show myself out."

She was halfway to the door when his voice stopped her. "Strickland won't give me the information about my brother unless I bring you with me when we meet."

Marianne whipped around. "He wants to *see* me?"

"Yes."

"You mean he is here—in London?"

"No, he is on the Continent. He said he will meet us in a small town just east of Metz."

"Why in the world would he think I would go all the way there because *you* asked me to go?" She held up her hand. "Never mind. I don't know why I even asked that question—it doesn't matter what he thinks or why. I don't want to see him. Ever. And he must know that, which is why he didn't bother sending *me* a letter, because I would have disposed of it without opening it."

Marianne looked away from Staunton's too penetrating stare, annoyed at the guilt that pooled in her belly. "I can see he has led you to believe that my presence is the key to your brother's freedom. He is lying—there is nothing left between us, and he knows that better than anyone. If he says that he wants to see me before he gives you any information, then what he really means is that he wants more money and has used his outrageous demand—which he knows I would never accede to—as a bargaining device. Trust me, Your Grace, you don't need to bring me to him to get your brother; just offer him more money." She turned and strode to the door, expecting him to call her back, but he remained silent.

One of the footmen closed the door behind her after she'd exited the library, and she stood in the middle of the corridor, staring at nothing, her mind a frantic whirl; Dominic was still alive.

"May I show you out, sir?"

"Hmm?" Marianne blinked and turned.

"It is this way, sir," the footman said. He gestured in the opposite direction, so it was just as well that he'd spoken because her wits were so scrambled that she couldn't recall how the devil she'd gotten there.

The butler was just entering the foyer when she descended the grand staircase, making her wonder if the duke had somehow notified the man.

"Go see that a groom brings Mr. Simpson's mount round, Gerald," the butler—Buffle, Staunton had called him—said to the young footman who'd accompanied her.

"Of course, sir."

Buffle held up her overcoat. "Here you are, sir."

"Thank you." Marianne slipped into the coat and was buttoning it up when the knocker sounded on the front door.

"Pardon me a moment, sir." The butler strode past her to open the door. "Good morning, Lord Carlisle," he said, stepping aside to usher in a man who was as handsome and tall as the duke, but dark where the duke was fair.

The peer smiled down at the butler, the genuine expression causing attractive crinkles at the corners of his warm whiskey eyes. "Good morning, Buffle." His friendly gaze shifted to Marianne. "Am I interrupting something?"

"No, my lord," Buffle said, handing Marianne her hat. "His Grace is in the library."

Marianne pulled her gaze from the dark-haired god with some effort. She had never seen the man in person before, but she had read about Gaius Darlington often enough. He was a staple of society writers—who had, rather unimaginatively, dubbed him The Darling of the *Ton*. He was also first in line to inherit his grandfather's dukedom. She knew far too much about him thanks to Cecile, who had an insatiable appetite for all things *ton*.

Too bad she couldn't tell Cecile that she'd actually seen The Darling in person and that he was even more beautiful than the rhapsodizing descriptions of him.

Marianne scowled at the unfairness; why were some people born with so much? Wasn't it enough that these men were wealthy and controlled the destiny of everyone else? Did they have to be stunning as well?

She settled the high-crowned beaver hat on her head, smiled tightly at the butler, ignored Lord Carlisle entirely, and left before any more handsome, powerful peers poured into the duke's foyer.

Once she was outside, she paused to pull on her gloves, glancing up at the door she'd just exited. Lord Carlisle stood at the sidelight, watching her through a diamond of beveled glass. He was no longer smiling.

Chapter 4

Gaius Darlington, Marquess of Carlisle and heir to the Fairhurst Dukedom, didn't wait until the library door closed behind him before saying, "Good Lord, Sin, if I'd not received your message warning me that she was here, I would have thought that was a man I met in the foyer."

Only Guy—St. John's oldest friend—still called him by his childhood nickname now that his brother Ben was gone.

"That *was* her—the Boxing Baroness—wasn't it?" Guy prodded.

Some newspaper wag had given Simpson the cruel nickname after she had claimed to be Strickland's legal wife. Now that he had met the serious, proud young woman, Sin had a difficult time imagining her even speaking to Strickland, much less becoming his lover.

"Yes, that was Miss Marianne Simpson."

"She looks a bit different without all that face paint, doesn't she? More delicate, somehow. Why in the name of all that is holy does she dress like a man?"

"The subject didn't come up."

Guy chuckled and dropped into the chair Marianne Simpson had just vacated, reminding Sin of the provocative manner in which she had lounged, her long, shapely legs spread wide, her leather breeches pulled tight over—

"So, did she get choked up and weep all over you when she heard about the resurrection of her old swain?"

Sin jolted at the question, grateful for his friend's interruption. The last thing he wished to do was entertain sexual thoughts about Marianne Simpson.

"She refused to read his letter."

Guy gave a raucous hoot and slapped his thigh. "She didn't even want to *read* it? What a cold-hearted bitch. And incurious, too. Are you sure she's even female?"

St. John thought back to the oddly potent woman he'd just spoken to. Yes, she was certainly female. Too female for his comfort.

"I don't think I've ever met a woman who didn't want to know everything about everything," Guy said when Sin didn't answer. "Lord, I couldn't resist reading Dom's letter myself, even though I loathe the bastard."

Guy's loathing had not always been the case. Once, years ago, Sin, Guy, Dominic Strickland, and two other friends—Elliot Wingate and David Norris—had been as close as brothers, the five of them teasingly referred to as The Brotherhood when they were at Eton.

Until today, Sin had believed there were only three of them still alive: himself, Guy, and Elliot.

David was incontrovertibly dead—a victim of the same enemy ambush believed to have killed his brother Ben—and Dominic had been reported dead in a fire almost a year ago.

"Do you think Simpson might be working with Dom on this scheme?" Guy asked. "Maybe her refusal to cooperate is just a way to drive up the price for information on Ben's whereabouts."

"No. I think she was as startled at the news that he is alive as we were."

"What about her uncle—do you think he is involved?"

"That, I don't know, but Elliot put a man to watch Farnham's house right after I received my letter, and he reports that Farnham has neither sent nor received any letters from Strickland. If the two are in cahoots, one would expect communication between them."

Guy nodded. "One would think. Oh, Elliot is on his way over, by the way."

"At this time of day?" Elliot worked for the Home Office and rarely socialized during daylight hours.

"He told me he didn't want to get your hopes up, but he might have found the file on Simpson and Farnham."

"I thought he said there wasn't one?"

"Lord, who knows with that secretive bunch? I doubt they even know most of what is going on, themselves."

So, the Home Office was collecting information on her. Before that revelation, his suspicions about Marianne Simpson—specifically about her connection with the smuggling enterprise her uncle and Strickland had operated—had been just that: suspicions. But the British government did not investigate people for no reason.

"What's she like?"

"Hmmm?" St. John murmured.

"Miss Simpson—what is she like?"

"She is remarkably well-spoken," Sin said after a moment's deliberation. "I also found her astonishingly direct." That was an understatement.

The library door opened, and a dark-haired, rapier-thin man entered without formal announcement. "Good morning, Staunton, Carlisle."

"Good morning, Elliot," Sin said. "Guy tells me you might have a surprise for me."

Elliot shot Guy a look of resignation as he took the chair beside his friend and roommate. "You are a worse gossip than Mrs. Onions."

Mrs. Onions was the charwoman at the men's shared lodgings. Her ability to talk without pause was legendary.

Guy shrugged. "What? You didn't tell me the information was a state secret."

Elliot ignored him and set his battered leather satchel beside his chair. "So," he said, turning to Sin, "was she cooperative?"

Sin quickly filled in the other man on his brief meeting with Marianne Simpson.

"It is interesting that she refused to read the letter," Elliot said. "But perhaps not so surprising given how Dominic treated the women in his life." He opened his satchel and removed a slender file. "The gentleman who delivered this to me was not one of ours."

By *ours* Elliot meant the Home Office, which was where he was employed—doing what, Sin could never discern.

"Not *yours*?" Guy gave a frustrated groan. "Then who the devil does the man work for? And how did he know you wanted information about Farnham?"

Elliot shrugged. "He might be with the Alien Office. Or the Admiralty. Or perhaps even the Secret Office."

"Secret Office? Is that some sort of jest?" Guy demanded.

Elliot ignored the question. "The existence of this file confirms my suspicion that somebody was investigating possible connections between Farnham and Strickland and Simpson." He handed Sin the file and then said, "I do wish you'd give me permission to tell them about Dominic's resurrection."

"For my brother's sake I'm going to take Dominic's warning seriously," Sin said. "And—no offence to you, Elliot—but I've heard far too many *government secrets* bandied about at balls and dinners to have much faith in anyone's discretion. Once Ben is safe, I will tell your superiors anything they wish."

Elliot sighed. "I understand, but I had to try."

"Do you really believe that Dominic would refuse to help Ben if the government discovered he was still alive?" Guy asked. "Surely even he couldn't be so low and without honor?"

"The man sold secrets that he knew would end in death—or at the least capture—of our soldiers," Sin reminded him. "And now he is extorting ransom money for one of the very men his spying endangered. I think it's safe to say he'd do anything."

Guy scowled with disgust "What a vile, soulless bastard he is to set up a cottage industry ransoming his own people."

"We don't know for sure that Dominic was involved in those

other cases," Elliot pointed out. "None of the three men who've returned mentioned an Englishman being one of their captors."

"Is there any evidence at all to indicate Dom was involved?" Guy asked.

"There are a number of similarities. The Earl of Wells paid ten thousand pounds to recover his son, the same amount Dominic is demanding from Staunton. The threat about government intervention was the same. In all three cases only one person was allowed to collect the captive and deliver the money. I can see Dom disappearing—and taking all information about Ben with him—if he feels threatened. From his point of view, getting captured means a trial for treason."

Guy turned to Sin. "I know you're worried about Dominic finding out, but if he has a whole network in place, we might find ourselves overwhelmed with just the three of us." He shrugged. "A few soldiers might help even the odds a bit."

It was Elliot who answered. "That is out of the question. Already, with only the three of us, we are courting trouble from our government."

"Why would our plan cause trouble? How can our government *not* want to get their hands on a treasonous bastard responsible for the deaths of two of our soldiers, who might now be involved in ransoming at least one of them back? They should be paying *us* to bring him back."

"They might *want* to go after him but matters on the Continent are tense. You know how volatile the negotiations in Vienna have been. The mood in France has changed dramatically since Napoleon's abdication. As relieved as the French people were to escape more war—and him by extension—they've now had almost a year under Bourbon rule and Bonaparte's popularity is once again soaring. It is tearing their nation apart. This peace is fragile, Guy. Britain cannot simply send soldiers into a foreign country whenever we choose. At least not without setting off a fresh round of hostilities."

"I have no intention of jeopardizing my brother's safety by bringing in the government," Sin said, not wishing to pursue the subject. "Even if Dominic *hadn't* forbidden it. The only people I trust with Ben's rescue are the three of us." He raised his eyebrows. "If either of you don't agree, I will under—"

"I'm with you," Elliot said, cutting him off.

"So am I," Guy said.

Sin left it at that and opened the file Elliot had given him.

"Will you read it aloud, Staunton?" Elliot asked.

Sin nodded and began reading:

"Nothing is known about Marianne's father other than his name, James Simpson.

Marianne's mother, Sandrine Dupuy, was born in Marseille, France.

Prior to moving to Dover Sandrine worked for ten years as a lady's maid to Désirée Clary."

Sin looked up. "Désirée Clary? Why does that name sound familiar?"

"Because she was once engaged to Napoleon Bonaparte," Elliot said.

Sin's eyes widened. "Didn't she later—"

"—marry Jean Bernadotte, one of Napoleon's generals?" Elliot cocked an eyebrow. "Yes, she did. Several years after Napoleon—in a very ungentlemanly fashion—broke off their engagement to marry Joséphine de Beauharnais."

Guy sat up straighter. "Bernadotte? Wait, that's—"

"Charles John, the Crown Prince of Sweden."

Guy whistled softly. "Well, well, well. Marianne Simpson's mother was the maid to a future queen. There's an interesting little tidbit."

"Indeed," Sin murmured.

"Marianne's mother died of an influenza when her daughter was eight. Barnabas Farnham arrived to collect Marianne, claiming to be Sandrine Simpson's brother. That was the first recorded contact between Farnham and Marianne Simpson.

"At the time of Sandrine's death, Barnabas was part of a financially unstable theatrical troupe called The Mayfair Players. After collecting his niece he went to London and—with the help of a lump sum of money that was

anonymously deposited in a Barings bank account—purchased a rundown theater on Newcastle Street.

"Every year, continuing to the present, an anonymous donor has deposited fifteen hundred pounds in the same account on the fourteenth of July."

Sin looked up. "If the first amount was deposited in 1804, in total that would be—"

"Almost fifteen thousand pounds," Elliot said.

"That's a bloody fortune," Guy said.

"And deposited on Marianne's birthday," Elliot pointed out.

"You think the money is for her?" Sin asked.

"Farnham gains access to this money shortly after collecting her?" Elliot shrugged. "It seems too coincidental, otherwise."

Sin agreed.

"Farnham opened Farnham's Newcastle Street Theater in 1805 and by late 1809 the theater enjoyed solid bookings.

"At the peak of the theater's popularity Farnham inexplicably shuttered the business and accepted an offer to manage a small theater in Deal, where he spent two years."

"Why the devil would he do that?" Guy demanded.

"Keep reading," Elliot said.

"The Deal theater was owned by a Gerald Mimsey. Subsequent investigation into Mimsey found the man did not exist. There is sufficient evidence to suggest Dominic Strickland and Gerald Mimsey are the same person."

"Well, well, well," Guy murmured.

"During his two years in Deal, Farnham participated in a 'smuggling war' that took place between two local fishermen. Farnham's smugglers eventually gained control of the area around Deal in the summer of 1811. Interviews with servants who worked for Farnham in Deal indicate the baron visited Farnham on numerous occasions."

Sin laid down the first page and paused. "So, Marianne has known Strickland since she was a young girl?"

"She was away at school and only came home on the holidays during that time. It is quite possible the two never met," Elliot said.

"She went to school?"

"Yes, and a good one, at that," Elliot said.

That would explain her refined speech.

Sin picked up the second page.

"Farnham returned to London and purchased the building behind the theater for two thousand, one hundred pounds and has since used it as a residence.

"He re-christened his operation Farnham's Fantastical Female Fayre. Over the next few years he hired only women acts: magicians, jugglers, trapeze artists, two prizefighters, and a sharpshooter.

His niece, Marianne Simpson, came to work for him after leaving Miss Nolan's Academy for Young Ladies."

Sin paused. "It seems like I've heard that name."

"It's an excellent school. All six of my sisters went there," Guy said. "It's considered the best lady's finishing school in Britain."

"So at least Farnham spent some of the money on his niece," Sin said and then continued reading.

"Simpson applied for a number of positions after leaving school but evidence suggests she was unable to gain work as a governess or companion due to her connection to the circus. Simpson trained with Jack Nelson for ten months and had her first public boxing match in late 1812.

"The first confirmed contact between Strickland and Simpson was in early 1814, when the two had dinner, with Farnham in attendance. Over the next few months Strickland dined with Farnham and his niece several times and purchased a front row seat for all Miss Simpson's fights. According to a source near Farnham, Strickland and Simpson were married by special license in the family chapel at Strickland's estate outside Chatham at the end of March.

"No record of either a license or marriage lines have been found.

"Simpson lived with Strickland until May 20, when she returned to her uncle's house after a London newspaper made mention of a Lady Caroline Strickland, née Amherst, who claimed to have married Strickland secretly, in Coldstream, Scotland, the year before.

"Almost immediately after Simpson's departure, Strickland returned to his captaincy in the Royal Berkshire Militia.

"While Strickland and Simpson were at his country house, six French

prisoners escaped from the prisoner hulk, The Captivity, *on May 11. The ship was anchored at nearby Chatham.*

"Strickland and a tall, thin, red-haired man—a description that fits Emil Beauvais, one of the escaped prisoners—were seen talking several times between the twelfth and fifteenth of May at the Rusty Scupper Pub in Chatham.

"On May 24 Strickland, in his militia capacity, received information that at least one of the prisoners who'd escaped from Chatham was hiding in a house outside Dover. Strickland entered the house, leaving his four subordinates outside. Shots came from inside the house just before the building caught fire. Neither Strickland nor anyone else escaped the fire. Two badly burned bodies were discovered in the wreckage.

"One trusted source in Paris confirmed that Beauvais had been smuggled out of Deal on May 17, aboard a fishing vessel used by the same smugglers Strickland and Farnham did business with years before.

"The day after arriving in Paris, Beauvais left for Toulouse, accompanied by four men. On May 28, weeks after the armistice and two days before the Treaty of Paris, Beauvais and his men attacked a safehouse occupied by intelligence agents Major Lord David Norris, Captain Lord Benjamin Powell, and Lieutenant John Doset.

"Only Norris and Doset's bodies were recovered.

"Beauvais disappeared afterward and his four accomplices were never identified.

"Farnham was brought in for questioning in the Beauvais escape but was cleared of suspicion as he was in Birmingham at the time."

Sin reached the bottom of the page and realized his hands were crushing the parchment. Any death during this interminable war had been a waste, but for his brother to be killed in some sort of rogue militia skirmish weeks after the war had ended was beyond tragic.

He composed himself and placed the paper on top of the others before looking up. "This is all you have on Marianne Simpson and Farnham?"

"I'm afraid so," Elliot said.

"This hasn't answered any questions—it has only raised more."

"I know."

Sin forced a smile. "I sound very ungrateful—what I should be saying is *thank you*."

Elliot paused and then said, "I do have a bit more information that's not in the file—probably equally unhelpful—about Farnham's most recent employee, Josephine Brown."

Guy grinned. "Ah, yes—the knife thrower. Brown is her name? That seems a terribly mundane name for such a mysterious woman."

"Why do you have information about Brown?" Sin asked.

"After you received Dominic's letter, I asked around about Farnham, his circus, and anything connected to it. I didn't learn anything new about Farnham or his niece, but I *did* discover that Miss Brown was a *subject of interest* in a naval case a few years back."

"Subject of interest?" Sin asked.

"That usually means we've received information which has raised questions about an individual or their associations, but don't have enough evidence to open an official case on them."

"That's . . . vague."

Elliot smiled dryly. "Welcome to my world, Staunton. In any event, Brown was cleared of any wrongdoing." His forehead furrowed. "Still, there's just something . . . *off* about the woman. She possesses a remarkable facility with bladed weapons of all kinds, and there is absolutely no information about her past, where she came from, or who taught her such skills. She's a bloody enigma."

"Is that admiration I hear in your voice, Elliot?" Guy teased.

"Maybe a little. In my experience such anonymity is exceedingly hard-won."

Sin gestured to the file on the desk, steering the discussion back on course. "Nothing I read indicates Miss Simpson was involved in either her uncle's smuggling or that she knew what Strickland was up to with Beauvais—even though she was living with him at the time."

"That is true," Elliot conceded.

"Why in the world does Strickland want to see her so badly?" Guy asked, echoing the question that Sin had asked himself at least hourly since receiving Dominic's letter.

"Maybe he's in love and sorry for what he did and wants a chance to woo her back," Elliot suggested.

Guy laughed and even Sin couldn't resist a tired smile.

"This is Strickland we're talking about," Guy said. "I think she's dirty and so is her uncle," he added with uncharacteristic vehemence. "I think they're probably both involved in this current business with Dominic, too."

Sin and Elliot stared at him.

"Why are you looking at me like that?" he asked.

"I've been monitoring Farnham's mail," Elliot reminded him. "There's been no proof—"

"You only started going through his mail after Sin received Dominic's letter, right?"

"Well, yes."

"What if Dom sent him a letter *before*?"

"Of course, that's poss—"

"Or what if he's sending and receiving his correspondence using somebody else? Maybe another accomplice in this ransom scheme?"

"Yes, that's—"

Guy leaned forward in his chair. "We have an older smuggling connection between Farnham and Strickland—"

"But there's no evidence that Farnham did anything more than smuggle goods, Guy," Elliot said. "Certainly nothing linking him to Beauvais's escape."

Guy scoffed. "You think Farnham was up to his neck in smuggling in Deal yet didn't know what else Strickland was doing using the same network?"

"I agree it seems likely Farnham knows more than we've been able to discover," Elliot conceded. "But we have no evidence on Simpson—none. I need proof before I accuse a man—or woman—of treason."

"We're not condemning her to hang, Elliot, we just want something we can use to convince Simpson that she *has* to go with us and talk to Dominic."

"By convince, you mean *force*," Elliot said.

Before Guy could answer, Sin said, "Putting aside the fact that we shall have to force Simpson to go along with this"—he glanced at Guy—"and that is a significant issue to put aside, makes you so sure Strickland doesn't have something nefarious planned for her if we hand her over to him?"

"Surely her uncle wouldn't allow anything to happen to her?"

"You're assuming that Farnham is involved in all this. What if he's not? What if this is all Dominic?" Sin shook his head irritably. "This is a bloody tangled mess, with something very rotten at its core. Why does Dominic want to see her so badly?"

Guy waved a dismissive hand. "It doesn't matter what he's got planned because we'll be there with her; we can protect her."

"I wouldn't be so certain about that. Dominic Strickland's brain is murky and devious. We can't hope to guess what he's got in mind," Sin said. "The man has never done anything for nothing. If he wants to talk to Simpson, he has something to gain. It is only conjecture, but I doubt he means the woman well. Besides," he added, "it will only be the three of us if we encounter trouble. If Dominic is behind this rash of ransom demands, then he is probably not working alone. *Somebody* has to be holding these men prisoner. Who knows how many people are involved or what we might be facing? He might have a bloody army."

The other two men digested that possibility for a moment.

"I still think we should bring our own army," Guy said. "Not actual soldiers," he corrected hastily at Sin's look of annoyance. "We should hire some—"

"Absolutely not," Sin and Elliot said at the same time.

"Fine," Guy said. "Let's go over this again. You said that your office has been investigating Dominic for years—and that he was suspected of selling secrets before whatever happened with Beauvais?"

Elliot nodded.

"Then I'd say it's fair to assume that Farnham—whom we *know* smuggled goods alongside Strickland in Deal for several years—was also involved. And then there is Miss Simpson, who was conveniently living with Strickland at the time of Beauvais's escape." Guy turned to Sin. "The way I see it, Simpson *owes* you her cooperation if she wants to save her uncle's hide and clear her own name. If she won't help you willingly? Well, then I think you have every right to force her. Hell, you're not asking for the world—you only want her to take a few days out of her tour and go with us to Metz." Guy raised his eyebrows. "Not a whole lot to ask to save a man's life, is it?"

Sin looked at Elliot.

"I agree with Guy," Elliot said. "If her presence is a nonnegotiable part of the price to find out where Ben is being kept then . . ." He shrugged, not needing to spell it out.

If Sin wanted to save Ben's life, he needed Marianne's cooperation. Sin's choice was clear—and extremely distasteful to him: If she wouldn't come along willingly, then he'd have to resort to force—regardless of her guilt or innocence.

Wouldn't that make him just as bad, if not worse, than Dominic Strickland?

Chapter 5

Sin lurked in the shadows of the chilly theater and waited, feeling like a hole-and-corner pervert.

It had cost him a sizeable sum of money to bribe his way into Farnham's Fantastical Female Fayre while Miss Marianne Simpson practiced with her trainer. It was fortunate that the same servant Elliot was using to go through Farnham's mail was now firmly in their pocket and could not refuse Sin's demand.

He felt like a bloody idiot hiding behind stage curtains and miscellaneous props, but he had tried every other way—both reputable and non—to speak to Miss Marianne Simpson. It was easier for Sin to gain an audience with the King of England than a female pugilist. But short of having her arrested and dragged from her home or place of work, he'd run out of other ideas.

So, here he was, *lurking*.

The practice area was the same stage that was used for the actual matches. The only differences between this morning and a regular business night were the lack of a roaring all-male crowd, fewer candles to light the huge space, and the addition of two boiled-leather punching bags of the sort he often used himself at Gentleman Jackson's.

The scenery and props that usually concealed the backstage area were absent, exposing various ropes, pulleys, cupboards, and a stove that occupied a small brick niche, losing the battle to warm the cavernous area.

Sin had been waiting since five o'clock and had fallen into an uncomfortable doze while standing.

The sound of the stage door opening snapped him awake. He was about to step out from behind the curtain when he saw that it wasn't Miss Simpson, but her trainer, Jack Nelson.

Damn it! The servant had said nothing about the trainer being there, although Sin should have guessed. Jack Nelson operated his own boxing parlor and Sin had, wrongfully, assumed Marianne would go there to train with him.

Sin doubted the man would be pleased to find him trespassing, or amenable to giving Sin a few minutes with Miss Simpson. It was far more likely that Sin would find himself engaged in an impromptu mill with the huge man.

Nelson had a leather bag over one massive shoulder and an armload of linen, which he dropped onto one of four chairs lined up against the back wall. The man was a bloody giant—easily six feet three or four—and must weigh upward of eighteen stone. His blunt features had suffered significant rearrangement over time and hands the size of Christmas hams hung at his sides as he strode to the largest cupboard.

Jack opened the cupboard, exposing stacks of dumbbells, and bent low. When he stood up, he had a fat roll of mattress-ticking tucked beneath one arm. He carried it to the front of the stage and kicked it open, unrolling a thin pallet.

From his satchel he extracted two wine bottles and some other items Sin couldn't identify from where he stood. Jack was still rooting about in the bag when Marianne Simpson entered.

Rather than buckskins and a coat, she wore a simple straw bonnet and a gown and cloak, both a serviceable gray wool.

Jack looked up from the bag he'd been rifling through. "'Mornin', ducks."

A huge yawn distorted her face. "Good morning, Jack." She plucked at the ribbon under her chin and pulled her hat from her short brown curls.

Once again her pleasant, cultured voice—that of a gently bred woman—startled him, even though he now knew where she'd acquired it.

She strode toward Jack with loose-limbed, animal grace. Her movements were economical and fluid as she stripped off her gloves and then untied her cloak, shrugging it from shoulders that were well-formed, even without a claw-hammer coat accentuating them.

She yawned again and began to unbutton the row of wooden buttons that ran down the front of her dress.

Sin blinked. Good Lord, did the woman intend to disrobe right *there*?

After unfastening the last button, she pulled her gown over her head, exposing short stays over a chemise and a single petticoat.

Her skin was so pale that the bruises scattered on her torso stood out in stark relief. An odd tightness seized Sin's stomach at the mute evidence of the beatings her body endured week in and week out. The marks ranged from faded yellow stains to brown splotches to the still angry purple and black bruises on her breastbone and jaw.

So, her bouts were more authentic than he'd believed.

When Jack turned back to her, she held out a sleekly muscled arm and closed her eyes, as if she were finding it difficult to stay awake.

"Tired?" Jack asked, efficiently wrapping her left hand with strips of fabric.

"A bit." She didn't open her eyes.

Jack lowered her left and lifted her right hand, then began wrapping it. "I said you should 'ave slept in this mornin', Annie."

"Uncle wanted me with you three times this week." Her tone said this wasn't the first time they'd had this discussion.

"Aye, aye, I know what Barney wants." The big man snorted rudely, causing her bowed lips to curve into a charming smile that exposed the dimples Sin had suspected. "Does yer 'ead 'urt?"

"A little," she admitted, opening her eyes now that he'd finished wrapping her hands.

"I told you to avoid that narsty fizzy brew."

She laughed, the sound surprisingly girlish, and then winced slightly. "I think you must be the only person who thinks of champagne in those terms. Besides, it was Cecile's birthday celebration, so I had to drink it."

Jack grunted and turned back to his satchel. "You warm up good this mornin', lass—it's cold as a witch's tit and I don't want you pullin' nothin'."

She yawned, sighed, and then commenced to engage in the most rigorous series of exercises that Sin had ever seen—and he was no naïf when it came to athletic endeavors.

Like every young aristocratic man, Sin had been obsessed with milling in his youth. While at Eton he, Guy, Elliot, David, and Dominic had started the Gymnos Club.

As *gymnos* was not only the root word for gymnasium but also the Greek word for "naked," it had been their brilliant idea to engage in physical exercise while naked, just as the ancient Spartans and Olympians had done.

They'd quickly discovered that outdoor athletics in the Greek climate was a good deal different from attempting the same pursuits in an English one. Even after they'd capitulated to the exigencies of the English weather and donned appropriate clothing, they had continued to engage in a rigorous schedule of training as espoused by the ancient Greeks. That had included: thrice weekly swimming—no matter the season—footraces, riding, climbing anything and everything, from trees to buildings, utilizing dumbbells for strength training, and skipping rope and calisthenics for endurance.

Although Sin no longer embraced the grueling routine of his youth, he still worked his body hard at Jackson's three times a week and rode most mornings. But what Marianne Simpson did over the next hour and a half . . . well, he had never seen the like.

She warmed up by skipping so fast the rope itself was a blur, not stopping until sweat poured down her temples. Next, she lifted the dumbbells so many times, and in so many ways, that it made his own muscles scream just observing. After that, Jack used his considerable strength to fling a hard leather ball at her midriff for ten minutes.

Lastly, she did sit-ups, press-ups, lifts and various stretching-type exercises that Sin wasn't familiar with.

By the time Jack called a halt to the brutal series of lifts she was doing—using a trapeze bar that he'd lowered—her thin muslin garments were almost translucent with perspiration.

Jack handed her a towel and she walked a circuit around the stage until she had cooled down.

"I've got a new one for you today," Jack said. "Raw and not up to yer level, but frisky enough to keep ye on yer toes."

Marianne nodded, drying her face before toweling her shoulders and arms.

Jack pulled the bung from the wine bottle he'd taken from his bag earlier—which Sin assumed held water—and handed it to her. She put the bottle to her lips, tilted back her head, and swallowed repeatedly, the action flexing the long muscles of her throat.

Sin couldn't pull his gaze from her; she was . . . well, he didn't know what she was. Certainly unlike any female he'd ever seen. He tried to picture her with longer hair, wearing silks and jewels.

He couldn't visualize it.

She wiped her mouth with the back of her hand and took another gulp, giving him more time to gawk. The muscles in her shoulders and back were defined and elegant rather than bulky. Her arms, on the other hand, were as muscular as many of the men who sparred at Jackson's. When she raised the bottle to her mouth her biceps bulged, the pronounced tracery of veins a shocking blue beneath her almost translucent skin.

It was cold in the cavernous building but his skin was hot and prickling. Conflicting emotions churned inside him and sent blood pumping to all parts of his body. Marianne Simpson was sculpted and muscular and she moved with the physical confidence of any of the great athletes he'd seen: *male* athletes.

Women, in Sin's experience, were soft, curvaceous, and well-padded. And yet his groin had stirred while he watched her work through the grueling training, until he was now erect and aching, more aroused than he'd been for a woman in . . . well, he couldn't recall when he'd last been so hard.

What the devil was wrong with him to feel desire for such a mannish woman?

No—*mannish* wasn't the right word. For all her musculature, she was undeniably female. Her small breasts were delicate swells pressed fetchingly against a corset so loose it hardly merited the name. Although her hips were slender and compact, there was a distinctly feminine curve to them—

He wrenched his mind and gaze off the too-entrancing woman and focused on the brutish man, instead.

Jack peeled an orange and handed it to her. She relaxed while she ate it, staring at nothing in particular as Jack bustled about the stage.

"I'm ready," Marianne said a short while later, thankfully yanking Sin away from thoughts he did not wish to entertain now or ever.

She stood and dropped her hands to the tapes that held up her petticoat.

Jack cocked his head. "It's cold, luv—you sure you wanna strip down?"

"I'm burning up and will soon be even warmer."

She pushed down the petticoat, and Sin's pulse pounded as the thin white muslin floated to the floor.

He squinted. *Were those—*

Yes, his eyes were not deceiving him: she wore men's inexpressibles along with her chemise and stockings.

Why should that shock him at this point?

Indeed, the cotton drawers fell to just below her knees, so there was actually less skin showing than if she'd worn only a chemise.

Yet the knowledge that she wore men's undergarments was enough to send his already elevated body temperature soaring. Intellectually, he found his body's reaction ridiculous, but that made it no less powerful.

Jack opened the door to the stove, tossed in a handful of coal, and then shut it with a clang. "I'll go get 'im, then."

Him?

Marianne took a fresh towel off the stack and vigorously scrubbed at her short, damp hair. When she'd finished with her hair, she pulled up her chemise.

Sin hissed in a breath as she exposed her taut, sweat-slicked stomach, which was not only flat, but ridged with muscles. The drawers she wore rode low on her slender hips, the dark shadow of her sex visible beneath the thin cotton.

"*Good God*," he whispered, unable to look away.

By the time she finished drying her belly, her normally pale skin was rosy pink. As casually as she'd raised the hem of the chemise, she dropped it, hiding her mesmerizing midriff.

And then she pushed down the straps of both her stays and chemise with two practiced flicks.

Sin's jaw sagged.

Turn away, you cad.

His body was frozen, and not from cold.

She grabbed the front of her stays with one hand and yanked the stiff garment down, taking the chemise along with it and exposing small, exquisite breasts.

Sin swallowed as she roughly toweled the two delicate white mounds—the only part of her that seemed to have any softness at all—the tips a pinky-brown that quickly pebbled in the cold air. A painful-looking bruise was the only thing that marred their perfection.

She tossed aside her towel and jerked up the chemise and stays as quickly as she'd pulled them down.

The burning in his lungs alerted him to the fact that he'd been denying his body air for longer than was healthy. He inhaled shakily and loosened the fingers of both hands, which had fisted at the astoundingly erotic display. No mistress had ever made him ache so fiercely, so fast, and she had not even expended any effort.

Of course, she hadn't known that she was performing for a despicable, lurking bounder.

Sin decided to feel bad about that later.

She turned to the door as it opened and called out a friendly, "Hello," as she approached a man who appeared to be a few years younger than her own twenty, his body caught in that awkward stage between boyhood and manhood.

The lad returned her pleasant greeting with an insolent smirk that caused Sin to bristle. Marianne, on the other hand, appeared amused rather than affronted.

The young man turned to Jack. "'Ere then," he said in a grating, nasal voice, "she ain't exactly moy weight, is she? Wot if I 'urt 'er?" He eyed Marianne's lithe, stripped-down body with an insultingly dismissive look.

He was right that he outweighed Marianne by a stone at least and was perhaps two inches taller. Sin wondered if the trainer was not a bit mad to put a woman with a man, no matter that the man in question couldn't be more than seventeen.

"Just worry about yerself, Tommy," Jack advised the lad with a wry look. "Do you need a bit o' time to loosen up?"

Tommy sneered, his beady eyes flickering derisively over Marianne. "Nah, I reckon I'm good the way I am."

Sin's fists clenched at the younger man's obnoxious disrespect. Why he felt offended on Marianne Simpson's behalf, he had no clue, because she certainly didn't seem to notice the lad's behavior.

"Awright, then." Jack gave an abrupt nod. "Strip down and I'll wrap yer 'ands before I tie on your mufflers."

"Wot?" Tommy demanded, halting in mid-strut. "You 'spect me to wear *mufflers*?"

Jack's jaw tightened ominously. "I told you that already. If you want the money, you'll wear gloves. Now, either shut yer gob or get the fuck out."

Tommy held up both hands in a placating gesture, his expression tinged with healthy fear. "Awright, awright, gov."

Marianne turned her back to Sin so Jack could tie on the padded gloves boxers called mufflers. The rounded swell of well-developed buttocks pushed against the thin muslin of her chemise when she moved.

The drawers and chemise hid her thighs, but her thick woolen stockings couldn't disguise calves that were both shapely and muscular. Once again, features that would normally have appeared masculine and unappealing to him were tempered by the presence of dainty ankles.

Sin scowled at his body's unwanted response and wrenched his gaze upward to rest on her shoulders as Jack tied on her glove.

Sin's attitude toward boxing—like so many things—had altered as he'd grown older. Back in his youth, he'd reveled in bloody, bare-knuckled fights. Now he found such exhibitions repellent and barbaric—for either gender.

The athleticism of boxing was just as rewarding to watch without having the combatants bloody and permanently damage each other. Yet even with wrapped fists, the activity was brutal, the bruises on Marianne's body telling their tale most vividly. How Farnham could do this to a member of his own family—or any woman, for that matter—was beyond Sin.

Curb your crusading spirit, old man, this woman's occupation is none of your concern.

No, it wasn't. But in Sin's world, gentlemen protected women; they didn't exploit them.

Oh, is that what goes on in all those brothels that supply little girls to wealthy "gentlemen": protection?

He couldn't deny the accusation. It shamed him that men he'd grown up with could prey on the weak and powerless.

As you are about to prey on Miss Simpson?

Sin silenced the voice. There would be plenty of time to wrestle with his conscience later—after he'd freed his brother.

Once Jack finished with Marianne, he moved to Tommy.

Marianne kept her muscles warm by stretching as she waited,

her body limber and supple rather than muscle-bound as was the case with many male boxers.

Sin's own body tensed as he waited for the sparring to begin; he was not looking forward to this. It didn't matter that Tommy had a youthful, slender build. He was a man and men were stronger than women.

Or at least that was what he'd always thought.

But once the sparring started, it took less than a minute to see that Tommy was sorely out-classed when it came to skill and speed.

The younger man's aggressive insouciance changed so quickly it was comical. One minute he was smirking and swaggering, the next he was staggering back from a ferocious crosscut he'd never seen coming.

Sin was flabbergasted by the woman's speed. Her fist was a blur, her loose and relaxed posture giving away nothing of her intentions before her arm shot out.

After the second hit, Tommy tightened his stance and raised his guard, no longer strutting, his expression intent—and perhaps even a little respectful—rather than jeering.

Once he took his opponent seriously, the fight was more closely matched, but even so, Tommy only got in one hit for every five or six of Marianne's. She possessed a lethal combination of intelligence, skill, and endurance. Sin was impressed by how subtly Marianne drew out the young man's weaknesses and used them against him, until Tommy was winded, his punches increasingly wide of his target.

By the time Jack stopped the sparring, both fighters were breathing hard and sweat-slicked, but Tommy was clearly the worse for wear. As they toweled off, drank, and prepared for a second bout, Jack spoke softly to Marianne for a moment before turning to Tommy, who was drinking far too much water for a man about to fight.

The older man wrenched away the bottle. "Much more and you'll be shootin' the cat." He leaned close to Tommy's face, studying his right eye, which had already begun swelling. "You good for anovver go, or do you need more time?"

Tommy's already flushed face darkened. "'Course I'm awright!"

Before the two could resume sparring, the stage door opened, and Barnabas Farnham bustled into the room. "Ah, good—I caught you between bouts," he said in his barely accented English. He turned his shrewd, dark stare on Tommy, frowned at the younger man's swelling eye, and then glared at Jack. "This is the best you could find?"

Jack looked pained and Tommy flinched, as if he'd been punched in the face.

The trainer opened his mouth, but Barnabas waved an impatient hand. "Never mind, I don't have time right now." He turned to Tommy. "Does Jack know how to get hold of you if we need you?"

The lad nodded.

"Good. Now leave. *Go,*" he added when Tommy hesitated.

Tommy scowled and stalked toward the chair, snatched up his clothing, and then stormed out the stage door.

"Oi, we're not done 'ere, *Barny,*" Jack said. "Can't it wa—"

"No, it can't wait," Barnabas said, already striding impatiently toward the door. "I need to talk to you right now. Also, since you aren't condescending to join us on our tour, have you found replacements for you and Andy?"

"I've been talkin' to some blokes, but I need to bring 'em in to meet Annie and make—"

"I don't care. Just get it done." Farnham snapped his fingers. "Now, come along, I've not got all day."

The huge boxer looked fit to explode at being called to heel like a dog. He opened his mouth, no doubt to deal the other man a proper blistering, but Marianne interrupted him.

"It's fine, Jack," she said, sounding mildly amused. "I'm tired."

The two exchanged a speaking look and Jack nodded before turning back to Farnham. "I need to gather me things."

"I'll give you one minute," the Frenchman snapped. "And then I want you in my office."

"Bloody 'ell." Jack shook his head after the other man had stormed off.

"I'm sorry about this."

"It ain't your fault, lass," the huge man rumbled as he untied her mufflers.

"Part of it is. I've put you off twice about interviewing your replacement. I can't seem to make myself do it because I'll miss you so much. But I know why you're staying. I promise I'll meet all your lads and hire somebody before next Friday." She yanked down his head and gave his cheek a smacking kiss.

Jack was red-faced, but Sin could see he enjoyed her casual affection. "'Ere, ducks." He held out her petticoat.

"Thank you," she said, quickly stepping into it. "I'll put everything away here. You'd better go and talk to Uncle."

Sin waited until the door closed behind Jack before he stepped out of the gloom. "Good morning, Miss Simpson."

Chapter 6

Marianne shrieked as she spun around.

The Duke of Staunton stood across from her, dressed in linen as white and fluffy as a cloud, tight fawn pantaloons, a coffee-brown claw-hammer, and Hessians the color of melting caramel. He looked as if he should be in a lady's sitting room rather than on a circus stage.

Her eyes swiveled from his person to the curtain he must have been hiding behind.

"How did you—" Marianne stopped and then frowned as she considered his vantage point, and what he would have seen: her without her chemise.

He stopped in front of her. "I'm sorry if I startled—"

Her fist flew before her brain even knew what it was doing, striking the duke in the side of the mouth and whipping his head back hard enough that she heard his neck bones pop. He stumbled back a step, steadied himself, and then lifted his hand to the side of his face. They both looked at the smear of blood on the tip of his finger before their eyes locked.

Marianne was vaguely aware that she was breathing heavily, more winded than she'd been after going one round with young Tommy.

And her hand bloody *hurt*.

The duke's mouth pulled up at the corners. The movement was infinitesimal—you'd have to be watching closely to catch it—but it was, nonetheless, a smile.

"You think this is amusing?" she demanded. "To trespass and spy on a person?"

"Actually, I was thinking that I deserved what you did." His words were as effective as a jolting uppercut. "I'm sorry," he said, finishing his one-two punch with an apology.

A duke apologizing? To *her*?

He dabbed at his bleeding, rapidly swelling lip with a handkerchief he'd produced from his coat while Marianne absently shook out her aching hand; it had been a long time since she'd thrown such a powerful leveler without a muffler.

The duke's handkerchief was edged in intricate navy stitching, a coat of arms painstakingly embroidered in one corner. He folded the square to hide the blood before tucking it back into his coat. "I thought this would be a good opportunity to speak to you. I didn't expect, er—" He made a vague gesture to her person.

He wasn't babbling by any means, but she suspected that he rarely felt as wrong-footed as he did at that moment.

A sense of power suffused her as she observed the slight breach in Lord Flawless's composure. To be honest, she didn't care about his seeing her naked—a person soon lost their physical modesty working in a circus—so much as invading her privacy.

Even so, she couldn't help being amused that it had taken only a glimpse of her bare breasts to make one of the most powerful men in Britain blush like a maiden.

Amusement aside, she felt at a disadvantage standing before this impeccable creature while she was sweaty and half-clothed. She turned and snatched her dress off the back of the chair.

"You might be a duke, but you are still trespassing on private property." She threw the words over her shoulder before slipping the gown over her head. Once she'd buttoned up the loose bodice, she turned to him. "Or are you above the law, Your Grace?"

"You may call the constable after I've spoken to you, Miss Simpson. I will pay the price for my trespass."

"Oh, may I? Thank you so much for telling me what I *may* do. But first I *must* speak to you, even though I've told you repeatedly that I don't wish to do so?" She crossed her arms over her chest to keep from physically lashing out. The more she thought about his sneaking around, the angrier she became.

"I want your cooperation on a few matters, Miss Simpson, and you shall be generously compensated for your efforts."

"Because money is all my sort cares about, is it not?" she shot back.

"That's not—"

"I already know you want me to talk to Strickland, so that's one thing. What else do you want?"

"I understand your uncle will be leaving on a tour of the Continent at the end of next month."

Marianne blinked at this unexpected tangent. "Yes, what of it?"

"I want him to allow me and two others to accompany you."

"What?"

"We will only travel with you as far as Metz."

"We are not going to Metz," she blurted, as if that had anything to do with his ludicrous request.

"I know. We will leave the circus at some point before then."

Marianne rubbed her temple, which had begun to pound. "When you say *we*, you mean—"

"You will accompany us to the meeting with Dominic Strickland."

She snorted with disbelief at his arrogance. "Let's just say, for the sake of discussion, that I agreed to go with you. Why in the world would you want to travel with a touring group? We will keep a grueling schedule and use caravans to travel. You are a wealthy man. If you want to see Dominic so badly, why not take a coach and six and travel in comfort? Why not—" Marianne stopped and shook her head. "I cannot believe I am having this conversation. Perhaps Tommy hit me harder than I thought," she said to herself.

The duke raised an eyebrow.

"Are you addled, Your Grace? I feel that I must ask." She exaggeratedly looked around. "Have you escaped from your keeper? Is he or she searching for you?"

He took a few steps toward her, until he stood close enough to strike her, if he were so inclined. Marianne refused to step away and had to crane her neck to look up at him.

"What I want from you is twofold. First, the cover of your circus. Second, I want to keep you close at hand; I don't wish to go running all over Europe when the time comes to see Strickland. We can argue about this all day long, Miss Simpson. But know this: I will not be deterred. *Ever.*"

It was all she could do not to back down from his cold, implacable gaze. "No."

He stared.

Marianne stared back, astounded—and disgusted—when her skin began to prickle with sweat under the weight of his icy eyes. "If you think you can glare me into submission, you are sorely mistaken, Your Grace."

He reached into his breast pocket. "Perhaps you might want to look at this."

Like a child, she put her hands behind her back. "I told you I didn't want to read the baron's letter—"

"It is not Strickland's letter." He held a thick wad of mismatched papers bound with a piece of twine.

"What are those?" she asked as he untied the bundle.

He pulled one piece from the pile and held it up so that she could read it.

Marianne immediately recognized the familiar signature. Her eyes widened at the figure on the chit. "That is my uncle's name." She looked at the numerous pieces of paper still in his hand. "How much—"

"A great deal, I'm afraid. In fact, I would hazard that everything Farnham owns will not be enough to clear these debts."

"I don't believe you." Marianne snatched the papers from his hand.

Some fluttered to the floor, but her gaze was riveted on the dozen or so that she held.

She raised her free hand to her mouth. "My *God*, there are thousands of pounds owed here." When he didn't respond, she looked up.

Something flickered in his inhumanly cool gaze—pity?

Marianne sorted through the chits, which had obviously been issued on different days and likely to different people. "You bought these, didn't you?"

"Yes."

Marianne wanted to cry—it had been years since she'd done so, not even during the wretched debacle with Dominic.

"So, what you're telling me is—"

"If you do not do as I ask, I will call in these debts and your uncle will go to prison. For a very, very long time. I will take everything he owns, and I will close down the circus."

Her fist tightened around the papers and blood thundered in her ears. "You vile, odious, execrable—"

"If you do as I ask, I will hand everything over to you once you've spoken to Strickland. These vowels are worth tens of thousands of pounds. You may call them in—or not." Impossibly, his beautiful face hardened even more. "You should realize that whether I bought these debts or not, they would come due sooner rather than later and your uncle would not be able pay them. The opportunity I am offering you is beyond generous."

Marianne stared at him through a red haze of fury. She hated him more for being right; his offer was generous. Insanely so. That didn't make her feel any less like a trapped animal. "Why did you pretend that I had choice? Why this—this—*farce* of asking for my help? Why didn't you just tell me I was at your mercy from the beginning?"

"That hardly matters, does it?" The words—not taunting, but toneless—only made her want to hit him more. And keep hitting.

"You're right; it doesn't matter." She lifted the vowels she still held. "That doesn't mean I'm just going to take your word for all this. I want to talk to my uncle."

He remained as motionless as a predator observing the futile struggles of its wounded, dying prey. "You are scheduled to leave England on March first, are you not?"

"Yes."

"So that means there are five weeks remaining before your departure. I will give you until the night of your next bout to speak to your uncle and confirm what I have told you."

Marianne chewed her lower lip; she felt as if she'd been struck hard on the head.

"Did you hear me, Miss Simpson?"

When she didn't answer, Staunton stepped closer. Rather than retreat, she squared her shoulders and took a step toward him, until their chests touched; Marianne would be damned before she cringed from this man.

"What if I tell my uncle about you and he scarpers off to the Continent, leaving you with a handful of useless paper?"

"That would be inadvisable."

"That sounds like a threat."

"You and I know that your uncle has been involved in illicit activity for *years*."

Marianne's throat shrank to the diameter of a pin, and it was difficult to breathe. What did he know?

He nodded at her flushed cheeks, as if she'd made some sort of admission, a harsh smile taking possession of his angelic features.

"I have no idea what you are talking about, Your Grace."

"Then perhaps I should send a message to the Customs Office? I daresay they'd be fascinated by the contents of your uncle's cellars, Miss Simpson. I could have agents here within the hour."

Marianne held his harsh gaze; she would not quail. "If buying smuggled brandy was a jailable offence, the prisons would be stuffed to bursting, Your Grace—mostly with men from *your* class."

"I'm not talking about buying smuggled goods, and we both know it."

Her stomach lurched sickly at his words and accusing look. "You—"

"Yes, yes, I know—I am vile, odious, et cetera. You needn't repeat yourself. Instead, think on this: If keeping your uncle out of debtors' prison isn't enough to persuade you to cooperate, perhaps keeping him from being transported or hanged might be sufficient reason?"

Marianne could only stare. What did he know? More importantly—what exactly had her uncle *done* with Dominic? Oh, she knew the two of them had been up to their necks in smuggling in Deal, but she'd never wanted to know just how far they'd gone. But now—

The duke's next words shook her from her miserable introspection. "After your next fight my carriage will collect you and take you somewhere we can discuss your plans for the next few months." He paused, the planes of his face hardening. "If you are not waiting for me, I will ensure that the requisite authorities collect your uncle. Am I understood?"

She chewed the inside of her cheek until it was ragged.

When she did not answer, his frown deepened. "Do not test my patience on this matter, Miss Simpson; you will find I have none. Tell me you understand," he repeated.

"I under*stand,* Your Grace." The words were like broken glass in her mouth. "Is that all?"

"No. There is one more thing. Tell your uncle I want to see the letter and the locket."

"Letter and locket? Should I know what you are talking about?"

"Your uncle will know."

He turned and left the way he'd come—through the door that led to the prop room, and then to the back alley.

Marianne watched him go before she spun and hit the leather man. "*Bastard!*" she hissed, pummeling the boiled-leather punching bag with her bare fists until her knuckles stung and burned.

Only when she saw a fresh smear of blood on the coffee-colored leather did she grab the bag and collapse against it, blinking her eyes rapidly, as if that could stop the tears that were already falling and blurring her vision.

Yet again a man was controlling the direction of her life. Unlike Dominic, who'd only destroyed her reputation, the duke would destroy the lives of everyone who depended on her uncle and the work he provided. Dozens of workers and their families would suffer if Marianne told the duke to go to the devil. Thanks to her uncle's rash involvement in smuggling over the years, he might get transported or even *die* if she denied Staunton what he wanted.

Yet again a man was giving her a choice that was no choice at all.

"I don't understand, Uncle. How *could* this happen? Is it really all gone?"

Barnabas Farnham's pale, papery skin had turned brick red. Never had she seen her uncle look so ashamed.

Fear arrowed to her chest at the desolation in his eyes. "Oh God. You used my money, too, didn't you?"

He bit his lower lip.

Marianne squeezed her eyes shut. "All my money is gone, isn't it? All my pay—which you were supposed to invest for me. Instead, you gambled it all away."

When he didn't answer she opened her eyes.

Her uncle's expression was one of profound shame. "I'm sorry, Marianne. I'd planned to replace it all—to have it back, with interest—before you even noticed."

Marianne had no words.

"How did you find out?" he asked.

"Does it matter?"

He swallowed. "No, I suppose it doesn't."

"This must have been going on for years," she said.

He licked his lips. "I had been managing the debts—borrowing to pay off the ones that came due, but then, I had a bad run of—"

She raised a hand. "Please, spare me the sordid details."

"What are you going to do, Marianne?"

She laughed and her uncle flinched at the almost demented sound. "What are my choices, Uncle?"

"There must be some other—"

"I know that you sent me to school hoping that I could find respectable work, but if nobody would hire me as a governess *before* I started boxing, they're hardly likely to do so now that I'm the Boxing Baroness, are they?" she demanded, fury and desolation battling inside her. They'd been naïve and foolish to expect that a decent education would offset her association with a circus. Six months of applying for positions—even in far-flung parts of Britain—had convinced her there was only one way to earn a living.

"I had hoped to quit fighting in three years—now I will be forced to continue for another six, at least. I am wondering what will be left of me by that time and if quitting will even matter by then."

"I can make it up to you, my dear. I swear. It is not the end of things. I will be able to . . ."

"What?" she demanded when he stopped.

"I can get you the money. It will just take some time—"

"I hope you do not mean smuggling, because that is—"

"No, no—it's not—"

"Then you think to win everything back at the tables?"

"No."

She flung up her hands. "Then what?"

"I—I can't tell you just yet, but I swear on my mother's eyes that I will get back your money. It will just take a little time—"

"We don't *have* time, Uncle." Marianne didn't even want to know what he was scheming.

"How did you learn about this, Marianne?"

His question reminded her of the man behind this conversation. "The Duke of Staunton came to me—he bought up all your vowels."

Barnabas goggled in a way that might have been amusing any other time. "Staunton? But—but *why*? I've never played cards with him in my life." His brow furrowed. "Is this about closing us down for moral reasons—is that why he's done it?"

Marianne knew she should tell her uncle the whole of it, but she was too angry to be fair to him just then. Besides, she couldn't bear to bring up Dominic or the fact that he was still alive. Her uncle and the baron had brought out the worst in each other; the last thing she wanted was to bring them back together again.

"He did it because he wants to force me to cooperate with him."

"Cooperate, about wh—"

"Staunton mentioned a locket and a letter—do you know what he is talking about?"

Barnabas's jaw sagged and the color drained from his ruddy cheeks.

"Uncle?" she said sharply when he only stared. "What letter and locket is he talking about?"

"Er—" He swallowed and met her angry gaze. "I don't know?"

"That sounds like a question, Uncle."

"No, of course not," he blustered. "I don't know anything about it. You've just unsettled me, Marianne. I don't appreciate you accusing me of things."

Marianne employed Staunton's trick of staring without speaking.

"I am your uncle," he said piteously. "I swear I am telling you the truth—I know nothing of any letter or locket. Surely you believe my word over a stranger's?"

She held his watery gaze for a long moment. "Of course, I do, Uncle," she said with a tired sigh. It wasn't quite a lie, yet it wasn't the truth, either. But the locket and letter were the least of her concerns: Her entire future had just crumbled in a matter of minutes. Her uncle had gambled away the money she had entrusted to him.

"Whyever would Staunton be so interested in me? In us?" Barnabas asked, almost of himself. His mouth was compressed into a worried frown and his gaze had turned inward.

When Marianne didn't answer, he met her angry stare. "You needn't do anything he says, Marianne. I'm sure we can contrive a way to get the money. Perhaps I could—"

"Never mind," she said wearily. She could just imagine the sort of muddle he'd *contrive* if left to his own devices. "I'll take care of it." She pushed to her feet and turned to the door.

"But how?" he asked behind her. "You don't have the money—other than that horse, you've never even spent any of your earnings on jewels or anything of value that you could sell, my dear."

Oh, she had one thing left to sell: her pride.

Chapter 7

The door to the dressing room opened and Cecile bustled into the room, slammed the door, and leaned against it. "He's out there again tonight, Marianne."

She didn't need to ask who *he* was.

Marianne squeezed the charcoal stick she was using to darken her eyebrows. "Blast," she muttered as small black fragments rained over the pots of face paint on her dressing table.

"Did you hear me?" Cecile asked.

It would be difficult not to, but Marianne kept that observation to herself. "His being here has nothing to do with me," she lied.

Cecile turned her dark eyes to stare at Josephine Brown, who had performed before Marianne tonight.

Marianne didn't know the reserved and mysterious woman very well—nobody in the circus did. Josephine had simply appeared at the Newcastle Street address one day and then commenced throwing knives until she'd gained Barnabas's attention. He'd hired her on the spot to be his third big attraction on the Fayre's non-theatrical evenings.

If there was a knife or sword in existence the lethal woman hadn't yet mastered, Marianne hadn't seen it.

Usually, she did her act and disappeared, never socializing with the other employees. But, for some reason, Josephine was loitering in the dressing room even after she had removed her face paint and the scandalous outfit she wore for her act: black leather breeches, a black superfine tailcoat, black linen, and black riding boots, topped off with a black leather mask that covered the top of her face. The outfit was especially dramatic when combined with her fair skin, pale gray eyes, and corn-silk colored hair.

Not to mention the huge black bird that accompanied her at all times.

Angus, her raven, was as quiet and mysterious as his owner. The two were inseparable, and Angus was an integral part of her knife routine. He'd been trained to hold playing cards up for Jo to impale with her daggers, among other things.

The bird was also something of a thief—at least that was what several members of her uncle's troupe believed. Small things—not always valuable—had gone missing over the past four months since Josephine and Angus had joined the troupe. And although nobody could prove Angus was the culprit, he and his mistress were the focus of much suspicion.

Her uncle billed Jo as *La Sabreuse* and kept her identity a secret. Not that any of the people working at the circus knew much more about Josephine Brown than the punters did.

"Did he watch you tonight?" Cecile asked Josephine, who was lazily sharpening one of her knives, a pastime that seemed to fill a great many hours, given the quantity of knives she kept on her person. Angus was perched on a pile of clothing that had been tossed over the arm of the settee, his feathers fluffed up and his massive head tucked beneath his wing.

When Josephine didn't answer Cecile clapped her hands, the sound like the report of a pistol in the small room. "Blade! *Écoutez-moi!*"

Neither Jo nor her bird turned so much as a hair. Or a feather.

Instead, a dull hiss filled the silence as Josephine scraped the knife down the whetstone once more before looking up, her strange opal-gray eyes slumberous, as if she'd just woken from a deep sleep.

"I beg your pardon?" Her voice was soft, her accent not exactly refined, but without any regional inflection. She spoke much like an upper servant—perhaps a housekeeper or governess. Dressed as she was right now, in a plain navy wool gown, with her striking hair braided into a thick rope down her back, she reminded Marianne of the milkmaids who kept their herds in the park and offered cups of fresh milk for sale. Her appearance was wholesome and pure.

Until you looked more closely.

Never had Marianne met a person so devoid of emotion—*any* emotion—as Josephine Brown. Not even the Duke of Staunton could compare. At least with the duke, Marianne had sensed anger, irritation, and derision roiling beneath his polished façade. With Blade—a nickname that suited her in more than one way—she sensed only an eerie void.

Cecile made a sound of annoyance and snapped her fingers in Josephine's face when it appeared the woman had forgotten about her question. "*Mon Dieu!* You live in your own little world, eh? I asked you about Staunton," she said before Jo could confirm or deny her rude question. "Was he watching you tonight?"

Blade never did or said anything hastily, and Cecile's rough treatment didn't hurry her. Instead of answering, she stared at the wicked dagger in her left hand. Her elegant, tapered fingers looked incongruous holding the heavy, black, leather-wrapped hilt.

"No, I don't think he was out there," she finally said, still not looking up, her thumb moving over the edge of the blade in a slow, thoughtful caress. "At least not that I noticed."

"*Pffft!*" Cecile flung up her hands and gave the pale blonde a disgusted look before turning to Marianne. "It is as I thought—he has arrived just in time to see you." Her beautiful features shifted into a crafty, contemplative expression. "This is an interesting development. He is a wealthy and powerful man. If he wants to speak to you, perhaps—"

Marianne turned back to the mirror and dipped her finger into the small pot of rouge; she wished the excitable Frenchwoman would leave the subject alone.

"Maybe he's here to see *you*, Cecile. After all, I'm not the last act tonight."

Cecile gave Marianne a look that spoke volumes and made Marianne's face heat.

Marianne should have sent Staunton a message after talking with her uncle. Why not? It wasn't as if a few days made any difference. But she'd felt mulish about it and took all the time he'd offered. And now she had to deal with his presence at her place of work and its effect on everyone else—or at least the females. And probably her uncle when he learned his creditor was in the audience.

Cecile snapped her fingers in front of Marianne's face and she jolted. "You are like the other one. Off in your own little world." She jerked her head toward Blade, who was not paying them any mind, but stroking the feathers on Angus's neck and whispering softly to the rapt bird, who made soft croaking sounds, giving every impression of conspiring with his mistress.

Marianne finished applying her lip coloring and blotted off the excess. "What do you want me to say, Cecile? So what if Staunton is here to see me or you or Blade—sorry." She grimaced and looked at Josephine, but the woman didn't appear to have heard the nickname. "He has a right to watch, just like any of the other punters who purchase a ticket."

"I *know* that, you nonny."

"Ninny," a quiet voice corrected.

Cecile and Marianne both turned to Blade, but she wasn't looking at them. Instead, she'd picked up one of the cloths they used to remove their face paint and calmly sliced it in half with barely a touch of her blade.

"Barnabé will yell at you for that," Cecile warned her.

That was true. It drove her uncle mad to find slashed bits of cloth, paper, and anything else around the theater—a sign that Blade had been there, absently cutting objects.

Of course, it also drove her uncle mad when anyone called him by the French version of his name, but that didn't stop Cecile from doing it.

Blade looked up at Cecile, her fingers lazily spinning the knife with jaw-dropping grace.

When Jo remained silent, Cecile jabbed a finger at Angus, who'd gone back to sleep. "He is standing on my dressing gown—has he done his business on it?"

"Angus has better manners than that," Jo said mildly, resuming her sharpening. "He likes the feel of silk under his claws."

Marianne thought that might have been the most information the quiet woman had ever volunteered.

Cecile growled and shook her head before turning back to Marianne.

"Don't let him distract you tonight, *chérie*. You need to remember what happened to you the last time."

Marianne didn't tell her friend that she no longer needed to steal looks at the handsome peer. She'd get to see more than she wanted of him for the next two months.

The duke's carriage—a huge, glossy black beast without any escutcheon on the side—was waiting in front of her uncle's house when Marianne stepped outside an hour and a half later.

The bout—her third with Nelly O'Grady, a woman from Dublin— had been a tough one. Nelly was smaller than Marianne, but she was fast, and it was like boxing with a hornet; Marianne felt as if she'd been stung all over her body. She was exhausted and in a foul mood; she wanted to have a long soak in her tub and go to bed, yet there she was, getting into his bloody carriage.

Well, the duke might be able to bend her to his will, but that didn't mean she had to capitulate gracefully.

Marianne smiled at the thought of making the man suffer. A silver lining.

A servant wearing luxurious livery hopped off the back, opened the door, and flipped down the steps as Marianne approached the carriage. She wore her riding kit—breeches and a coat—so the groom didn't try to hand her in as she climbed into the interior of the huge vehicle. Like the gentleman he was, the duke had taken the back facing seat. The footman closed the door, and soon they were rumbling away.

"Good evening, Miss Simpson."

"Where are we going?" she asked, not feeling inclined to pleasantries.

"I own a small house not far from here."

Marianne raised an eyebrow.

The duke sighed. "I have no designs on your person, Miss Simpson. However, what we are about to engage in is not something I want connected to my name." He cocked his head. "We will be spending a good deal of time together over the coming weeks and months, Miss Simpson. Is it your intention to be combative that entire time?"

She propped her elbows on her knees and leaned forward, closing the gap between them. "I don't see myself warming up to my extortionist anytime soon, Your Grace. So, *yes*, I will likely be combative for the foreseeable future. Is that going to be a problem for you? Perhaps you might want to change your mind and find somebody else to strongarm into doing your bidding?"

His lips curved into a smile that made the hairs on the back of her neck stand up, but he didn't speak. Marianne turned away and they rode in silence. Less than five minutes later, the carriage stopped in front of a three-story redbrick house.

The duke opened the door, put down the steps, and then turned to help her.

She ignored his hand and hopped out.

"After you." He gestured for her to go first.

Marianne glared up at him. "I dressed like a man so that I might retain what little vestige of my tattered reputation that remains, Your Grace." She didn't wait for a response but strode ahead. The door opened before she could grab the handle.

Lord Carlisle stood in the doorway, his full lips curved into a smile that promised sensual delights. But his eyes were as hard as stone.

"Hallo, Staunton," he said, not taking his gaze from Marianne as he stepped back. "And this must be Miss Simpson."

Marianne pulled off her gloves before removing her hat and

dropping them inside. She tossed it to Carlisle, who reflexively caught the hat and then frowned.

"Ta," she said, unbuttoning her coat, shrugging out of it, and holding that out to Carlisle, too.

He took the garment, his expression sardonic. "It's my pleasure to serve you, Miss Simpson."

"How delightful to encounter an aristocrat with a desire to be useful," Marianne said, earning a bark of laughter from the gorgeous peer.

The duke ignored their exchange and laid his own hat and gloves on a console table, then took the stairs two at a time, not waiting for Marianne this time.

"After you," Carlisle said, handing the garments to the footman who'd followed them into the house.

"Second door on the left," Carlisle instructed when they reached the first floor.

The room held not only the duke, but another man. Unlike Staunton and Carlisle, this man was neither tall nor strikingly handsome. He had medium brown hair, dark blue eyes, and regular features. Indeed, if she'd been asked to describe him, she would have said he was almost exceptionally average.

Or maybe that was just how he looked when compared to his two godlike associates.

"Good evening, Miss Simpson, I am Elliot Wingate." He bowed.

Marianne ignored his greeting and strode to where a fire crackled, dropped into the nearest seat, and propped her booted ankle on her knee. "It is late, and I am tired. Can we get on with this?"

Wingate cocked an eyebrow and the duke compressed his mouth into an even thinner line. Only Carlisle appeared delighted by her rude behavior. He took the seat nearest her, visibly entranced by her mannish clothing. It was a reaction she'd encountered far too often from aristocratic admirers to find charming.

"Drink, Miss Simpson?" The duke gestured to a silver tray that held several decanters.

"No, thank you."

Staunton sat without pouring anything for himself.

The three men stared at her, each of them intimidating in his own way.

Marianne couldn't help feeling as if she was facing some sort of tribunal. She was almost afraid to ask, but . . . "As I am being *forced* to do your bidding, I think I should know what was in the letter from Baron Strickland."

She'd hoped the duke might say he didn't have the letter—or that it had spontaneously combusted or been stolen—but she was not so lucky.

He reached into his coat and extracted a small rectangle. "I brought it along, thinking you might wish to read it."

She sighed, took it, and unfolded it.

Staunton,

I hope this letter finds you well. It has been over a decade since we last spoke—so much water over the dam. No doubt you have looked at the signature on this page and have already contemplated notifying the authorities or throwing it into the fire. I hope, for your brother Ben's sake, that you do neither.

There, that caught your attention, didn't it?

Yes, I've recently discovered that dear Ben is alive, although not perhaps in the pink of health.

First off, let me assure you that he is, for the time being, safe. When you come to collect him, however, you should bring a caravan or the like to transport him as he is not fit for riding.

The gentleman in whose care he resides requires compensation for his time and effort. He wants £10,000. It seems a great deal, but I assured him it was well within your means. Especially for your only remaining brother.

As proof of my claim, I've included your brother's ring and a letter from him, in his own hand.

I am not asking for money for my part—I will take you to where Ben is convalescing in exchange for a favor.

I wish to see a woman named Marianne Simpson, who works for a man named Barnabas Farnham.

There are important things I need to say to Miss Simpson. Bringing her to see me won't be as difficult as it seems as Farnham's company will be touring the Continent exceedingly early this year, presumably to get a head start on his imitators, who will likely have the same idea.

Marianne looked up to find all three men watching her intently. "How does he know about the tour?"

"He was an associate of your uncle in the past. Is it possible he is in communication with him now?"

Marianne's first response was anger—indignant anger—and she opened her mouth to defend her uncle. But the words wouldn't come. How *did* Dominic know about their tour? Who would have told him if not Barnabas? But how could her uncle do such a thing after everything that had transpired between her and the baron?

She felt sick to her stomach at the possibility of Barnabas being so disloyal.

Marianne met the duke's gaze. Was that pity she saw in his eyes? "I don't know if they are in communication," she admitted.

The duke only nodded.

Marianne turned back to the letter.

If you bring Marianne to me, I will take you to Ben.

She won't want to see me—it will likely prove a struggle to get her here. If she requires motivation, tell her to ask Barnabas about the locket and the letter. Once she sees those, she will have many, many questions. Tell her I have answers to all her questions; that will make her eager to see me.

I know what a law-abiding, upright citizen you are, my dear St. John, but do curb your desire to notify the authorities of my existence. If I get so much as a whiff of Elliot or his associates within one hundred miles of me, I will be deeply chagrined.

And Ben will die.
Be at the Iron Helm Inn on April 15th, and I will find you.
Show up even one day late and I will be gone, and Ben will die.
Dominic

Marianne folded up the letter, proud that her hands barely shook. If there'd been any doubt that Dominic was alive, this letter had put it to rest. Not only did she know his handwriting, but she was more familiar with his tone than she would like to be.

She looked up and gave the duke the letter. "Perhaps you might tell me what it is that you have in mind, Your Grace."

Chapter 8

"Are you absolutely barking mad?" Marianne Simpson's eyes bulged in a manner that almost made Sin smile.

"No, not mad, Miss Simpson."

She looked from Sin to Guy to Elliot; neither was smiling.

"Then this is some sort of prank? I know aristocratic men like to make ridiculous wagers to alleviate the boredom in their pointless lives. That's what this is, right? A prank?"

"No. It is not a prank or a wager. It is a serious request. You need to get the three of us jobs with your uncle's circus. You read the letter—we will need to carry a great deal of money with us as well as bring my brother home in some sort of conveyance. Nobody will notice an extra caravan along with your uncle's circus."

"Fine. Then why can't you simply follow along behind in your caravan?"

"Because two peers and a servant of the Crown showing up armed in a foreign country—at this particular time—would cause no small number of political difficulties. And you read what Dominic said about Elliot. We must appear to blend in and not raise any eyebrows. If the other members of the circus saw a caravan with men who did nothing, *that* would raise eyebrows. We need jobs. We need to go unnoticed."

She gave a breathless laugh and shook her head. "My uncle has already engaged everyone he needs for the tour. With the war over, there is brisk competition for crews. We aren't the only ones who are taking advantage of the first opportunity to tour in decades. The people he's hired are skilled and strong and accustomed to long days and back-breaking work. They know how to move props and people speedily and efficiently."

Sin remained silent.

She flung up her hands. "Even if you *did* possess the skills necessary to do those jobs and I could persuade my uncle to hire you, what, exactly, am I supposed to do with the people my uncle has already engaged? Give them the sack because a couple of peers have decided it would be a lark to play at work?" Her angry question echoed in the room for a moment, and St. John could feel Guy and Elliot's stunned reactions to Marianne Simpson's raw aggression.

"I do not expect anyone to suffer by my actions," he said mildly, refusing to be insulted by her imputation that the three of them were lazy, useless weaklings. "I will generously compensate anyone who is displaced, Miss Simpson. I will pay them double what your uncle pays—just to sit at home and do nothing for the rest of the year. Would that suffice?"

She inhaled deeply and then let the air out in a noisy gust. "Even if some of the workers might accept that offer, what is it that the three of you are fit to *do*? All the jobs are either menial—meaning lots of toting, lugging, fetching, cooking, cleaning, and carrying, or they require a great deal of skill, like a carpenter or seamstress." She smirked. "Do any of you sew or paint theatrical sets?"

He ignored her dig. "I daresay we could manage toting, lugging, fetching, and so forth."

She laughed.

"Perhaps you might share the joke, Miss Simpson?" Sin asked coolly.

"I'm sorry, Your Grace, I'm just imagining you taking orders from circus employees—people who would certainly notice your lack of experience even with simple tasks. But assuming they *don't* notice, I'm picturing you—a duke—willingly and obediently fetching and carrying *and so forth*." She spoke the last three words in a deep-voiced, fair approximation of his accent.

"I am no stranger to physical exertion."

"It's not the exertion part that I'm concerned about." Her lips twitched. "I have to admit there is something appealing about the thought of you carrying my luggage."

Guy burst out laughing. "Lord, you two! Perhaps you need to tie on mufflers and go at it for a few rounds to sort matters out?"

Sin cut his gregarious friend a stern look; Miss Simpson needed no encouragement when it came to behaving obstreperously.

Fortunately, she didn't even appear to hear Guy—which was strange. It was an unusual woman who didn't notice Gaius Darlington, a man who was widely considered one of the most attractive and eligible bachelors in Britain.

Marianne Simpson was proving herself singular in several ways.

"Let us say that I can manage to find three *extremely* menial positions for you, how can you believe that you will go unnoticed?"

"I can alter my appearance," Sin assured her.

Again, she laughed, but this was more of a disbelieving snort. "Well, I'll have to take your word for that, I suppose."

"Yes, you will, Miss Simpson. You should also take my word for the fact that I will *not* change my mind about this. Nor do I wish to keep arguing the matter. It was my understanding that your presence here tonight indicated we had reached an arrangement."

"That is because I thought you just wanted to—oh, I don't know, bring your own caravan and follow along behind us. I didn't know you actually wanted *jobs*."

"Well, now you do know."

Her mouth opened, but no words came out.

"Now," Sin went on, "as for claiming that all the positions have been filled, I recall your uncle mentioning that you've dragged your heels about hiring Nelson's replacement—and some other man, too. Andy, was it? So that is two unfilled positions."

To Sin's surprise, she didn't tell him to get stuffed. Instead, she chewed her lip, her gaze turning thoughtful. A moment later she said, more to herself, "Perhaps that isn't such a bad idea."

"I beg your pardon?"

She looked up from her thoughts and met his inquiring gaze. "As you are wealthy men of leisure, I take it you all know how to box?"

Sin exchanged an amused glance with Elliot and Guy, neither of whom could be called wealthy, but both of whom most certainly knew how to box.

"We do," Guy answered for all three of them.

She turned to Elliot. "Will you please stand?"

Elliot's eyebrows arched, but he stood.

Miss Simpson rose from the chair in a sinuous motion and strode toward Elliot, prowling around him and eying him much the way a man might inspect a piece of horseflesh.

Elliot's normally inscrutable face flushed at being treated like an animal up for auction.

A muffled choking noise came from his right, where Guy was red in the face, attempting to suppress his chortling.

When Marianne stopped in front of Elliot, Sin noticed that his friend wasn't too much taller than she—perhaps two or three inches, although Elliot obviously outweighed her by at least a stone.

The two looked similar enough to be related: both lithe and compactly built with pale complexions and short, dark brown hair. Both moved with a predatory grace that hinted at latent strength in their slender forms.

"So, you can box?" she asked him.

The nostrils of Elliot's slender nose flared slightly. "Well enough."

"He was twice champion of the lightweight class at Eton," Guy volunteered, earning a filthy look from Elliot.

"I am in the presence of greatness, am I?" Miss Simpson asked, amusement clear in her voice. "Do you have a problem wearing mufflers or sparring with women?"

Elliot's brow furrowed. "No, to both."

"Can you come to the theater on Friday, first thing?"

"I can."

"Good. I'll make sure Nora and Lucy are there, too, and we'll see just what you have to offer."

Elliot's flush deepened at her provocative words.

She turned to Sin. "It'll be too much bother to find sparring partners while on the road, so my uncle wanted to hire somebody for the three of us. If your friend is as good as you say, then Jack will recommend him to my uncle. The job includes sparring, taking care of our equipment, serving as knee or bottle man, and whatever else needs to be done." She scowled at Elliot, as if he had argued. "This is a *real* position—do you understand what I'm saying? If you can't take us seriously and do the work required, I don't care what pressure His Grace brings to bear—you will need to find another way to get to Metz."

"I understand, Miss Simpson," Elliot said quietly.

She turned to Sin, giving him the same brash once-over she'd just given Elliot, stroking her chin as she studied him. "And what about you, Your Grace?"

"What about me?"

"Were you also a champion boxer at your posh boy's school?" she taunted.

"He was our—"

Sin cut Guy a sulfurous glare and the other man's mouth snapped shut.

"What are you getting at, Miss Simpson?" Sin asked, furious that his skin was heating under her mocking gaze.

"You were right; as neither Jack Nelson nor Andy Leonard will be coming on the tour, I'll need somebody else. I should have engaged someone already, but I've not been satisfied with the men so far." She smiled, an expression that held no humor. "It appears that my satisfaction is irrelevant."

Sin refused to rise to the bait.

"Whoever takes this position will serve as my knee man and supervise my training." She scowled at Sin. "This is also a *real* job."

"Is there a third position?" he asked with a mildness he was far from feeling.

"I'm taking my horse with me. I had planned to pay the lads taking care of my uncle's animals to look after Reggie, but I could engage a groom without raising any eyebrows. Since taking care of Reggie won't be a full-time job, whoever takes that position can also drive the caravan I'll share with Cecile and Josephine. That means he'd be transporting our luggage, running our errands, and whatever else needs doing."

She crossed her arms and gave him a belligerent look. "So, there are three positions. Whoever takes the first two will have to pass muster with Jack. The groom job is one I can bestow myself."

"Staunton boxes with the Gentleman thrice a week—he's your man when it comes to training," Guy said quickly, smirking at Sin. "I think I'm best suited for the groom position."

Sin gave the other man a look that promised retribution. Thanks to Guy, he would be closeted with a hostile woman for hours every day.

Marianne regarded Sin from beneath heavy lids but said nothing.

"I will take Jack's position," he said, as if he had any choice.

"You know that we cannot keep your identities from my uncle?"

"I trust it will go no further?"

"I'm not eager to share the news, nor will he be. So, unless anyone else recognizes you—and I can hardly be held responsible for that, can I?—nobody else will know."

"Nobody will recognize us," he assured her.

She gave a skeptical-sounding grunt. "I hope you understand that I will actually need you to *do* at least some of these tasks?"

"Yes, you may have mentioned that four or five times. In the past five minutes."

She gave him another scathing once-over. "You look as if you might be fit enough, but this is going to be real work, not *sparring with the Gentleman down at the club thrice a week*."

Guy made a sound like a dog whining as he tried—unsuccessfully—to repress his laughter.

"Yes, Miss Simpson," Sin shot back acidly, "I *understand*."

"Also, I'm not going to pay any of you. Indeed, I'm wondering if you shouldn't pay *me*."

Out of the corner of his eye, St. John saw Elliot bite his lip and look down at the floor to hide his expression. On his other side Guy was now snuffling and snorting like a truffle-hunting pig.

Sin sighed. "How much do you require?"

She looked displeased by his easy compliance. "Never mind about that. I don't need your money." She turned to Guy. "Lord Carlisle—I can hardly call you that. What name will you go by?"

"Guy is fine." He smiled. "Guy Darling."

She looked amused by that. "Fine. Guy, you won't need to do much of anything until a few days before we leave. You can collect the caravans—both mine and one you three will share. While you needn't come with the other two on Friday, you should make an appearance sometime next week so I can introduce you to Cecile and Josephine, both of whom you will also be"—she gave him a mean, slit-eyed look—"*serving*."

"Yes, Miss Simpson," he said meekly.

She eyed him suspiciously before turning back to Sin. "I asked my uncle about the locket and letter, and he knew nothing of them."

Sin wondered if she could really be so naïve as to believe a word that came out of Barnabas Farnham's mouth.

"Go ahead and look as disbelieving as you like," she said, reading his expression accurately. "He is my uncle and if he said he doesn't know, then he doesn't know. Are you going to have him imprisoned just because he doesn't have what you want?"

He did not dignify that with an answer. "When will you want me to start . . . *serving* you?"

She grinned, and it disturbed Sin that he found the expression more than a little taking.

"You should come along with Mr. Wingate so Jack can meet and approve of you. My guess is that he'll want you both to assume your duties immediately so he can keep an eye on you."

"He will expect us to start before we leave?" Sin asked, trying to keep his annoyance out of his voice but—judging by the smirk on her face—failing miserably.

"Oh, I'm so sorry," she said with an utterly unconvincing show of remorse. "Will this new job that you've just bullied and black-mailed your way into be an imposition for you? Do you find the notion of doing actual physical work six days a week unappealing? Perhaps you have changed your mind, Your Grace? I'm sure you can—"

"You want us there at six o'clock?" Sin ground out, losing the fight to keep his temper.

"On Fridays we meet at ten, so make sure you're there on time—I despise tardiness."

"Is that all, Miss Simpson?" Sin asked icily. "Or do you have any other instructions for me?"

"No, that is all. For now. But since you are now my employee, Your Grace, I suggest that you become comfortable with following my orders—and that you learn to do so quickly and with a smile on your face."

The door had scarcely closed behind Miss Simpson before Guy broke out in helpless laughter. "Lord, Sin, that woman is going to make your life hell for the next two months. An absolute *hell*."

Sin ignored him.

"Well, that was easier than I'd imagined," Elliot said, trying not to smile and failing. "The good news is that if we're expected to start right away, that means I'll have access to the theater, which is only a short step away from Farnham's house."

"You think it wise to investigate Farnham's place yourself?" Sin asked.

"I can take a good look around without getting caught," Elliot assured him, turning to Guy. "In spite of what Miss Simpson just said, I think all three of us should take every opportunity to spend time at the theater and get to know the employees. The more com-fortable they are with us, the less they will notice us, which means the more freedom of movement we shall have. But neither of you should make any effort to poke around. When it comes to getting into Farnham's office and house—"

"We shall leave all that to you," Sin assured him.

"Good," Elliot said. "Because Farnham will have his eye on you, Staunton, waiting for you to do something suspicious. The same with you, Guy."

"And you think that you will escape his notice?" Sin asked.

"Maybe not escape it, but I'm far less interesting or noticeable than either of you."

"Have a care, Elliot. People who've had dealings with Farnham and Strickland in the past have died," Sin reminded him. "Are you sure you really need to get into his office and house?"

"I feel that we are operating in the dark; and Farnham, with his past connection to Dominic, is the best hope we've got of digging up any information. There may be nothing to find, but there are too many unknowns not to at least make the effort."

"What can the two of us do to help you?"

"Get Farnham—and the girl—to lower their guard. And the way to do that is simply to show our faces, get them accustomed to our being there. Hell, let them think this is a lark for us. She already thinks we are self-indulgent arseholes looking for entertainment." He snorted, amusement glinting in his dark eyes. "I'm guessing she's going to make all three of our lives hell in the hope that we'll just give up."

Sin wished her good bloody luck with her plan. Until he had Ben safely home, he'd be stuck to Miss Marianne Simpson tighter than a limpet to a rock at low tide.

Chapter 9

Marianne was changing from her breeches and boots after her Friday morning ride when the dressing room door opened and Cedric, one of the stagehands, popped his head into the room.

"There's two blokes out here to see you. You want to talk to 'em?"

Marianne smirked at the duke's punctuality. "Send them in," she said, stepping out from behind the screen and fastening the big wooden buttons on her gray work gown.

Cedric opened the door wider. "Go on in, gents."

For a moment, Marianne thought it was somebody else—not the duke and his friend, at all.

One was tall, broad, brown-haired, with silver-rimmed spectacles. He wore old tweed trousers tucked into battered hobnail boots. On top he wore a black-and-white checked neckerchief, a worsted dark green coat, and a hideous gold and green vest beneath it.

Marianne couldn't help gawking when she reached his face—specifically, his jaw. He'd not shaved for a few days and the stubble was a shocking ginger interspersed with patches of silvery-blond. He looked . . . mottled.

In fact, he was all but unrecognizable.

Wingate wore a similar outfit and he'd shorn his thick, dark brown hair down to about an inch, until it looked like the velvety pelt of an animal. The short hair made his cheekbones as sharp as blades and exposed slashed black eyebrows that gave him a menacing aspect.

Marianne had to admit that she'd only recognized the men because she'd known they'd be coming today.

She met His Grace's pale green stare—there were some things a person couldn't hide, like the distinctive color of their eyes. "I am impressed," she said grudgingly, her gaze lingering on his hair, which was no longer a silky pale blond but a flat, mid-brown that was somewhat incongruous with his copper beard.

That beard; Marianne couldn't help smirking. "Lord, that goes well beyond ginger to an almost flamelike orange, doesn't it?"

He did not look amused by her observation.

"How did you get here today?" she asked. "Because if you came in that black behemoth of yours then all this"—she waved a hand at their persons—"was for naught."

"We engaged a hackney."

Marianne winced at the crisp, hard-as-diamond syllables. "You might look like a regular bloke but you still sound like a nob."

"You sound a bit like a *nob* yourself," he retorted coolly.

Marianne grinned at his acerbic response and his eyes widened, as if he didn't expect a pugilistic strumpet to possess a sense of humor.

"Fair enough," she conceded. "I've been accused of sounding like a toff more than once. I suppose it's not unheard of for the lower orders to ape their betters."

He narrowed his eyes at her emphasis on the word *betters*.

Now that the first shock had passed, Marianne noticed two more things that gave him away; his commanding stance and proud posture, which were those of a man who owned a goodly chunk of Britain.

Still, a person had to choose their battles. There was probably no way to beat the duke completely out of him. No matter how much she might like to.

"You have a few weeks to soften your accent a bit and also work on your posture."

"What is wrong with my posture?" he asked, stiffening and looking even more ducal.

"You look like you have an iron rod up your . . . er, well, you are as stiff as a poker. Take a look at the men you will be rubbing elbows with for the next few months and try to emulate them."

She could see by his haughty scowl that he didn't fancy the notion of emulating riffraff.

Marianne narrowed her eyes at him. "It might surprise you to learn that you are not the only one who doesn't want to be discovered playing at being a working man. I would prefer never to have my name linked with another aristocrat's. There would be only one conclusion people would draw if they found out that I had smuggled you into my uncle's circus. So, if you don't mind, I would be grateful if every person along our tour route didn't learn that you are a duke."

His eyes glittered dangerously at her disrespectful tone.

Marianne knew she was enjoying baiting His Grace far too much, and that her petty behavior did not reflect well on her character. She didn't care.

"Fine," he grated. "Who are we supposed to be then?"

"Given your accent, I think we'll just tell people that you used to be a butler in a lord's house. They're even starchier than their employers, aren't they?"

Elliot Wingate chuckled, the sound unexpectedly soft coming from a man who bore more than a passing resemblance to a satyr with his sharp features. "She's got you there, Staunton—er, sorry, Sin. Buffle is far more intimidating than any of the royal dukes."

"Sin?" Marianne asked.

"It is a pet name," His Grace said frostily, looking more displeased by the moment.

"*You*—the morally upstanding and noble Lord Flawless—have the nickname *sin*?" Marianne laughed. "Is it supposed to be ironical?"

The duke's eyes narrowed to dangerous green slits.

"It's a boyhood shortening of his Christian name," Elliot explained hastily, as the tension in the room thickened.

"What name is that?" she asked, and then cut the duke a sneer. "Or is it forbidden to share such information with a mere commoner?"

"St. John." The name came out somewhere between a low snarl and a hiss.

Hmm. Yes, he certainly looked like a St. John. "Isn't the name *Sin* something that a bunch of other toffs will associate with you?"

"No," Elliot said, while the duke seethed. "Only two others have ever called him that."

"Hmph." Marianne pondered for a minute, trying to come up with something that didn't scream *nob* but at the same time was familiar enough for Staunton to answer to. "How about we just say Sin is short for a more normal surname—like Sinclair. John Sinclair?"

"Fine," the duke said shortly.

She smirked. "Good—we already have a Squeaky, a Bazzer, and a Chook, so you'll fit right in."

"Why would a former butler join a traveling circus?" the duke asked, ignoring her dig.

"I'm sure you've sacked more than a few servants. Think of a reason."

He bristled visibly at her accusation but didn't refute it.

"Why do servants lose their jobs?" Marianne asked. "Fighting, wenching . . . stealing." She stopped. "Stealing. Hmm—"

"No," he said firmly. "I refuse to bear the stigma of thief for the next nine weeks."

His pinched expression amused her. "Fine, so, not a thief." She pursed her mouth and twitched her nose from side to side as she considered possible reasons for his downward social trajectory. "Let's say you were discovered quenching your thirst in your employer's cellar—not for the first time—and he discharged you without a character reference."

"So, I am a dipsomaniac."

Marianne smiled.

The duke sighed. "Very well. And how is it that I heard about this job?"

"We'll say you heard about it from Charlie Whittaker, who used to be a footman before he was a fighter: Handsome Charlie, he's often called."

"And won't this Charlie person deny knowing me?"

"Fortunately, he returned home to Glasgow not long ago. We can say you both worked for the same master years ago."

The duke nodded.

Marianne turned to the shorter man. "And you—what name do you want to go by?"

"Elliot will be fine."

"Elliot? *Elliot?*" She laughed. "No, I don't think so. That's almost as bad as *Sinjin*. And Wingate won't work."

"How about Smith, is that *normal* enough?" Elliot suggested with a wry look.

"A boxer would never go by Smith. Can you answer to Smithy?"

"I believe I could do that."

"Are you from London?"

"No, Bristol."

Marianne grinned. "Ah, the home of champions! Hen Pearce, Tom Cribb, and Jem Belcher." She surveyed his whipcord-lean body from head to toe. "So, we'll say you've just moved here from Bristol. I met Pearce once and you've the look of him. Why don't we tell people that you used to work for a butcher but got the sack when you cast your gaze too high—upon your employer's daughter. You've boxed since you were a lad, but you took a proper fibbing a few years back and you've not had a money bout since. Can you remember all that?"

He gave her another of his faint smiles. "I think I'll manage, Miss Simpson."

"You'd better get accustomed to calling me Marianne." She looked at the duke. "Both of you."

"And your trainer will not mind your hiring such reprobates—and without any character recommendations?" the duke asked.

"Unlike your sort, Your Grace, Jack doesn't expect people to be papered like racehorses. He knows what it's like to earn his crust and believes people deserve a second chance."

"Perhaps you should cease *Your Gracing* me and call me Sin, *Marianne*."

She doubted that she'd ever be able to call him by such an intimate name. She would avoid calling him anything at all.

"So, let's get to it then, shall we?" She moved toward the door, but the duke reached it first.

She stopped and glared up at him rather than going through the now open doorway. "You're no longer a gentleman. Women like me open our own doors."

"I refuse to be discourteous, simply because everyone else is."

"It will make you stand out even more than your speech and dukely posture."

His nostrils flared at her mockery "I believe the word you are searching for is *ducal*."

"No, is it?" she asked with exaggerated surprise. "I suppose you would know."

He cut her a scathing look and strode through the door ahead of her, no doubt suffering an agony of self-recrimination at his ungentlemanly behavior.

Sin knew she was just trying to goad an angry response from him—and she was damned good at it, too. If he bickered with her, then he'd just be giving her what she expected. He needed to ignore her childish digs and jabs.

That was easier said than done.

Jack Nelson was just shrugging out of his overcoat and an older man—yet another pugilist by the look of his battered visage—was in the process of hanging up one of the leather bags.

"'Mornin', luv," Jack called out to Marianne when they entered. His dark eyes flickered curiously over Sin and Elliot.

"These are Sin and Smithy," she said. "The ones I mentioned to you."

Nelson strode toward them. "Annie says you've both done a bit o' fightin' and know your way about a mill."

Elliot spoke first. "Aye, sir. I fought at The Hatchet and trained with Jemmy Wallace when I was a lad."

Sin blinked at his friend's sudden, incomprehensible, accent.

Whatever it was that Elliot had said brought a smile to Jack's face. "I squared up against Jemmy years ago." He pursed his lips and shook his head. "A damned shame what 'appened to 'im."

"Well, he always did like the ponies a bit too much," Elliot agreed. Both men took a moment of respectful silence.

Jack turned to Sin; his eyes narrowed. "I 'aven't ever seen a fighter with specs before."

"They are recent. I didn't wear them back when I fought in Leeds." Sin had conceived of a past for himself before coming today, choosing Leeds because he owned an estate just outside the big northern town and had often sneaked into mills with a cousin when he'd been a lad. "I had a few big money bouts at The Jolly Taxpayer, but that was years ago."

Jack's eyebrows—one of which was bisected by not one, but two white scars, shot up. "Blimey, listen to you." He turned to Marianne, who'd watched their exchange with ill-concealed amusement. "Didja find a bleedin' *dook* to replace me, luv?"

The little shrew grinned. "Nobody could ever replace you, Jack. Mr. Sinclair talks like a duke because he used to butler for one. He got sacked for being on the tipple."

"Oh, aye?" Jack asked, giving Sin a second, more piercing, look. "Which one'd ye work for? Tell me it wasn't that arsehole Lord Flawless?"

Marianne coughed and then said in a choked voice, "Er, not him, Jack. It was some other arsehole—a Scottish duke." She surveyed Sin with laughing eyes; it was an engaging, charming expression that hadn't been turned his way before. "It was Handsome Charlie who told him about the job."

Jack looked pleased by that information. "You know that old rascal Charlie, do ye?"

"Yes, I do," he lied.

"Quite the lad, old Charlie, eh?"

"Oh, yes," Sin agreed. "Ah, the stories I could tell."

The big man chuckled. "Aye, I imagine so. Well," Jack said, rubbing his two huge paws together, "if Charlie says yer awright, I reckon that's good enough for me. Come in on the mornings I'm 'ere—Fridays, Mondays, and Wednesdays and I'll show you the ropes with Annie. You know how to ride?"

Sin blinked. "I'm sorry?"

"Ride. Can ye ride an 'orse?"

"Er, yes."

"You'll need to go on 'er runs. Rent an 'ack and give Barney the bills."

He glanced at Marianne, who raised her eyebrows at him, as if daring him to demur.

"I can do that," he said.

"Good. You can work out the days and such with Marianne. Nora and Lucy are the other lassies, but Nora's brother Ted works with 'er and Lucy most of the time, so they'll only need you in a pinch."

"I think he should come in and train with Lucy and Nora, too, Jack. He should be familiar with all three of us," Marianne said, smirking as she filled up his days.

"Aye, yer right, lass. So then," Jack said, eyeing Sin. "You good comin' around every day till you leave?"

Sin cut Marianne an exasperated look. "Of course, if that is what you need."

"Good. You'll need to talk to them to find out what time to come in." He paused and frowned. "If clutch-fisted Barney makes any noises about not payin' you yet, why, you just send 'im along to me."

Sin nodded.

"All three are damned good pugs." Jack cut Marianne a fond look. "Marianne's been trainin' a while and knows 'er business, but she'll slack on her runnin' if you let 'er."

Marianne made an undignified squawking sound. "I don't—"

Jack smirked and ignored her. "I want 'er doin' five days a week—you'll need to crack the whip and make sure she keeps up to snuff, aye?"

It was Sin's turn to smile. Judging by the way Marianne flinched, it was a less than pleasant expression.

"It will be a pleasure to make sure Miss Marianne stays up to snuff." He looked down at the woman in question, whose earlier grin had turned into a glower. "As for cracking the whip?" His smile grew until it exposed his teeth. "That is something I will do most vigorously. And enjoy it."

Jack laughed and clapped Marianne on the shoulder with a huge paw. "It looks like you've found yerself a regular taskmaster, lass."

Her eyes narrowed at Sin.

"Now," Jack said, turning to Elliot. "Let's see what Smithy 'as to offer you, Annie."

Marianne was gasping for air after three rounds with Elliot Wingate.

"Awright, awright, that's good for now," Jack called out just when she thought her lungs might explode.

She groaned and dropped her hands to her knees, gasping.

"Somebody 'asn't been doin' 'er runnin'," Jack said in a sing-songy voice that made her want to punch him.

Marianne was too winded to answer.

"Yer right 'andy wiff yer fives," Jack said to Elliot.

She looked up in time to see Elliot's already flushed face darken. "She kept me on my toes," he said—kindly, in Marianne's opinion. The truth was, if Elliot hadn't pulled his punches, she wouldn't have lasted even a round with him. He was *fast* and incredibly strong, his body wiry, hard, and trim.

"So, what do you 'ave to say about our girl, Sin?" Jack asked the duke, whom Jack had told to study Marianne's form while she sparred.

Marianne glared at His Grace, *daring* him to open his mouth.

He crossed his arms over his broad chest and rocked back on the heels of his battered boots, the casual pose strange for such a stiff, upright man. "She drops her left."

"I do *not*," she retorted.

Jack chuckled. "Aye, lass—you know you do." He nodded at the duke. "You've a good eye, Sin. Now, what I want to talk about is some changes in 'er trainin'—"

Marianne scowled as the two men began to discuss her as if she weren't standing right there.

"You're good."

She turned at the sound of the quiet voice to where Andy was untying Elliot's mufflers.

"You're better," she said, pleased she didn't sound as grudging as she felt.

Elliot just smiled.

The stage door opened and Josephine entered. She glanced around the room, her strange, pale gray eyes flickering over the people in it. As always, Angus rode on her shoulder, his crafty black eyes as sharp as his mistress's were vague, taking in the room and its occupants.

"Good morning, Jo—did you need something?" Marianne asked when it seemed the other woman wouldn't speak.

Jo's gaze fixed on Elliot, who stared right back at her. Both went strangely still, and Marianne was put in mind of two alley cats. If they'd had fur, it would be standing on end.

"Er, Jo?" Marianne repeated.

"Your uncle said you'd hired new volunteers. I wanted to meet them," she said, her gaze still on Elliot. A wicked looking dagger appeared in her right hand, as if from thin air, and she deftly rolled it over the back of her hand and caught it, the motion smooth and hypnotic.

"Volunteers?" Elliot repeated, raising one black brow.

"Aye," Andy said as he finished untying Elliot's gloves and moved on to Marianne's. "All the lads take turns."

Elliot looked from Jo to Marianne. "Take turns doing what?"

"Oh, didn't I mention that part of your job—the volunteering part?"

Jack and the duke had stopped talking to listen to their conversation.

"No, you didn't mention anything about volunteering," Staunton said in a tight voice—no doubt wondering if he'd have enough time left every day to eat or sleep.

Jack patted His Grace's shoulder. "Don't worry, Sin, the lassies are both professionals. Trust me, you'll get used to it." He snickered. "After a while."

"Get used to *it*? What is *it*?" the duke repeated.

She had to bite the inside of her cheek to keep from laughing. "You'll be one of the volunteers in Jo's knife-throwing act."

"*Volunteer*," Angus intoned, sounding so much like Jo it was eerie.

Elliot looked from the bird to Marianne. "You keep saying *volunteer*. What exactly does that mean?"

"She means that I'll throw knives at you," Jo said in her low, toneless voice.

"*Knives*," Angus echoed.

The two men's heads whipped around to stare at Jo—or perhaps Angus—neither of whom paid them any mind.

Jo now held a second, identical, knife in her left hand and was simultaneously spinning both. Angus was grooming the feathers of one wing, his huge beak making a *fffffft, fffffft* sound.

It was Andy who broke the shocked silence. "And Cecile will shoot an apple off your 'ead," he said, pulling off the second of Marianne's mufflers. "Just about soiled myself the first time she did it," Andy muttered under his breath.

"She'll also shoot the pips out of playing cards while you hold them," Jack chipped in, clearly enjoying the men's startled expressions.

"Between your teeth," Andy clarified.

Staunton and Elliot slowly turned away from Jo to Marianne.

Marianne met their outraged glares with wide-eyed surprise. "Did I neglect to mention that?"

"You did," the duke said in a voice that was all silky menace. "Is there anything else we should be aware of? Do we have to swing from a trapeze? Juggle flaming torches?"

"Oh, nothing like that." She found that she could no longer hold back her laughter. "Although you might need to step in for the clowns, on occasion."

Chapter 10

Marianne tossed the jarvey a coin and rubbed her hands together as she headed toward the footpath that ran along the river. It was cold—freezing, even. Her uncle was a bit mad to plan this tour so early in the year, but he was right about his two chief competitors getting the jump on him. John Dornan's all-female circus had already left for Paris in December, and Melvin Pickle's far smaller circus was leaving just a week after Farnham's.

Everyone—not only circuses and businessmen, but aristocrats by the drove—was headed to Europe now that the war was over. Of course the performers who worked for Farnham's would hardly be rubbing shoulders with the crème de la crème who were reported to have gathered in cities like Paris and Brussels.

Marianne chafed her upper arms through her worn woolen coat and glanced around, looking for the duke as she jogged in place on the hard-packed soil.

How disappointing that she'd broken his resolve so quickly.

The last time she'd seen him had been at four o'clock yesterday when she'd passed through the theater looking for Cecile. She'd seen the duke loading up the dirty linen that Jack had allowed to build up.

She'd lingered long enough to hear Jack send him to the laundry and remind him to come back at eight to observe Nora's fight that evening.

Marianne chuckled at the memory of the high-and-mighty Duke of Staunton reduced to toting dirty laundry.

Well, she didn't need him in order to run; that was just a precaution Jack insisted on—

The clop of hooves came from behind her, and Marianne turned.

And immediately laughed. "Where did you get *that* nag?" she asked once she'd stopped chuckling at the sight of the imposing, dignified Duke of Staunton seated on the sway-backed, spavined old horse.

"I believe you *commanded* me to avoid notice," he reminded her icily.

"That's even worse than the horse Andy usually rides." Andy was the one who accompanied her on most of her runs. "If you got him from the livery Jack told you about, I think they might be having a laugh at your expense."

"As much as I hate to disappoint you, I didn't rent the animal."

"You *own* a horse like that?"

"I do now. As I didn't care to be lingering around a livery before dawn five days a week, I purchased *Dobbin*."

"Where? From a glue factory?"

"Very droll."

"Your stable master must think you've run mad to bring back such an animal."

"Of course I do not keep him at Berkeley Square."

"Of course not," she said in a soothing voice, grinning broadly as her gaze moved over Staunton and his steed. The duke was dressed in rugged clothing like that he'd worn yesterday. His hair was hidden under a battered tweed flat cap and his face even scruffier. In fact, he looked rumpled, as if he'd barely had time to wake up. His overcoat was a nondescript brown homespun that had been liberally patched and his heavy hobnail boots barely fit in the stirrups.

"You sound a bit crabby this morning, Your Grace. Is this earlier than you usually are up and about? Or was it the long day you had yesterday? I hope your new job isn't interfering with your busy, ducal schedule?"

The duke just stared, rather than responding. She noticed that he did that quite a lot. No doubt he was accustomed to his lofty position, imposing stature, and hawkish glare intimidating all his underlings.

But Marianne wasn't his underling, so he could stare until his eyes fell out.

Which he appeared more than willing to do.

"Let's see if you can get that beast up to a trot." She started down the path at an easy lope. "Try to keep up," she called over her shoulder.

A moment later his horse clattered up beside her.

Marianne put him out of her mind and fell into a rhythm.

The first ten minutes of every run were always miserable, but by the time she neared the end, usually around three-quarters of an hour, she would wonder why she'd made such a fuss.

"How long will you go?" the duke asked, his deep voice startling her from her from a pleasing fugue.

"What time is it?"

He took out a battered tin watch. "Half-past six."

"Until a little after seven."

"Jack said you do this five days every week?"

"Jack would *like* me to run five days every week, but I generally don't do more than four."

"If I'm your new trainer, then I say you will do five days a week—I shall meet you here tomorrow at the same time."

Marianne laughed. Let him try to make her do anything. "The same time tomorrow," she said, agreeably.

She'd be in Hyde Park.

His eyes widened at her easy acceptance and he looked quite proud of himself for having *cracked the whip*.

"Jack has his own boxing parlor, does he not?" the duke asked, more agreeable than she'd heard him sound before.

"Yes. And a wife and five children, with another on the way. He likes to schedule my time before he opens."

"Why don't you train at his place of business?"

"We tried that—at first. But—"

"You garnered too much attention?" he guessed.

"Something like that." Marianne glanced up at him. He wasn't frowning at her—as he usually seemed to do. He wasn't exactly *smiling*, but at least he wasn't looking at her as if she were something stuck to the bottom of his boot.

They didn't speak for the rest of the run, which was just as well as she was too winded to talk.

"This is it," she said in a breathy voice as they approached Temple Gardens. She slowed to a walk, taking a few minutes to cool down. Once she'd caught her breath, she walked back to where he waited, surprised when he pulled a wine bottle from a saddlebag, pulled out the bung, and held it toward her.

She drank a quarter of the bottle before handing it back. "Thank you."

"Shall I hail you a hackney?"

"No, that's not necessary. I'm going to walk over to Water Street. You can go."

"I'll accompany you."

Marianne frowned. While she wanted to pull him out of his warm bed and servant-filled house at the crack of dawn, she didn't want to share her breakfast with him.

"I'm just going to get something to eat," she said. "No training involved. Consider it a reprieve—a chance to go back to your warm bed."

He re-corked the bottle and slipped it into the bag before dismounting. "I shall accompany you," he repeated.

"Why? I am only just—"

"I cannot *go back to my warm bed* as I will be meeting Lucy at the theater in an hour—thanks to your kind suggestion that I show up *every day*. Or one of your suggestions—because I believe you were the reason I spent two hours yesterday polishing every single dumbbell—"

"They were dirty," she said, not bothering to hide her smile.

"—and also the one who convinced Farnham that Elliot and I should move every single chair and bench in the stalls because you'd conceived of a new seating arrangement that would accommodate more punters? Which it didn't. So then we had to move them all *back* the way they were initially."

She shrugged. "There can be no progress without failure."

He gave her a look that made her skin burn.

"Besides, I will not leave a gently bred woman in this part of the city unattended. No matter what you have to say about it." He raised an eyebrow at her, a supercilious action that irritated her almost as much as his presumptuous, arrogant, masculine assumption that she needed his protection. Or, indeed, that she needed anything from him.

You're the one who insisted he be here . . . .

Marianne gritted her teeth at the unwanted reminder. Instead, she spun on her heel and marched down the road.

Sin led the ancient horse and followed her. Although she didn't speak, anger vibrated off her like the hum from a tuning fork.

That was too damned bad. It had been her idea to run him ragged, so now she could deal with the fruits of her labor.

Sin almost smiled at the irony; *hoisted by your own petard, eh, Miss Simpson?*

He smelled the bakery before he saw it. Although it was early, a short queue had already formed, so they joined the line. She pointedly ignored him while they waited.

The baker's assistant, a pretty dark-eyed brunette, leaned on the ledge of the Dutch door and gave Marianne a worshipful smile that said the two had met before. "Hallo, Mr. Simpson." Her eyes flickered to Sin and widened. "Ye've brought a friend today."

"Mornin', Sally," Marianne said gruffly. "Two of the pork, please."

"Anythin' for *you*, Mr. Simpson." The girl smirked and ducked back inside.

How in the world could anyone believe Marianne Simpson was a man? Her features were decidedly feminine, as were her mannerisms, but all most people seemed to see was her clothing.

When the girl returned with two paper-wrapped packages, Marianne gave her some coins. "Ta, luv."

"See you next week, Mr. Simpson?" she asked in a breathy, hopeful voice.

Marianne just smiled, shoved one of the packages at Sin, and then stalked back to the post where he'd tethered Dobbin.

Sin stared at the warm, fragrant package, his brow furrowing. She had bought him breakfast.

"What's wrong?" she asked, unwrapping her food and scowling up at him. "Are you too good for growlers?"

"No, I'm not too good for a growler," he snapped, too exasperated by her relentless sniping to hide his irritation. "It's just that I've not had one for many years," he added pointlessly.

And never in his life had a woman bought him . . . anything.

Take hold of yourself, St. John. It's not a wedding ring, old boy. It's just a pork pie.

"Well, sorry if the location isn't up to your usual standards, but these are the best in London," she said, and then set about devouring hers.

Sin ignored her dig and unwrapped the brown paper, the savory smell making him woozy. "I've only heard them called growlers in Yorkshire," he said, and then took a bite and was ashamed of the noise he made.

She grinned up at him, the open expression transforming her from a scowling hoyden into a lovely young woman, and temporarily robbing him of breath.

"I told you they were good. Our cook taught me that term—she's from Leeds," she added, still smiling.

He chewed and swallowed and hoped that she didn't notice his flushed face. Or, if she did, that she attributed it to enjoyment of his meat pie.

The pies were better than good—they were sinfully hot and

delicious on a freezing morning. They also brought back fond boyhood memories he'd not thought about in years.

They leaned against the side of a horseless wagon that was resting on its shafts and ate their meal in companionable silence.

Marianne finished first and looked up at him, her smile gone. "You are a duke. Surely you have other things to do—important things. How is it that you can spend entire days playing at work?"

"I do have lots of things to do," he admitted. And the list was only getting longer thanks to her meddling, but he kept that to himself. "But there is nothing more important than my brother's life." He frowned down at her. "If you are hoping to drive me into quitting by running me ragged, then you are severely misguided. I will fulfill my obligations to you, just as I promised I would," he said, amused by the mulish expression his words had created.

He ate the last mouthful of pie and cut a yearning glance across the street at the bakery; the line was three times as long.

"I wouldn't bother," she said, reading his mind far too easily for his comfort. "The pork ones go quickly. They'll be out of everything except loaves of bread by the time you get up to the front again." She stepped toward the street and raised her hand to hail a hackney. "Next time it will be your turn to buy breakfast."

To her surprise, the duke was waiting for her when she arrived to pick up Reggie the following morning.

Today he was clean-shaven, dressed in his regular, impeccable clothing, and rode the same stunning stallion he'd been astride the first time they'd met.

Marianne gave the stable lad a coin and swung into the saddle before turning to Staunton.

"What are you doing here?" she asked, urging Reggie on his way.

"Why? Were you hoping I was wandering around on Dobbin, looking for you down by the river?" He fell in beside her.

She smirked.

"I thought you might be here, but I sent Guy to wait for you by your running path, just in case."

That made her laugh.

"I'm pleased it amuses you to waste our time," he said coolly.

Marianne didn't deny it. "Well, you can leave now that you've delivered your message," she told him. "Hyde Park is hardly dangerous. I do not require protection here. Nor do I need somebody to *crack the whip* and make me ride." Nor did she want him there. As much as she wanted to drive him to quit and leave her alone, she enjoyed her solitary rides too much to wish to share them.

"I ride most mornings around this time, so it is no inconvenience to me."

"Why aren't you riding Dobbin today?"

He smiled—true, it was small—but the sight startled her so much that she almost fell off her horse. Had he smiled before? Not that she'd seen. A sneer once or twice, but no smile.

"Won't people wonder who you're riding with?" she asked, shoving away thoughts of his disturbing almost-smile.

"I rarely see anyone I know this early. If I do, I'll tell them you're the son of a friend."

"Don't you have to go to Parliament and speechify and make laws to control the rest of us?" she asked as they rode down the almost empty street toward the park entrance.

He ignored her.

"Don't you have vast properties to manage? Servants to order about? Parties to grace with your presence? Women to charm?"

"I can still do all those other things and spare a few hours for you every day, Miss Simpson."

"How fortunate for me."

They rode in silence.

"I'm going to want to run once we are inside the park," she warned him as they neared the gates.

"Of course."

His pleasant acceptance was annoying. It was not easy to keep insulting somebody when they would not rise to the bait. She eyed his mount. "That is a lovely animal," she said grudgingly.

"Yes, Cassio is one of the first pleasure horses to come out of a stud I acquired several years ago."

"Cassio?" She laughed. "Interesting choice of name. I trust you aren't planning to name any of your other horses Iago?"

He patted the stallion's neck. "Probably not."

"Have you only recently begun breeding horses?"

"I've only acquired this particular farm recently. It was given over to breeding racehorses, but I have no interest in racing, so I am taking the stud in a different direction."

"An aristocrat who isn't interesting racing?" she mocked. "I didn't think that was allowed."

He turned to face her. "Do you always classify people so rigidly, Marianne?"

She experienced an annoying fluttering low in her belly at the sound of her name on his tongue.

"We are here," she said, ignoring his question. "It's time to run."

Chapter 11

By the fifth day, Marianne was beginning to have a little respect for the Duke of Staunton. He might have lived the life of an entitled aristocrat, but he was not going to break easily.

By the eighth day Marianne had begun to suspect that the duke would not be put off by a constant stream of menial, pointless, or disgusting jobs.

By the end of the second week, she had all but given up trying to break his will. It simply took too much effort. Besides, when she could make herself forget who he really was for a few minutes, he was actually an excellent trainer—not to mention a fine boxer, himself—and had improved her performance in more than a few areas.

They hadn't become friendly, of course, but she had stopped sniping at him. Well, at least she'd cut the number of snipes in half.

One morning at the beginning of the third week Marianne showed up at the livery stable to find the duke waiting for her on a new horse—this one a gorgeous silvery-gray gelding. Beside him, saddled and ready, was Cassio.

"Is somebody else joining us?" she asked, peering into the dimness of the stables and looking for the lad who worked the early morning.

"No, I thought you might enjoy riding him."

Marianne spun around. "*Me*?"

The duke nodded.

Marianne looked at Cassio, who looked back at her with, she would have sworn, a haughty, skeptical equine sneer—as if the magnificent stallion couldn't believe his master would dream of loaning him out to such a plebian.

She turned back to the duke. "I couldn't."

"You are worried you will not be able to handle him?"

"Of course I'm not worried about that!"

The faint smirk on his lips told her he'd been taunting her and she'd snapped at the bait.

Well. Who knew His Grace had a sense of humor?

"What I meant to say," she explained, "is that the animal is too valuable. What if I damaged him? I'd never be able to repay you."

"Damage him? How?"

"I don't know—what if he threw a splint or I ran him into a rabbit hole?"

Both blond brows went up. "A rabbit hole on the Row?"

She threw him a look of pure exasperation. "You know what I mean, Your Grace."

"I didn't peg you for a coward, Marianne."

Marianne snorted. "Does that sort of taunt work on your two friends, Your Grace?"

"I loan out my mounts all the time and most of the people I loan them to are not half the rider you are."

Marianne was momentarily rendered speechless by his unexpected compliment.

"I've made my offer clear—the decision is up to you. If you don't wish to ride him, Emmett"—he gestured to the groom holding his reins—"can ride him back to my stable."

She slowly exhaled. "Oh, well, there's no need to put Emmett to extra work," she protested disingenuously. "But if anything happens—"

He looked painfully bored as he inspected the handle of his crop.

Marianne stroked Cassio's neck, looking him in the eye. "You will have an easy morning with me—no hulking brute to haul around."

Emmett coughed and glanced away, but not before Marianne saw the smile on his face.

Marianne mounted and took the reins from the groom. "Thank you, Emmett," she said, smiling down at the man. Goodness! It was amazing how much higher up she felt, even though Cassio couldn't be more than a hand and a half higher than Reggie.

"Ready?" the duke asked.

They rode out at a sedate pace and Marianne was immediately aware of the difference between Reggie and the duke's horse.

"Well, blast," she muttered after a minute or so of gliding along on Cassio. "I'm not sure I'll ever be satisfied with poor Reggie after this."

"Yes, Cassio is a gem."

Marianne gestured to the horse he was riding. "Is this another of your new horses?"

"No, Bay Rum didn't come out of the new stud, I've had him a good ten years at least. He has been here in London for the past year. When I leave, I shall send him home to enjoy the country." He patted the horse's neck with an affection that surprised her, coming from such a cold, unemotional man.

"Where is your home?" she asked.

"Derbyshire."

"Pretty."

"You've been there?"

"There is no law to keep people of my kind out of the provinces."

Marianne immediately regretted her unpleasant response—especially since he'd gone out of his way to please her with the loan of his horse.

"Marianne. Must we—"

"I'm sorry, Your Grace."

His eyebrows jumped in obvious surprise.

"What? You don't think I can apologize when I've been rude?"

"It has not been my experience."

Marianne chuckled, earning another startled look. "I deserve that. As to Derbyshire, I stayed there one Easter with a schoolmate."

"Where did you go to school?"

"I went to Miss Nolan's Academy for Young Ladies."

"I've heard of it. An excellent school."

"You're probably wondering how I managed to get in?"

He gave her a pained look.

"Sorry, that sounded a bit, er, snappish."

"A bit. But yes, now that you mention it, I thought the school had a waiting list."

"It does." Marianne cut him a shrewd look. "I was fortunate in receiving a recommendation from the Countess of Morecombe."

The duke frowned, his expression that of a man cudgeling his memory. "Isn't that—"

"Dominic's maternal grandmother."

"You've known him since you were a girl, then?"

"Not personally. It was my uncle who arranged that. I didn't actually meet Dominic until after I'd left school." She watched with interest as he absorbed that information. Just what would the duke ask next?

But when they reached the park gates, he surprised her by saying, "Did you wish to run?"

"Not just yet." She gave him a sheepish smile. "I'd like to get used to Cassio first."

He nodded.

After a moment, he said, "I am glad to hear Dominic was able to use his influence for good."

"For a change?" she added.

"Well, you were the one who said it first—that Dominic was motivated solely by money."

"I did say that," she admitted. "And that's why he talked his grandmother into lending her support. He owed my uncle for something or other. I'm fortunate that Barnabas thought to seek repayment in such a form," she said, meaning it. Her uncle, for all his faults, had managed not only to get her into the best school for girls in Britain, but also to scrape together the not insignificant funds for it.

"Did you enjoy your time at school?"

"Surprisingly, yes."

"Why surprisingly?"

"Come, Your Grace, you must know what a cuckoo I was in that particular nest. I wasn't one of the few scholarship students—whose lot in life was significantly worse than mine—but neither was I accepted by the fashionable crowd."

"I can't see you cultivating their approval. And before you bite my head off, I just meant that you do not strike me as a tuft-hunter."

"I'd have had as much chance of scaling such social heights as I would flying. But I found my level—mainly among the daughters of merchants. Although even some of them were leery of associating with the niece of a circus owner. My uncle had advised me to lie about my background, but I saw no point in falsifying my life to please strangers. I never went so far as to invite friends to visit me, of course, but several girls were kind enough to have me on the holidays."

"Do you still keep in touch with them?" he asked.

"When I began boxing in my uncle's circus, that was the end of most connections." She chewed her lower lip when she thought about Deborah Barton, her best friend at school. "I severed the last of those friendships myself after Dominic—" She cut him a wry look. "I'm sure you've read or heard about all that."

He didn't leap to deny it, as many people did. Instead, he said, "You are not what I thought you would be." He spoke more slowly, and carefully, than was usual for him.

"What did you imagine? A loud, brash strumpet who dressed in red satin, cursed like a sailor, and drank gin by the pint?"

To her astonishment, the starchy Duke of Staunton laughed. It was as if a bolt of sunshine had just burst through the clouds, the sound low and velvety and *sinful*.

"Well, yes, actually. I suppose I pictured somebody along the lines of Letty Lade."

"Do you know her?" Marianne asked. "Dominic mentioned her more than once, but I think he disliked her for besting him in some race or other."

"Yes, she trounced him badly and won five hundred guineas in the process."

Marianne laughed. "How wonderful! So, I'm not like Letty, then?"

"No. You're not like any of the women I saw Dominic with over the years. And before you ask, that is a compliment."

"Your Grace! That's twice in one day," she teased, hoping he attributed her flush to the freezing wind.

He turned his far-too-piercing gaze on her. "Yes, well, I shouldn't—"

Marianne barely squeezed Cassio's flank and he leapt forward. "Race you!" she shouted over her shoulder.

And then she was flying.

Something cold landed between Sin's collar and neck and he looked up; the snow that had been threatening since he'd awakened that morning had finally begun to fall.

He grimaced. He was a fool to be sitting there in the snow, mounted on the sorriest sack of bones he'd ever seen, waiting for a woman who wished him—with good reason—to the devil.

The spavined horse shifted beneath him.

"Sorry, old man—did I say that out loud?" Sin asked. He leaned forward to scratch the shaggy beast between the ears. "It seems that I pulled you out of your warm stall for nothing, Dobbin. It appears Miss Marianne is a fair weather—"

A battered hackney turned onto the street and rumbled toward them. It shuddered to a halt not far from Sin, and Marianne hopped out. She tossed the hackney driver a coin.

"I didn't expect to see you out here this morning," she said as she jogged toward him.

She wore a dark green knit hat pulled down over her short hair and a hideous red, blue, and yellow scarf. On her hands were periwinkle blue-and-pale pink-striped mittens.

Sin knew his mouth was open, so he shut it. But not before she noticed.

She gave him an open smile that disarmed him, looking up at him through the falling snow, flakes of which were sticking in her ludicrously long eyelashes.

Eyelashes. Hell. When was the last time he'd noticed a woman's—

Sin squashed the thought before it could fully form. "Warm enough?"

"I know, I look quite hideous. Cecile made the set for me—she is only learning how to knit—and it would hurt her feelings if I didn't wear it."

"Yes, but perhaps not all at once."

She laughed. "As mismatched as it all appears, it is incredibly toasty, so I'm glad I wore it." She rubbed her hands together and then engaged in a series of stretches, one of which included bending over and pressing her hands flat on the ground.

Good Lord.

He'd spent almost every day with her for weeks but still was surprised by the sheer athleticism she displayed.

After a few more minutes warming up, she started to run, taking several minutes before she loosened up and fell into a comfortable stride.

The snow fell harder and the world around them turned white.

"It's so beautiful, it's almost worth the discomfort of being out in it," she said, echoing his thoughts. London when it snowed was a magical place. Tomorrow, or even later today, it would be a nightmare of slush, ice, and muck, but right now it was a wonderland.

"Talk to me," she said, just when he'd fallen into a comfortable fugue.

She made the same demand every time she ran. "It helps the time pass, and I despise running," she had explained.

At first, he'd been almost offended by her peremptory demand.

But now he knew she barely listened to the words themselves; she just liked hearing the sound of another person's voice. Even if that person was Sin.

"What shall it be today?" He'd spoken more on her morning runs—and on a wider range of topics—than he could recall ever doing in his life. He never knew what subjects she'd come up with: the current status of the peace negotiations in Vienna, whether he liked Brighton or Bath, the war in America, and on and on. The only subjects she avoided were personal ones—much to his relief.

"Tell me about the Season you will be missing while you're off on tour."

Well, so much for avoiding personal subjects.

"What do you wish to know?" he asked warily.

"What is it like? Describe a day."

Sin considered her question—he especially considered whether to answer it honestly or not.

Once she'd stopped trying to make his life miserable and drive him to quit, an odd acquaintance had sprung up between them—although he couldn't really call it a friendship—and her company had grown on him. Although he made a point of not surrounding himself with sycophants, he knew his status intimidated all but a few people in the nation. Most of those people were other peers. And now, Marianne.

"Come, Your Grace," she teased, clearly sensing his reticence. "Will you go to Almack's? Will you chauffer young ladies about in Hyde Park in a yellow bounder? I'll never be part of your world. This is the only chance I'll ever get for a peek into the *ton*."

He considered mentioning that she'd once been the lover of a baron but didn't want to spoil her cheery mood.

"Very well," he said, pulling the brim of his hat lower to keep the snow off his nose. "Yes to Almack's. Yes to driving ladies. Usually, I would attend no more than one, maybe two functions per day—"

"Functions?"

"Balls, dinners, routs, and the like."

"Usually—what do you mean by that?"

Oh, she was so sharp, Miss Marianne—she picked up on that one word, which he already regretted inserting.

"Would it have been different this year?" she prodded. Before he could answer, she turned to him, her eyes wide. "Were you going courting this Season, Your Grace?"

Naturally his blasted face heated at the exceedingly personal nature of her question.

She grinned. "You were, weren't you? You're a bit long in the tooth to just be starting on that, aren't you?"

Sin snorted but didn't take the bait.

"How old are you?"

"How old are *you*?" he shot back.

"I'll be twenty-one in July. Your turn."

"Thirty-two."

"Hmph."

"What does that mean?"

"I just thought you were older."

Sin frowned down at her.

She laughed up at him. "I'm just teasing you, Your Grace."

"Hmph," he said, giving her own response back to her.

"I have the impression most people are too intimidated to tease you."

"You've met Guy," he pointed out drily. "Does he seem intimidated? Or Elliot?"

"Yes, that's true—especially about Guy. He is a bit of a pest and has already driven Cecile halfway mad with his teasing. So, back to your wife hunting."

"I didn't say I was going *wife hunting*, to use your vulgar expression."

"But you are, aren't you?"

"Not this year."

"But you *would* have been if you'd been in London?"

"I refuse to answer such a question."

"As the heir to a dukedom, shouldn't you have been married already?" she persisted, undeterred.

Sin's jaws tightened.

She glanced up at him, and her good-natured smirk disappeared in a heartbeat. "Lord. I've put my foot in it, haven't I? I'm sorry."

"You've nothing to be sorry about," Sin said stiffly. "It was a long time ago." Half this woman's lifetime, in fact. "She died in childbed, as did our son."

How fascinating that a man could sum up the most catastrophic event in his life with only eight words.

She ran in silence for perhaps ten minutes, and then tugged at the hideous scarf around her neck.

Sin held out a hand. "Throw it up here. I will keep it for you."

She tossed him the scarf and with it came a whiff of her scent: soap, fresh air, and the clean, salty tang of sweat. Why did female sweat smell so much nicer than male sweat?

"You're not talking," she said, her voice a bit breathier than before. "Tell me about your friends—Guy and Smithy."

That was painless enough.

"I've known Guy since we were both in our cradles. His family is far larger than mine: he has six sisters and is the only son."

"Ah, the darling of the family as well as the *ton*, then."

"Yes, he is terribly spoiled, if that is what you are asking."

"And he will be a duke one day, too?"

"Yes."

"But Elliot is just a plain mister?"

"He is the younger son of an earl, so, no, he has no title."

"Slumming, are you?"

Sin frowned down at her. "I don't know that word."

"I believe it is fairly new, used to describe the way *your* people come to observe the 'umble entertainments that *my* people get up to. Sort of like watching the animals at Astley's, except with commoners rather than tigers and elephants."

"Just who do you think your people are, Miss Simpson? Given the school you attended and the way you speak, I don't think you're one of Jack's people."

She smirked at his acerbic tone, clearly pleased to have drawn a rise from him. "So, Elliot will never be a lord, then?"

"Not unless his three elder brothers and four nephews predecease him."

"He has no title and he's poor."

"Why do you say that?"

"Because he has a job."

"He told you that?"

She cut him a strange look. "How else would I know?"

For some reason it surprised him to think of Elliot and this woman exchanging personal information. Elliot was not exactly the most forthcoming of men. But the other man spent almost as much time with Marianne as Sin had over the last few weeks. Could it be that Elliot was not untouched by Marianne's rough but appealing brand of charm?

Sin found he did not care for that thought. And he cared for *that* thought even less. It was no affair of his what, if anything, Elliot and this woman got up to.

"You met him at school?"

"I'm sorry?" he said.

"Elliot, or Smithy, rather—I asked if you met him at school."

"Yes."

"He was friends with you, Guy, and Dominic."

He turned to look down at her, but she was staring straight ahead. "How did you know I was friends with Strickland?"

"Why?" she shot back. "Was it supposed to be a secret?"

"It is not a secret," he said, exasperated by her sarcasm. "I'm just surprised you know. Did Strickland tell you?"

"Yes. He mentioned you." The way her mouth curled, Sin could guess what his erstwhile friend had probably said. "But he said you'd had a falling out." She paused, clearly hoping he would expand on her knowledge.

"Did he tell you what it was about?" Sin asked, even though he knew he shouldn't.

"He said you were self-righteous and judgmental and always trying to run his life. And that you got angry when he wouldn't let you."

Sin just bet he'd said something like that. Dominic would have known that the truth would not have pleased the woman beside him.

When he didn't speak, she went on. "He said you'd been close— you two and three others. That you went by some name in school."

"The Brotherhood."

She laughed.

"Yes, it does sound rather idiotic," Sin admitted. "But do keep in mind that other boys called us that—and they were only ten when they coined the name."

"So that's you, Smithy, Guy, Dominic—and who else?"

"A man named David Norris."

"Hmm, David Norris. Am I going to need to find a position for him in my uncle's circus, too, Your Grace?"

"David is dead."

She glanced up at him, her brow puckered. "I'm sorry. The war?"

"Yes."

She nodded and turned to face the road.

They finished the remainder of the run in silence.

Once she'd finished cooling down, Sin slipped from the horse and handed her the water. When she'd had her fill, she returned the bottle and glanced up at the sky. The snow was falling more heavily now.

"Do you want to brave the weather?" she asked him.

"Yes, I'm hungry."

They walked in companionable silence, not speaking until they reached the place where he usually tethered Dobbin.

"It is my turn today," Sin reminded her. "How many for you? I'm getting three."

She grinned up at him, her joyous expression causing yet another blast of unwanted warmth in his belly. "*Three*! That's a bit piggish, isn't it?"

"I made the mistake of mentioning them to Guy. He considers himself something of an expert on pies and believes these can't possibly be better than those we used to buy from the village near my house." He didn't tell her that as hungry and cold as he was, the third pie might not make it back to the other man.

"One will be fine for me," she said and then shivered.

Sin took her hideous scarf out of the bag where he'd stuffed it. "Here," he said, lowering the scarf onto her shoulders and then wrapping it around her neck twice. He was about to tuck the ends between the lapels of her coat when he realized what he was doing and dropped the scarf ends like hot coals.

Her eyes seemed darker and larger than normal when they looked up at him.

"Thank you," she said, a strange, taut expression on her face.

Sin stared down at her for a long moment while neither of them moved.

When had her face become so familiar to him? When had he come to enjoy these painfully early mornings on a miserable old horse?

What was happening to him?

"Right, pies," he said foolishly, wrenching his gaze away.

Sin turned and hurried toward the line with unwonted haste. Some part of him wanted to keep right on going.

Chapter 12

"Yer guard, lass! Mind yer guard," Jack shouted at Marianne, prowling around the sparring fighters and muttering to himself in between yells.

Marianne dutifully raised her left hand, cursing her inattention.

The source of that inattention stood beside Elliot with his arms crossed over his broad, powerful chest, booted feet shoulder-width apart, and watched her with eyes that made her feel like an insect pinned to a board.

One would think she'd have become used to the duke's unnerving attention after almost three weeks, but, if anything, she was jumpier around him with every day that passed.

Instead of finding reasons to drag Staunton into work more often, she was now looking for ways to get away from him.

It made no sense.

When he'd been an arrogant arse to her, Marianne had done everything in her power to keep him near. Now that he was being almost . . . human—all right, so he was being more than human, he was kind, even—she couldn't get away from him fast enough.

But all her attempts to keep him from her training sessions or runs had come to naught. Jack had become as irritable as a bear when Marianne had insisted she didn't need him there.

"Lord, Annie! Yer leavin' in only a few weeks. 'Course you need yer new trainer lookin' on and learnin' yer ways."

Ha. The duke learning her ways was the last thing she wanted.

No, that wasn't true, the last thing she wanted was to be the focus of his intense gaze while she fought. He made her feel anxious, jittery, and—ultimately—sloppy.

And why is that, Marianne? Could it be you've done that thing you swore you'd never do again? Do you fancy the Duke of Staunton? Could you be so foolish?

She wanted to punch that mocking voice right in the face. Unfortunately, it was inside her own head.

Marianne refused to believe that she was becoming infatuated by the most perfect man in Britain.

Refuse it all you like—it's still the truth.

Ugh. It was.

She wanted to weep at her stupidity. How could she be so weak and foolish? Hadn't one tragically humiliating affair with an aristocrat been enough?

Apparently not.

"Marianne!"

Jack's angry voice jolted her out of her internal misery just in time to parry a jab from Lucy's fist.

"Criminy!" Jack hollered.

Marianne paid attention for perhaps five seconds and then, as if her eyes were on lead strings, her gaze slid back to Staunton.

The duke was supposed to be observing Lucy while Jack watched Marianne. But Marianne felt the weight of his stare. And every time she snatched a glance at him—which was far too often for her safety—she found him watching her with his brooding eyes.

Like Jack, Andy, and Elliot—all of whom were there today—the duke had stripped off his coat and rolled up his sleeves, baring surprisingly muscular forearms that were dusted with ash-blond hair, the veins on the back of his long-fingered hands a pronounced blue beneath his pale skin.

His forearms were distracting enough, but that wasn't the worst of it.

Lately, he'd taken to wearing ancient, butter-soft buckskins, the breeches so worn and thin they clung like silk to his muscular thighs, taut hips, and firm buttocks.

Marianne snatched a quick glance at said buckskins and barely dodged a cross from Lucy.

"Annie!" Jack shouted, all but frothing at the mouth.

Marianne gritted her teeth and yanked her mind away from the duke's hips and thighs.

But like a willful, untrained hound, her thoughts veered back toward him only moments later.

It was a disgrace. Dressing like that in public! How was a woman supposed to concentrate when he insisted on parading about in—

Lucy's fist struck Marianne's chin and drove her head back hard enough to make the bones in her neck pop.

"Bloody 'ell!" Jack shouted as Marianne staggered back from the hit. "Where's yer 'ead, Annie?"

Marianne doubted he'd like the answer—that it was on the duke's buckskins. Or worse, *in* the duke's buckskins.

She shook herself, blinking to clear her trebled vision.

"Time!" the duke called.

Marianne spun and scowled at him—or at least at one image of him. "I don't need—"

"Oy!" Jack said, setting a huge paw on her shoulder. "When Sin calls time, you listen to 'im the same as you listen to me, my girl."

Marianne's face heated at the uncharacteristic chastisement. "Sorry, Jack," she mumbled, her vision still blurred.

"No, 'tisn't me you need to be sorry with." Jack jerked his chin in the duke's direction.

"That's not nec—" His Grace began.

"I'm sorry . . . *Sin*." She pushed the words through clenched teeth. Saying his name, which she'd thought plenty but had never spoken aloud, made her already warm face flush hotter.

Jack patted her gently. "That's my lass." He tilted Marianne's chin up and winced. "You'll have a proper bruise tomorrow." He cut a glance at Sin. "You were right to call time. Annie's mind is somewhere else. That's enough for today."

"You've got one more fight before you leave," Jack said, speaking to Marianne, "and I'll be wantin' Sin to take my place."

Marianne blinked; she couldn't have heard him correctly. "What?"

"This Tuesday I want Sin with you," Jack repeated.

"But—why? You'll be here, won't you? How come—"

Jack's eyes narrowed and he took her by the upper arm and marched her toward the wings, far enough away that the duke wouldn't be able to hear them talk. "Has Sin done somethin' wrong to you, lass? 'Cause you're mighty prickly with 'im."

"No, of course not, Jack. It's just—"

"It's just?" he prodded.

It's just that I can't stop looking at his breeches, his forearms, his perfect face and—

Marianne clamped her jaws shut, horrified she might actually spew such idiocy. She cleared her throat and shoved the duke and his breeches from her mind. "I'd hoped you'd be with me on my last fight before we leave," she said lamely. "You're my good-luck charm, Jack."

Jack smiled and cupped the non-aching side of her face with one big paw. "I'll be there—watchin' from the wings," he assured her. "Yer a bang-up fighter, Annie. You don't need luck."

Marianne hoped to heaven that he was right.

But something told her that being forced to perch on the duke's knee in between rounds—as every fighter did with their knee man, whose thigh served as a seat—enduring his touch on her body, his breath hot on her ear—all the things she'd never noticed with Jack or Andy—would play bloody havoc with both her wits and her luck.

She'd get slaughtered on Tuesday.

Sin was helping Lucy remove her mufflers when he saw Marianne break away from Jack and stalk toward him.

"I need to talk to you," she said to Sin.

"I'll be—"

"*Now*. Excuse us," Marianne said to the startled woman. "Jack can take care of you, Lucy." She set a hand on Sin's back and all but pushed him toward the stage door.

"Where are we going?" he asked as she elbowed past stagehands and other performers.

"We'll go to the dressing room."

"Why?"

"Because I need to talk to you in private." She reached the door and then stopped, cutting him a pointed glare.

"What?" he asked, cocking an eyebrow. "I thought I wasn't supposed to open doors for you?"

She raised her hands, which were still bound in mufflers.

Rather than be annoyed by her abrupt behavior—which had gone well beyond rudeness into the realm of abusiveness—Sin had to bite back a smile as he opened the door and she shoved past him.

Marianne Simpson truly did not care about his status, money, or the fact that he would be eating dinner with the Prince of Wales that very evening.

She displayed more courtesy toward street sweepers than she did with him. When he'd once confronted her on that issue, she had cut him one of her cheeky smirks and said, "Street sweepers perform a valuable function. Dukes, however . . . well."

With each day that passed, he was more impressed by her intelligence, tenacity, and fire. He now knew that her fights were as real as any of the dozens of mills he'd seen over the years.

Although Sin despised Farnham more than ever for earning money off his niece's pain, his admiration for Marianne was rapidly beginning to threaten his objectivity.

Hell. Who was he trying to fool—what objectivity? He'd been impressed by the woman since the first morning he met her. First, he'd been taken by her directness and—he couldn't lie—her incredible rudeness.

But in the almost three weeks that he'd spent with her, he'd come to admire her more and more. She was smart, loyal, witty, kind, and honest. Any suspicions he'd had about her being Strickland's partner in crime had slowly dissipated.

Sin now wondered—as he looked at her angrily pacing the tiny dressing room and glaring at him—how he ever could have suspected her of such duplicity.

"Are you mad?" she demanded.

"You like to ask me that question, don't you?"

She shoved her hands at him, wrists up.

Sin plucked at the double knot that held the thick cowhide gloves on her hands, standing close enough that he was surrounded by her now-familiar scent. No other woman smelled like her; an intoxicating blend of clean sweat, leather, and lavender. He couldn't remember why he'd ever found expensive perfumes appealing on a woman.

"You cannot serve as my knee man on Tuesday."

Sin glanced up. "Why not?" he asked as he removed the glove, marveling—as always—at the delicacy of her wrist.

She yanked her gloveless hand away. "Why not?" she repeated, pulling a haughty face and aping his accent in a way that almost made him smile. But he caught the expression in time, compressing his lips in a stern frown.

"What an excellent imitation of me, Marianne. I'm flattered you've taken the time and effort to study my voice and mannerisms so carefully."

She scowled. "I'm not in a jesting sort of mood."

He picked at the tight double-knot on her second glove. "Why are you suddenly fighting this after forcing me to spend almost every minute of my days either chasing behind you on Dobbin, cleaning up after you here at the theater, or serving as your general dogsbody?" Sin now knew more than he ever wanted to know about laundry and looked at his own snowy-white linens with newfound respect.

"May I remind you, Your Grace, that if you get on that stage Tuesday, you'll be in front of hundreds of your closest chums. Men you've gone to school with, caroused in your clubs with, and whored at brothels—"

Sin's head whipped up, and he was no longer amused.

Her tirade stuttered to a halt when their eyes locked.

"You think you know everything about me, don't you, Marianne?"

She flinched at the quiet menace in his tone.

Sin pulled off her glove and tossed it to the floor. And then he lowered a hand onto the wall on either side of her shoulders, effectively caging her in.

"Or perhaps it just amuses you to insult me by accusing me of being a hypocrite? Lord Flawless—a stuffy, overly righteous, self-important twit who rails against public immorality in Parliament and denies other men and women sensual pleasures but does not hesitate to sate his own base appetites?"

She swallowed and his gaze was drawn to the taut musculature of her throat. Moisture flooded his mouth at the sight of her slick, pearly skin. And the scent of her . . .

God. She smelled so damned good.

She licked her plush lower lip, the simple gesture making him hard in a heartbeat.

"I, er, don't—"

Her broken babbling yanked his attention away from her tantalizing mouth and the wicked thoughts that he had almost put into action.

"Yes, Marianne?"

She shook her head, the short, sweat-damp brown curls that framed her face dancing. "Er—"

Sin leaned closer to her, the sudden movement startling her. He inhaled her scent, filling his lungs to bursting and holding it.

When his chest began to burn, he reluctantly exhaled. The room was quiet but for the sound of their labored breathing and the muted noises coming from beyond the dressing room door. A strand of hair had become tangled in her lush eyelashes and he carefully teased it out and tucked it back with the others, his hand shaking ever so slightly.

"I am no saint, Marianne," he said gruffly. "I have never claimed to be. I am not without flaws, by any means. And I am a man with physical desires." He allowed his eyes to roam her face and throat, lingering on the pulse that pounded at the base, before meeting her gaze again. "My reasons for the anti-brothel sentiment I espouse in Parliament are the same reasons I don't use prostitutes to satisfy my own sexual needs."

Her hazel eyes darkened as she stared up at him, her fascinating bowed lips slightly parted.

Temptation and restraint warred inside Sin's body and his iron-hard shaft throbbed against the placket of his buckskins. There would be no concealing his condition when he forced himself to step away from her.

But step away he did, and it was perhaps the hardest step he'd ever taken.

Sin stared down into her hooded eyes—was that a hint of disappointment he saw? Or was it relief?

"Stop baiting me, Marianne," he said, his voice harsh with the effort of the struggle he'd just endured. "I know you never wanted me in your life, but I'm in it—at least until April fifteenth." He pivoted on one heel and strode toward the door, not bothering to turn as he said, "I shall see you bright and early tomorrow morning at the park."

Marianne felt as if she'd just been run down by a mail coach. She held up her hands and wasn't surprised to see they were shaking.

She lowered them to her sides and then closed her eyes and let her head fall back against the wall with a *thunk*. Good Lord, if he'd not come to his senses and stepped away from her, she very well might have launched herself at him and—

Marianne stopped the thought before it came to fruition. No use borrowing trouble; he *had* come to his senses.

But it had been close.

She lightly banged her head against the wall, as if that might jar some sense into her.

But it was pointless. She was physically attracted to the man—how could she not be. He was rich, powerful, handsome, and—it appeared—honorable.

Marianne groaned. How had this happened? How had he gradually chipped away at her resistance until he now occupied a sizeable portion of her thoughts?

What was wrong with her? Yes, he was caring, gorgeous, and principled, but he was also an aristocrat—that breed of man who believed they were better than everyone else and took what they wanted, suffering no consequences but leaving pain and wreckage in their wake.

And yet . . . although Staunton was undeniably a member of that exclusive circle, he did *not* live by their credo.

That just made him all the more attractive.

"Lord," she whispered, staring sightlessly at the ceiling.

How was she ever going to make it to April fifteenth without doing something disastrous?

Like fall in love.

Chapter 13

Suzi Fisk delivered a punishing jab to Marianne's jaw just seconds before the bell rang, ending the fifth round.

Marianne staggered back from the blow, shaking her head to clear it of stars.

Two large hands settled on her shoulders. "Here, come sit down," the duke shouted as he guided her back to her corner. The crowd—which was always raucous—seemed even more bloodthirsty than usual.

The reason for the enthusiasm was two-fold: his would be the last performance until next winter, and Suzi was always a favorite with crowds. She was remarkable in the world of women pugs for her beauty, and her manager—also her husband—knew how to play up her appearance and dressed her in gowns so low that it wasn't unusual for a breast to pop out in the middle of the fight, a prospect that always drove ticket sales through the roof. Marianne couldn't recall seeing the theater so full—even the aisles were packed with men—and knew her uncle had shamelessly oversold tickets.

The duke lowered himself to one knee and gently pulled her down onto his other leg. It was the fifth time she'd sat on his thigh that evening. Even with her head ringing and jaw aching, her entire body tensed at the hardness of his thigh beneath her bottom and the tantalizing scent of him. She inhaled deeply, savoring the faint odor of some cologne—likely expensive—mingled with wool, sweat, and leather.

"Are you listening, Marianne?" His deep voice rumbled against her temple, accompanied by a hot puff of air and the faint scent of citrus—likely from the oranges he always brought with him. The way he asked the question made her realize it wasn't the first time.

She opened her eyes, relieved to see only one of everything. "Yes, I'm listening."

"Here, give her this." Elliot pushed through the heavy velvet ropes that made up the boxing ring. In his hands were a bottle and half an orange, cut into quarters.

"Thank you," Sin murmured, holding the fruit in one hand while he handed Marianne the bottle of water.

"Listen to me," he repeated as she drank. "You can't take many more hits like that last one."

"Believe me, I know. She caught me on the same spot Lucy did when we sparred."

"And why is that?" Sin asked, more than a little sarcasm in his tone.

"I know, I know," Marianne said, wiping her mouth with the back of her hand and wincing at the soreness in her jaw before handing the bottle to Elliot. "It's because I keep dropping my left."

Sin gave her one of the orange pieces and then briskly toweled her neck and the damp hair at her temples while she ate, leaning closer. "Do you remember Rule One?"

He was referring to the rules in the great Mendoza's book, *The Art of Boxing*. She'd read it at least a dozen times, but it had been years since the last time she'd thought of it. Rule One was that you should always watch your opponent's face—unless not doing so brought you an advantage.

"Of course, I do," she said.

"You've a tendency to hold your opponent's gaze and Suzi knows that. Now would be a good time to use her knowledge against her."

"You want me to feint?"

He grinned fiercely, and it was like a second punch to the head.

His face was beautiful in repose—but with a smile like that, he was almost painful to behold.

"—only the once," he said.

Marianne stared. "I'm sorry?" What was *wrong* with her? It wasn't like her to be so bloody distracted.

"You weren't paying attention, were you?" His stern expression caused its own collection of disturbing effects to cascade through her body. "Do you need me to tell your uncle to call this—is your vision impaired?"

"No, you absolutely cannot call this fight. I'm fine, I just, er, well, I wasn't listening. But I'm listening now."

"I was saying that I also noticed she always drops her right just before she throws her left, leaving herself unguarded."

"I hadn't noticed," Marianne admitted.

"That is why I'm here: to notice." He handed her the other orange segment. "Next time she does it, don't parry. Instead, move to the right and then hit her straight on."

Marianne nodded.

"Here, turn a bit," he ordered, his hands on her waist, shifting her until she was facing away from him, straddling his thigh.

Marianne bit her lip to keep from groaning as the sensitive flesh of her sex pressed against hard bone and muscle. Did the man have any notion how that *felt*?

"You're tight," he said, leaning forward so close that his lips brushed against her ear.

Marianne's jaw dropped.

"I'm going to loosen you up a bit." Strong fingers dug into her shoulders as he kneaded the taut, knotted muscles and . . .

Oh, God. Marianne knew that she should be ashamed of the small, whimpering noises that slipped from between her lips, but she was past caring.

Who knew that hands so beautiful could be so powerful? And how could a man who'd never done a day's work in his life have such strength?

The orange rind slid from her limp hand as he worked new life into her, his magic fingers getting her blood flowing and infusing her muscles with vigor, until she was all but vibrating with energy.

All too soon he stopped and shifted her again, turning her body perpendicular to his thigh. "Look at me."

She forced up heavy lids and looked at the man it was getting harder and harder to remember was a duke. She was as close to him as she'd been during their argument in the dressing room, but this time the lights over the stage were blazing, illuminating his eyes behind his spectacles. A complex constellation of greens made up his irises—from juniper to moss to peridot, along with countless shades she couldn't name. This close, his eyes didn't look cold and reserved at all but burned with intelligence and life and . . . something else: desire.

Marianne was no stranger to that expression, but never thought to see it on this tightly controlled, proud man's face.

The duke desired *her*.

That was bad.

What was even worse? She knew her eyes had the same hot need shining from them.

"Marianne?"

She shoved away the shocking knowledge and nodded. "I'm listening."

His mouth—his stern, serious lips—twitched into a tiny smile that held more than a hint of savagery. "You can finish her in this round," he said. "She's bigger and slower and a couple good hits like those we talked about could put a stop to this."

"But my uncle—"

"I know; he likes to drag things out to seven rounds and give the punters their money's worth." He scowled, his hawklike eyes sweeping over the raucous crowd, light glinting off his reddish-gold stubble. "They've already had their money's worth. And more."

The bell rang and his hands dropped to Marianne's waist. He gave her a gentle squeeze, nodded, and then lifted her off his knee as if she weighed nothing. "Get in there and end this, Marianne."

★ ★ ★

"I said I was sorry, Uncle," Marianne repeated for the third time.

Barnabas was pacing the dressing room, his wiry body jerking with agitation as he repeatedly shoved his fingers through his thin gray hair.

"It's not that I don't understand how hard you work, Marianne, but if these men don't get what they pay for, they get angry." He shivered. "You weren't here in '12 when—"

"I know, I know—*Puss in Boots*."

Those three words sent chills up and down the spines of anyone who'd been with Farnham's Fayre when a violent riot had erupted during a bad play—a riot that had closed the theater for half a year.

"Those men—*aristocratic* men—didn't just rip apart the theater, Marianne," Barnabas said. "They were deranged beasts, attacking stagehands and even the poor linkboys I'd let watch from the gods. It was—"

She'd heard all this countless times before, how every part of the theatre—from the stage all the way up to the cheapest seats, or the gods as theatrical folk called it since it was so high up as to be in the heavens—were subjected to the anger of the maddened crowd. "I understand, Uncle."

"I haven't even mentioned how much ending a fight early costs us when it comes to loss of sales. You know these men buy more drinks with every—"

"*I know.* And I'm sorry about tonight. It won't happen ag—"

The dressing room door banged open, and the duke stepped inside.

Barnabas, who'd passed through the haranguing stage and moved into the pleading stage, would soon have left Marianne in peace.

Instead, he got puffed up all over again when he saw the man he believed—rightly—responsible for his loss in revenue. "And *you*. It's your job to see that she doesn't—"

"Are you speaking to me?" the duke asked, his voice so cold and his gaze so haughty that Barnabas cringed from the much larger man, suddenly recalling exactly who it was that he was hectoring.

Marianne stood up from the dressing table where she'd been removing her face paint. "Let me talk to him, Uncle." She stepped into a small gap between the men.

Emboldened, Barnabas straightened to his full height, which was still half a head below the duke. "Hmph. See that you do." His eyes narrowed as he glared up at Staunton. "And perhaps you might remind His Grace that he is only here on sufferance."

The duke stepped closer, the front of his body pressing against hers. "And perhaps I might remind you that you'd better find the locket and letter I asked you for weeks ago."

Marianne hadn't known the duke had asked him.

"I've already told you I have no idea what you are talking about."

Marianne could hear the lie in her uncle's voice and could tell by the duke's expression that he heard it, too.

"Your friend Strickland says otherwise."

"I find your—"

"Please, Uncle. Go," Marianne said, cutting off his bluster.

Barnabas made a strangled sound of displeasure, pushed past her, and stomped out of the room, leaving the door open, as was his wont.

Marianne shut the door and locked it so they'd not be interrupted, and then turned to the duke.

He winced when he saw the swelling on her jaw. "Good Lord." He reached for her, but she slapped away his hand.

"Don't," she snapped.

He sighed, crossed his arms, and leaned back against the wall in the pose of a man who was about to tolerate an outburst from an overwrought woman.

It was a good look to receive just then—because she had, foolishly, softened toward him over the course of the evening. Other than Jack, the duke was the only man who'd ever tried to protect her from pain or seemed to care that fighting for a living was a hard, dangerous job. Marianne had discovered that she liked his solicitous attitude far too much.

Both his protective instinct toward her—and her appreciation of it—had to stop.

"You need to accept that this is what I do, Your Grace."

His lifted a brow.

"If you cannot do what you are here to do—keep me in a fight for seven rounds and preferably help me win—then I need to find some other occupation for you on this journey."

He merely stared.

Suddenly, his remoteness—his untouchability—combined with his chaotic effect on her body and mind, were unbearable. She stepped toe-to-toe and poked him in his surprisingly hard chest with one finger. "I know you consider my life brutish and low but—"

Rather than look at her offensive finger, his gaze dropped to her mouth, and then his jaw tightened. She knew what the look meant because she was feeling the exact same way: clenched.

And then his head dipped down an almost imperceptible amount.

Without hesitation Marianne pushed up on her toes, bringing her face closer to his.

This is a mistake, a voice whispered in her head. But like a piece of flotsam tossed and battered by waves, the voice was speedily borne away.

Marianne didn't need the voice; she already knew it was a mistake.

But she no longer cared. Instead, she pushed up that last fraction of an inch.

And he covered her mouth with his.

Chapter 14

It turned out that the duke's firm, severe mouth was not hard, at all.

In fact, it was soft as he crushed her lips. His hand, strong and familiar, slid around her waist and fingers splayed against the base of her spine as he pulled her body close.

His other hand cupped the back of her head, and his tongue, slick and warm, stroked over her lower lip. He kissed just the way she'd known he would: with utter command.

Marianne did what she'd been wanting to do for weeks and slid her hands over the warm buckskin that sheathed his hips. A moan slipped from her mouth to his as she dug her fingers into the tight weave of muscle. He felt even better than she'd imagined—and as good as he looked. Marianne pulled his hips tight to her body and massaged his buttocks, grinding her pelvis against the hard ridge of him.

He grabbed her waist with both hands, lifted, and turned her with startling ease, not stopping until she was pinned against the un-yielding wall where he'd just been leaning. His mouth roamed from her lips to her cheek, to beneath her ear, the bridge of his elegant, aristocratic nose nudging the sensitive skin of her neck as he inhaled deeply, his chest expanding against her as he filled his lungs.

"You smell so good." His deep voice vibrated from his chest to hers, his words drenched with desire. His lips, eager and hot, parted over her throat and his slick tongue caressed her skin. "You taste even better," he muttered almost angrily, trailing kisses until he reached the hollow of her throat.

Marianne caught her lower lip with her teeth to keep from making a mortifying noise as he took a mouthful of delicate skin and sucked hard, the pain oddly pleasurable. Some distant part of her brain pointed out that he would likely leave a mark, but she couldn't bring herself to care.

His knee pushed between her thighs, and she eagerly spread her legs for him.

This time, she didn't catch the mortifying whine that slipped out of her as he nudged her mons. He pressed harder and she ground against him like a back-alley tart, mindlessly chasing her pleasure.

He released her skin with a soft sucking sound. "Marianne," he whispered, the word dark with need. He claimed her mouth and gripped her hips as he lifted his knee.

Marianne bucked against him, the soft, swollen folds of her sex rubbing against the unforgiving muscle of his thigh.

He pulled away just far enough that he could see her face, his green eyes hooded and heavy and dark as they drank in her pleasure, his knee working her as his hands slid up her waist to her ribs. When his thumbs flicked the hard tips of her nipples, she cried out, her eyelids fluttering as she took in the harsh, hungry lines of his face.

Once again, he claimed her mouth, rhythmically rocking his knee, his palms cradling her breasts, and his mouth catching the animal grunts and whimpers that she couldn't restrain.

A bolt of exquisite pleasure struck her core and her body clenched, spine arching, and—

Something moved at the other end of the room; the tangle of blankets and costumes piled on the old sofa rose up and a head emerged.

Marianne shrieked.

Sin spun around, keeping Marianne's body between his and the wall.

His eyes widened; there was a head sticking out of the pile of garments that perennially covered the old settee.

It was Josephine Brown. She blinked owlishly up at them and then yawned. "Oh," was all she said.

Marianne scrambled out from behind Sin, her face a fiery red. "How is it that you didn't hear Barnabas come in, yell at everyone to get out, and then harangue me?" she demanded.

Brown—or Blade as everyone called her—merely pushed the tangled pile of costumes and clothing off her and swung her feet to the floor.

Sin had not seen her this past week, since she'd apparently taken time away from the circus to visit an ailing relative.

Given what Elliot had said about her—that she had no family—the sudden appearance of a cousin was suspicious. Elliot had arranged for somebody to follow her to wherever she'd gone, but the man he'd sent had lost her trail. Sin couldn't recall ever seeing his friend so furious.

Although Sin had rehearsed with her four or five time, he hadn't realized just how odd looking she was. The lighting had been dimmer during rehearsals and any other time he'd caught a glimpse of her, she'd been performing and wore a mask that covered most of her face.

The part that hadn't been covered by the mask—her jaw, chin, and mouth—had been disguised by the heavy face paint all Farnham's entertainers wore.

Looking at her now, in the well-lighted dressing room, he could see she was virtually colorless. Sin had ash blond hair, but hers was the corn silk white of a towhead. It was a hair color that was fairly common among children but rarely persisted into adulthood.

Her eyes were a pale, true gray, devoid of any hints of blue or green, resembling an agate.

When she rose to her feet, he could see she was wearing one of the functional gray woolen dresses the circus women seemed to prefer while at work. She was shorter than Marianne by several inches, her figure slight and girlish although Sin would have placed her in her mid to late twenties.

"When did you get back?" Marianne asked, still sounding strained, but no longer looking furious.

"Just a few hours ago." Her voice was low and husky for such a slender woman. There was a barely discernible accent, and he supposed it was what remained of her childhood in Yorkshire.

"How about your cousin?" Marianne asked. "Is she—"

"Better."

Blade's eerie gaze drifted from Marianne to Sin.

Drift: that was a perfect word to describe her—no sudden movements, only a gradual drifting.

She tilted her head slightly as she looked up at him. "Hello . . . Sin."

Something about the way she was looking at him—strangely . . . knowingly—made his face heat slightly. He inclined his head. "Good evening, Miss Brown."

"You can call me Blade." Her lips twitched but didn't quite make it into a smile. "Everyone else does."

"Nobody means any harm," Marianne said hastily. "I can ask everyone to stop if you—"

"Oh, I don't mind," Blade said mildly.

Another awkward silence filled the small room.

Sin was just about to take his leave when Marianne said, "Where is Angus?"

"He's got a bit of a sniffle, so I left him at home tonight."

Sin had never realized birds could get *sniffles*.

Blade cocked her head, her unnerving gaze still on Sin. "You look familiar to me."

Was the woman jesting? "Er, I've been practicing your routine with you for several weeks," Sin reminded her.

She gave a low chuckle. "No, I meant before you came to work here."

"I don't think we met until a few weeks ago." That was the truth—Sin wouldn't have forgotten meeting a woman like her.

His attention was drawn to a movement at her side, where a six-inch blade had appeared from nowhere. Sin knew she'd not been holding it a moment earlier because she had smoothed down her skirts with both hands when she'd stood.

Her fingers were as pale and slender as the rest of her, and they moved almost languidly, the knife spinning around the back of her hand before she caught it in her palm, around and around and around.

The three of them stood frozen, like figures in a statuary garden, the only movement that of the knife glinting and flickering.

"Well," Blade finally said. "I suppose I should go and find Barnabas and tell him I can work tomorrow. Goodnight."

Sin and Marianne murmured their *goodnight*.

When the door closed behind her, Marianne sagged against the dressing room table, sending bottles and pots clinking and rattling. She looked absolutely wrecked, the corners of her beguiling mouth turned down in an expression of self-loathing. When she looked up at him, he saw confirmation of her shame in her eyes.

Sin could guess what she was going to say before she said it.

"In spite of the way I just behaved, I hope you don't think I'll become your whor—"

"Don't."

Her eyes flashed. "Why not? I'm sure it's what you're thinking."

"How about we have an agreement, Marianne. You don't tell *me* what I'm thinking, and I shall do you the same courtesy. Because invariably, we would both guess wrong."

"Fine. What *are* you thinking?"

"Several things, actually. My first thought—dishonorable though it might be—was that I am sorry we were interrupted."

Her jaw sagged and her eyes widened.

Was it petty of him to enjoy putting such an expression of surprise on her face? Probably.

"But right behind that thought is a second one: I am sorry for my lapse in self-control."

Her charming, wide-eyed look swiftly shifted to a mocking, jaded smirk that did not suit her nearly so well as the other expression. "Ah, yes—Lord Flawless should be above such earthy behavior."

Sin studied her through narrowed eyes.

Slowly, like a sunset, her cheeks pinkened under his gaze.

"I have never claimed to be flawless, Marianne," he said quietly. "As I've already confessed, I am a man who has physical desires, just like any other. I do strive to keep control over those desires, but I would be a liar and a hypocrite if I didn't admit that I found you attractive almost from the first moment I saw you."

Rather than look flattered by his admission—as any other woman in his experience would have done—she scowled up at him. "It is only the novelty of me that attracts you, Your Grace. A boxing woman—how quaint and unnatural, like a talking cat."

She *was* a novelty. But she was also so much more: She was intelligent, clever, witty, and kind—to everyone except Sin and Guy. He had also seen her be generous with weary street sweepers, aged rag pickers, and hungry urchins.

Marianne Simpson was more nuanced and complex than any person he'd ever met.

But the last thing she needed—*they* needed—was for Sin to tell her exactly how much he had come to admire her.

She had just given him the excuse he needed for his rash behavior of a few moments before; he could lie and agree that was exactly how he saw her: as a novelty.

Such an admission would serve to reinforce her low opinion of aristocratic men in general, and Sin in particular, but, in the long run, it would be a kindness. Because there could never be anything between them. At least nothing that would do her reputation—or his conscience—any good.

Even though it was for her own benefit, he'd couldn't make himself verbalize his agreement. But neither did he deny her accusation. "I thought you should know that I am leaving tomorrow for a week. I have already told Jack."

Her gaze shuttered, telling him that she'd received his message.

She turned away. "Fine," she said, snatching up a cloth and turning to the mirror before realizing she'd already cleaned off her face paint. She flung the rag into the overflowing hamper.

"I shan't be back until the day we leave for Dover."

She spun on her heel to glare at him. "Fine," she said again. "You may leave now."

Sin's body responded before his mind could stop it. He grabbed her arm and yanked her to him, until their bodies were flush against each other. And then he lowered his lips over hers.

She opened to him without hesitation, and he took what she offered, plumbing the depths of her hot, soft mouth until he was forced to come up for air. He stared down into her hooded eyes, breathing hard, furious with himself for doing exactly what he'd told himself he'd never do again only moments before.

"You should know that your pert, ill-mannered behavior doesn't anger me, Marianne," he said in a voice roughened by desire. "It just makes me want you more."

He kissed her again for emphasis, hard, and left her standing there, looking every bit as stunned as he felt.

Chapter 15

After their torrid exchange in the dressing room, Sin was eager to put some distance between himself and Marianne Simpson. As hard as he'd tried to scour from his mind the memory of her kisses and the feel of her body, he'd not been able to stop thinking of her.

He could have paid a visit to his mistress—Lady Alanna Galhart, the eager, lusty widow he'd been seeing for almost two years—to sate his desire, but the thought of bedding one woman while fantasizing about another left him with a sour taste in his mouth.

He chose distance rather than Alanna. While distance wasn't a complete cure for Marianne's appeal, it was better than spending five hours a day with the source of temptation.

Sin had never left England for such a long period of time before and the list of things that needed to be done before his departure seemed to grow daily.

The item at the very top of his list was a visit to his aunt Julia and his steward, William Talbot, both of whom lived at Wortham, his family seat. While he was home, he would of course see his mother, not that she would notice.

Talbot had worked for Sin's father and knew as much as Sin did about all eight of his estates, not just Wortham.

Sin had initially planned to tell Talbot the same lie he was telling everyone else: that he was going to North America. But the more he considered the matter, the more he decided that Talbot was one of the three people in his employ—his valet, Phelps, and his secretary John Morland, being the two others—who should know where he'd really gone, and why. After all, this journey was not without danger. If he were to die, Talbot would need to take measures to locate Ben, if possible, or notify the next in line, his cousin Wendall.

Sin's aunt Julia, on the other hand, could not know anything about his real plans.

As he looked at her now, on the last morning of his visit, he felt an odd tightness in his chest. She was so very dear to him, his mother in all but name.

His father's only sister had once, before the pox, been an extremely lovely woman. Even now, in her seventh decade and with the ravages of her illness marking her face, she was still beautiful.

But both her health and appearance had taken on a dangerous edge of fragility since she'd heard the news of Benjamin's death last year.

She had already suffered so much in her life: the loss her husband from an illness when she'd been only twenty-three, two stillbirths and a miscarriage, and the deaths of her elder brother, oldest nephew, and youngest niece—a child who'd borne her name—from the very illness that had left her scarred.

No, Sin could not add to her grief and worry by telling her that he was putting his own life in jeopardy by confronting a dangerous traitor without enough scruple to fill a thimble.

Nor did he want to tell her about Ben just yet. He could not share such information when he wasn't sure he believed it to be the truth. It would be beyond cruel to raise her hopes only to dash them if Strickland was lying.

"But, darling, how can you think about going to America right now?" Lady Julia asked—not for the first time these past five days—as they sat eating breakfast on his final morning.

It wasn't accurate to say she was eating; rather, she was desultorily dipping a finger of dry toast into the weak tea she favored.

"It is time I made a visit, Aunt. It has been years since anyone has gone, not since Father's visit in 1784."

She pushed away her cup, her tea and toast largely unconsumed. "I would have some gruel," she said to her favorite footman, Charles, who was never far from her.

"Right away, my lady." Charles bowed, his exit from the room soundless, courtesy of the thick felt booties all the indoor servants wore.

Sin grimaced; it was never a good sign when his aunt wanted gruel.

"America is such a *dangerous* place, St. John," she fretted, pulling her teacup back toward her, but only to fiddle with the handle.

Fiddling was yet another bad sign.

"I've seen the stories in the newspapers—they are at war, my dear."

Sin reached over and laid his hand over hers, the bones as fragile as a bird's.

An image of Marianne Simpson's hands—not so much larger, but eminently stronger and more capable—flashed through his mind. He'd felt those hands on his body, those fingers digging into his arse and hips . . .

Sin caught himself, yet again, and banished the unwanted image. It would not stay banished, of course, but he would keep trying.

Instead of fantasizing about Marianne, he applied himself to soothing his aunt, a woman he thought of as his mother, even though his mother still lived in the east wing of his house. If you could call her existence living.

He squeezed Lady Julia's hand gently. "The conflict you are thinking about is in the far south, Aunt Julia—in the Florida territory. Our timberland is near the northern border with New Brunswick. Indeed, a good deal of the property is actually in our colony. There is no danger of war there."

Lady Julia pursed her lips, thwarted, but not routed by any means. Sin was returning to London after breakfast, so she only had a few hours left to mount another assault.

"It will be fine," he promised her, patting her hand before releasing it.

The door to the breakfast room opened and Keller, who'd been the butler at Wortham since Sin was a lad, entered, bearing a salver. "These just came for you this morning, Your Grace."

"Thank you." Sin's gaze was already on the distinctive feminine writing on the top envelope.

He sighed. Alanna. Yet one more item on his list of matters to attend to before he left.

Below her letter were several others forwarded from his secretary in London and one other letter with no return direction, written on cheap parchment, and sealed with a putrid gray wafer.

"You really must talk to Phelps about whatever it is that he is using on your hair, St. John."

He looked up from the letters. "I'm sorry, Aunt?"

"Your hair," Lady Julia said, her pale green eyes—so like his own and his father's—narrowing. "It looks almost . . . dirty."

"I think it might be the new pomade Phelps is using," he lied, silently begging his valet's forgiveness.

Elliot had given Sin a coffee-based paste that darkened his distinctive ash-blond hair. How his friend knew about such things was a mystery he wasn't sure he wanted to solve.

Phelps, his valet, had been appalled when Sin brought him the coffee mixture the first time and instructed him to apply it.

Elliot had assured Sin that the color would wash out easily. That had turned out to be something of an exaggeration. Fortunately, Phelps had concocted a vinegar rinse that had stripped off most of the color when soap and water had failed to do the job.

Poor Phelps. If his valet had been stunned about darkening Sin's hair, he'd been close to apoplexy when Sin had told the man where he was really going for the next few months.

And where *Phelps* was really going.

Although his valet had not questioned the order to pack and prepare for a journey to America—a trip which Phelps would be taking with Sin's secretary—Sin had sensed the other man had been as close to speaking out as he ever had in the almost twenty years that he'd served him.

Well, it couldn't be helped. Phelps and Morland's journey was necessary to preserve the façade of his trip to America. Besides, his secretary *did* have business to attend to in Boston, although it could just as well have been accomplished by letter.

Sin turned his attention to Alanna's lavender missive first. The paper was impregnated with her signature scent and lilac drifted up to tease his nostrils.

Sin had enjoyed a mutually beneficial arrangement with the lovely widow, but he'd been poised to bring the relationship to a close for some time now.

Before he'd received Strickland's letter, his plan had been to apply himself seriously to finding a wife. It was not a process that he'd been looking forward to. Not because he was opposed to marriage—he had enjoyed his brief marriage to Vanessa, even though they'd hardly been more than strangers when they'd married.

No, he wasn't looking forward to finding a wife now because he would still be expected to choose a young woman in her child-bearing prime even though he was thirty-two. He'd gone to enough balls over the past few years and danced with enough young women to know the gap between thirty-two and eighteen was more than one of mere years.

Nevertheless, he had drawn up a list of suitable candidates. It had been his intention to become acquainted with the young women— all of whom were of impeccable background—over the course of the Season and make an offer before he left for the family seat at the end of June.

Now, he would have to put aside his plans for marriage.

Because he found the notion of courting a wife while bedding a mistress a repugnant one—not to mention disrespectful to both women—he had planned to end his arrangement with Alanna be-fore the Season.

Alanna would not take kindly to the news. He suspected she held hopes that he might extend her an offer of marriage. She was the widow of a viscount, and her lineage was adequate. Her three male offspring suggested she was suitably fecund, although at thirty-six she would likely not be able to give him more than a few children.

Still, that was no reason *not* to marry her.

And yet . . .

And yet he could not see himself living with her as his mate. She was surpassingly lovely and also a lusty, uninhibited, and demanding bed partner.

Unfortunately, she had no desire for anything other than pleasure. Not even her children seemed to interest her, and she had given them over to her mother-in-law to raise.

Sin had grown up with a selfish, reckless, pleasure-seeking father and a damaged mother; he wanted better for his own children. He wanted a woman with more than just fashion, jewels, and entertainment on her mind.

He had hopes that he might come to love whatever woman he married. Because once he wed, he would remain faithful to his wife and demand the same.

Well, all of that would have to wait, now. And he couldn't say that he didn't feel some relief at postponing the monumental decision.

He opened Alanna's letter.

Darling,

It has been more than three weeks since you have come to me, Staunton. I am beginning to think you do not like me anymore. You will be gone soon, I know, and I shan't see you again for ages.

You know how thin town has been of late. And the weather is so miserable this year. I am languishing from your neglect. I will be at Lady Conrad's soiree tomorrow night. I do hope to see you there.

Yours,

A.

Sin folded the paper back into its neat little rectangle. He supposed tomorrow night was as good as any. He'd been planning to go to the Conrad soiree, in any case. It would be the last formal entertainment he'd attend before leaving.

Sin turned to the final letter and cracked the ugly gray wafer.

Duke,

I know you are offering a reward for information about a certain event that took place in May 1815. I will be at the Three-Legged Dog after eleven o'clock on February 27. Come alone and bring twice the money that was promised if you want to hear what I know. I know what you look like and I will find you. If I think you've been followed or if you bring anyone along, you will never hear from me again.

Sin stared down at the roughly written letter. Elliot had used his connections to put out the word that they were looking for information about Dominic's possible connection to the French escapee Beauvais, and this was the first response they'd had. February twenty-eighth would be his last night in London.

Why did Sin feel that the date—right before he was leaving—was more than just a coincidence?

Chapter 16

It was snowing February twenty-eighth, the day they departed London.

Marianne considered that an omen—although what kind of omen, she wasn't quite sure.

The first caravans bearing sets and props—one of two such groups—had left for Dover a few days earlier and would already be on their way to their first performance in Lille by the time Marianne and the other performers arrived on French soil.

Almost all the circus employees were making the journey in caravans, and a few, like Marianne, were bringing horses. Her uncle, however, was traveling in his coach, an obscenely cumbersome thing that must have belonged to some lord or other because there was still a gold shadow of a poorly removed escutcheon on the doors.

She knew it would be Sonia—his longtime lover—who'd demanded such an extravagance. It made Marianne weary to think how much money—money they didn't have—he must have spent on the vehicle.

Barnabas had offered Marianne a place inside, but she would much rather ride Reggie, even in the snow. The only activities her uncle and the mercurial Sonia seemed to engage in were squabbling or billing and cooing.

Marianne found witnessing either activity fatiguing.

She loved her uncle, but she could barely tolerate Sonia—a feeling that was mutual. Although Marianne had lived with the other woman from the day her uncle had saved her from having to live in an orphanage all those years ago, Sonia had never made it a secret that she resented Marianne's presence in their lives.

Cecile had tried to convince Marianne more than a few times to move out of her uncle's house and share lodgings with her. But whenever Marianne had mentioned moving to Barnabas, he'd always begged her to stay.

Since this business with the duke had started Marianne was actually relieved that she and Cecile hadn't left to get their own lodgings. For weeks she'd been avoiding being alone with the inquisitive Frenchwoman—not an easy or pleasant task since Cecile was her closest friend—all because she couldn't lie about what was going on with the three peers.

Marianne had resolved to ask the duke if she could tell Cecile at least part of the truth. She was tired of keeping secrets from a woman who was as close as a sister to her.

The sound of galloping hooves interrupted her thoughts, and she turned, her hand resting on the pistol she kept tucked in the waistband of her buckskins; the Dover Road was dangerous, even in broad daylight.

She squinted through the snow at the approaching horse and rider. Although he was dressed in his "humble man" outfit, she could easily recognize the duke, who had an excellent seat and held himself as if he owned the road. Knowing him, he probably did.

He slowed as he approached her. She'd not seen him since the night of their tussle in the dressing room, and her heart fluttered like a bird trapped in her chest.

Even dressed in old clothing he looked like a god. And now that she knew what he felt like beneath those clothes—as hard as granite—she knew he felt like a god, as well.

"I thought you'd already gone down with Smithy and Guy yesterday," she said by way of greeting.

"I had one final matter to attend to last night."

His eyes, when they met hers, were so cold that Marianne flinched.

She frowned. Was he angry about what had happened in the dressing room? He certainly hadn't seemed angry when he'd left.

Or was he concerned that she might fling herself at him if he behaved with the same cordiality he'd exhibited before that fateful Tuesday?

Shame burned inside her at the thought. Well, he needn't worry about fending off her advances.

"That was Barnabas I just passed riding in the Earl of Charring's old coach, if I'm not mistaken?"

"Yes, Barnabas and Sonia, his housekeeper," she said, every bit as coolly as he.

The duke cocked a dark blond eyebrow. "He is bringing his housekeeper with him?"

"Keeping house is only one of her duties."

He opened his mouth—as if he were going to ask what the other roles were—but then shut it, a faint blush spreading over his cheekbones. "Ah."

Marianne couldn't help being amused by his prudish reaction. Well, she supposed the wholesome young women he was acquainted with didn't speak of—or even hint at—lovers. He should know—especially after their last encounter—that she was not a wholesome virgin.

"Is her presence in the carriage the reason you are riding?" he asked.

"Partly. But I also prefer being on Reggie to being tossed around in a coach, no matter how well sprung."

"Even in the snow?"

"Even in the snow. What about you? Why aren't you in a curricle speeding your way to a warm, dry room at the Ship Hotel?"

"I am striving to stay in character, Marianne."

Marianne didn't like the way her body responded to the sound of her name in his mouth—even when he said the word as unemotionally as he just had. She'd given up on his ever speaking less succinctly and precisely—he was a duke all the way to his bones.

Hearing her name spoken in his diamond-hard accent was . . . well, distracting to say the least, dangerously stimulating at worst.

Dominic's accent had been every bit as crisp, although he had never sounded stern or severe. She doubted Dom had a stern bone in his body. Selfish, reckless, thoughtless, and careless bones? Yes, by the score.

"How are your ribs?" he asked, startling her out of her musing.

"What do you know about my ribs?"

"Elliot told me Nora got under your guard."

Why did it make her feel so strange to know he was talking about her with his friend? By now she'd realized that the man never did anything by halves. At first she'd thought making numerous demands on his time would drive him to quit. She'd soon begun to suspect that he would have taken the position and his responsibilities seriously, even without her riding him.

"Marianne? Your ribs?" he said.

"Oh, they're fine—just a bit sore."

She didn't tell the duke that the reason for her wandering attention was riding beside her. Actually, it wasn't the duke himself who'd distracted her but her memory of a dream she'd been having when she woke up that morning. An extremely vivid, colorful, *erotic* dream.

Her face heated at the mere thought of it.

Marianne was no blushing virgin; she knew what she was feeling was sexual attraction—it wasn't emotional, it was animal. Her body's reaction to the Duke of Staunton was beyond mortifying. She wanted to bang her head against something hard and pound some sense into it, but her head wasn't the problem; it was her body betraying her.

Marianne didn't know what it was about Staunton that made it so difficult for her to concentrate. It was more than just his handsome face, because his friend Lord Carlisle was far prettier and more pleasant, and yet Marianne felt nothing around him.

Whatever it was that was scrambling her wits, she needed to get herself under control, because she would soon be sitting on the duke's knee on a weekly basis. He would be wiping sweat from her body, tending her injuries, and generally taking care of her. She could hardly throw herself at him every time as she'd done two Tuesdays ago. Her pride would not survive another rejection.

"Do you have family in France?"

She blinked at the abrupt change in conversation. "None that I know of." She hesitated and then added, "My mother and uncle were the last of their family."

"Did they move here together?"

"Barnabas moved to England first. Then my mother married an English sailor and moved here after I was born."

"So, you are French?"

Why was he asking her these questions and wearing what she thought of as his "raptor" look—not the sort of expression a person wore when trying to make pleasant conversation.

"By birth, but I consider myself an Englishwoman."

"Do you." His lips curved in an unpleasant smirk.

Marianne frowned at him. What the devil was he getting at? "What about *you*, Your Grace?"

"What about me?"

"You want to talk about my family. Well, I want to talk about yours. Since your brother is the reason for your presence in my life, perhaps you might share what happened to him?"

"You don't know?"

She gave him an exasperated look. "How could I?"

"My brother was an Exploring Officer for Wellington. He and two others were ambushed by a group of men acting on information smuggled out of England. My brother's body was never found, but the other two were brought home."

"How do you think Dominic found out about your brother?"

"How do *you* think he found out about him?" the duke countered.

Fury boiled inside him at her confused look. What an actress she was!

"Me? How would I know anything about this?"

"You were Strickland's lover—I'm sorry, that's right: you

claimed to be his *wife*"—he scoffed—"only weeks before he arranged his death and disappeared. Surely you must have noticed something untoward."

Her jaws clenched and her nostrils flared at his crude taunting. "Actually, his *wife* was with him only a few days before he supposedly died. Why don't you ask *her* if she knew what he was up to?"

He held her glare, looking for guilt, fear, or shame—any sign that she knew what her ex-lover had been up to during those final weeks. But all he saw was anger, confusion, and hurt.

If what he'd learned last night at the Three-Legged Dog was true, then she was a remarkable performer.

"My brother and the other two men were captured because of information the French received from one of their own agents— a man who'd been held on one of the prisoner hulks anchored at Chatham."

Naked fear flickered across her face at the word *Chatham*, but was quickly suppressed. "What are you trying to say, Your Grace?"

"I'm not *trying* to say anything. I'm telling you how the information passed from Whitehall to a prisoner on a hulk in Chatham to somebody in France. And led to the death of two men and the possible imprisonment of the third."

Her gaze flickered away, and then back. "Dominic's family seat is outside Chatham."

"Yes."

"I was there—in May of last year."

"Were you?" he asked with mock surprise.

"You know I was—don't you? That's what all this is about. You think Dominic had something to do with all this." She gave a huff of disbelieving laughter. "You think *I* had something to do with this. You're saying Dominic smuggled the man out—a spy with secrets that led to the murder of British soldiers."

"Did you?"

She stopped her horse in the middle of the road, snow swirling around her. "How *dare* you accuse me of such a thing?"

"I'm not accusing—just asking."

"It doesn't sound like a question," she snapped, bright spots of color on her pale cheeks, white flakes of snow caught in her eyelashes. "That's what all this is about—isn't it? You're using me to get to Dominic because you think I helped him spy. Maybe I'm *still* helping him?"

He merely stared at her. "Are you?"

"Why bother asking when you won't believe my answer?"

"Make me believe you, Marianne."

"Why should I? Just what is going to happen when we meet Dominic, Your Grace? If you think I had something to do with treason, you're not just going to bring me to him to have tea and crumpets, are you?" Her mouth tightened and she swallowed audibly. "If you think I was involved, you probably think my uncle was involved, as well."

Telling her the truth will hardly help your cause.

He knew that. But he couldn't bear to look at her after what he'd learned last night.

He was not trained as a spy—somebody who could prevaricate convincingly when it came to treason and traitors, a friend's death and his brother's capture.

"I do," he said.

"Then what are you going to do with us?"

"I'm going to find out the truth."

"What if I told you that I know nothing about any of that?"

When he didn't answer, she snorted. "Never mind, I can see your answer on your face. What's to stop me from turning around right now and going back to London?"

"I will stop you."

"What? You'd grab me and drag me to France in chains?"

"Yes. And your uncle, too."

Her body vibrated with anger. "You wouldn't dare."

"If it's a choice between my brother and you, my brother will always win."

She stared at him for a long, furious moment and then said, "Have you ever wondered just why Dominic wants to see me so badly?"

"I have," he admitted. "Why don't you tell me?"

"Because I don't know," she said through clenched teeth. "I was just as shocked as you to learn he wasn't dead." Her eyes raked over him. "But I do know one thing for sure, Your Grace."

"What is that?"

"If Dominic is going to all this trouble to see me, it won't be for any good reason." Her smile was bitter. "Don't worry, I'm not going to make you use brute force on me. I gave my word I would go, and I don't lie, despite what you might think."

"Neither do I."

"Oh? And what about my uncle? Because it sounds like you just threatened to put a noose around his neck after promising me in London that you would not take action against him about the smuggling if I did as you bade me."

Sin ground his teeth. After what he'd learned last night, the two of them—uncle *and* niece—should be drawn and quartered.

"Well?" she taunted.

"My promise regarding your uncle applied to the smuggling of expensive fripperies, Miss Simpson. I will not condone treason and murder. Both you and Farnham will stand trial for your crimes—along with your lover, whom I *will* bring back in chains."

"My crimes." She laughed, the sound without mirth, and turned her mount.

"Where are you going?"

"Don't worry, I'm not running away. I'm going to ride with my uncle. Suddenly a trip in his rattletrap coach with a woman who despises me is far more appealing than a ride with you."

"But he's miles back. This road is unsafe—a man and his valet were robbed and shot here only last week, in broad daylight."

"What? Are you worried that somebody will shoot me and deprive you of the joy of watching me hang?" She didn't wait for an answer, but kneed her horse into a gallop, leaving Sin alone in the middle of the snowy road.

Chapter 17

The crossing from Dover to Calais was remarkably smooth. The circus was comprised of too many caravans for just one packet, so their group was spread across several.

Marianne hadn't seen the duke since leaving him in the middle of the Dover Road the day before. She knew that he and his friends must be on this packet because she'd watched as the crew loaded their caravan on board. They had bought their wagon somewhere else—not at the place where her uncle had commissioned the rest of them—and it was a lovely glossy red with black trim and gold lettering on the side. The duke must have spent a fortune on it, but then, Staunton had a fortune to spare.

It was just as well that she hadn't seen him because she wasn't sure she could look at his face without punching it.

Cecile came up beside her and leaned against the packet's high railing. "What is wrong, *chérie*? You've looked like a storm cloud ever since you got to the hotel last night. Were Barnabé and Sonia dreadful on the ride down? I told you that you should have come with me, Nora, and Lucy. They talk, talk, talk—those two—but at least they do not fight the whole way."

"Josephine didn't come with you?"

"No."

"How did she get to Dover?"

Cecile shrugged. "I am not that one's keeper. I have enough of a job looking out for you."

Marianne stared out over the water. "You don't need to look out for me. I'm a grown woman."

"I thought we were friends?"

Marianne looked up at the hurt in the other woman's voice. "Of course, we are. I'm sorry I'm so peevish."

Cecile waved away her apology. "That is not what I mean. For weeks I have waited for you to tell me what you are doing with these men."

It surprised her that Cecile had waited so long to dig into this subject. "You recognize them?"

"Them? No, I don't recognize the slender fellow you call Smithy. But the duke, of course I know that face—those are not eyes a woman would soon forget. As for the other one—*Guy.*" Cecile's full lips curled and she pronounced the name in the French fashion, so it sounded like *Ghee.* "Naturally I recognize that big, dark-haired, dumb—"

Marianne laughed. "Dumb? I'd call him many things: arrogant, flirtatious, smug, superior—oh, I could go on—but dumb? No."

"Very well. Perhaps dumb is not the right word."

"Has he been difficult about volunteering for your routine?" she asked, suddenly curious. She'd assigned all three men their *volunteering* duties but hadn't checked with either Cecile or Blade to see how the performances had gone.

"No, no, he's shown up and done what I told him."

"Then what is it? You look disgruntled."

Cecile ignored the question, gazing out over the Channel.

"I would have thought you'd be happy to have him at your beck and call."

The Frenchwoman's head whipped around. "What do you mean?"

"Well, you did like reading about him in all those gossip—"

"You didn't *tell* him that, did you?" Cecile demanded, dark eyes flashing.

. "No, of course not. I haven't told him anything about you."

"Why? Has he been asking questions about me?"

Marianne gave a startled snort. "No, he hasn't asked anything and I wouldn't tell him if he had. What's wrong? Why do you look so . . . anxious?"

Cecile turned away again. "Nothing is wrong."

Marianne didn't believe her, but she wasn't feeling energetic enough to press the matter.

Personally, Marianne rather liked the happy-go-lucky Marquess of Carlisle. At least he'd not accused her of treason and murder.

"When did you first recognize them?" Marianne asked.

"*Pffft!* The first time I saw them I knew. Do you think I am stupid? That I can't see through a bit of hair dye and cheap clothing?"

"Barnabas didn't recognize either of them until I told him who they were."

Cecile snorted. "That fool. How you came to be the relative of such a stupid man I will never know."

Marianne couldn't help laughing, even though she felt guilty about it. But Cecile was right—how in the world could her uncle not have noticed immediately that the men looked and behaved like English lords? Even Smithy—who did a fair enough job with his Bristol accent—looked far too sleek and healthy to be an ex-butcher pugilist.

"I don't suppose you will tell me why they are traveling with us?" Cecile frowned at Marianne's bonnet and then reached for the bow beneath her chin.

Marianne tried to pull away, but Cecile held tight. "Hold still and let me put this right," she muttered, tugging on the navy-blue ribbon until it was longer on one side, and then ironing the wrinkled ties with her fingers before fashioning a new bow beneath Marianne's ear. She stood back to admire her work. "*Bon.* Why do you insist on dressing like such a down?"

"I think you mean a *dowd*."

Cecile gave one of her elegant Gallic shrugs—which seemed

to communicate so much more than the standard English shrug. "Don't try to evade my question."

"Which one? The one about the men or about me being a dowd?"

"You are *not* a dowd. You try to be one."

"I cannot tell you why they're traveling with us, and I'd ask that you not tell anyone else their true identities."

Cecile's offended scowl told her what she thought about such a superfluous warning. But, to Marianne's relief, she didn't pursue the topic. A person never knew with Cecile. Sometimes she could dig in like a wood tick.

"Good afternoon, ladies."

They turned to find the Marquess of Carlisle grinning down at them. He swept off his tweed cap and gave them a court bow.

Cecile sniffed.

"Hallo, Guy," Marianne said, amused by the Frenchwoman's reaction.

"I see you're both good sailors." He leaned an elbow on the rail. "Have either of you been seasick before?"

"This is my first trip on a packet." Marianne frowned. "Actually, that's not true; it's my second. But the last time I was barely a month old, so I don't recall." She turned to her friend, who was looking at Guy with such intensity it was amazing that his head didn't burst into flame. "What about you, Cecile? You must recall your last crossing?"

"Yes, I was fourteen. And no, I did not become ill."

"And how long ago would that have been?" Guy asked.

"That is as bad as asking me my age."

"I'll tell you mine if you tell me yours."

"I don't care how old you are," Cecile retorted.

"*Oof!*" he said, grabbing his heart. "That's hitting below the belt."

"Then I think you should be grabbing something lower."

He laughed. "It seems pistols are not the only deadly weapons you wield."

"Speaking of deadly weapons, have you seen Josephine?" Marianne asked, interceding before Cecile shot the teasing peer.

Guy pulled his gaze away from Cecile with obvious effort. "No, I've not seen her since last Friday—when she was throwing knives at my head."

Marianne chuckled.

"I'm pleased to amuse you," the marquess said tartly. "But I'm not so sure I would have taken this position if I'd known women were going to be using me for target practice."

"You should be pleased to be useful for a change," Cecile snapped.

Guy opened his mouth, but then his attention was caught by a tall, familiar, and unwanted figure coming toward them.

"Hallo, Sin."

The duke nodded at Cecile and Guy and then turned his cold gaze on Marianne. The atmosphere chilled considerably.

"How is Smithy feeling?" Guy asked after it was clear that neither Marianne nor his friend had any intention of speaking, even though they were locked in a glaring war.

The duke blinked slowly at Marianne and then turned to Guy. "Wretched. Although I think that his misery is more from mortification than actual illness. He said he's never been seasick before."

"It happens that way," Guy said. "Even sometimes to seasoned sailors." His gaze slid to Cecile, who was frowning from Marianne to the duke, and back again.

The four of them stood in uncomfortable silence until Cecile broke it. "I must go and see to something."

"Er, I'll go with you. I need to see to something, too," Guy said. At Cecile's raised eyebrows he amended, "I mean something else."

The two hurried off and Marianne turned her back on Staunton and propped her elbows up on the railing.

Rather than leave, as a normal human would, he leaned beside her, so close their shoulders brushed. "It's going to be a long journey if we are constantly at daggers drawn."

"Maybe you should turn around in Calais and go back home, Your Grace."

He turned to her, but she stared straight ahead, the endless water soothing her jangling nerves.

"The night before last I spoke to a man who'd been a footman in Strickland's house in Chatham. He was there the same time you were."

"So?"

"He said he was with you and Strickland when you picked up a French gentleman down by the docks and drove with the man to Deal."

Marianne turned to him. "What of it? The man was a French architect—an émigré by the name of Olivier Monet." She had purposely blocked out memories of her time with Dominic, but she remembered the day—and journey—quite well.

They had been arguing. Well, she had been arguing and Dominic had been drinking. It was only a few short weeks after their supposed marriage and he had filled his Chatham house with people who'd worked for him at his version of her uncle's circus, a business he'd started the year before, which he called The Caligula Club. The name was well-suited as Dominic's circus had murky undertones: his female fighters were harsh, beaten-down women who smelled strongly of gin. None of his boxers—male or female—wore mufflers, and the fights weren't finished until there was only one person standing. She had also heard rumors about other, less savory, events being held for select patrons: like a rat pit in which he didn't only employ terriers, but children.

When she had confronted Dominic about what she'd heard, he had asked her to go for a ride in his carriage. She'd thought they were going to discuss her accusations. Instead, he had picked up Monet.

"I remember Monet," she finally said to the duke, who'd waited patiently. A sour stew of fear and dread swirled in her belly as she recalled that day. "We collected him from a dilapidated house several streets off the harbor in Chatham." She met his intent gaze. "Why are you asking about him?"

He reached into his pocket and extracted a letter. "Is this your handwriting?"

The envelope only bore two words: *Robert Slattery.*

"It looks like my handwriting." She glanced from the letter to the duke.

"You know Robert Slattery?"

"I didn't *know* him as such." She chewed her lip as her mind raced. "And before you ask, yes, I knew that he owned a ship—the *Defiant*—that ran smuggled goods back and forth across the channel."

The duke opened the letter. "Let me read it for you: '*We've received the money. The package will be at the old rope warehouse on May 17ᵗʰ.*'" He looked up at her. "Do you remember writing this?"

"No." His eyes narrowed and she hastened to explain. "I'm not denying that I wrote it, but I don't remember that specific letter."

"This is a letter Strickland's footman said he was sent to deliver a few days before you and Strickland drove the Frenchman to Deal."

"*What?* That's a lie. I didn't—Wait," she said. "If this man was paid to deliver it, then why did he still have it?"

"He said he managed to steal it back after the man read it."

Marianne snorted at that. "How convenient."

The duke frowned, but she could see he, too, thought the story rather flimsy.

Marianne pushed the thought aside. "What does all this mean? What are you getting at?"

"May seventeenth of last year was the day at least one of those escaped French prisoners was smuggled out of Deal, Miss Simpson."

Marianne flung up her hands. "I swear on my life that I never sent a letter on May 17, 1814."

"I'm sorry, but how can you be so sure?"

"I can be sure because the last time I wrote any of those letters— all of which were about smuggled goods, not people, by the way— was back when my uncle still lived in Deal, at least five years ago, when I was down from school visiting him on a holiday."

*　*　*

Sin stared into her angry eyes. "Explain."

"Why should I bother? Will you believe me?"

"Tell me and we'll find out."

She heaved an exaggerated sigh. "My uncle has a difficult time with written English. Actually, he has a terrible time with written French, as well. I often write letters or messages for him in both languages."

"If you wrote it, you must have been helping him smuggle."

"Yes. I was helping him smuggle," she admitted, her cheeks reddening at the admission. "It is wrong—I know that—and I knew it then, too. But—"

"But what?"

"He said the reason he'd been forced to move to Deal was because his solicitor had made a muddle of the deed for the London theater. He claimed he would lose all his interest in the building if he couldn't get together a sum of money and—"

She groaned and shook her head. "Lord, the story sounds so idiotic in light of the gaming debts you are so graciously holding over my head. But back then I believed him. I was terrified that we would lose the theater. Besides, what Barnabas wanted to do didn't seem so terribly wrong. You must remember what it was like back then? It seemed that everyone who lived in a coastal town was smuggling. A person was actually suspect if they *weren't* running something. But I mean spirits, lace, silk, and what have you. I swear that I never heard of anyone selling information or smuggling people. So, yes, I wrote that letter—but long before the escape of this prisoner you're talking about."

Sin was disturbed by how badly he wanted to believe her. "Tell me about this jaunt to Deal with Strickland and the architect."

"Tell you what?"

"Tell me everything and anything you remember—no matter how minor it may seem."

She stared skyward, as if searching the attics of her memory. "He was very tall and thin. I remember he looked . . . ill. He was gaunt, with an unhealthy pallor. His hair was the same ginger as your beard."

She had just described Beauvais perfectly.

"Why were you taking him to Deal?"

"He needed money and was willing to work cheaply on a building for Dominic. You knew Dominic—you must have known what he was like."

"Yes, I knew him—a long time ago. Tell me what you mean."

"He always seemed to have *arrangements* with people. Agreements that weren't exactly illegal, but somehow . . . shady. He loved to barter, largely because he never had any money, I suppose. I assumed this ill-looking architect was somebody who would do the work for a fraction of the cost because he was French and desperate. That was Dominic, always willing to take advantage of another person's desperation if it could make him money."

Sin agreed; Strickland had always operated on the fringes of propriety. Their friendship had been severed by one such venture, which had crossed the line into illegality—not to mention immorality. "What else do you recall?"

"That is all. I'm sorry, but I had my mind on other matters that day." She gave him a searing look. "If you know as much about me as you seem to know, then you'll have realized I left Dominic's house not long after that carriage ride. Let's just say that architects—French or otherwise—were not foremost in my mind at that point."

Sin hated how curious he was about the relationship between her and Strickland. The more he knew her, the less he could understand her falling in love with such a man. Oh, Dominic could charm a bird out of a tree, but he was . . . superficial.

Sin had come to believe—at least before talking to that bloody footman two nights ago—that Marianne Simpson was exactly what she appeared: a smart woman forced into a brutal line of work by circumstances.

"I know you think I am no better than a whore because of what happened with Dominic. And I can't blame you for thinking me a criminal since I've admitted to smuggling. But you have my word of honor—the only thing I really have—that I never smuggled either people or secrets. That letter was from years before, and Dominic apparently found it and used it for his own purposes. I suppose he wanted to be sure that it would not be in his handwriting if it were ever discovered."

"I believe you," he said quietly.

Her expression was bitter rather than relieved. "But you think I might have aided spies unknowingly."

"It is possible." Indeed, it was almost certain.

Her shoulders sagged. "What I helped my uncle do was foolish and reckless. But I refuse to believe Barnabas would have been involved in smuggling secrets. Not because he is especially patriotic," she said with a bitter snort. "But because he would have been too scared. Barnabas, for all his bluster, is, I'm ashamed to admit, something of a coward."

Sin heard the pain in her voice at the admission. She was loyal to her uncle, but not blind to his faults.

They stared out at the water, which was eerily smooth for such an overcast, stormy-looking day.

When she finally turned to him, her expression was grim. "If Dominic smuggled that man out of the country, using my letter to deflect suspicion from himself, then I want to know," she said quietly. "I know at first I was resistant to seeing him, but I am eager to speak to him, now. I'll talk to him. And I'll find out the truth, Your Grace."

Sin believed her. He only hoped that the truth didn't doom her as well as her treasonous ex-lover.

Chapter 18

Barnabas had booked rooms for them in a humble but clean inn on the outskirts of Calais

Their first performance, three days hence, was in Lille, a solid two days' journey from Calais. The heavily loaded prop wagons that had come across with them would never be able to make the journey that quickly, so it was fortunate that another set of wagons had departed for Lille several days ago.

The caravans that had arrived with them would bypass Lille altogether and continue to the next city on the tour. If nothing went wrong, this manner of leapfrogging should mean a full crew and set of props would await them at each stop.

Her uncle had made sure the itinerary was lighter at the beginning, which meant they would stay a full two weeks in the towns that made up the first part of the tour to allow for bad weather delays. Starting in May they would be stopping in many smaller towns where they'd offer shows with only one of the main acts each evening; that was when they'd begin to get more use from the caravans rather than staying at inns.

It was unseasonably cold the morning they set out, and, as the day wore on, the sky became even darker and the rain began to develop into sleet.

Marianne had decided to ride Reggie rather than make the journey inside the caravan she shared with Cecile and Jo. They were fortunate there were posting inns at regular intervals, where they'd be able to break their journey throughout the day. But if the sleety rain continued to fall so heavily, they were not likely to make it to their midway point, the town of Blendecques, before dark.

"You should be riding in the caravan with the others."

Marianne turned at the sound of the familiar, haughty voice. The duke was mounted not on Dobbin or Cassio, but on a sturdy-looking chestnut gelding better suited for uncertain terrain and long rides. She suspected the horse had cost the duke a pretty penny, but it didn't look out of place—as Cassio would have done—among some of the other mounts her uncle's employees were riding.

Marianne lowered her ugly scarf just enough to crack the shell of ice that had formed over her mouth. "Why don't *you* ride with Smithy?"

Like the duke, the other two men had mounts, but Elliot was driving their caravan while Guy drove the one with Cecile and Jo. Cecile could have driven it perfectly well, but that was part of Guy's job and the Frenchwoman enjoyed making the big marquess work.

Jo rode inside the caravan along with Angus.

"You won't be much use in Lille if you are ill," the duke said.

Marianne couldn't help smiling. "You can't bear the fact that I don't obey your orders, can you?"

He glared at her, only his pale, sea-green eyes familiar. He'd stopped shaving entirely and the copper and blond scruff that covered his face rendered him unrecognizable.

Marianne's gaze flickered to his hair. "Your hair looks darker."

He hesitated—as if he were going to persist with his scold—but then he seemed to think better of it. "I started using a dye made from black walnuts."

"What were you using before?"

"Something made from coffee. Smithy says this will last longer."

"No more spectacles?" she asked.

"I don't think I'll need them here."

Marianne didn't think so, either. With the darker hair, even his mother might not have known him.

His mother. Hadn't he said his mother was alive? But that an aunt had raised him? There was a story there, she suspected. But his elegant, aristocratic profile told her he'd have no interest in sharing confidences.

Since when did Marianne care what he wanted? Why not probe? What else was there to do on such a dreary day?

"Did you see your family on your week away?"

His jaw flexed and he didn't turn. For a long moment, she thought he'd not answer. But then he said, "Some of them." He must have realized how churlish he sounded. "I'd already visited with my sisters at a christening a month ago, but I saw my aunt and mother."

"They didn't go to the christening?"

He turned to her. "No."

Marianne held his cold gaze and raised her eyebrows.

He sighed and wiped the accumulated moisture from his face.

"My mother is not well, and my aunt cannot leave her." There was a finality in his tone that told her she'd get no more from him on that subject. "I believe we shall have to stay in a smaller village than planned this evening," he added as the rain began to fall in large, sludgy drops.

"I warned my uncle that touring at this time of year was madness. He says he's made allowances for such delays. I suppose we shall soon see if he's made enough of them."

"To be fair to your uncle, it is unseasonably cold for this part of France."

His defense of Barnabas—a man he clearly loathed—didn't really surprise her. The duke was almost biblical in his fairness. She could easily see him seated on a throne, ordering a child to be cut in half.

No, that wasn't accurate. He was fair, but he wasn't cruel.

"The weather in April might not be much better than this," she said, moving the subject away from her uncle. "We will have to make sure to leave the Fayre in time to get to your meeting with Dominic."

"I'm afraid you shall have to miss one of your bouts since the meeting itself is on a Tuesday," he said. "But I believe I can get you to Dijon for the next one."

"You don't have to *get* me anywhere, Your Grace. Once you have your brother, you will wish to return to England with all possible haste."

"I will see you safely to Dijon, first," he said in his cool, implacable way.

Marianne rolled her eyes—or at least tried to, but it was too bloody cold.

"I've arranged to have a new trainer meet you in Dijon."

Her head whipped around at that. "You did what?"

"One of the men on Jack's list—Dexter Fielding—will be in Dijon to accompany you on the rest of the tour. I have already paid his wages."

She snorted. "You can't help yourself, can you?"

"Jack said you liked Fielding."

"I *do* like Dex, but that's not the point. The point is—" Honestly, Marianne didn't know why she even bothered to try to argue with the man. He could pay the Prince Regent to show up in Dijon, but that didn't mean she had to abide by his decisions.

"Never mind," she said, and then clucked her tongue to urge Reggie ahead, leaving the duke behind her.

Sin didn't know why he even bothered to argue with the woman. He should have just let matters run their course. She would have shown up in Dijon to a fait accompli.

He scowled as he watched her ride ahead, pulling her horse up beside her caravan. Although Guy was driving it, the Frenchwoman—Cecile—was sitting beside him. The last time he'd stopped to tell Guy something, the two had been locked in a fierce argument about guns, of all things. The woman had looked on the verge of pulling out a pistol and shooting Guy, so Sin had come to ride beside Marianne, hoping to have a normal conversation after their rapprochement on the packet. But the woman was as stubborn as a badger.

Sin slowed his mount until Elliot, who was driving the last caravan in a group of four, came up alongside him.

"Lovely day," Elliot said, smiling at Sin from beneath his battered hat. He looked profoundly untrustworthy with a week's worth of growth on his face.

Sin gestured to Marianne. "Why the devil is she riding in this weather instead of traveling in one of the caravans?" he demanded and then immediately wished he hadn't when he saw Elliot's faint smirk.

"Why are *you* riding in this weather?"

"Because I'm a *man* and riding in such weather is nothing to me."

"Perhaps it is nothing to her, either."

Sin made a scoffing sound.

"I think we will not make it to our destination this evening if the road gets much worse," Elliot said, the comment an obvious gambit to change the subject.

Sin glanced down at the muddy ruts, which had become deeper by the hour. "Did you look at the map?" Elliot had brought along excellent government maps of all the areas they would be travelling through.

"I did," Sin said. "I think we can make it to a town called Longuenesse by dark."

Ahead of them, the back window on the women's caravan slid up and Josephine Brown stood in the opening with her raven Angus on her shoulder. Her lips curled into a slight smile.

Sin couldn't see where she was looking, but suspected Elliot was her target.

"What is it with you and that woman?" Sin asked. "You never took your eyes off her at breakfast this morning."

"There is something . . . off about her," Elliot said in a musing tone.

Sin barked a laugh. "There are about a dozen somethings *off* about her. Starting with that beast of hers."

As if the raven heard him, it turned its head and made a rusty sounding *quork, quork* that was audible even over the rumble of the wagons.

"I've never known anyone to keep a raven as a pet before and I had no idea they could talk," Sin said. The bird sounded exactly like his mistress when he spoke; it was more than a little disturbing.

Elliot chuckled. "Angus is her familiar."

Blade leaned toward her bird, her lips moving.

The big black creature hesitated a moment and then launched itself into the gloomy, drizzly day, disappearing into the dense trees on the side of the road.

"Now, what was all that about, I wonder?" Elliot asked.

Blade gave them a last look and then slammed the window shut.

Sin couldn't help noticing that his normally serious friend was smiling, his sharp, speculative gaze lingering on the caravan.

Chapter 19

There were three inns in Longuenesse, the town where they were forced to stop for the night, and all of them were small. So they split into three groups: Barnabas, Sonia, the duke and his two friends, and Marianne and Cecile took rooms at the first inn; Jo and the three jugglers shared rooms at the second; and Nora, Lucy, and Ted took the last two rooms at the third inn.

"What were you and Guy arguing about all day long?" Marianne asked as she stripped out of her soaking wet clothing.

"That one! He thinks he knows everything."

Marianne smiled at the irony of Cecile making such a statement; it was like the pot and the kettle since Cecile was a bit of a know-it-all herself and would argue about anything and everything.

"If he bothers you so much, why didn't you ride inside the caravan with Blade?"

Cecile snorted. "What? And talk to myself all day? At least I get *some* conversation if I sit up front."

It was true that Blade was extremely reserved. Angus was probably more talkative than his mistress.

"Besides," Cecile added, "Arguing helps to keep one warm and also makes the day go faster."

Marianne glanced at the pile of luggage Cecile had brought up to the room. "Why so many bags for just one night?" she asked. But before Cecile could answer, she laughed. "Wait—I know. You had Guy bring up every single bag you packed, didn't you?"

Cecile, who was sitting at the dressing table repairing the minimal damage to her hair and clothing, smirked faintly. "It is what he is good for, that one."

"That's not really fair—he's amusing and rather pretty to look at, too."

"*Pfft.*"

That was one of the Frenchwoman's favorite responses for those times when she was finished with a subject.

Marianne pulled out one of her gray wool dresses.

"Oh, no," Cecile said, shaking her head. "Please. Not that—that—*chiffon hideux.*"

She turned to Cecile. "It is *not* a hideous rag. It's simply a—"

"*Chiffon hideux,*" Cecile repeated, going to her open trunk and rooting about before pulling out a navy dress and then tossing a thick, fleecy cream shawl on top of it "Here. This is good for your coloring, and you will need something warm. It is snug for me, so it will be perfect on you."

Perfect was a bit of an exaggeration, although what Marianne lacked in bosom she made up for in breadth of shoulders and back.

"You're very kind, Cecile, but why should I—"

"We are not in England any longer, *chérie.*"

"I *know* we're not in England. What are—"

"Put it on." Cecile turned back to the mirror and resumed screwing in her earbobs.

Marianne looked at the dress—which was simple in design and yet so soignée, like all the garments the Frenchwoman owned.

She imagined the duke's expression if she showed up looking—for once—feminine.

Her face heated at the thought and she glanced up at Cecile, as if the other woman might know what Marianne was thinking.

Her friend met her look in the mirror, her full lips curved into a wicked smile. "It will make those beautiful eyes of his roll out of his head."

"I don't know who you're talking about," Marianne said weakly.

Cecile laughed.

Marianne groaned. "Lord. Is my foolish infatuation really so obvious?"

"Yes. But it is not only *you*, Marianne. The two of you make sparks when you rub against each other."

"We do not *rub* against each other," she lied.

"Put on the dress."

Marianne's gaze slid back to the dress. Well, why not? It was just a dress.

The dining room of the Poule et Coq inn was small but cozy. Although it was separate from the taproom, the door had been left open to allow for the heat from the huge hearth—complete with a roasting pig—to circulate through the two rooms.

Barnabas, his housekeeper-slash-lover, Sonia, and his coachman, Yves, were already seated at a large table when Sin entered the dining room.

The Frenchman gave him a pinched look but gestured to the open seats. Sin lowered himself into the chair across from Sonia, giving her a brief smile in response to her simpering and eyelash fluttering. The older Frenchwoman was attractive in a lush, over-ripe way, but he disliked her flirtatious, cloying manner and had needed to excuse himself from her presence twice already, once on the packet, and again last night at dinner in Calais.

"Did the ostler find places for the caravans?" Farnham asked.

"He's keeping one of them at his brother's house for the night. Smithy will sleep in it after he's had some dinner." There was too much money and too many weapons secreted in the caravan to leave it unattended. Although it had shutters with padlocks and double-thick doors with metal inlaid panels, they couldn't risk somebody breaking in or even stealing it.

"How are you enjoying your trip to France . . . Sin?" Sonia asked when Farnham turned to respond to something his coachman said.

She wore the same sly smirk whenever she spoke to him, clearly bursting at the seams to tell him that she knew exactly who he was. He suspected the only reason she hadn't said anything was because Farnham had warned her against it. Sin doubted she was the sort to heed her lover's warnings for long.

"It is colder than I'd hoped," he said mildly. "Which part of the country do you hail from, ma'am?"

She looked pleased by his interest. "I'm from L'Estaque, but I've lived in England for twenty years, now."

"L'Estaque? I've not heard of it." Sin nodded his thanks to the waiter who'd delivered a glass of wine.

She chuckled, the action jiggling her considerable bosom and taxing the tensile strength of the fabric that made up her low-cut gown. "I'd be surprised if you had, monsieur. It is a tiny bit of a place north of Marseilles."

"Will you be visiting family while you are in France?"

An evasive expression flickered across her handsome face so fast that he thought he might have imagined it.

"I am the last of my family." She shrugged. "But I have a new family now." She glanced at something over Sin's shoulder and her mouth tightened. "Ah, here is one I think of as my own daughter."

Sin stood and turned, his gaze landing first on Cecile Tremblay and then, standing behind her, Marianne.

His mouth opened in surprise.

"Is there room for us?" Cecile asked.

Sin yanked his startled gaze off Marianne. "Yes, of course." He pulled out two chairs beside him.

Cecile said. "Here, you take this chair beside Sin, Marianne."

Marianne didn't turn toward him, but he saw that her pale cheeks were flushed.

"You almost resemble a young woman tonight, Marianne," Sonia said, not looking especially pleased about the fact.

Marianne smiled faintly, unperturbed by the dig. "Thank you, Sonia. You look very nice, too." She turned a sideways glance at Sin. "Thank you for seeing to Reggie for me."

He'd all but needed to wrench the reins from her frozen fingers before she had allowed him to help her.

"It was my pleasure," he said, unable to stop staring.

She lowered her eyes.

"Some wine?" he offered, unsettled by this new, almost demure version of a woman who was usually so fierce and direct.

"Please."

Sin raised his hand and summoned the waiter.

Sonia and Cecile discussed what was probably going to happen in Lille, the two women speaking rapid French, and leaving him with Marianne.

"You look very nice."

Well, that sounded tepid.

"Er, quite pretty," he amended, and then wanted to chew out his own tongue when she raised her startled hazel eyes, giving him a disbelieving look.

"What?" she retorted, her cheeks flaming. "Did you think I wasn't a female, Your Grace?"

Rather than be offended, Sin grinned at her hostility, pleased and relieved that she was still her acerbic self, no matter what clothing she wore.

Her eyes widened as they flickered over his face.

"What?" he mocked. "Did you think I was incapable of smiling?"

"As a matter of fact, I did. *Merci*," she said to the waiter.

Sin saw her wearing dresses often—she fought in a dress and showed up for her training sessions in the gray woolen gowns she favored. The only real difference in her person tonight was the color and cut of the gown—the navy flattering to her skin tone—and some dainty pearl earbobs. She'd also done something to her hair—although he couldn't tell what.

She *did* look pretty, but mostly—he realized with some surprise—she looked different, certainly no prettier than she did when garbed in breeches and a cutaway coat. In fact, that might be his favorite-outfit on her—although for reasons that were not exactly honorable.

"What do you think of France?" she asked after taking a sip of wine.

"I've been here before."

"Oh, when was that?"

"It was only briefly, a long time ago, and I was quite young—not much more than ten, I should think. My father took me with him to look at some horses. I don't recall the town, but it was outside Paris. I do remember how woeful my schoolboy French was."

"I heard you speaking to the ostler—it sounds as if you've gotten much better."

His eyebrows shot up. "Praise from you, Marianne?"

She flushed. "I'm not—"

The door to the outside flew open hard enough to bounce off the wall, almost hitting a passing waiter. The man who stumbled into the room was soaked to his skin, pale as parchment, and shaking. He gazed around the room with wide, almost crazed eyes, and then shouted, *"Napoléon a quitté l'île d'Elbe; il se dirige vers Paris!"*

Napoleon has left Elba; he is marching on Paris!

Sin and Marianne turned to gawk at each other while the room exploded as everyone spoke at once, shouting questions to the visibly harried man.

The messenger climbed onto a chair and waved his arms. *"Il a appelé tous les Français fidèles et patriotes à le rejoinder."*

At the news that he was calling on all loyal, patriotic Frenchmen to join him, people began pouring in from the courtyard—villagers who must have followed the half-mad man as he rode into the tiny town.

"Could this be true?" Marianne asked Sin.

"I hope to God it is some kind of jest," he said. But a heavy sickness settled in his belly as he studied the messenger. He was as pale as a corpse, but there was a fervor that burned in his eyes. It did not look like the face of a man who was bent on a jest.

If Napoleon had truly escaped Elba and was raising another army, that meant the hell of the last two decades was about to begin all over again.

And they would be caught right in the middle of it.

Chapter 20

They left before the cock crowed the following morning, the weather even more miserable than the day before.

Barnabas Farnham steadfastly refused to believe what they'd heard in the dining room.

"The English would never allow him to escape, and Frenchmen would *never* want him back," he'd insisted when Sin had asked him what his plans were if the country were to erupt in war. "We will keep to our schedule until we receive more reliable information."

So they trudged on to Lille through the heavy rain.

But it became clear, the closer they got to the city, that rumor of Napoleon's escape had already spread far and wide.

By their third night in the small, but vibrant, city there was no denying the truth of what they'd heard: L'Empereur was on the march toward Paris, and he was gathering an army along the way.

Sin had served as Nora's knee man that night since her brother had caught a nasty cold and was keeping to his bed.

After the boxing match finished and he'd seen to Nora's few injuries, Sin went looking for Elliot and Guy, whom he'd barely had a spare moment to talk to since arriving in Lille.

He spotted Guy watching Blade's routine from the wings.

"I thought it was your turn to *volunteer* tonight," Sin said, going to stand beside him. They'd finally decided the best way to deal with the unpleasant task of having guns fired and knives thrown at their persons was to alternate, from week to week.

"It was," Guy admitted and then winced as Blade threw a knife through the center of a playing card that Elliot held between his fingers. "But Smithy said he'd take all Blade's acts from now on." He cut Sin a knowing smirk and dropped his voice to a whisper. "I'd say our Elliot might finally have developed some interest in the gentler sex." He snickered like a twelve-year-old boy. "I think this might be our Elliot's twisted notion of flirtation."

Sin snorted as another knife *thwacked* through a playing card, pinning it to the colorful board behind Elliot's head.

Blade turned to her audience, as if to take a bow, but Angus called out, *One more!* in French and flew another knife over to his mistress, earning an outraged squawk and angry glare from Elliot; which made the crowd howl with laughter.

Blade's show ended a few minutes later, and Sin nodded to Elliot when he came off the stage. "We need to talk."

"Follow me," Elliot said, leading them to a relatively quiet corner not far from the back door to the theater.

"So," Sin said, looking at Elliot. "Do you have any news for us from your friend in Paris?"

"I received a message just before Josephine's routine. My contact said all the diplomats who've been working in the city are rapidly being moved to Brussels or home. He seemed to think the response was overcautious—that Bonaparte would be easily stopped before things got too far."

"What do you think?" Guy asked.

"Honestly? I just don't know—but the next few weeks will certainly be critical."

"Do you think I should tell Marianne that I've changed my mind? That she should just go back to England?" Sin asked.

"It would certainly be safer for her. The three of us can still make our way to the meeting place. I'm ready for whatever you decide, Sin."

Guy nodded. "Me as well."

"You don't have to make up your mind right now," Elliot added. "But sooner, rather than later."

"Let's give it a bit more time," Sin finally said. "I'm not going to drag Marianne into the middle of a war zone to please Dominic. No matter how dire the repercussions."

"Look at this!" Barnabas was waiting by the stage door after Marianne finished—and won—her fight.

She paused, sweat rolling down her face and her head aching from an especially hard hit to the temple, and squinted out over the audience. Her uncle had been complaining about the poor sales from the moment they'd arrived in Lille and had become more agitated with each day that passed. Now, on night six, he was downright frantic

"Barely half the seats are occupied." Barnabas looked ready to cry. "If this keeps up, we'll—"

"She needs to put ice on her eye," the duke said abruptly, setting a large hand on Marianne's shoulder.

Barnabas's mouth snapped shut at the other man's menacing tone.

"Come along," Staunton murmured to Marianne, the kindness in his voice all the more noticeable in contrast to the frosty tone he'd used with her uncle.

The duke pushed his big body between Marianne and her uncle, nudging Barnabas ungently out of their way.

Marianne allowed him to guide her toward the dressing room that she shared with at least seven other women. "You shouldn't be so harsh to him," she chided, even though just speaking made her head pound harder.

Staunton gave an angry laugh as they navigated around Francine Gordon, the magician, who was cradling her rabbit, Henry, and frowning down at the snowy white beast with worry.

"Is Henry still under the weather?" Marianne asked, her question cutting off whatever it was the duke had opened his mouth to say—likely something unpleasant about Barnabas.

Francine looked up from her rabbit, a notch between her huge blue eyes. "He's even sicker." Her rosebud mouth puckered into a worried frown. "Do you think Barnabas would mind if—"

"You've got the interlude before Blade?" Marianne asked. The interludes were shorter performances between the main acts.

Francine nodded.

"I'm sure either Lizzy or Lu-Lu can fill in for you." Those were the two jugglers. "Go ahead and take Henry back to the inn and I'll tell my uncle."

"Thank you so much, Marianne!" Francine pulled a fancy silk handkerchief from thin air and daubed at her eyes.

Marianne smiled and glanced around, looking for a stagehand. Instead, she saw Guy, who was leaning beside a wall of rigging, chatting up a pretty woman Marianne didn't recognize.

Marianne raised her hand to summon him, but Sin took her wrist and pulled her arm down. "You go into the dressing room and sit down. I'll talk to Guy." He turned to Francine, gesturing to the heavy trunk that served as both a container and prop for her show. "Don't worry, we'll take care of your prop case."

"Oh, thank you, Sin—you're a love." Francine stood up on tiptoes and kissed the duke on the cheek. "Say *thank you*, Henry." She held up her rabbit, who merely surveyed Staunton through its pink eyes, its nose and mouth twitching.

"Er, you're both welcome," Sin said, a charming blush spreading beneath his scruffy red and blond beard.

Once the magician was gone, Sin turned back to her. "What are you doing still standing here?" He waved to Guy without turning away from her. "Go sit down before you fall down."

"Quit telling me what to do," she snapped, each word like an icepick in her head.

"Go. Sit. Down," he ordered in a low, firm voice.

"You needed me?" Guy asked, strolling up beside the duke.

"Can you make sure Francine's trunk gets locked up with all the others?"

"Of course. But it's called a prop chest, Sin."

"And find me some ice—quickly, please."

Guy raised an eyebrow but asked no further questions as he easily picked up the heavy case by the leather handle and hauled it away.

"Why are you still standing here?" the duke demanded. "You are swaying on your feet." His was tone accusatory. "Quit being so stubborn for once, Marianne. Just pretend I'm Jack and *listen* to me. You need to sit." He strode toward the dressing room and yanked open the door.

Marianne gave up arguing and followed him into the room, which was, thankfully, empty.

There were several tables and stools, but only one chair. "Here." He shoved a pile of garments and costumes onto the floor, ignoring her squawk of indignation.

She began to lower herself into the chair, but a wave of blackness flooded her vision and her body turn liquid.

Powerful arms closed around her and held her tight against a hot wall of hard muscle.

"Damnation, Marianne!"

And that was the last thing she heard before the darkness pulled her under.

Sin wanted to wrap his hands around Barnabas Farnham's neck and squeeze. Unfortunately, he had an unconscious woman in his arms.

He gently lowered her into the chair and then took two long strides to the door, which he flung open, startling a passing stagehand—Phil, he thought the man's name was. "You," he snapped. "Go fetch a doctor."

The boy's eyes were as round as coins. "A doctor?"

"Yes. A doctor."

"But . . . where?"

"Ask the manager. *Now*. And be damned quick about it!"

The lad sprinted off in the direction of the theatre manager's office.

"What's wrong?"

Sin turned at the sound of the quiet voice to find Blade, dressed head to toe in black leather, half her face concealed behind a matching black mask.

"Marianne took a bad hit to the temple, right beside the eye socket. She's just lost consciousness."

Blade stepped into the dressing room without speaking and Sin shut the door behind him while she crouched next to Marianne's chair, pulled off her black leather gauntlets, and lifted Marianne's eyelid. "How long ago did this happen?"

"When she sat down—less than a minute. She was flushed— even more than usual, and then suddenly lost color." Sin's own pulse was pounding loudly enough to make his head throb. "Are her pupils dilated?"

"They seem to be adjusting to the light," she said, looking at one eye and then the other before examining the swelling on Marianne's temple, her pale, slender fingers deft and light. She finally dropped her hands and looked up at him as she stood. "I've seen people with head injuries before. Even if she is concussed there's not much you can do other than keep her comfortable and warm."

Not until she was standing beside him did Sin realize just how small Jo Brown was. Her head barely came up to his shoulders. With her slight figure, snug black outfit and crown of thick white-blond hair she looked otherworldly, her pale gray eyes almost silver beneath the mask.

"If she could quit fighting, that would be a good start," Sin muttered, his eyes fixed on Marianne's pale face. Lord. She looked so bloody fragile lying there. She had won her bout tonight, but the other woman had been huge. He didn't understand why Barnabas would arrange a fight between his niece and such a big woman. While she'd not gotten in many hits, those that had connected had caused some damage. Marianne had relaxed her guard after a stumble—just for a second—but it had been enough.

"I think we'll all get to quit pretty soon," Blade said.

He looked up at her words. "What do you mean?"

"Napoleon went through Grenoble and the Fifth Infantry apparently joined him, and they are on the march to Paris."

"The Fifth? But aren't they solidly—"

"Royalist?" she asked with a slight twist of her slick carmine lips. "It seems they had a change of heart."

"Bloody hell," he murmured, and then recalled whom he was talking to. "I beg your pardon."

Amusement glinted in her pale eyes at his apology.

"How did you hear about this?"

"They sent carrier pigeons out and there was an announcement in the town square just after dusk. Already half the town seems to be making plans to head to Paris and meet him when he arrives."

"Good God," Sin breathed. His mind could gain no purchase; Bonaparte was free. The nightmare was beginning all over again.

She pulled on her gloves. "I wish I could stay, but I'm on after the interlude."

Sin nodded, raking his hand through his hair. "I've sent one of the stagehands for the doctor."

"I'll come back after my show." She gave Marianne a last glance before turning to the door.

She'd only just left when the door opened again. This time it was Guy.

He gawked at Marianne's unconscious form and held out an ice bucket with only a few jagged chunks inside. "This is all I could find quickly."

Sin took the bucket.

"She seemed fine just a few minutes ago. What happened?" Guy asked.

"She fainted when she tried to sit." Sin took one of the cloths the women used to remove face paint and wrapped a chunk, making sure the ice was covered.

He was about to lower the cloth when she moaned and shifted, her eyes fluttering open. "Wha—what happened?"

"You fainted," he said, carefully lowering the cloth over the nasty swelling.

She winced.

"I'm sorry," he said. "I know it's cold, but hold it there for a few moments. I've sent for a doctor."

She opened her mouth.

"Don't argue, Marianne. Close your eyes and rest."

For once, she did as he bade her.

Guy sidled over to him. "I just heard—"

"Blade already told me," Sin said.

Behind them, the door opened, and they turned as Elliot entered.

"I just saw Blade and she told me what happened to Marianne. Can I help?"

Sin shook his head. "I've sent for a doctor."

"I take it you've both heard?" Elliot asked.

Sin and Guy nodded.

"This is worse than you expected, isn't it?" Guy asked.

"Yes—and it's also happening far faster than I expected. Even so, there are still enough of the army's generals on the king's side. They might stop him in Paris—although I'm not optimistic."

"What do you think is going to happen?" Guy asked.

"War," Elliot said, his mouth thinning into a grim line. "I think war is going to happen."

Chapter 21

It was dark when Marianne awakened. Although *awakened* didn't seem quite the word for the slow, sluggish journey to the surface of consciousness.

Her head throbbed as she gingerly felt around the source of the pain. Ah, yes, the last decent hit Berta had got in on her before the final bell. Her eye was a bit swollen, but not as bad as she would have thought.

Worse than her head was her thirst.

Marianne slowly swung her feet off the bed, which was when she saw somebody had changed her into her nightgown.

"What are you doing?"

She yelped and her head whipped around—and then she almost threw up from a wave of nausea as the room rocked and swayed around her.

Strong, but gentle, hands landed on her shoulders. "Do you feel faint?" the duke asked, only a shadow above her in the darkness. Although it wasn't completely dark, now that her eyes were adjusting, she saw a glow from the fireplace and the lazy flicker of flames, which had been blocked by what she now realized was a wing chair. That must have been where the duke had been sitting.

"Marianne?" he asked, concern evident in his deep voice.

"I didn't know anyone was here," she said, her voice scratchy and hoarse, as if she'd not used it for a long time. "What *are* you doing here, Your Grace?" She still hadn't been able to bring herself to call him Sin, even though everyone from the seamstresses to the boot boy called him by the nickname.

"The doctor didn't think you had a concussion, but he wanted somebody with you for at least tonight, preferably for forty-eight hours." He released her, and she immediately wanted his hands back.

Fool! a voice in her head accused.

She was, indeed.

"Cecile and I are sharing this room. She can stay with me."

"If Jack were here, would he leave you?"

"Yes," she blurted.

"*Tsk tsk*, Marianne. Lying does not become you."

"Fine. Jack would have stayed. But Jack is—"

"I'm staying." He didn't raise his voice or change his tone, but she heard the steel behind his words.

"Where is Cecile?"

"I gave her my room, and Guy will bunk up with Elliot. Come, sit down." He took her by the elbow and guided her to the chair nearest the fire.

Marianne wanted to argue—just because she always argued—but the truth was that her legs were feeling less than steady.

"Are you hungry?" he asked once she was seated.

"I'm thirsty—that's why I was getting up. But I'm also starving." Her hunger probably accounted for at least part of her jittery weakness. She'd not cared for the sweetbreads that Barnabas had ordered for dinner earlier, so all she'd eaten were a few pieces of the delicious bread baked at the inn.

She heard the clinking of glass, and then the duke's hand appeared holding a glass of water.

"Thank you," she said, her hands shaking as she took it.

"I'm going to ring for a servant."

"Won't the kitchen be closed?"

"It's late, but I'm sure they'll still have something." He took a spill from the mantel to light some candles.

"Not too many, if you don't mind," Marianne said. "The light hurts my eyes."

He took the candelabrum to someplace behind her before lighting it, causing a soft, warm glow to fill the room.

"Did you undress me?"

"No. Cecile did that before she left." He leaned against the door and surveyed her with his far too piercing eyes.

"Where is Cecile?"

"At the meeting your uncle called, with all the other employees."

"So late?"

"Well, he had to wait until the show was over."

"Is he thinking to leave already?" she asked.

"Yes. You probably didn't hear it before you lost consciousness, but Bonaparte has gathered even more soldiers and is marching on Paris. The town has begun to faction. There have been fights in the streets—even in the dining room tonight—and tempers are high on both sides."

"Royalists and Bonapartists?"

"There is no great love for this king, so I think it's not so much Royalists as those who are sick and tired of war. But Bonaparte's appeal seems . . . well, let's just say that a year of bickering in Vienna and some foolish actions on the part of Louis have made more than a few people nostalgic for the Corsican."

There was a soft knock on the door.

Sin opened it and Marianne saw it was her favorite maid, Yvette.

She smiled warmly when she saw Marianne. "Ah, you're feeling better?"

"Yes, thank you."

"Would it be possible to get something to eat?" the duke asked. "Mademoiselle Simpson did not have any supper."

Yvette cut the duke a saucy look. "Either did you, monsieur." She turned to Marianne and jerked her head toward the duke. "This one was so worried for you that he didn't go down to dinner—even when Mademoiselle Tremblay offered to sit with you."

Marianne looked at the duke, her eyebrows arched.

Thanks to his beard she couldn't see much of his face other than the tops of his cheeks and the tips of his ears, but those parts she could see turned a pinky red.

He ignored her inquiring look. "What choices do we have for supper?" he asked Yvette, who was openly grinning at Marianne.

Once they'd settled on stew, bread, some cold game bird, and one of the magnificent fruit tarts the chef was known for, Yvette said, "Would you like me to bring up some hot water for you, mademoiselle?" Her gaze lingered on Marianne's hair, which was no doubt a bird's nest.

"That would be lovely," Marianne replied.

Once the door shut, Marianne asked the duke, "What options is my uncle going to offer tonight?"

The duke moved the chair so she wouldn't have to twist around to speak to him. She couldn't help noticing that he was wearing her favorite outfit—yes, it was pitiful that she knew all his clothing—the soft, worn buckskins, a dark green vest, a black neckerchief, and a rough cotton shirt rolled up to expose his delightfully muscular forearms.

Marianne had never believed a man's arms and hands were sensual, but even a glance at the duke's was enough to start a fire in her belly.

"Your uncle didn't confide in me, of course," the duke said with a wry smile. "But I would guess—based on what I know of him—that he is hoping to proceed by skirting whatever army Bonaparte is gathering."

"Surely that's not wise?"

"No. I think it's madness to do anything other than get out of the country. The coalition will re-form and once the powers that be declare war on Bonaparte, we will be citizens of a hostile nation, stuck in France. The entire country is poised to erupt at any minute." The candlelight picked out the blond highlights in his hair where the walnut dye had begun to fade. His green gaze slid from the fire to her. "This could be a disaster, Marianne."

"Surely the French government will stop him before another coalition is necessary," Marianne said. "The king—"

"Louis is weak at best and useless at worst. No, Bonaparte will not be stopped by any force within France. There will be war. Again. The wise thing is to get out of France now—before we are caught in the middle of it."

"You want to return home?" She couldn't keep the disbelief from her tone.

"I said that would be the wise thing to do." His lips flexed into a faint, wry smile. "It's not what I'm going to do. I can't. But you need to leave, Marianne."

"What about your brother?"

"I shall have to take my chances."

"But Dominic said—"

"I know what he said. I am not dragging you into the middle of a war, Marianne."

She blinked at the vehemence in his tone.

"It's bad enough that you're here in the first place." His eyes sparked with anger. "You cannot keep boxing. The doctor who came to look at you said the sort of hit you took often leads to a swelling of the brain and when that happens you could *die*—"

"Do you think I am ignorant or stupid, Your Grace?"

"You know I don't," he retorted.

"Then why are you telling me something I already know?"

"Because you are stubborn, Marianne—not stupid or ignorant, but loyal and stubborn and so damned young that you don't realize how precious your life is or how quickly you could lose it." He stopped abruptly, looking even more surprised than Marianne felt at his emotional outburst.

"I gave you my word on the packet that I'd go with you, Your Grace. And I *will* go with you."

"I forbid it. It is too—"

"You *forbid* it?" Her voice was loud in the small room.

He heaved a sigh. "Perhaps *forbid* was the wrong word."

"Perhaps," she agreed icily.

"What I should have said is that you will not come to this meeting."

"You can't stop me—I know where and when it is going to take place and I will—"

"You never wanted to see Strickland. Now you don't have to."

"It's not just about your brother now. If Dominic was using me to help that man escape the country, I want to know."

"I can tell you about that later—after I return to England. You don't need—"

"I can go with you, or I can go without you. Those are your choices."

He gritted his teeth, his expression closer to a scowl than anything she'd yet seen. It occurred to her that the duke was gradually losing his ability to dissemble. Or perhaps she was learning to read the subtle cues he let slip. Either way, she could see he was on the brink of raising his voice.

"Besides," Marianne added in a less combative tone, "for all you know, Barnabas will want to finish the tour, so I'll be going that way, anyhow."

He gave a bark of laughter. "I wouldn't be the least bit surprised if he blundered right on through a war."

"Your meeting with Dominic isn't for weeks," she pointed out. "What will you do for all that time?"

His raptor-like stare seemed to burn a hole through her. He wasn't accustomed to anyone going against his word—no doubt this was a painful experience for him—but she could see he was torn. They'd only known each other a matter of weeks, but their association had been, by necessity, a close one. He should know by now that she was not going to relent.

Finally, after what felt like an hour, he said, "I'll head straight to Metz and hope to avoid any hostilities that erupt. Dominic is not a stupid man; he will know what this news means to your uncle's tour. I daresay he'll expect me to show up early."

"I don't think this will be a good time to travel as an Englishman."

"We'll have the caravan, so we can maintain the fiction that we are some sort of traveling troupe."

"An English circus?"

"I'm sure we could get somebody to change the name on the caravans to something French."

All the caravans they'd brought with them had *Farnham's Fantastical Female Fayre* painted on the side.

"To what?" she asked.

"I don't know, I'll think of something."

"I don't mean to be insulting, but the only one of you who could pass for French is Elliot."

His eyes narrowed. "What point are you trying to make?"

"I think that *you* should go back to England. If anyone stays, it should be me, Elliot, and perhaps we can talk one of the stage-hands into accompanying us. We can take your caravan and bring the money. We can also bring your brother back."

He gave her a look of stunned disbelief. "Absolutely not."

"Even if it will jeopardize your brother's life to travel with Englishmen?"

"You have *no* idea what Strickland has planned for you," he said, skirting her question entirely. "And I have *no* intention of going anywhere but to Metz. So let's consider that discussion closed."

She'd not really believed that he'd assent to such an idea, but it was worth a try. "So that means I'll join the three of you, then. We'll only take the one caravan and my horse."

"Marianne."

"Hmm?" she asked, her mind racing. They'd be cramped, and it wouldn't be—

"You don't have to do this."

His quiet voice jerked her away from her busy thoughts, and she looked up. He wore an expression she'd never thought to see on his face: uncertainty.

It didn't take a genius to guess what he was uncertain about. Part of him had to want her to come along—his brother's life was at stake. But he was an honorable man who wouldn't put her in danger.

His face—for all that it was covered with copper scruff—was still the same haughty, beautiful, aristocratic face she'd seen that first night in the crowd. But his eyes were no longer harsh or opaque whenever he looked at her. Somewhere along the way he'd begun to care what happened to her—and he made no effort to hide it. He was a decent man who'd given Jack his word that he would take care of her. That's all this was—his word mattered to him.

Nobody had extracted such a promise from Marianne. She had no excuse for caring about him.

Now was her chance to run as far from him as she could, and yet she wasn't taking the opportunity.

The reason she was insisting on going along wasn't because she wanted to find out the truth from Dominic. At least not entirely— the duke would make sure Dominic got what he deserved. No, *he* was the reason she insisted on going.

Somehow, without her noticing it, he had carved out a place for himself in her life. She had begun to rely on him, to trust him, and believe he really was what he was playing at: a man who cared for her.

But he wasn't a boxing trainer. He was a duke, and she was a female pug in a circus. They might as well be two different species.

She met his concerned gaze, her heart beating unsteadily as she accepted the truth: She simply didn't care who or what he was—he could be the King of England for all that it mattered to her. She wasn't willing to let him go. Not yet. Not when she might spend another few weeks with him.

She'd have the rest of her life to live without him.

Marianne smiled. "I'm going, Your Grace. Let's not discuss it again."

Chapter 22

"I forbid it, Marianne!" Barnabas shouted.

Marianne met the duke's amused gaze and knew he was thinking the same thing she was: that her uncle was the second man to use exactly the same words in less than twenty-four hours.

"You can't forbid me to go, Uncle."

"I can! You are only twenty. You are still under my care."

The duke snorted and Barnabas whirled on him. "You mock me—but *you* are the one wanting to drag her into danger."

"I already told her to stay. But she is right, Farnham; she is her own woman."

"Oh, *now* she is her own woman. But in London, you were singing another tune—then she had to do what you ordered. Then she was your pawn, or else you would pull everything down around our ears."

The duke's mouth flexed into an especially unpleasant smile, and he stared at Barnabas as if he were a roach that he was looking forward to crushing. "And who was the man she sacrificed herself to save, Farnham?"

Her uncle gave a squawk of inarticulate rage, and Marianne thought the top of his head would blow off.

The duke's presence—how ever well-meaning—was not helping with this difficult conversation.

"Can you please give us some privacy, Your Grace?" Marianne asked. They were sitting in her chambers, which the duke had stubbornly continued to occupy all night, leaving only long enough for Cecile to help her bathe and dress this morning. Not that she *needed* help with those things, but the duke had insisted on that, too.

Staunton looked unhappy at her request, and he jabbed a finger into Barnabas's shoulder, making him squeak—and then flush at his undignified reaction. "You don't let her out of this room, Farnham—do you understand me? The doctor wanted her to rest at least one more day."

Marianne took the duke by the elbow, and his big body jolted beneath her hand.

"I'm not going anywhere," she said before her uncle could commence yelling again. "Come, Your Grace." She led Staunton slowly but inexorably toward the door.

"Fine, I'll leave," he said. "Just don't allow him to talk you into helping load up all the wagons—or any other kind of exertion. You haven't been downstairs and seen the pandemonium. If you go down there, you'll be pulled into all the madness."

"No exertion," she promised.

Staunton opened the door but then paused. "For once, Farnham is right. You should go back with him, Marianne. That would be—"

"Yes, thank you." She gave him a gentle shove and shut the door before turning to her uncle.

Barnabas was waiting for her, his arms crossed over his chest, his expression mulish. "You can't do this."

"I have to do this. A man's life is at stake, Uncle."

"But that is not your fault!"

Marianne wondered if the discussion she was about to have was even worth her breath. She knew her uncle had lied to her about the smuggling, the gambling, and probably dozens of other matters. It was unlikely that he would tell the truth now, but she had to try.

"Why are you looking at me like that, Marianne?"

"Not long before he staged his death, Dominic helped smuggle out a French prisoner of war, a man named Beauvais."

His eyes bulged. "Surely you don't think I—"

"I don't want to know, Uncle. I really don't. Because then I'd have to make sure you answered for such a crime and doing that would surely destroy me."

Barnabas opened his mouth but must have seen something in her eyes that made him close it.

"You rescued me after my mother died and took care of me when I couldn't take care of myself. You sent me to school when I know you needed that money for yourself. I owe you. And I will gladly pay what I owe. But I could not stand by without saying a word if I learned you were involved in anything treasonous. So, if you were, you need to leave *now*—get as far away from Staunton as you can."

His face, which had been flushed only a few moments before, had turned an unhealthy gray.

"I've done things I'm ashamed of—you have no idea how much shame I carry, Marianne. But I swear that I knew nothing of this Beauvais you are talking about. I heard about the way Strickland was supposed to have died—chasing these French prisoners—so I assumed he was—" he broke off and worried his lower lip, his chest rising and falling like that of a man who'd been running. "Never mind about that. I need to tell you something—perhaps it will change your mind about going."

Marianne's stomach fell.

"A few things, actually." He gestured to the two chairs in front of the fire. "Sit for a moment. You look unsteady on your feet."

She was, but not because of the hit to her head.

Once Marianne sat, Barnabas lifted the strap of his battered leather satchel over his head and removed the bag. Her uncle never went anywhere without his bag. It contained his calendar, his ledger, and numerous other items too precious to leave anywhere. He wore it crosswise over his chest and it was his habit to fiddle with the straps and buckles when he became agitated.

He pulled the bag onto his lap and looked up, his fingers playing with the straps. "I received a letter from Strickland in November of last year."

Marianne closed her eyes.

"He is the reason I have brought the Fayre to the Continent so early. He said he wanted to see me."

Barnabas stopped speaking and she opened her eyes, suddenly seeing more clearly than she had in her life.

"He is holding something over your head." It wasn't a question. "He is blackmailing you."

Barnabas nodded.

It explained so many things. Marianne couldn't believe that she'd been ignorant for so long.

"What?" she asked.

"He has a notebook that holds an account of my, er, smuggling activities. It was made by an agent for the Crown and is very detailed."

Marianne wanted to scream. Instead, she asked, "Is this from when we lived in Deal? Because Dominic was involved, too, and—"

"No, no, this is from long ago, when I first moved to England. It is an old, old story that goes back many years. Strickland used the notebook to get me to introduce him to the smugglers I knew then—"

"I'm listening," she prodded.

He swallowed. "I will need to go back a bit, to when I lived in Paris as a younger man. I became entangled with some men who were . . . well, not the sort you want to cross. I owed them a lot of money, gambling debts, more than I could repay. They knew I could speak English—" He blushed. "I had lived with an English woman for several years and she taught me. Anyhow, they said I could repay my debt if I did something for them." He paused and licked his lips. "They paid my way to England and gave me some money to live."

Please, Uncle, don't say what I think you're going to—

"At first they wanted help making contact with men interested in doing business along the coast."

"The fishermen smugglers?"

He nodded. "But after a while, they wanted me to tell them things I noticed." His eyes darted to hers, and her stomach roiled at the guilt she saw. "They arranged for me to work with a touring troupe called the Mayfair Players, even though I'd never worked in the theatrical business before—"

"You said that you and my mother had grown up working in a theater—that my grandmother was a costume maker and my grandfather an actor?"

"I know what I said," Barnabas said wearily, "but that was a lie. I'm not what I've claimed to be, Marianne." His eyes brimmed with shame. "I was a criminal. My mother was a whore, and I never knew my father."

Marianne could only stare.

"As for *your* mother . . ." He reached into his bag and brought out an exquisite enamel box the size of his palm.

Memories exploded like fireworks at the sight of the familiar jewel-toned colors.

She gasped. "That belonged to my mother. I remember—she showed it to me once." Marianne had forgotten all about it—even now, it seemed like something from a fever dream.

She squeezed her eyes shut and tried to catch hold of the fleeting memory of her mother. She'd been ill, yet she was digging in the garden, and she'd fainted. In the folds of her skirt had been the glitter of something sparkly along with a thick, gold chain. But Marianne had been too scared to care what it was; she'd been terrified that her mother had died.

She opened her eyes to see Barnabas taking a large locket from the box and holding it up by a long, heavy gold chain. The locket was a rectangle, with the edges squared. Even though Marianne knew nothing about jewelry she could tell this had been made by a master craftsman. In the center was a large red stone that looked like it might be a ruby. Radiating out from it were eight rays. The rays were composed of small canary-yellow stones.

"It is hundreds of years old and worth a great deal of money.

Your mother left it buried behind her cottage—in case I didn't get there before she died. Take it." Barnabas offered it to her.

Her hands shook as she reached for it. "It's so heavy," she murmured, surprised by its heft and how it filled her palm. There was a tiny lever on one side and a hinge on the other. Marianne pushed the lever and the locket popped open with a soft *snick*.

Inside was a miniature of a dark-haired, brown-eyed stranger who had the same shape eyes and face as Marianne. Inscribed on the other side of the locket were the words: *Avec tout mon amour, N.*

With all my love, N.

Marianne looked up. "Who is this? What does the N stand for?"

"I have always believed that is your real mother. As for the N?" he shrugged. "I do not know her name."

"My *real* mother?" she demanded. "What are you talking about, Uncle?"

He swallowed convulsively. "Er, I'm not your uncle. I didn't have any sisters—at least not that I'm aware of."

Her gaze was drawn again and again to the miniature in her hand. The eyes were the same shape as hers, but brown where hers were hazel. And the woman in the picture shared the same pearly complexion and dark brown hair as Marianne.

The longer she looked at the painting, the more she saw a resemblance. Certainly more than she'd resembled the woman she'd always believed to be her mother.

Her mother.

Those words conjured up a heart-shaped face with tawny hair and blue eyes.

"Who is this woman?" she asked.

"I don't know."

"You don't know?"

He flinched at the disbelief in her voice and raised his hands in a placating gesture. "I give you my word that I'm not lying."

"That is rich indeed—your word."

He clenched his jaws but remained quiet.

"Tell me everything you do know, Uncle—" She gave a dismissive snort. "I suppose I can call you what everyone else does, now, Barnabas."

"Please, Marianne, don't—"

"Everything."

He sighed. "There isn't much to tell. I first learned about you when I was with the Mayfair Players. Sonia received a letter from Sandrine, saying that she was dying and that somebody needed to come and claim you."

"Sonia? Why Sonia?"

"She was a cousin of your mother's—" He grimaced. "Er, I mean Sandrine Simpson's cousin."

"So why didn't Sonia come claim me? Why you?"

"We agreed it would be better if a man were to make the claim—"

"Why?"

"I don't remember the reasoning," he said, sounding utterly unconvincing.

"Why would you do such a thing?"

His eyes slid away and then back slowly. "Sandrine's letter promised money."

She laughed. "Ah, now that is motivation I believe."

He flinched at her bitterness.

"This is a bizarre story—you realize that, don't you?"

"I know. But it is the truth."

"And so you took me in for money?"

He nodded miserably.

"How much?"

"Five hundred pounds."

"Five hundred pounds!"

He winced, and then nodded again.

"That is a fortune! But, having seen your bills recently, I'm sure you went through that quickly enough. Why didn't you just drop me off at an orphanage once you had the money?"

"I can't believe you'd think me capable of that!"

She raised a hand. "Don't. Please. I'm not a fool and I'm tired of being taken for one." Before he could reply, she said, "What about this locket? Where did you find it?"

"It was inside the enamel box. Sandrine was very sick the last time she wrote to Sonia. She worried she'd be dead before one of us could come collect you. So, she buried the box and locket and told us where to find it. As things turned out, she was unconscious by the time I came to get you and was being nursed by a neighbor woman."

Marianne turned the locket over in her hand. "So, this must be the locket Dominic wants. What letter does he mean—the one from my mother—er, Sandrine?"

"I don't know which letter he wants."

"Are you lying to me?"

"No! I don't know what—"

"Where is the last letter from Sandrine?"

He swallowed. "I don't have it."

She narrowed her eyes.

"I swear to you, Marianne! I'm telling the truth this time."

"Oh, *this* time." Marianne was stunned by the fury that surged in her belly as she stared at this stranger—this *lying* stranger. "And how does Dominic even know about this locket?"

"He went through my things. You know how I always keep this bag on me, but if anyone could have found their way into it, that bastard Strickland was the man to do it."

"You've kept all this in your bag all these years?" she asked, openly skeptical.

"No, of course not. But until we had the house, I didn't feel that there was anywhere safe enough, so—"

"You're lying to me, Barnabas! There is something you're not telling me about all this." There were probably dozens of things.

"I'm not, I swear," he wailed piteously.

"Why did Dominic write you last year?"

Barnabas dropped his head in his hands. "He wanted to make sure I brought you." His voice was miserable and muffled. "He swore this time that he'd give me the bloody smuggling notebook if I did."

"This book must be fairly damning if you are willing to do all you've claimed."

"It is not . . . good," he muttered.

Marianne shuddered to think what Dominic was holding over Barnabas's head.

"Where is Dominic's letter? I want to see it."

"I destroyed it."

Of course he had.

Marianne scowled at his bowed head. "I assume the woman in this portrait is wealthy—certainly the miniature and the locket would suggest it. And the fact that she and I share a resemblance tells me I am probably her child. The five hundred pounds would also indicate she was rich and paid a lot of money to see that I was taken care of. No doubt Dominic—with his finely honed sense for exploiting people's weaknesses—believes he has found a woman he can squeeze for a great deal of money."

Barnabas nodded. "Yes, that was my thought, as well."

Marianne laughed.

"I don't see the humor in any of this."

"Oh, it's a dark sort of humor, but amusing all the same. I knew there was only one reason Dominic would ever want to see me again: money. And it turns out I was right." She fixed him with a cold look. "You can go now."

"Wait," he begged. "What are you going to do?"

"I told you. I'm going with the duke to see Dominic."

"Then I'm going with you."

"Why would you—oh," she said, comprehension dawning. "You want your book back." She shrugged. "Do whatever you want, Barnabas. But you won't be coming with me."

"Marianne, please, don't be this way. I was going to tell you everything on your birthday, when you would finally be an adult."

"You mean more of an adult than when you urged me to marry Dominic? Was that why you were so persistent and persuasive— why you worked away on me, convincing me it was either marriage to Dominic or a life spent taking weekly beatings?" Her eyes narrowed. "Did you know in advance that the wedding ceremony Dominic arranged was fake, Barnabas? Did you agree to sacrifice me to get your precious book back?"

"No! How could you believe I would ever—"

"Just go home, Barnabas. I'll get your book of nasty secrets back for you."

Marianne was suddenly so weary she could hardly keep her eyes open. So she closed them, and laid her head against the back of the chair.

For a long moment, there was no sound.

"I'm so sorry," Barnabas said softly. She heard his feet cross the floor and then the opening and closing of the door. And then she was alone.

Marianne opened her eyes. Her uncle—no, Barnabas—had put the enamel box on the end table, right beside the locket.

Marianne took the locket and opened it again, staring at a picture of her mother, hoping for some sense of recognition. But she felt nothing other than grief that Sandrine Simpson—the mother she'd loved all her life—had probably been like Barnabas, just somebody else the woman in the picture had paid to take care of her.

It *was* darkly humorous. As if Marianne had not sunk low enough in the world after her affair with Dominic, it seemed she was now illegitimate.

What else would Barnabas tell her before this mess with Dominic was all over?

Chapter 23

Sin watched as Marianne's eyelids got heavier and heavier, even though she was hardly halfway through the meal Yvette had brought for them.

"Tired?" he asked, setting his fork and knife down on his mostly empty plate.

"I'm tired, but my mind won't stop racing." She yawned and then cut him a quick look, her pale cheeks flushing. "I'm sorry, that was rude."

"I'll forgive you this time."

Her mouth pulled up into a charming, lopsided grin. "What you really are thinking is that you're accustomed to my rudeness by now."

Sin's lips twitched at her accurate assessment. He was relieved to see her talking and smiling—even if she looked worn and ragged. After Barnabas had left her that morning, Sin had returned to find a woman who'd aged five years. Not only that, but she'd appeared ill—not from a knock on her head, but from despair.

He had not asked what had happened, and she'd not offered to tell him. Instead, she'd crawled back into bed even though she'd earlier complained about sleeping too much the day before. She'd slept all day and into the evening, once again missing dinner.

Sin hadn't eaten, waiting for her to wake and hoping he'd have a chance to talk to her before morning, when she would no longer be under doctor's orders and he would no longer have an excuse to be parked in her room.

For the second night in a row, he paid the innkeeper an exorbitant amount to keep the kitchen open. Finally, just before eleven, she'd woken.

"This is lovely," she said, pushing away her half-eaten plate. "But I can't eat another bite."

Sin stood and rang for a servant to come and clear the remains away.

"I'm ready to hear what happened today while I was sleeping," she said. "And I want to know what our plan is."

He lifted the bottle of port he'd ordered sent to her room, but she shook her head, so he poured a glass for himself. "Almost everyone left today," he said. "The only ones remaining are you, me, Guy, Elliot, Cecile—"

"Cecile? Why is she here?"

"She says she is staying with you."

"Did you tell her that was foolish and dangerous?"

He gave her a wry look. "Yes, I told her that and more. She obeys as well as you do."

For once, Sin was relieved when Marianne's tired expression shifted into more familiar, mulish lines. "She'll change her mind tomorrow, once I've had a chance to talk sense into her."

Sin doubted that.

"If she comes along you'll have a caravan, so at least you won't be forced to share ours," he pointed out.

"Perhaps Blade will want it? Or has she already left?" "Elliot said she rode out before first light this morning. Just her and the bird." Sin snorted. "Well, and likely a few dozen knives."

"What about the rest of her belongings?"

"Cecile said she left her baggage in the caravan."

"That is odd."

Odd, indeed.

Sin didn't tell her that Elliot had followed the woman—before she'd managed to lose him about ten miles down the road—and that she had not been headed back to Calais with all the others.

"So, just our two caravans, then?"

"And your uncle's—he is driving it because he sent his coachman back with his carriage."

She scowled, suddenly looking wide-awake. "Barnabas is not coming with us."

"He says he is. So is his, er, housekeeper."

"Sonia is not coming, either—in fact, I'm thrilled to say I'll never have to speak to her again."

"Does this have something to do with whatever you two talked about this morning?"

"Neither of them are coming," she insisted, ignoring his question.

"Marianne, we can hardly stop them—it's a public road. We might as well let them come along—at least that way we can keep an eye on them."

"No." She crossed her arms.

"Think on it a moment," he urged. "If Barnabas is trailing along behind us, it will look . . . strange."

"I don't care."

He recognized the signs of what he thought of as her *badger* persona. He would deal with it later.

"Elliot found a scenery painter who works at the theater here to change the names on the caravans from English to French, so that will hopefully attract less attention on the road."

"What are we called now?"

"Foire aux Femmes Fantastiques de Fuchs."

"Fuchs?"

"It was a name your uncle came up with."

"He's not my uncle. He's just some stranger my real mother paid five hundred pounds to take care of me." An expression of gut-wrenching desolation twisted her features. "He's been lying to me—about almost everything. He's not even related to the woman who claimed to be my mother. For all I know, *she* was paid to take care of me, too."

Sin carefully considered what he should say. Clearly she knew about some of the money Barnabas had taken—but did she know the full extent of his thievery? Probably not.

Looking at her miserable expression, he decided now wasn't the time to tell her that she had never needed to turn to fighting to make a living. That she could have lived like a gentlewoman. That it was Barnabas's fault she'd fallen prey to Dominic.

Instead he asked, "Who is your real mother?"

"He doesn't know." She gave a bitter laugh. "Not that I can believe a word he says. Oh, by the way, there is a locket from my real mother."

"A locket?"

"Yes, Barnabas confirmed that it is the one Dominic wants—yet another lie he told me."

"And the letter?"

"He still insists there is no letter, but he lies so much I wouldn't be surprised if it magically appears at some point. He thinks Dominic hopes to find my real mother and blackmail her. I think that is a fair assessment."

Sin was, yet again, appalled and stunned by Dominic's depravity, even though he knew he shouldn't be.

"If Barnabas doesn't know who she is, how does Strickland hope to blackmail her?" he asked.

"I doubt Barnabas has opened his budget fully with me. I wouldn't be surprised if he knew exactly who she was—and probably my father, too."

Sin suspected she was right. He watched her chew her full lower lip, a strange ache in his chest as he looked at her forlorn expression. He wanted to help her, but there was nothing he could do—at least nothing that wouldn't make her life—or reputation—worse.

Finally, she shrugged and met his gaze. "All I can think is that Dominic recognized the portrait when he saw it."

"Portrait?"

"Oh. Didn't I tell you there was a miniature in the locket?"

Sin smiled at that monumental oversight. "No, you didn't mention that."

"Do you want to see it?"

"If you don't mind."

"I don't mind." She snorted. "At least I don't have to worry about you blackmailing me. The locket is on the dresser inside that enamel box."

The box in question was lovely and looked costly as well as very old, although Sin was no expert on such matters.

He lifted the lid, momentarily startled at the size of the locket. It had the look of the late sixteenth or early seventeenth century. The ruby on the front—if it was genuine—would be worth a fortune.

"I can't believe Barnabas didn't strip it and sell the jewels," she said.

That had been Sin's thought, too.

He pushed the small catch and the locket popped open. The miniature was the work of a master, the rendering so lifelike that you almost expected the woman to be breathing.

Sin opened the built-in frame, which was hinged opposite to the hinge that closed the locket. Running along the bottom righthand curve of the miniature was the name: *C. Horneman.*

Sin hadn't heard of him, but then the only miniatures he knew much about were the dozen or so that hung in the gallery at Wortham. Most of those were several hundred years old. If this was indeed Marianne's mother—and the resemblance was clear—then the painter was a contemporary.

He looked up to find her watching him.

"She looks like me, doesn't she?"

"Yes, the same shape of eyes and face." And also the same lovely, pearly skin, which the painter had captured with a slight flush. "Did your uncle say where the other miniature was?"

She frowned. "What other miniature?"

He walked over to her chair and dropped to his haunches. "See here—" He opened the frame around her mother's picture.

"Oh, I didn't realize you could do that." She glanced up at him. "Do you think it would damage the picture to take it out?"

"I shouldn't think so." He took his pen knife from his pocket and handed it to her.

The miniature popped out easily.

"It's thicker than I thought," she said, turning the tiny painting over in her palm and lifting it closer to her face. "It looks like ivory."

Sin glanced from the miniature to the wide-open locked. "Look, Marianne. There's another inscription behind it." He squinted, struggling to read the small writing without his reading glasses. "Can you read it?"

"*Tu es le gardien de mon coeur. D.*," Marianne read aloud.

You are the keeper of my heart. D.

She looked from the locket to Sin. "Is she D? Or N?"

"I don't know," he admitted, "but the presence of two inscriptions indicates the miniature was part of a pair."

Marianne stared down at the picture, her expression blank.

Sin had questions, dozens of them, but she looked so very vulnerable and tired that he didn't have the heart to ask them.

"Come, why don't you lie down," he said, gently taking the heavy necklace from her unresisting hand and returning it to the dresser.

She scowled up at him when he offered his arm to help her up.

"I'm fine—you heard the doctor say that himself earlier—after I *told* you that I was fine and that you were *not* to send for him," she added.

"He said you probably didn't have a concussion, but that you still needed to rest."

She scowled even harder and slapped his arm away. "I'm not a cripple. I can get up on my own."

Sin bit the inside of his cheek to keep from smiling and took a step back. He couldn't recall when he'd begun to find her rude treatment r appealing rather than offensive.

"I'm going to wash my face and clean my teeth—if that is permissible?"

"Yes, by all means," he said mildly. "The water from earlier will be cold. Do you—"

"It's fine," she snapped. "You don't need to stay in my room tonight."

Sin ignored that comment and settled into the wing chair, listening to the evocative sounds of splashing behind the screen and trying not to think of her slipping off her nightgown and wiping her body with the cool water. He forced himself not to imagine how her nipples would stiffen and—

He groaned, readjusted his erection, and took out his watch; it was almost midnight. Hell. It would be a long night.

When Marianne came from behind the screen several minutes later, she'd removed her robe and was garbed only in a whisper-thin nightgown.

Sin stood and slipped the old watch back into his pocket, his pulse pounding like a herd of horses as the light behind her illuminated her body, temporarily robbing him of the power of speech.

"I was serious, Your Grace. You needn't stay," she said as she climbed into her bed and pulled the heavy blankets up around her chest. "I don't need anyone to watch over me."

"I'm sure Cecile is already settled in my room." Actually, he had a hunch that Cecile had joined Guy in the Caravan. But he kept that information to himself.

She opened her mouth—probably to argue—but then closed it.

Sin smiled and she saw it.

"You like that, do you? Having people follow your orders?" she asked, visibly peeved.

"I'll admit I feel a certain sense of achievement getting you to obey without argument."

"Hmph. Well, don't become accustomed to it."

"Good night, Marianne," Sin said by way of answer, snuffing the candles.

Once the room was dark, he resumed his seat in front of the fire. He stretched out his legs and closed his eyes, trying—and failing—to banish the image of her from his mind's eye.

"You may light some candles to read," she said. "It won't keep me awake."

"Thank you, but I'm fine." His thoughts were far too turbulent to read. Or sleep. And it wasn't Bonaparte he was thinking about, but the woman on the bed. Even battered and bruised and hostile, she fired his imagination and sent his blood rushing.

Sin dropped his head to the chairback. How had he allowed himself to become attracted to such an inappropriate female? Was there, in all of Britain, a woman less suited to him? And yet no matter how often he told himself that she was not for him, he still wanted her.

He could not, in good conscience, even offer her a carte blanche, as he'd done with Alanna. Although Marianne was better educated—and likely smarter—than Alanna, she was not of the *ton*. Indeed, she was vocal in her dislike and distrust of male aristocrats. And rightfully so after her humiliating entanglement with Dominic.

Over the past month he'd changed more than he'd done in the prior ten years. Perhaps that wasn't entirely surprising given this journey he was on, but it left him unsettled and unsure, two feelings he'd not experienced since he was seventeen, when he'd been in love with a different, but equally inappropriate, woman.

He'd made the right decision all those years ago when he'd given up Jenny, but the cost of that decision had been almost unbearable at the time.

Now, as a man with fifteen years more experience, Sin knew how precious and fleeting life could be. The temptation to grab what happiness he could was nearly overwhelming.

The prospect of spending weeks with Marianne—without the annoyance of her wretched job—set off a chain reaction in his body: joy, anticipation, and even a bit of fear. Fear that he'd not be able to do the proper thing and leave her be.

For weeks now he had imposed such rigid control over his mind and body that his very muscles ached from it. He was exhausted from battling his own desires. It had been many years since he'd wanted a woman so badly. Not since Jenny—and he wasn't even sure if what he'd felt at seventeen could compare to what he was feeling now. He'd loved Jenny, but he'd never—

"I'm not tired."

Sin startled at the sound of her voice.

"Are you asleep?" she asked when he didn't respond.

"No."

"Are you worried about what will happen?"

Sin didn't need to ask her what she meant. "I am not unworried," he admitted. "Wandering deeper into a country about to be at war is not one of my wiser decisions."

"How can one man turn the entire world upside down? Bonaparte must possess unparalleled appeal to the French people."

"He must," Sin agreed. Although he, as an Englishman, failed to see the attraction.

"If he makes his way to Paris—as seems to be his goal—he will wrest control of France from a king. I know France has beheaded one king, already—but that was the will of many. For *one* man to topple a king is inconceivable, isn't it?"

"Inconceivable but—unfortunately—not unheard of. I would not be surprised if France were not headed for civil strife yet again, as well as war."

They sat in silence for so long that he thought she must have fallen asleep.

"Poor France," she said.

Poor France, indeed. Whatever happened over the coming weeks and months, one thing was certain—the common men and women of France would suffer and die.

Sin waited perhaps half an hour before getting up to check on her. There was a gap in the drapes and enough light coming in from the courtyard that he could see she had fallen asleep, her lips slightly parted, her breathing even.

At first, his attraction to her had terrified the hell out of him. Now, it just left him feeling as battered and bruised on the inside as she was on the outside.

Even in this light he could see the swollen, bruised skin around her eye.

Fury clawed at him, as well as helplessness, at his inability to do anything to stop the abuse she endured.

It was no surprise that he wanted to rescue her from such a life. He would want to spare anyone—man or woman—from such a brutal existence.

But Sin didn't just want to rescue her. No, he wanted to explore all the facets of her character, which she was only now beginning to share with him. He wanted to make her laugh the way he'd seen her friends do. He wanted her to smile at him with pure, unadulterated joy shining from her eyes.

In short, Marianne Simpson—with her grit and her grace even in a life filled with brutality—was exactly the sort of woman that he wanted to share his future with.

He smiled bitterly, darkly amused at the irony of his situation. For the second time in his life, he wanted someone desperately. And, for the second time, he'd chosen somebody he could never, ever have.

"I can practically *feel* you thinking."

Sin jolted and met her gaze in the gloom. "I thought you were sleeping."

"I don't want to sleep," she said, her expression solemn as she pushed back the blankets and swung her feet to the floor. "I've already slept far too long."

He suspected she wasn't speaking literally.

She held out a hand. "I want you."

Not for the first time did she render him speechless.

Her hand wavered when he didn't take it—as if she might pull back—and his hand shot out, lacing their fingers together as he stepped closer, pushing her knees apart, not stopping until his thighs touched the mattress.

And then Sin did something he'd wanted to do at least once a day for weeks; he reached out and lightly ran the knuckles of his free hand down her jaw.

"Your skin is so soft," he murmured. So unspeakably soft. "Just like a pearl."

Her lips parted as she stared up at him, and the raw desire in her gaze ignited a fierce hunger within him.

Sin slid his fingers to her chin and traced the sensual curve of her wicked lower lip. She opened her mouth to him, touching the tip of her hot, wet tongue to his thumb. He stifled the groan that was trying to force its way out, his self-control hanging by a thread.

"But your head," he protested weakly. "You shouldn't—"

"My head is not your concern. Or don't you want me?"

He groaned. "You know I want you, Marianne, but I cannot—"

"I know. There can be no more than this between us." She released his hand and set both of hers on his hips, her fingers stroking the worn leather of his old buckskins. "I don't care. *This* is all I want." Her hand slid from his hip to his pulsing shaft, which was thrusting eagerly against the placket of his breeches.

He sucked in a harsh breath as she closed strong fingers around his girth and gave him a firm stroke over his clothing. Sin willed his hips to stay still—not to thrust into her hand like a desperate boy, but even with the leather between them it was impossible to suppress the passion surging inside him.

Still holding his gaze, she pushed him away, stood, and then opened the few buttons that fastened the high neck of her prim gown. And then she pulled the thin cotton over her head and let it flutter to the ground, standing naked before him.

Sin gorged on her.

How had he ever believed her mannish?

She was exquisite, her skin so pale she could have been a marble statue come to life, her proportions as divine and perfectly sculpted as Leonardo's *Vitruvian Man*, but with a feminine potency that made him ache.

She shuddered slightly when he lowered his hands to her waist, and cut him a quick, shy glance as she stepped into the circle of his arms, her hands roaming over his body with a boldness that thrilled him.

Sin lowered his mouth to hers and she opened to him without

hesitation. Unlike the last kisses they'd shared, these began gently, a sweet exploration. Her lips were every bit as soft and welcoming as he remembered. They engaged in a give-and-take, an advance and retreat, an erotic jousting of tongues. But her body vibrated with the same desperate hunger as his and soon they were squeezing and biting and thrusting.

She growled and shoved him away. "I want to see you," she said, reaching for the buttons on his waistcoat, her fingers pulling and jerking, until the last button was free and she yanked the garment down over his shoulders.

Sin took one hand from her body to pull off the simple neckerchief he wore. Her hands dropped to the catches on his fall while he pulled the shirt over his head and flung it aside.

"Boots," she muttered in an almost feral tone, shoving him down onto the bed and crouching low, her deft fingers making short work of the laces on the heavy boots he wore.

Once he'd toed them off, she removed his stockings and sat back on her heels as Sin stood, flicked open the last buttons on his breeches and shoved them down along with his drawers.

Before he could kick them off his feet, a cool, strong hand closed around his hot shaft.

"Bloody hell," he muttered, looking down just as she smirked up at him and then lowered that decadent mouth of hers over his cock.

Chapter 24

Maybe Marianne had decided to take what she wanted because of what Barnabas had told her that day—that she was a bastard and no man would want to marry her, even if they could have ignored her less than glorious reputation.

Or maybe she had finally realized there was no point in not taking what she wanted. Resisting the duke just because he was a duke was foolish.

Besides, if there was one thing she knew about the Duke of Staunton that hadn't been true of Dominic, it was that the man she'd be giving herself to was worthy of whatever pain she would experience afterward.

Marianne chuckled at the hissing gasp he made when she wrapped her hand around a shaft so thick that her fingers didn't meet. Good Lord. Not only was Sin decent and honorable, but his body was a work of art.

"Bloody hell, Marianne." His voice was ragged and his hips jerked as she gave him an exploratory stroke, learning the delicious length and girth of him, excited by the slick moisture already leaking from his crown and wildly aroused by his clean, musky scent.

Marianne flicked the small slit with her tongue and grinned at the explosive curse that burst from His Grace's stern, shapely lips.

His arm shot out to the side so abruptly that she thought he was having some sort of fit.

What he did was grab the heavy drape and yank it open so roughly that the room was filled with the sound of tearing fabric.

The light from the courtyard lamps illuminated the small room with a warm glow.

"Much better." He slid his fingers into her hair, his thumbs coming to rest on her lips, which were stretched taut around his shaft. "I want to see your beautiful mouth wrapped around me."

Marianne shivered at his raw words. His lips were parted and his fine nostrils flared, giving him a wild, feral aspect. He stroked her mouth, his gaze heavy lidded, his pupils so huge she couldn't see even a sliver of iris.

Marianne took him deeper, enraptured by the play of emotions that spasmed over his normally inscrutable face: wonder, adoration, and lust among them.

His eyes widened as she went down, down, down, not stopping until the wiry curls tickled her nose and he was fully sheathed inside her.

Dominic had been selfish, greedy, and immoral, but he had, at least, given Marianne a great deal of pleasure in bed.

He had also taught her a great deal about giving pleasure during their brief faux marriage.

She swallowed, earning a guttural groan, and then slowly drew off.

"God. Marianne."

Marianne worked him in earnest, the memory of what Dominic had taught her coming back—muscle memory—and for once without the attendant shame.

His body jolted and stiffened.

Before she realized what he was doing, he leaned down, slid his hands beneath her upper arms, and lifted her to her feet.

She gave him a quizzical look when he pushed her onto the bed.

He cupped her jaw with firm but gentle fingers. "Lie back, sweetheart," he said, straddling her body on his hands and knees as she lowered her head to the pillow.

Marianne's belly clenched at the endearment. Never would she have believed such a sweet word and tender tone could come from such a severe mouth.

He pushed up onto his knees, towering over her and affording her a glorious view. She'd spent the last few years around some of the fittest men in Britain, but never had she seen such a beautiful, elegant body. He lacked the bulk of a professional pug, but he was hard and sculpted and perfect.

He rubbed his hand over her belly, an odd smile curving his mouth.

"What does that look mean?" she asked, her gaze dropping to his jutting cock as she stretched out her hands to stroke from his knees up his thighs, rough springy hairs giving way to smooth hairless skin.

"It means I'm happy." He smiled in earnest, the action exposing a dimple on his right side, making her realize she'd never seen such an open—yes, *happy*—expression on his face.

His big warm hands slid to her breasts and Marianne whimpered encouragement.

"Good?" he murmured, his clever fingers plucking and tweaking her already hard nipples.

She could only nod, arching her back for more.

And then he took her in his mouth and all rational thought fled.

As delicious as she'd felt and looked wrapped around his shaft, Sin couldn't last a minute longer without touching and exploring her.

Having her stretched out before him, a feast for his greedy eyes, was even better than the filthy dreams that had plagued him night after night.

Her lean, strong body bucked helplessly as he suckled her sweet little breasts. He pulled away from one taut nipple with a nip that made her whine. "Sensitive?" he asked, even though he already knew the answer.

She growled and caught his head in a firm grip to pull him back down.

While he pleasured her with his mouth, his hands found their own diversion, one stroking the firm lines of her waist and compactly muscled hips while the other found its way between her thighs.

She opened for him without hesitation, and it was his turn to growl when he slid his fingers into her curls.

He looked up from his labor of love as he stroked between her slick, swollen lips. "Is this for me, Marianne?" he teased, lightly pinching her engorged bud between two fingers.

She pushed her hips against his hand. "Please—don't torture me . . . you can do that later."

Sin laughed.

"Right now, I want you." She shuddered. "Need you inside me. Please."

Her plea—desperate and raw—was the most sensual thing a lover had ever said to him. Sin pushed her knees wider and took his shaft in his hand, lowering his hips until he could stroke the wet petals of her sex with his crown.

She shuddered and spread wider, the fascinating muscles of her stomach and thighs flexing and shifting.

"God. Marianne." Sin shook his head in wonder. Just looking at her was enough to make him climax. If he didn't get inside her soon, he'd make one hell of a fool of himself.

"Please." She raised her hips off the bed and Sin did as she bade him, entering her with a powerful thrust.

Marianne bit the corner of her pillow to muffle her shout, but Sin suspected she was still audible several rooms away.

So much for discretion, he thought as he held her pinned to the bed, giving her time to adjust to him.

"Are you all right, Marianne?" he asked, his voice rough with need.

She opened her eyes and gazed up at him from beneath heavy lids, a wide, slumberous smile the likes of which he'd never seen before spreading over her face. "Mmm, perfect. More."

Sin gave a choked laugh at her earthy, demanding response. "As you wish," he said tightly, withdrawing all the way and then working her with deep, measured thrusts.

She stroked up his stomach to his chest, scratching him lightly with her fingernails.

When she grazed his nipples, he yelped.

"Too rough?" She grinned, and then pinched him.

"You *witch*."

She flexed her inner muscles and drew him deeper. "Please."

He gave in to his desire and rode her hard, grinding his pelvis against her sensitive bud each time he pumped into her.

As much as he wanted this to last—he knew it wouldn't. He was gritting his teeth and thinking about crop drainage, labor legislation, and the Catholic issue when she pushed her hips up in silent pleading.

Sin's control began to slip and he pumped into her with strokes so powerful they shook the bed. "I've imagined sheathing myself inside this beautiful body for weeks, Marianne," he gritted through clenched teeth.

The headboard banged loudly against the wall with each driving thrust.

Thud.

Thud.

Thud.

She tilted to take him even deeper and Sin almost wept, his body shaking with the effort of holding off his impending climax.

Her back arched and she cried out as she came apart, bucking and shuddering.

"Yes!" he hissed. "Come for me, Marianne."

Sin captured her passion in his mouth and then hilted himself with a savage thrust, their bodies clenching and convulsing together as he emptied himself deep inside her.

Marianne woke to the feel of something soft and hot stroking her belly. She lifted her head just enough to see the duke—the *duke*!—tracing the ridges of her abdomen with his lips and tongue.

He looked up at her. "Ah, the sleeper has awakened."

"Was I asleep long?" she asked and then yawned.

He shook his head, his tongue dipping into her navel.

Marianne laughed as he sucked on the sensitive flesh.

"Tickles?"

She nodded. It did tickle, but she missed it when he put an end to his explorations and came up to lie beside her.

He propped himself up on an elbow and looked down at her, pushing a lock of hair away from her bruised temple, his mouth tightening. "I'm not much of a nurse—did I hurt you?"

"I rather like your bedside manner."

His mouth flexed into a slight smile, but his eyes were serious as he stroked her midriff. "I don't like seeing you hurt, Marianne."

She captured his hand, bringing it to her mouth and kissing each knuckle.

His pupils flared, but his lips compressed into a stern line. "You have been fortunate thus far, but your luck will not hold out forever. You need to find some other way to support yourself before you take permanent injury."

She lowered his hand and glared at him. "Do you have some *position* in mind?" she retorted, regretting her aggressive words before they were all the way out of her mouth.

"You know I'd never suggest anything like that between us."

"I'm sorry. I know you wouldn't. But tell me, since you've raised this topic, what kind of a job do you think I'm fit for? I can't be a governess or companion with my reputation—I couldn't find a position teaching even *before* I began working at the Fayre, which is *why* I'm boxing. Just what do you think I should do?"

He opened his mouth, paused, and then closed it.

Marianne nodded. "Now you see my dilemma."

"There are jobs in your uncle's—er, Barnabas's—business that do not require taking a weekly beating. Can you not find something else?"

She was tired of this subject and lifted his hand to her mouth again. Instead of arguing, she took his index finger and guided it between her lips, lightly tonguing the pad.

His jaw tightened as she sucked, working his finger suggestively.

He shook his head, his mouth curving into a grudging smile. "You are an expert at distraction, but I am not finished with the subject."

Marianne smiled around his finger, her tongue stroking as she sucked, and then paused. "But you are for now."

He growled. "I am for now," he agreed, and then pulled his hand away and shifted his body until he was on top of her, holding his weight on his elbows while his knees nudged between her thighs.

She spread for him eagerly and groaned when he thrust into her. He was almost painfully thick and long—much bigger than Dominic—and she squirmed slightly as he held her full.

"Am I hurting you?" he asked, nuzzling her jaw and trailing kisses back to her mouth.

Marianne shook her head

"Mmm," he hummed as he gently pulsed his hips, angling himself exactly right and rubbing her swollen, sensitive nub. He paused. "What a brute I am taking you again so soon. Are you too sore?"

She was, but she didn't care. "I'm not too sore," she lied. She tilted her hips and pushed up against him. "More," she commanded.

Their eyes locked as he pushed up onto his knees and hooked his arms under her legs, lifting her higher, his eyes greedy and dark as they settled on her sex.

"I wish you could see this," he murmured as he pulled out slowly and then gave her his entire length again. "You look so beautiful wrapped around me."

She reveled in his hungry stare, shivering and bucking under his touch as he worked her over the edge, her climax catching her in a convulsive grip.

He sucked in a harsh breath as he pushed himself infinitesimally deeper and then stilled. "I can feel your pleasure," he marveled, his shaft flexing inside her as she convulsed around him.

He lowered her feet to the mattress and covered her with his body.

Marianne grabbed his buttocks with both hands and pulled him closer as she tightened around him.

He groaned while she massaged him with her inner muscles. "Mmm, what's that you're doing to me?" he asked with a breathless chuckle, their faces only inches apart.

He began moving again, but more slowly and deliberately this time, his gaze burning through her, his jaw tighter with each measured thrust. The room was too dim to see the color properly, but his pupils had swollen so huge there was very little iris to see.

"Lord, what are you doing to me?" he repeated in an oddly shaken voice. And then he drove himself home and flooded her with warmth.

Marianne held his big body while he shuddered with his release. They were pressed so close that she could feel the pounding of his heart in her own ribs.

Had she ever been happier? If so, she couldn't recall when.

Pure contentment flowed through her body like sweet, slow-moving honey. He was everything she'd hoped for and more: a thoughtful, decent man, a loyal, caring friend, and a passionate, tender lover.

She squeezed her eyes shut when she felt the telltale prickle of tears.

And he could never, ever be hers.

Chapter 25

It was dawn when she next woke, and the bed beside her was empty.

Marianne pushed herself up and squinted into the crepuscular light.

The duke was sitting in the chair nearest the fire, fully clothed, lacing up a boot.

"What time is it?"

"Half-past six." He finished and sat up in his chair, rolling down his sleeves. "I will have a bath sent up for you."

"That sounds divine."

"Would you like me to send up breakfast, as well?" He stood and took his coat from a peg on the wall.

"No, I will come down."

Sin buttoned up his coat and then strode to the bed and sat down beside her.

Marianne met his gaze warily.

He smiled at her—the rare expression setting her heart fluttering. He reached out and cupped her chin, smoothing his thumb over her lower lip. The desire to take him into her mouth and pull him back into the warm blankets was strong, but he was already clothed, and ready to leave.

And she needed to collect herself.

"I meant what I said last night," she said, her face heating under his hawklike gaze. "I have no expectations."

"I know you meant it." An uncharacteristic look of uncertainty spasmed across his features. "Last night was . . . well, I shan't lie, Marianne: I want to do it again. And again." He lowered his hand with obvious regret. "The decision to continue this must be yours. I will not importune you."

"But I may importune *you*? Again."

Heat flared in his icy eyes. "I hope you do." He raised her hand from where it rested on the blanket and lifted it to his mouth, kissing not the back, but the palm, the tender, erotic gesture obliterating her wits.

He left before Marianne could speak—not that she had anything to say that wasn't gibberish.

She slumped back against the headboard, her face flaming as she recalled how loudly the duke had made the heavy wood pound against the wall last night—more than once. And how loudly she'd cried out. She raised her hands to her heated face. Lord. Her uncle had the room next to hers. What if he and Sonia had heard?

She dropped her hands and gritted her teeth; Barnabas was *not* her uncle. And even if he were, he was the one who'd all but shoved her into Dominic's bed, so he'd have no right to comment on what she did now.

Marianne looked at the door the duke had just passed through. So, he would not come to her; she would have to go to him.

She chewed her lip as she considered his words. Last night had been more wonderful than she'd ever hoped. She had known he'd be a generous and caring lover in bed, but his passion and uninhibited zest had stunned her. As had his earthy language and open hunger for her body.

And he wanted to do it again. And again.

Marianne couldn't recall a time in her life when she'd both wanted something fiercely and yet feared it at the same time.

Would she go to him—importune him?

Honestly, she didn't know.

★ ★ ★

They stayed in Lille for five more days. They might have stayed longer if the allied coalition had not declared war on France. But after that happened, the townsfolk—even the friendly innkeepers—chilled toward them.

Sin had not returned to Marianne's room and she had not come to his.

He had waited in vain for her every night.

During the day she behaved as if nothing had ever happened between them. Sin told himself he should be grateful for her sophisticated attitude.

Instead, he felt as if he were slowly being eaten away from the inside out.

He wanted her. That one night had done nothing to assuage his desire for her. It had only made things worse now that he knew she was a sensual, bold, and demanding lover. He wasn't surprised that he'd never had another woman like her. There *was* no other woman like her.

He should never have given his word that he'd leave her alone.

Yes, you should have.

Sin sighed. Yes, he should have. He'd already behaved in a way that brought him shame—although he couldn't regret his time with her.

But to continue such a relationship—to deepen it and explore it—would only make the inevitable ending all the more painful. He would not tire of her in a week a month or even a year.

And he did not have a year. He'd already left marriage and children too late. A year from now, he'd be courting some woman, planning his life with a stranger.

The thought left him empty inside.

"Sin."

He turned at the urgent voice, frowning up at Guy, who sank into the chair beside him. He'd been sitting in the taproom, drinking a pint of French ale while going over the route they would be taking.

"What is it?" he asked.

"We need to leave. Now."

"We're leaving in the morning."

"No, that's not soon enough." Guy's gaze slid to the doorway between the taproom and dining room. The innkeeper, one of his ostlers—the biggest one—and a stranger were staring at them. And their looks weren't friendly.

Sin and Guy stood up as the stranger came toward them, the other two men in his wake. "You need to leave," the man said before he'd even come to a stop.

Sin glanced at the innkeeper, who wouldn't meet his gaze. "We're paid until tomorrow."

"If you don't leave within the next hour, you won't be leaving at all."

"Who are you to tell us what to do?" Sin demanded, stepping closer, looming over the man, who was a good five inches shorter than he.

"I'm the mayor, Etienne DuBois," he said, taking a slight step back and swallowing hard, his eyes jumping from Sin to Guy to Sin. "And by speaking to you I am putting my own life in jeopardy. We have groups here—I suppose you would call them militias—who have power over us, like the army or constabulary. Some are legitimate groups that report to the army, but others . . . Well, these particular men take orders from no one. They are called the Red Cats and they are over one hundred men strong. They consider this area their territory. It is unlikely you would have run afoul of them before, er, well, before the current hostilities, but now they have no reason not to apprehend you if they see you. You are the enemy."

Sin and Guy exchanged looks. "I've heard a few stories about them," Guy said quietly. "They're led by an ugly character named Garnier. The woman who warned me about them said they've been pillaging the area with impunity for years. Only recently, with the end of the war, have townsfolk dared to deny them whatever they wanted. But now—"

Guy didn't need to explain. Now, with order breaking down, there would be nobody to hold them in check.

Sin nodded and turned to the Frenchman. "We will go. How long do we have?"

DuBois looked almost faint with relief. "Two hours, maybe three—no more. You must go south from town because they are coming from the north."

Going south was always their plan. "We shall be gone in less than two hours."

DuBois inclined his head and the three men scurried out.

"Elliot was with me when we heard about this Garnier character," Guy said, walking beside him as they left the empty taproom and headed upstairs. "He's gone to get the caravans ready to go."

They paused on the landing. "Have you seen anyone else?" Sin asked—meaning Marianne.

Before Guy could answer, the sound of footsteps on the stairs made them both turn.

It was Farnham, and his wild eyes told Sin he'd already heard the news. "We need to leave now before—"

"We know," Sin said shortly.

Barnabas glanced at the door to Marianne's room. "Will you—"

"I'll tell her," Sin said.

Barnabas nodded and hurried to the room he shared with his lover.

Sin turned to Guy. "I'll find the women and alert them that we are leaving."

Guy nodded. "I'll just collect the few things I left in Elliot's room and then bring the women's caravan around."

"See you in an hour in the courtyard?"

Guy nodded and disappeared into a room down the hallway.

Sin was just about to knock on Marianne's door when he heard more feet coming up the stairs.

The moment she saw him she said, "We need to—"

"I know," Sin said. "You'll need to make haste; we have barely an hour.

★ ★ ★

Marianne was still shaking three hours later, even though the town of Lille was already several miles behind them.

She heard horse hooves and turned to find Sin cantering toward her.

"Nobody is following us," Sin said before she could ask. "Or if they are, they're more than an hour behind us."

She exhaled a shaky breath.

"Tell me what happened," he said quietly when he drew up beside her.

The two of them were riding behind the three caravans, while Elliot rode ahead to make sure they weren't traveling into a worse mess.

"How do you know anything happened?"

He gave her a dry look.

"We were in that little café on the Rue Comtesse when a group of men came in. They had red scarves around their necks and were armed with truncheons. They recognized me, and started taunting me, saying they wanted to see me fight one of their number—a man. We were fortunate that some men from a rival gang came into the café and the two groups started to argue. The waiter was kind and led us out through the bakery onto the back alley. It was . . . terrifying."

"It's not too late for you to go home, Marianne."

"No. I've come too far, and I want answers—answers that only Dominic seems to have. Besides," she added, "there's no saying the people we met on our way to Calais would be any better than the ones we'll find on this road. In any event, I think we have a fair chance of passing for French as long as we don't encounter anyone who recognizes us from Lille."

Sin cut her an amused look. "And as long as Guy and I pretend we are mute."

He was right about that. The two aristocrats spoke adequate French, but their accents were atrociously British. Elliot, on the other hand, sounded like a native—he'd even managed to absorb the regional accent in the few days they'd been in the small city.

"Guy stocked both caravans with plenty of food and water, and Elliot will find somewhere for us to stay for a few nights—somewhere away from any town."

As far as Marianne was concerned, they could avoid towns for the rest of their time in France. It was horrifying how quickly people had turned against them in Lille and the speed with which lawlessness had pervaded the erstwhile idyllic town.

Marianne shivered; she had a new appreciation for her safe, predictable life in London.

"Are you cold?"

She looked up from her thoughts to find the duke observing her with a worried frown. "No, I'm just thinking about how hard life must have been in France—for a very long time."

"Yes, we've been fortunate and safe on our little island." He gave her a grim look. "Let's hope our luck continues."

The farm Elliot found for them was almost Eden-like in its perfection.

"I told the farmer we were a theatrical troupe whose schedule was destroyed by the impending hostilities," Elliot explained as they sat around their small cookfire and ate the meal that Sonia had prepared.

"How long are we staying?" Cecile asked, blowing on a spoonful of stew to cool it.

Sin couldn't help noticing how enrapt Guy was by the French-woman's actions.

"Just tonight," Elliot said. "We need to be on our way at first light."

"Do you think there will be fighting soon?" Cecile lowered her unfinished bowl to the stump that was serving as a table. "Perhaps we are worrying for nothing and the tide will turn against Napoleon in Paris?"

"No." The word was soft but certain.

Everyone turned to Marianne.

"You've seen the people on the road—even a small road like this," she said, looking from face to face.

They all knew what she meant. There'd been a constant trickle of people heading north—mostly men, but some women, too. Almost without fail they'd been vocal in their support of L'Empereur—the first emperor of France in over one thousand years. A man who'd had the audacity to crown himself. The French had had a brief taste of surrender these past months, and it was sour in their mouths. Bonaparte was offering them another chance, no matter how slim.

"Elliot is going to scout ahead and see what he can find out. If it looks good, we'll stick to our original route," Sin said.

"And if it doesn't look good?" Marianne asked.

"We have maps and lots of time before we need to get to Metz—we'll find a way—a safe way."

"Do you want me to go with you?" Guy asked Elliot.

"No. I can move faster on my own." He stood and nodded at Sonia before setting down his empty bowl. "Thank you for a delicious meal."

"You're leaving *now*?" Cecile asked. "In the middle of the night?"

Elliot gave her a faint smile. "I shall see you all in three days." He strode off in the direction of the horses. Within moments they heard hooves disappearing into the night.

Sin glanced around at the grim faces. "We should all get some sleep tonight. Tomorrow is going to be a long day."

Chapter 26

The six days after leaving Lille passed in a blur. They rose before first light and rode through the day and into the night, thanks to the moon, which was waxing gibbous.

The cold, rainy weather that had plagued them on their journey toward Lille moved to the north and the narrow cart track was dry by their third day.

They met up with Elliot not far from the town of Charleville, where they'd planned to stop and resupply.

"We need to go around it," Elliot said. "There is a royal armament factory in the town."

They were pulled off to the side of the road, watching as a slow but steady stream of people trickled by.

"A group of French soldiers have arrived and are spreading the rumor of a Prussian attack. The townspeople are boarding up their houses and people are frantic."

"Is an attack likely?" the duke asked.

"I think they have grounds for their fear," Elliot said grimly, unfolding the map. "You can go this way without losing too much time." Elliot traced over the route while he handed the map to Sin.

Marianne rode Reggie closer, and the duke held the map so she could look at it.

"How far is that?" Marianne asked.

"It'll take you at least five hours."

"What do you think?" the duke asked her.

She looked at Cecile, who'd been driving the women's caravan since they'd left Lille.

Her friend looked exhausted, but she nodded, as if she knew what Marianne was asking.

"We can do it tonight," Marianne said.

"Good. Stop when you are a few miles this side of Boulzicourt and I'll find you." Elliot turned to his horse.

"Why aren't you going with us?" Guy asked.

"I'm going back to Charleville; I want to see if I can get more recent news on Bonaparte's movements."

"You don't want to rest and eat first?" Sin asked.

Elliot had been going for days, and the dark smudges beneath his eyes said the strain was taking its toll.

"No, I'll find a few hours to rest once I've returned to town."

"Here." Sonia climbed down from the bench she'd been sharing with Barnabas and handed him a wax-paper-wrapped bundle.

Elliot's face lit up. "Thank you." He unwrapped the sandwich and handed back the paper, grinning. "I'll eat it while I ride."

Once he'd gone, Sonia passed out the sandwiches she'd made. The older couple kept to themselves most of the time, which was fine with Marianne. Every time she looked at Sonia, she felt like a fool. Dozens of snide comments the woman had made over the years came back to her, making sense for the first time.

Anger roiled in her belly as she snatched the food from Sonia. "I'm going to ride," she said to nobody in particular.

The duke fell in beside her a few minutes later, munching on his dinner. "Do you want mine?" she asked, holding the uneaten sandwich toward him.

"You need to eat."

"I'm not hungry."

His cool glance told her that he knew why she wasn't eating—because of who'd made the sandwich. Her behavior was irrational—she knew that.

She didn't care.

After a long moment, he took the food. "I'll hold on to it for you."

"How long will we stop?"

"If we can find somewhere safe and comfortable, I'm hoping we can rest for a few days."

"Good. Because Cecile needs a few days to recuperate. I wish she'd gone home; this is wearing on her."

"But not on you?"

"I'm tired, but I've spent the last few years training. Physically, at least, this is far easier for me. Besides, I have a reason to want to keep going."

They rode for a while in silence, the moon still low in the sky.

"Will you try to meet your mother if Dominic knows who she is?" he asked.

"I don't know. At first I was angry—furious—that she'd handed me off to strangers as if I were no more than a cast-off piece of clothing." She sighed. "But at least she tried to take care of me. Five hundred pounds is a great deal of money." She glanced at him. "She must have cared about me a little."

An uncomfortable look flickered across his face.

"I'm sorry," she said sharply. "Here I am burdening you with a sordid tale that you probably don't want to hear."

"I would not have asked if I had not wanted to know. Besides, you know the aristocracy specializes in sordid."

"Surely not Lord Flawless's family?"

He gave her a level look.

She bit her lip. "I apologize—that was uncalled for."

"My elder brother, Robert, was not my father's son."

Marianne blinked at his unprecedented offering of personal information. "That seems . . . unusual for an eldest child."

"*Unusual.* That is a good word for both of my parents."

"Did your father know—about your brother, I mean?"

"Oh yes. My mother told him. Theirs was not a love match," he said, staring straight ahead. "The dukedom was depleted, and my mother brought a great deal of money to the union. My father married her, but he was in love with someone else, and he never let my mother forget it. Her first few pregnancies ended in miscarriages. My aunt said my mother felt trapped and miserable and that my parents could scarcely stand to be in the same house together. As for my father, well, he had other consolations." He turned to look at her. "He kept his mistress right up until his death. I have eight half-siblings."

Good Lord. "Did your mother know?"

"Not at first. She found out about both the woman and the four children she'd already borne my father not long after her own third miscarriage."

Marianne could not imagine the humiliation. It was a dozen times worse than what Dominic had done to her.

"My aunt said she was deranged with anger when she found out," the duke continued. "She took a lover—my father never learned who—and waited until Robert was born to tell my father the truth. Of course, he was furious, but there wasn't a thing he could do about it except punish her. So he packed her off to the country. He dismissed her personal servants—maid, footmen, and her old nurse—and hired new ones. They were more like gaolers. She went nowhere and had no visitors. Well, except for my father. He would come home only long enough to breed her. I was born after two failed attempts, my sisters came one after the other, three of them in almost three years. My mother was grievously ill after my youngest sister's birth, but my father still came to her. He did it because he hated her, not because he wanted more children from her; I doubt if he even knew his daughters' names." He inhaled deeply, and then sighed. "A year after her illness, Benjamin was born."

They rode in silence. Just when she'd believed it couldn't get worse, he said, "My mother tried to kill herself right after Ben's birth. Suicide by horse. The horse died but she—well, she is alive, barely. She needs constant care and will do for the rest of her life."

"I'm so sorry," she said, not knowing what else a person could say to such a story.

"It all happened a long time ago, much of it before I was born. My aunt always lived with us, and she loved us when my mother and father could not. My childhood was not an unhappy one in that regard."

"Was your father unkind to your elder brother?"

"He never spoke to Robert directly—not that I ever heard."

Marianne winced, unable to even think about such cruelty.

"It was fortunate that Robert had a relentlessly sunny temperament—completely out of place in our home, where tempers were always frayed. He obviously inherited that characteristic from his natural father."

"*Your* temper never frays."

"It does; I've just learned how to hide it." He gave her a sideways look. "Although you certainly have tested me at times."

"You never show it. I've often considered your unflappability inhuman."

His lips twitched, but he didn't speak.

Marianne was suddenly wide-awake, wanting to know more. "You inherited the title," she said, tentatively. "Your older brother—did he—"

"He died on the same day as my father. The duke—who always spent the majority of his time in London with his other family—had neglected to see that his tenants or legitimate children were vaccinated for the smallpox. He must have believed himself immune, because he was never vaccinated, either. One of the crofter's children became sick and my aunt called on them. She brought the illness back to the house. Only Robert, my youngest sister, Ben, and—just by coincidence—my father were there. Francine, Mariah, and I were all away at school.

"The day after Father and Robert died, Sarah, my youngest sister, died. My aunt recovered but bears scars. Miraculously, Ben was spared."

"How old were you?"

"Fifteen."

Marianne had always felt more than a little self-pity that she had no siblings. But the thought of what he'd gone through—the pain and loss—made her almost glad that she'd only had her mother and uncle.

She paused at the thought; perhaps she *might* have siblings—half-siblings like the duke. Would they want to see her?

"Have you ever met your father's other children?"

His knowing look said he understood what she was asking. "My half-brothers all attended Eton, three at the same time I did. All my half-siblings have had Seasons and most have married—and done well for themselves."

"There is no stigma attached to their birth?" she asked, not hiding her disbelief.

"The natural child of a duke is welcomed by all except the highest sticklers. And even those would not have wanted to offend my father." He hesitated and then added, "Or me."

"You don't mind?"

"I have always behaved amiably toward them. After all, it is hardly their fault, is it? *They* did not swear an oath to my mother."

"That is an . . . enlightened viewpoint. And, I suspect, not a common one."

"No," he agreed, sympathy in his eyes. "I'm afraid it is not."

They found what seemed to be the perfect camping spot a few miles from the town of Boulzicourt. It was a large farm that had gone to weeds even though it had rich soil and abutted a sizeable stream.

The woman who owned the land was a widow with three small children. Her husband had been a soldier who'd made it all the way through the war but then died in a freak accident while plowing one of their fields.

Sin paid her well, and she was too concerned with her own affairs to wonder why they were camped behind her big, empty barns.

The first two days they slept most of the time, and Sin gave the woman money to cook and deliver their meals, giving her enough money to buy food for herself and her children, as well.

By the third day, everyone was rested enough to begin wondering what the next step would be.

"We'll wait here for Elliot," Sin said as they sat around the small fire eating the simple but delicious dinner of crusty bread, fresh butter, savory stew, and a tart made from dried apples.

"Shouldn't he be here by now?" Cecile asked, carrying the pot from person to person and offering more stew.

Sin was worried, but the last thing he wanted to do was scare the others. "I'm not concerned yet," he lied. "We've got ample time before we need to get to Metz."

Although he'd not told Cecile what they were doing in Metz, he assumed Marianne had. Or perhaps even Guy, who'd taken to loitering around the Frenchwoman's caravan even when his services were not needed as footman. It was obvious to all that his friend had fallen hard for the beautiful markswoman. Whether the two had consummated their passion, Sin couldn't say.

As for his own situation, he'd given up hoping that Marianne would come to him. He told himself that was just as well, but the thought lacked conviction and he wanted her more with every day that passed.

He was truly a fool.

"Cecile and I are going to the stream to wash some clothes."

He looked up from his lustful thoughts to find the object of his desire standing beside him, wearing one of her dreary dresses rather than the breeches and boots she'd worn while they'd been on the road. "Do you have anything that needs washing?"

"I'm sure we could pay Madam Blanchet to do our wash."

"Probably, but I feel the need to do something."

He raised his eyebrows. "Are you saying you miss running behind Dobbin?"

"I'm not that desperate. But I just need to be doing . . . something."

Sin stood. "I have plenty of dirty clothing. I will carry it for you."

To his surprise, she didn't demur. Instead, she turned to Cecile, who was engaged in a whispered but visibly heated argument with Guy. "I'll see you down there."

The Frenchwoman nodded at Marianne without stopping the angry flow of words.

"What are they arguing about?" Sin asked once they were out of earshot.

Marianne gave him a wry look. "What do you think?"

Amazingly, his face heated. "Oh. I didn't know whether they'd—"

"They have."

"And there is now a problem?"

"I don't know; I think they both just like to argue."

Sin laughed and she turned to him. "Why are you looking at me like that?"

"You never laugh."

"I laugh plenty."

"No, you occasionally snort—or maybe snicker—but genuine laugher? Not that I can recall."

Sin left the unwinnable argument alone. Instead, he said, "I saw you talking to Barnabas. Have you—"

"No. I just wanted to know if there had been another miniature in the locket. Both he and Sonia swore there hadn't been." She snorted. "For what their word is worth."

"Maybe your mother kept it?"

"Maybe. Anyhow, I suppose I should be glad."

"What do you mean?"

"If there was a picture of my father, then Dominic would have two people to blackmail."

Marianne was desperate for a bath, but the duke stayed after carrying their laundry to the river, and she didn't have the heart to ask him to leave.

She knew she should push him away, for both their sakes, but she'd already denied herself the pleasure of his body; surely, she deserved his companionship in exchange for such wisdom and selflessness?

It was very wise and selfless of you to launch yourself at him that night, the voice in her head pointed out.

Marianne refused to regret her actions. She would have shown up at his door the following night if she hadn't had a very enlightening discussion with the duke's friend, Guy.

Her mouth tightened at the memory of their brief chat, and she beat the shirt she was washing—one that belonged to the man in question—with extra aggression.

"You're going to tear that," Cecile cautioned from beside her.

Marianne threw the shirt at her, and it smacked the water harder than she'd intended, splashing Cecile in the face.

"Sorry," she muttered when the other woman's eyes narrowed enough to make her glad Cecile didn't have her pistols.

Marianne looked to where the duke was washing a towel, squinting at it as he pounded it on a rock, getting as much, if not more, water on himself in the process.

Cecile had flung the towel at the duke when he'd showed signs of settling beneath a tree and taking a nap. "Make yourself useful and wash that."

He'd given the towel a horrified look. "What if I ruin it?"

"It's an old, ragged towel, Your Grace. You cannot ruin it."

He'd frowned at her use of his title but—wisely—hadn't corrected her. Correcting Cecile about anything was never a good idea. Correcting her when she was in a *mood* could be downright dangerous.

Cecile had started calling both men by their titles a few days ago, and Marianne suspected she did so to remind not only herself, but also Marianne, of the great gulf between themselves and these aristocratic men.

She knew her friend and Guy had slept together the two nights Marianne had been with the duke because Cecile had told her.

"I want you to know so that you can slap me if I start behaving like a lovesick idiot," she'd said when Marianne had looked surprised by the disclosure. She'd known the Frenchwoman took lovers, but this was the first time she'd told Marianne about one of them.

"And I will slap you if you do the same," she'd said when Marianne hadn't replied.

"I won't need slapping," Marianne had assured her.

Cecile had only laughed.

But then Cecile hadn't heard the brief but illuminating discussion between the duke's closest friend—Guy—and Marianne.

The conversation in question took place the morning after her wonderful evening with Sin, when Marianne had been looking through her caravan for a good place to hide the enamel box and locket.

Guy, who'd been staying in the men's caravan, had popped his head out when he'd seen her. "Hello. What are you doing?"

"Something private."

"Oooh, I love private activities." He'd smirked so wickedly that her belly had fluttered. Although Marianne felt nothing for him other than amused tolerance, she couldn't deny he was a gorgeous specimen of manhood.

"What's that?" he'd asked, his sharp gaze on her hand.

She'd been on the edge of telling him that it was none of his affair, but then decided it didn't matter if he knew. What was he going to do? Steal the locket and blackmail her? He'd need to get in line.

"It's something that's very important to me," she said. "I need a place to hide it."

"Hide it from whom?"

"None of your business."

Predictably, he'd grinned. "Fair enough. I have an excellent hiding place."

"Where?"

He'd taken her to Sin's caravan and shown her the false bottom, which ran the entire length of the wagon and was a good ten or eleven inches high. It was also filled with weapons.

"Good God," she'd whispered.

"Clever, isn't it?"

It was. You'd never know the floor of the caravan was anything but a floor. "What are all those guns for?"

"It's private." His eyes twinkled with dark amusement as he echoed her words. "Want me to put your things in here? Because if this is broken into, the thieves can find anything."

She'd given him the enamel box and he'd tucked it away.

"Thank you," she'd said, turning to leave.

"He might seem cold, but he is the farthest thing from it. You could hurt him. Deeply."

Marianne had considered pretending she didn't know what Guy meant, but, again, decided it wasn't worth the lie.

"I think you've misinterpreted His Grace's feelings for me, my lord."

"I've known Sin a long time, and this is something different for him."

"What? Are you trying to tell me I'm the first lover he's ever had—aside from his wife?"

"No, he's had other lovers."

Marianne didn't want to hear that—even though she already knew it. "Then what?"

"He normally takes lovers from among the *ton*."

His words felt like a slap. "Well, don't worry, I'm sure he'll go back to the proper sort of woman soon enough. No doubt his recent decision was a result of his lack of options." Marianne had whipped around to leave, but he'd caught her arm.

"That's not what I meant."

"Then what do you mean, *my lord*?" She'd yanked her arm away.

Lord Carlisle was almost relentlessly charming, and rarely serious. He had quickly become a favorite among her uncle's employees—especially the female ones. She'd never seen his face so stern and severe.

"St. John's morality is not just a mask he puts on and takes off. He is an honorable man—through and through. I have known him since before either of us could walk. After he inherited the title—a title he'd never envied his brother—he became a different man. He was no longer St. John Powell, a younger son destined for the church—" He nodded at Marianne's look of shock. "Yes, the church. He already had his future mapped out while the rest of us were still getting into foolish scrapes at school. He fell in love—and fell hard—when he was fifteen, before his family was decimated."

Pain and jealousy had swirled in her belly; pain that the duke had lost somebody he loved—even as she burned with jealousy to think of him with another woman.

"I knew his wife died, but I didn't—"

"The woman he loved was not his wife."

Marianne hadn't believed she'd heard him correctly. "He kept a mistress while he—"

"Of course not! That is the last thing he would do after what his father did. You've been around him for weeks now—do you see him as the sort of man to inflict pain on others? Especially people who are dependent on him?"

No, she didn't.

"When he married Vanessa, he worked to make their marriage a happy one. I doubt she ever knew his heart had been given to another. They were happy together—even though it didn't last long. I daresay they would have come to love one another in time." Guy had shrugged, unaware that his words were like claws, shredding her.

"What about the woman he loved?"

"She was a vicar's daughter—sweet, gentle, and utterly unsuited to the life of a duchess even if Sin could have married her. She grew up in the village of Staunton, where her father was the vicar, a living granted by Sin's father. She was our age and we ran wild together before Sin and I were packed off to school. But even then—when we were just sprouts—it was easy to see that Sin worshipped her. He was different then—far less reserved. His father surely knew where his middle son's interest lay, and Sin would have had to fight to convince the duke to allow him to marry a vicar's daughter."

"You say even if he *could* have married her. Why couldn't he? Just because of their disparate statuses?" She scoffed. "It couldn't have been such a great love if society's judgment mattered more than their happiness."

"You are quick to disparage what you do not understand."

"Well, explain it to me—unless you think my brain is not sophisticated enough to grasp the complexity of *ton* marriages?"

He narrowed his eyes at her. "You have a larger chip on your shoulder than anyone I've ever met, Marianne. We are not all like Strickland, you know."

"I'm waiting, my lord."

"Sin's brother Robert had been betrothed to Baron Shereford's daughter—the marriage arranged when the two were still in the cradle. When Robert died, the bond passed to Sin."

"That's positively . . . *gothic*."

"Call it what you like. Not only was he honor bound to marry the woman, but the marriage brought a parcel of land with it—not a large piece, but one that was critical to the health of the village of Staunton. Without the land, the village would have withered and died. Thanks to the marriage, Staunton has access to a canal that has breathed new life into the area."

"Why not simply *buy* the land?"

"Because Shereford—a man who only came into his barony thirty years ago—didn't *want* money—he had oodles. He wanted a duke for a son-in-law. He wanted his grandson to be the next Staunton. Sin's choice was simple, albeit painful: He could dishonor his name and please himself, or he could better the lives of countless others who depend on the Dukes of Staunton for their livelihood."

Marianne had been appalled. "What a horrible decision—love or decency; happiness for two people or the good of the many."

"Exactly. No choice at all to an honorable man."

Marianne had been furious at Carlisle for sharing such a story. "Why are you telling me this?"

"Because I recognize the expression I've seen on Sin's face these past weeks—I've seen it before, back when he was in love with Jenny."

She'd flinched; now she had the name of the woman who'd

been fortunate enough to have the duke's love and tragic enough to lose it.

"You are wrong; he doesn't love me."

She had desperately wanted him to argue, but he'd only shrugged. "I don't know how far matters have progressed. But know this: He will not keep a mistress when he marries, and he will never choose his own happiness over his responsibilities."

She'd laughed then—a bitter laugh tinged with tears. "And a mistress is all I can ever aspire to, isn't it?"

"You may scoff and rail against it, Marianne, but it is a reality. Dukes do not marry circus performers. The sooner you end this, the easier it will be for both of you."

Guy had looked almost anguished as he'd said that last part.

Not until now did Marianne realize that he hadn't been speaking only to her—he was trying to convince himself. After all, Carlisle was heir to a dukedom, too, and it was evident to anyone who cared to look that Guy was—at the very least—infatuated with Cecile.

As for Cecile's feelings about him?

Well, that wasn't so clear.

Marianne looked at her friend, who was savagely washing one of Guy's shirts, her expression that of a person whose mind was elsewhere. Was Cecile thinking of her lover and the fact they would never see one another after this journey? Or was she contemplating accepting an arrangement from Carlisle? Marianne had not asked Guy if he were the type to keep a mistress after marriage. But based on all the newspaper stories she'd read about the marquess, it seemed like a possibility.

Could Cecile agree to play that role in his life?

Marianne didn't want to think what her own decision would be if she were in that position. Would sharing part of the duke's life be better than none? What if there were children—

Marianne shook away the thought. It would destroy the duke if he followed in his father's footsteps. And it would destroy her, too.

She sighed, sick of her whirling thoughts, and tossed the neckerchief she'd just rinsed into the basket for clean clothes.

St. John. That is his name. Can't you even call him that inside your head?

No, she couldn't.

St. John was not a man she knew. Sin—with his scruffy beard, worn clothes, and protective attitude toward a common female boxer—now *he* might be somebody she could get to know.

But St. John was a man who spoke to kings, a politician whose decisions shaped the world, and a duke who would one day marry a lady.

Marianne didn't realize she was crying until a tear landed on her bare forearm.

"Are you all right, *chérie*?" Cecile asked softly, her forehead furrowed with concern and something else . . . empathy?

"I'm fine," Marianne said, forcing a smile. "I just splashed myself in the eye."

There was one thing Guy had said that Marianne now knew was wrong: It was already too late to end things without getting hurt. Far too late.

Chapter 27

Sin couldn't sleep. Maybe it was the fact that they'd all slept so much when they first arrived. Or maybe it was the fact that he couldn't forget how Marianne had looked today, her skirt pulled up between her legs and tucked in her bodice—her pale, muscular legs bare and slick in the water.

He groaned and turned over.

"Bloody hell," Guy mumbled sleepily from the other bunk. "Go for a walk or a ride or a drink," he muttered, turning over and tucking his head beneath his pillow.

Sin swung his feet to the floor and slid them into his boots, not bothering to lace them up until he was outside. He plucked his coat off the hook and reached into Guy's pocket for the silver flask his friend kept filled.

It was a cool night, but not nearly as chilly as it had been. It had been an exceptionally warm sunny day—more early summer than spring.

He sat on the step on the back of the caravan and laced up his boots.

Sometimes, usually when he was engaged in a mundane task like dressing, he'd stop and marvel: He was dressing himself without a valet, shaving himself—well, not really—making tea on occasion, and even doing laundry. He stood up, smiling at that last item—

Cecile had called him less than useless when he'd handed her the product of his labor earlier today.

And that was another thing that was different—the people around him, especially these women—didn't simper and flatter and pursue him. They didn't give a rap who he was. In this life, what you could do was far more important than what your name was.

Movement in the women's caravan caught his attention—a flicker of light—and Sin instinctively hid himself from view as the door opened and he heard the murmur of female voices.

"I will," Marianne said, her tone the mildly aggrieved one she adopted whenever somebody gave her advice or instructions she didn't want.

She climbed down and closed the door, her arms full of something. A garment? No, a towel. She was dressed in her breeches and boots but hadn't bothered with a vest or neckerchief.

And she was headed toward the stream.

Sin frowned. The blasted woman was going to have a bath at—he fished his watch out of his pocket and squinted—almost one o'clock in the morning. By herself.

Didn't she realize the land was crawling with people—mostly men—on the move? Today three ragged-looking men had approached their caravans. Barnabas had given them some food and sent them on their way. Sin suspected they would not always be so fortunate.

Marianne might be a well-trained boxer, but she was no match for desperate men with knives or guns.

"Stubborn, foolish woman," he muttered, pocketing his watch and heading off after her.

Because you are not a danger to her person. Or virtue. Are you, Sin?

He scowled at the unwanted thought.

It was light enough to see as he made his way through the narrow band of forest that had been left to grow along the banks of the river.

She went to the same spot they'd washed clothing earlier, where a sandy-bottomed pool was kept fresh by a constant infusion of water. The river had warmed slightly in the sun but it would be frigidly cold—Sin knew that from experience since he'd bathed after the women had returned to the caravans.

She was lifting off her shirt as he emerged from the trees.

"Marianne."

She yelped and spun around. "What are you doing lurking out here at this time of night?"

"I couldn't sleep and spotted you wandering off—alone. You saw those men today—they won't be the only ones."

"So far the only thing I've had to worry about is a lurking duke."

"Very droll."

"I can take care of myself."

"Naked? In the water?"

She narrowed her eyes at him and then deliberately pulled her shirt over her head.

A gentleman would look away.

Sin wasn't so sure of that.

Besides, he didn't care what some theoretical man who wasn't there would do.

She smirked at him as she toed off her boots.

Sin's greedy eyes marauded over her lean, muscular body as lecherously as the men he'd just warned her about.

"Are you going to join me?" she taunted.

He opened his mouth to tell her he'd washed earlier and then shut it. What sort of idiot was he? A woman was asking him to bathe with her. And not just any woman—but a prickly, combative, gorgeous woman like Marianne.

Marianne herself, in point of fact.

Sin unbuttoned his coat.

Marianne's heart threatened to pound out of her chest as she pushed down her buckskins.

The duke's jaw tightened—the only sign that he was looking at a naked woman.

She should probably be offended by the lack of expression on his face, but the bulge in his breeches assured her he was not un-moved.

She'd undressed in front of countless people during her time in the circus, and not only females. Far too often male employees wandered in and out of the dressing rooms in the course of their work. And she'd stood in front of howling, screaming hordes of men once a week, her thin muslin dresses plastered to her body with sweat. Normally, being naked in front of somebody did not bother her in the least.

But then this wasn't *somebody*. This was the Duke of Staunton.

As badly as she wanted to cover herself back up, she forced herself to move casually, snatching a quick glimpse at the duke as she sauntered boldly toward the water.

She dipped a toe in the pool and winced; it felt far colder than it had that afternoon.

Marianne swallowed and then began to submerge one foot, hoping a gradual immersion would be less shocking.

It wasn't.

"Coward," he taunted. "You'll be all night at that rate."

She turned just as he pulled off his shirt, the rest of him gloriously naked.

And hard.

Marianne's eyes settled on his erection. No, her memory had not exaggerated; he was as beautiful and big as she remembered.

He freed his head and tossed the shirt onto the pile of clothes.

And then he came toward her. He should have looked ridiculous with that prodigious pole bouncing up and down in front of him, but Marianne had never seen anything even half so erotic in her life.

His eyelids were at half-mast and his lips were compressed in a forbidding line.

He stopped walking only when the hot, satiny head of his cock pushed against her stomach. And then his arms slid around her, and he captured her mouth.

What happened next probably wouldn't be called kissing. It was a savage joining, a clash of wills, a battle for supremacy. Marianne couldn't seem to get close enough to him, even though she was half-way up his body, a squirrel to his tree.

He came up for air but kept her crushed to his chest.

"I told you I'd not importune you," he said roughly. "I'm a liar and a scoundrel who can't keep his word." His lungs were rising and falling with unnatural swiftness, the moonlight silvering his skin. "You have bewitched me, Marianne." He took her mouth again, but more gently this time.

She gave herself up to his kiss, a leaf borne on a powerful current.

He licked and caressed and teased, until they were both breathing like winded coach horses.

"I want to be inside you," he said, kissing her nose, her cheek, her brow. "Come into the pool with me."

Marianne ground her hips suggestively against the indisputable evidence of his desire. "What about this? I thought they didn't like freezing water?"

He barked a startled laugh. "*We* don't care how cold the water is." He slapped her on the buttock and she squawked. Before she could reciprocate in kind he stepped forward and slid into the water, not diving, but submerging his entire body in one long glide.

She watched him swim a moment, marveling at the breathtaking sight. His was the sort of beauty that must have made the ancient Greeks believe gods came down from Olympus and played among humans.

He broke the surface of the water and shook his head, sending icy droplets glittering in the moonlight.

"How is it?" she asked.

"Lovely. Quit stalling."

She gritted her teeth and strode into the water, not stopping until they were once again chest-to-chest.

"You lied to me," she accused. "It's *freezing*."

His arms slid around her and his hard shaft—undaunted by the chill—thrust insistently against her midriff.

"I'll keep you warm." He nuzzled her neck.

"Your nose is like ice," she muttered, burrowing into his embrace.

Some part of her mind wanted to spoil this moment—knew she ought to get out of this pool and start running and not stop until she was back in London.

But Marianne ignored it. Whether she ran now, or walked away later, didn't matter.

She would suffer either way.

Before she suffered, she would take every last bit of him she could get—until she couldn't.

It *was* bloody cold. But holding her like this—suspended in water with nothing between them—was heaven.

She squirmed against him in a way that made his already hard cock stiffen even more.

"You feel so good," she said, her cold lips and nose on his neck, kissing and nipping and licking.

"Is that your teeth chattering?" he asked in disbelief.

"Mmm-hmm." She shivered and his eyes rolled back in his head as her hand slid between them and closed around his shaft. "Ahhh, you're as hot as a furnace." She bit his neck hard enough to make him start. "Put it inside me, Your Grace. Make me warm."

"Not until you say my name."

She stilled in his arms. "I always say your name."

He thrust his hips, making his shaft slide up and down in her fist. "Say it."

She groaned. "You're torturing me."

"Don't think that I haven't noticed that you've never said it—"

"Not even once?" Her hand tightened and it was his turn to groan. She tried to guide him between her thighs, but he stepped back and slipped from her grasp.

"Uuuugh."

Sin grinned at the genuine frustration in her voice.

She opened her eyes and scowled. "You are the devil."

"I don't understand why this is so difficult." Indeed, Alanna had incessantly made hints about his name—and how it should be a mistress's right to exercise such intimacy. But he'd left those hints unappeased.

Until this journey, Sin had only allowed those closest to him—his family and Guy—to use his nickname or Christian name. It was not a name for mistresses.

But then Marianne was not his mistress. Nor would she ever be family.

She was his lover.

"Marianne," he whispered, pulling her close again and flexing his hips, grinding shamelessly against her taut stomach, his actions a graphic, but wordless promise of what he'd give her.

"Sin." She growled the word into his collar bone and bit him.

"My *real* name."

Her mouth moved south, until she'd captured one of his nipples, and she bit him again.

He gritted his teeth at the sharp stab of pleasure but stood his ground. "Say it."

She said several very vulgar words.

"*Tsk*," he teased. "Such language. If you can say those words, surely you can say—"

"*Sinjinn*."

He gave a low, triumphant laugh. "There now," he said, sliding a hand between her thighs, pleased when she opened for him. "That wasn't so hard, was it?"

Her strong, slightly calloused hand pumped his shaft. "It's very hard, actually."

Sin felt her slickness even in the water. "I wish I could taste you," he murmured against her temple, kissing her while sliding a finger inside her tight sheath and making them both groan.

"Mmmm," she purred, her hand faltering and then releasing him entirely as he thumbed her stiff peak. "Oh, Your Grace," she sighed.

Sin snorted at her relapse to his title. "So. Stubborn," he grated through clenched teeth, using both hands on her now.

She wrapped her legs around his hips, bucking and thrusting.

"Yes, Marianne," he hissed as he felt the first tremors of her climax begin to roll through her body.

She dug her fingers into his shoulders and bit his chest as she cried out, her inner muscles clenching his fingers.

Sin cradled her bottom in his hands while she came down from the heights of bliss before asking, "Can you float on your back?"

"I don't know—should I?" she asked in a dreamy voice.

"Fill your lungs, lie back, and trust yourself to me."

She held his gaze, her eyes dark and heavy lidded. "With pleasure."

He bent his knees just enough to slide her legs over his shoulders.

She began to sink and laughed. "This is hard."

"You've not got enough fat to float easily," he agreed. "But I'll hold you up." He sank down into the water and drew her closer, until he bathed her with his hot breath.

"Ah, God. Yes, please, St. John," she murmured as he buried his mouth in her sweet sex.

It might not have been the easiest position to maintain—she had to remember to keep her lungs filled or she sank—but there was something magical about being pleasured so erotically in the moonlight.

She stared down her body, her eyes locked with his as he slowly teased her toward another climax, taking his time and working her toward the edge over and over before finally allowing her release.

Only when she was shaking and whimpering did he let go of her legs and slide her down his body. Marianne opened her thighs to him and he drove himself deep, filling her with his hard, silky heat. His big hands cupped her buttocks, pulling her closer.

"Warm enough?" he asked gruffly, his powerful hips beginning to pump.

"I'm perfect," she sighed against his throat, licking and kissing and nibbling the taut muscles of his neck as they bunched and flexed.

"You *are* perfect."

She squeezed her eyes shut, wanting to hold on to this night forever.

His thrusts were necessarily shallow because of the resistance of the water, but the water allowed him to do other things . . .

Holding her with only one hand he worked the other between them, caressing them where they were joined. "I'm going to make you orgasm while I am inside you, Marianne."

Marianne thrilled at his words. Even now—when he was naked, wet, and buried inside her body—she was unable to reconcile the fact that the man whispering such wicked intentions was the same man the rest of Britain knew as the untouchable Lord Flawless.

And he was hers.

Only Marianne saw this side of him—she knew that without a doubt. He might keep a mistress back in London, but she would know the sophisticated lover, a man who gave her jewels and mounted her between silk sheets.

She would never know the things Marianne knew about him.

How he hated that she boxed for a living and yet still took her seriously and did his best to see that she won.

How he'd sat beside her bed and cared for her when she couldn't care for herself—refusing to hand her over to another nurse.

How he'd mounted her in the water like a wild, passionate creature from mythology—a river Potamoi to her naiad—fierce and free of the crushing demands of society.

Marianne tightened her inner muscles around him.

"Marianne!" His clever finger paused only for a second, his hips drumming harder now, faster, as he rode her to a shattering, shared climax.

For the second time that day, her tears mixed with the river. In joy, this time.

But for how long?

Chapter 28

They stayed at the farm for six more glorious, idyllic days.

They were the best days of his life—an admission that increasingly shamed him. Not because he was ashamed of spending every waking hour—and a good number of sleeping ones—with Marianne, but because Elliot's absence suggested something bad had befallen his friend.

While there were still almost three weeks between now and the meeting in Metz, the roads had become even more clogged with traffic. Thankfully, most of the military movement seemed to be north and west, as opposed to south and east, which was their direction.

He would wait ten days for Elliot.

Until then, he worried plenty about his missing friend, but his concern couldn't rob the days and nights of magic.

But today was the ninth morning, and he could avoid the truth no longer.

They were eating their breakfast beside the cookfire, the day shaping up to be just as clear and sunny as the last six.

Sin was strongly tempted to take Marianne's hand and drag her toward the abandoned barn—where she'd surprised him by constructing a cozy, private love nest in the hayloft a few days earlier.

But that, alas, was not going to happen. He set down the half-empty cup of strong coffee Sonia had brewed and turned to his companions. "We're leaving tomorrow."

Marianne, Cecile, and Gus met his gaze and nodded, unsurprised.

"But your friend?" Sonia said with a frown. "Shouldn't we wait—"

"He'll know where we've gone if we're not here," Sin assured her, his glance going to Farnham. "You and Barnabas could stay here," he said, not bothering to try this argument on either Marianne, Guy, or Cecile—all of whom had put him in his place once already. "We could come back this way and—"

"We will go with you," Farnham said, his worried gaze on Marianne. The man looked so downtrodden and remorseful that even Sin was beginning to feel sorry for him, though he knew Farnham still hadn't confessed the worst of his infractions to the woman he'd wronged.

"Very well," Sin said. "We'll leave at first light. I want to cover this leg of the journey as fast as possible. I'd rather be early and wait for Strickland in Metz for a week or ten days than get held up somewhere and worry about being late. So, we'll be traveling hard." They nodded and breakfast broke up.

So much for a relaxing day in the hayloft.

Late that night, after all the washing, cleaning, packing, cooking, and preparing had eaten up the day, Marianne went to their meeting place in the barn.

It was past midnight and the duke had worked hard all day, as had the others, so she didn't really expect to find him there.

But there he was, waiting for her when she climbed up the wooden latter to the loft.

He stood and came to meet her. "I was beginning to believe you wouldn't come," he said as she walked into his welcoming arms.

"I thought it might be our last chance to be together for a while," she murmured into his hard chest, inhaling deeply and filling her lungs with his precious scent while he stroked her back. "Cecile told me I was a fool."

"Do you agree with her?"

"I might be a fool, but I'm right where I want to be."

He kissed her gently and deeply, the taste of him already so familiar and so dear. When his hands moved to the buttons of her dress, she shook her head.

His brow furrowed. "What's wrong, sweetheart?"

Marianne's body clenched at the endearment; Lord, how she hungered to take him inside her body.

"It's—well, my courses started today." Her face heated furiously at her admission, which was foolish after all they'd done together over the past few days.

He caressed her cheek, his eyes hot and loving. "I hope that doesn't mean that you are leaving? Because I want to hold you and sleep with you—at least for a few hours."

"I'm not leaving. There is something I've wanted to . . . finish, since that first night together."

"That sounds intriguing."

She walked him back toward the rough wall of the barn where she'd made their love nest. Her fingers made quick work of his breeches before she sank to her knees in the blankets, pulling his buckskins down with her.

She stared at his erection and then cut him a look of mock surprise. "Why, where are your drawers, Your Grace?"

He smiled down at her, exposing his elusive dimple. "My washerwoman says I'm wasteful, so I thought I'd do my part to cut down on the laundry."

"Very noble of you," she praised. "I think you deserve a reward." She slid her hand around his thick shaft and stroked him from root to tip.

"You will be the death of me . . . ." His hands slid into her hair, fingers lightly caressing her scalp.

She lowered her mouth and kissed the tiny slit in his crown.

His hips bucked and he groaned, his breathing uneven and heavy, his slumberous gaze greedy.

"You want more?" she whispered, lightly exploring his slick, salty offering with the tip of her tongue.

His jaws clenched as he struggled for self-restraint. "I want more."

"I want to hear you say the words. Tell me what you want," she ordered, stroking his shaft but leaving his crown untouched.

"Pleasure me with your mouth, Marianne."

She mouthed him gently, lightly. "Is that how you want it, St. John?" she taunted.

He clenched his jaws, his fingers tightening in her hair. "Suck me harder."

Her inner muscles clenched at his gruff command, and she smiled wickedly, licking his length far too lightly to do anything but tease. "Make me."

His heavy lids drooped even lower, his dark eyes glittering. "Do you know what you are offering, Marianne?"

"Oh yes." She lowered her mouth, taking him all the way to the root, her bold, challenging gaze locked with his.

He growled. "You would make a beast out of me, Marianne."

She nodded as best she could; she had fantasized time and time again about watching this proud, controlled man come apart.

His hands closed around her skull as he forced her mouth back down. "Open for me."

She obeyed without hesitation, her submissive posture a silent invitation to deepen his thrusting, her eager mouth fanning the flames of his primitive, masculine impulse to dominate—an urge that would, no doubt, shame him later.

"Yes, just like that," he praised, plunging into her deeply, slowly, and giving her his length with each thrust.

She explored his body with her hands while she used every trick another lover had taught her, massaging and sucking until his eyes darkened and grew almost crazed and his hips snapped harder and faster, raw desire eroding his polished veneer until scarcely any trace of the controlled, civilized, proper Duke of Staunton remained.

His thrusting became wilder, less controlled, his teeth bared as he struggled to hold back his need. "I'm going to—" He tried to push her away, a gentleman to the last.

She wrapped her arms around him, using all her strength to keep him close.

He bucked, his hands shoving at her shoulders even while his hips ground against her. "Marianne!" he shouted, losing the battle and thrusting wildly thrice more before hilting himself.

Marianne held him tightly while he spent in jerks that wracked his big body, emptying himself deep inside her as the last vestiges of his reserve shattered and the duke fell away, leaving only the man she loved in his wake.

Sin stroked her hair as they cuddled together under the blankets, his heart finally beating normally.

"Are you asleep?" he asked quietly.

She shook her head and pushed up, until she lay on her side, her head propped in her hand.

Sin stroked her lips, red and swollen from his rough handling, ashamed of the primitive, possessive throb that pulsed in his groin at this mute evidence of her desire to please him.

One side of that puffy mouth pulled up. "Don't," she warned.

It was a sign of how similarly their minds had begun to work that he knew what she meant. "I wasn't going to apologize for behaving like a savage and using you like an animal," he said, his own mouth curving into an answering smile.

"You liked it." She glowed with smugness.

"No. I adored it—and you. You have no idea how beautiful you looked taking me." He leaned forward to claim her mouth, tasting a hint of himself in their lingering kiss. "Marianne—"

"Please, don't say it."

He gave a huff of exasperation. "How do you know what I'm going to say?"

"You are a duke, accustomed to getting your way—"

"With *you*? Hardly."

"—*most* of the time," she amended "You think you can find a way to make this—*us*—last. But it cannot last . . . St. John. At least not beyond our time here, outside of the real world."

He knew she was right and yet it infuriated and pained him to hear her say it. "How can you give *us* up so easily?"

"Ending this won't be easy," she demurred, "but the decision to do so is." She slid a hand around his jaw, her expression raw. "The parts of you I respect and adore the most—your goodness, decency, and honor—are the same things I'd be destroying if I encouraged your line of thinking."

"What we have is perfection, Marianne, and if—"

"What we have right *now* is perfection," she corrected. "It will be far, far different when we both return to our lives."

He wanted to argue with her, but he knew she was right. Things *would* look different when they were back in London.

"It will hurt when this over—it will be agony," she said with a bitter twist to her lips. "But the alternative would be even worse. So, promise me now, Your Grace, that you will not tempt me. That this ends the moment we set foot on our packet home."

He held her gaze for a painfully long moment.

"Promise me," she urged softly, her hazel eyes glassy.

Sin sighed and lowered his forehead until it touched hers. "This ends when we set foot on the packet."

Chapter 29

Without Elliot to ride point for them, they found themselves again and again mired in congestion and entangled in chaotic snarls of people traveling on foot with everything they owned—swine, cattle, and poultry included—piled up into wagons of every description.

Most people were fleeing rumors of attacks on towns that bordered the areas controlled by coalition nations. Men of all ages were heading to Paris, flowing in an almost continuous stream.

There were no more private havens during the almost six days it took to get to Metz, and they drove for as long as they could each day before making camp among the floods of people.

While they received more than a few interested glances, none of the roving bands of armed men claiming to be soldiers bothered them.

To encourage that lack of interest, Cecile and Sonia bundled themselves in unappealing, heavy clothing and disguised any attributes that might attract attention.

Marianne dressed in worn breeches and stopped polishing her boots, wearing a tattered overcoat and battered hat that she'd acquired after their first day on the road.

There was no way to disguise the value of the wagons or their horses, but then they were masquerading as circus folk, so most people would assume the caravans were not only their businesses, but their homes.

Only once were they seriously delayed, when an overloaded wagon collapsed in the middle of the road, the two poor horses trapped in their traces while all traffic ground to a halt. Again and again they altered their route, sometimes taking roads that were barely visible to avoid potential trouble.

What Sin thought about Elliot's continued absence Marianne didn't know; they didn't see each other all day as he rode at the front of the procession and she took up the rear. At night, they barely had enough energy to eat before collapsing in their various caravans.

They reached the outskirts of Metz on the seventh day and skirted the city until they reached the eastern edge, where they located the Iron Helm Inn, their meeting place.

Once again, they were able to find a farm to park their caravans, although this one had been—abandoned years ago if the state of the house and outbuildings was anything to go by. Yet it suited their purposes admirably as it was away from the road, only a quarter of an hour from the inn, and had ample space to store and hide the caravans.

That night, for the first time in days, Marianne and Sin were able to get away after dinner. They made no effort to hide where they were going as they headed toward the dilapidated farmhouse after a late meal.

Marianne's body ached for him, and judging by the way he embraced her the moment he set down the lantern, the feeling was mutual.

"It has been torture looking at you every night and not having you," he murmured when he finally released her lips.

Marianne snuggled against his already dear body as he kissed her cheek, ear, neck, and any other part of her he could reach.

She glanced around their newest trysting place as she reveled in his attention.

It was a modest kitchen which had been stripped of everything except for a huge table that looked too big to fit through the door.

"I need you," he growled in her ear, his head swiveling to survey the room, his gaze falling on the table. He turned her and marched her backward. "Up," he ordered, his hands cupping her bottom and lifting her.

She'd thought ahead and changed into a dress before washing for dinner.

He flipped up her skirt and petticoat, and his nostrils flared as he looked from her naked body to her face, and then back again. "I'm afraid this will be a bit uncivilized."

Before she could answer he flicked open his breeches, shoved her knees apart, and positioned himself at her entrance.

They groaned as he sank into her.

"Oh, Marianne . . . how I have missed you." He held her full for a long moment as his erection throbbed inside her. "Lean back," he ordered gruffly. "I want to watch."

She lowered herself to her elbows and he tucked her skirts higher, exposing her to his view. "Yes," he hissed, his eyes on the place they were joined while he penetrated her with deep, measured thrusts. "So beautiful."

Marianne shuddered when he began circling the source of her pleasure with his thumb, skillfully driving her to one climax, and then a second, his pumping becoming wilder and less controlled before he gave in to his need and hilted himself deep inside her.

He heaved a sigh of intense satisfaction as the last spasm gripped his body, then smiled down on her with sated eyes. "There I am— behaving like a beast again."

She laughed weakly and lay back on the table. He lowered her skirts and then buttoned up his breeches before flopping down beside her, their legs dangling off the table.

"Do you think Elliot will find us?" she asked once their bodies had cooled and their breathing returned to normal.

"I have no rational reason to believe so, but I do," he said. "Elliot has been involved in government work for years. He never tells us what it is that he does, but whatever it is, it often requires long stretches out of the country. I think he knows how to take care of himself. If he's late, there is a good reason. But he will join us . . . eventually."

"And when do you wish to start waiting at the inn?"

"I'll go tomorrow—but you needn't come with me. If Dominic shows up early, I will tell him that I'll bring him to you."

"No, I want to go with you."

"Are you sure, Marianne? He might not show up until the appointed time, which means over two weeks of waiting."

"I have nothing else to occupy me," she said. "Well, not during the daytime, at least."

"Temptress." He chuckled softly. But his humor dissipated. "I don't know what he might do," he said. "He might ambush us outside the inn, for all I know. Which means I shall warn the others, so they won't be left wondering if we don't come back."

Sin turned to her and reached for a stray curl, tucking it back with the others. She had not run or trained since Lille and her face was already rounder, softer. It suited her.

"I wish you weren't caught in the middle of this," he said.

"I wish the same for you."

He took her hand and laced their fingers together.

"Part of me hopes he stays away until the day we're supposed to meet," she admitted, her hazel eyes locked with his green ones.

"Me, too. But then I think of Ben, and I am torn between my selfish desire for you and my need to see my brother."

They never talked about the person at the heart of this entire adventure—his brother—and she hadn't wanted to raise the subject. She hoped Dominic wasn't manipulating Sin, but she wasn't optimistic.

"You don't think he is alive, do you?" Sin asked, reading her thoughts in that eerie way he had.

"I hope he is."

"But you don't think so."

"I honestly don't know, Sin."

"You knew Dominic," he said. "What do you think?"

"You knew him, too."

"Ah, but that was such a long time ago."

"It's so hard to imagine that you were ever friends."

He smiled faintly but didn't answer.

"What happened between you? Did you have a single disagreement? Or was it a gradual estrangement?"

"It was both, although . . . to be honest, I don't think he ever liked me. Not even when we were lads at school."

"Why do you say that?" Although Marianne could guess: Sin was the better man, in every way, and Dominic, beneath his confidence and charm, was riddled with jealousy and envy.

"His father kept him on a short leash with money and it chafed at him. He thought I had everything: a generous allowance, the approval of my father, and then, after Robert died, I had the title. It ate at him." He snorted. "But none of that stopped him from borrowing money from me. Or stealing from me."

She grimaced. "Oh, Sin."

"I wasn't the only one—he stole things from Guy's grandfather's house once, when Guy had brought him home for the summer holiday."

"Was that when things ended?"

"No, not even then. At least not for me. Guy was finished with him after he had to tell his grandfather—the duke—what had happened. Although Guy's family is ancient, they are not wealthy. A lot of their financial problems are due to Guy's father, who was . . . well, rather profligate before his death. Guy and his sisters grew up with their grandparents, and the duke has always made him feel that it is up to Guy to make amends for his father's gambling. It must have been agonizing for Guy to admit that he'd brought a thief into their home."

He sighed heavily. "As for me, I could afford what he stole from me." He pulled a face. "I felt so *ashamed* for him that it was far easier to pretend it never happened rather than confront him. In the long run I think that just made him hate me more. After all, *it is human nature to hate him you've injured.*"

"Who said that?"

"The philosopher Tacitus, I believe." His mouth was compressed into a harsh line. "The incident that ended everything was when he sent me a message from a brothel, begging for help." He looked at her. "It is not a pretty tale. Are you sure you wish to hear it?"

She nodded.

"He'd gone to a virgin house. Whether the girl he took was a virgin or not, I do not know. But she was exactly that: a *girl*. He had no money to pay his way out and thought I'd take care of his debt, as I'd done so many times before. I refused. He was furious at me—accused me of being a moralizing prude and a bore and—well, you can imagine. The last time I saw him, he was being held by two huge bruisers, who were determined to get the money from him. He gave me such a look of hatred it was . . . chilling."

They lay together in silence, hands clasped, and stared at the ceiling, both of them remembering a man who could be so engaging and charming and loveable when he chose. And also so duplicitous and hateful.

Sin turned to her and squeezed her hand. "He did do one good thing."

"Oh?"

"If not for Strickland, I never would have met you."

Sin, Marianne, and Barnabas—who'd insisted on accompanying them—arrived when the tap room opened at the Iron Helm and occupied the corner table that faced the door.

There was so little business that the publican was satisfied if they bought pints every hour, even though they didn't drink them.

On their second day of waiting, Sin brought a deck of cards and taught her the card game piquet.

That had been yesterday.

"How much is it you owe me now?" Marianne teased as Sin gathered up the cards to shuffle them.

"As if you don't have the amount memorized." His eyes narrowed at her. "I think you're a Captain Sharp and have played this game since you were a child," he accused, secretly enchanted by her shining eyes and delightful smile.

"I hope you aren't allowing me to win, Sin."

"Never." *Well, maybe just a little.*

She cut a glance at Farnham, who sat in an almost trancelike state, just as he'd done for the prior three days. Yesterday he'd not even roused when Marianne asked him a civil question—something she'd not done in weeks—about his food.

Farnham neither drank nor touched the simple but hearty meals Sin ordered for both dinner and supper.

"What's wrong with him?" Sin asked when the older man got up to use the necessary, the only movement he'd made for at least an hour.

Marianne shrugged. "Who knows? I'm sure whatever it is, Dominic is at the heart of it."

"You think he won't turn over the journal if Farnham doesn't give him the locket?"

"Given how useful Dominic has found the book over the years, I'd be surprised if he gave up such an effective tool—even if Barnabas did give him the locket. After all, he doesn't really need the miniature if he already knows who my mother is." Her mouth tightened. "No, there is something going on between the two of them that Barnabas has not confessed."

"You think he plans to use Farnham for something else?"

"I wouldn't be surprised."

Farnham returned from his trip outside, and they lapsed into silence.

They were the tiny taproom's only customers for the two hours before closing. Sin ignored the scowl of the man behind the bar, and they stayed until the last chairs were stacked on their tables.

"He's not coming," Sin declared, and they gathered up their things.

It was late and dark, but the lanterns that hung from the hooks on the caravan made it possible to find their way slowly back to the farm.

Barnabas drove the wagon while they rode inside.

"This is going to be a long nine days," Sin murmured, holding her tight to his side and kissing her as the caravan rumbled down the rutted path.

"True," she admitted, standing up from the bench seat and straddling his lap. "We have another ten or eleven minutes alone before we get back."

"Good point," Sin said, and then went about making every minute count.

By the time they rolled to a stop in front of the old house—which they'd claimed for their own, preferring privacy to the comfort of either of their caravans—they were both breathless and sweaty and nowhere near finished with each other.

"Well, blast," Sin muttered, hastily buttoning up the bodice on her gown and rearranging the plain tucker she wore around her neck before opening the door and hopping out, taking her hand to help her down.

"You go ahead, darling," Sin said. "I'll help Farnham unharness the team. When I return I'll warm some water so you—"

The door to the house swung open, the squeaking hinge obscenely loud in the darkness, and Sin whipped around.

"Well, well, well. Look who finally showed up." Dominic leaned in the doorway, grinning, a pistol lightly clasped in his hand.

Chapter 30

"Sorry it took so long for me to get here," Dominic drawled, his bright blue eyes flickering over them and settling on the duke. "I thought you might come early, what with all the excitement going on."

Sin edged his body in front of Marianne. "How did you find us here?"

Dominic just smiled and stepped out of the house, followed by Cecile and Guy. Behind them came four more men carrying muskets, and behind them, was . . . Sonia—the only one of the three not bound.

Barnabas made a choked sound. "No," he said, his eyes wide with disbelief and horror.

Sonia had the grace to look embarrassed, but Dominic just chuckled. "I'm afraid so, old man. Sonia, here, has been helping me with little things for quite some time." He turned to the older woman, who regarded him with a look of hatred. "After you arrived, dear Sonia nipped over to the pub and left a message for me. If it's any consolation, she hasn't exactly been gracious about it, but—like you—she didn't have much of a choice."

"Why?" Barnabas asked.

"Oh, it's a long, tawdry story, Barney," Dominic said, his gaze on the duke rather than Barnabas. "But to cut it short, your lover has played you false since the first day you met her. She worked for the same criminals who sent you to England all those years ago. The notebook I've been keeping safe for you—well, that wasn't really written by an English customs agent, but compiled by Sonia herself, for her Paris associates. It was meant to keep you in line, should you ever try to buck their control." Dominic smirked. "But Sonia became smitten enough with you to claim that it was lost—that was the reason you were able to slip from their grasp." He grinned. "And into mine."

"He stole it from me, Barnabé," Sonia said, genuine anguish on her face.

Dominic nodded. "She's right. I did steal it. Although I've wondered why she would have held on to such an incriminating document when—"

"Enough." The duke's soft voice cut through the night.

Dominic's mouth tightened as he strode toward Sin. "You don't decide what is enough, here, Your Grace." His nostrils flared as he glared at the duke. "*I do.*" As he neared the caravan, the light from the lantern washed over him.

Marianne stared. It wasn't even a year since she'd last seen him, but he'd aged a decade. His handsome face, once rounded with too much good food and too many spirits, was gaunt, deep lines graven around his perpetually smiling lips. His eyes were still the color of a summer sky, but they appeared sunken, the skin beneath them papery.

"I told you not to bring anyone but yourself and Marianne, Staunton," Dominic went on when Sin didn't speak. "And yet I see Guy and the lovely Mademoiselle Tremblay!" He made a show of glancing around. "Is Elliot lurking around somewhere, too? Maybe a couple of his friends from the Home Office or a handful of well-chosen soldiers?"

"It is only we six," Marianne said, stepping closer to Dominic and putting herself between the men—both of whom vibrated with leashed violence as they glared at each other.

Dominic smiled. "Thank you, Marianne, for your sterling honesty. That is what Sonia told me, too." He glanced at the woman and pulled a thoughtful moue. "I can't believe she'd have any reason to lie, now would she?"

Dominic grinned, looking from Sonia to Marianne to Sin. "Fortunately for me, Sonia is not my *only* source of information where you are concerned, my dearest Duke."

Still smiling, Dominic backhanded the duke across the face hard enough to drive him back a step.

Marianne cried out and lunged for him, but one of Dominic's henchmen raised his gun and aimed it at her.

"Stay where you are, Marianne," Dominic said in a pleasant voice, still glaring at Sin. "I told you not to bring Elliot."

Sin wiped blood from the split in his lip. "What have you done to him?"

"I'm afraid dear Elliot might have had a run-in with one of the lawless mobs roaming the countryside."

"With some help from you, no doubt."

Dominic clucked his tongue in mock regret. "I'm afraid it is possible that the men I told about Elliot might have an axe or two to grind against our government."

Sin's face was expressionless. "And Ben?"

"Ah, poor Ben." Dominic gave an exaggerated grimace. "Well, I'm afraid I lied."

"Ben died during the ambush, along with the others, and you somehow happened on his ring and letters," Sin guessed.

"How clever you are, Staunton—but it has come a bit late, hasn't it?"

"Why me?"

"Why *not* you? God knows you have enough money." He grinned at Marianne. "And if anyone could bend Marianne to his will, it would be you. All I needed was a reason to persuade you to cooperate." He shrugged. "And since I knew about Ben—"

"You knew because you essentially murdered him."

Dominic's smile became strained. "*I knew about Ben*," he repeated, "because he and dear Norris had accidentally stumbled onto something far bigger than they. It wasn't a military secret that I smuggled out with Emile Beauvais—the war was all but over by then, you fool!" He laughed. "Well, so we thought *then*. I got Beauvais out because his brother paid me a great deal to get him back. You see, Emile and a few well-placed French and British officers decided there was a lot of money to be made while our governments squandered the lives of their citizens. Something far more lucrative than just selling boring military secrets." He paused and looked from face to face. "What? Nobody can guess?" He gave a snort of disgust and turned to Guy. "Staunton's ignorance doesn't surprise me—he was always a candidate for sainthood. But you, Guy, *tsk tsk*—"

"Why does any of this matter?" Marianne asked wearily.

Dominic cut her an annoyed look. "Art," he said, ignoring her question. "Paintings, sculptures—even the crown jewels from one of those useless duchies that litter Europe." His eyes glittered. "The wealth of nations. And it was all there for the taking—if you had the nerve and opportunity to take it, that is."

"This was never about selling secrets. My brother died so you could protect a ring of thieves," Sin said flatly.

"Essentially, yes. There are dozens of people involved. Your brother and Norris and that other chap were actually gathering evidence to destroy an operation that was making thousands of pounds for everyone involved. If Beauvais hadn't finished them off, somebody else—"

Sin lunged at him, but Dominic moved like a blur, the point of his pistol against the duke's forehead. "Don't be so predictable," he said through clenched teeth. "Step. Back."

Sin backed away, his eyes on fire.

"Keep two guns on His Grace," Dominic said to his men, his gaze sliding to the caravan that Barnabas had been driving—the one that belonged to Sin, Guy, and Elliot.

"If you made so much money then why all this?" Guy asked.

Dominic's face flexed into a petulant frown. "Well, things didn't go as well as I'd hoped."

Guy chuckled. "Ah, your criminal associates double-crossed you, did they? What a shame."

"I don't really *need* you, do I?" Dominic raised his gun and pointed it at Guy's face.

Guy just smirked, rather than look chastened or afraid.

Dominic sneered. "You always did have more looks than brains." He turned to Sin. "I'm hoping—for both our sakes, Staunton—that my ten thousand pounds is somewhere inside that caravan. Because we found nothing in the other two wagons or in this little love nest of yours. So, where is it?"

"It's easier to show you than tell you," Sin said calmly, as if their plan wasn't unravelling right before their eyes.

Dominic pointed to the men holding their guns on the duke. "Don't hesitate to blow his head off if he so much as twitches. Go on, Your Grace."

Sin went to the back of the caravan, opened the door, and then slid aside the panel that exposed the foot-high storage space. He stepped back. "It's in there."

Dominic motioned to a boy carrying an old musket that was almost as tall as he was. "Put that aside for a moment and go look."

The lad hurried to obey, squatting down and peering into the hiding space. "There's a trunk, sir."

"Well, *pull it out*, you fool."

The boy hurriedly reached inside and drew out a wooden strongbox reinforced with metal strapping. It hit the ground with a heavy *thud* that kicked up dust.

Marianne squinted into what she could see of the hiding place. Where was the enamel box? Where were all the pistols and rifles—at least a dozen of them?

She looked up and met Guy's gaze.

He winked at her before turning back to Dominic.

What did *that* mean?

"The key to the lock?" Dominic asked.

"I have it in my pocket," Guy said.

"Toss it to me—and don't try anything foolish."

Guy fished the key out of an inner pocket of his coat and threw it at Dominic, hard.

"Very amusing, Guy," Dominic said when the key bounced off his chest and fell into the dirt. "Pick it up and unlock it," he ordered the lad.

A moment later the boy flipped open the lid and Dominic gave a low whistle, a wondering smile on his face. "My, my, what a thing of beauty."

"It's a sad man who finds beauty in money, Dominic," Sin said. "But then you never could discern diamonds from dross, not even when you were staring right at it." He looked at Marianne.

Dominic followed Sin's line of vision and his jaw sagged.

He looked from Sin to Marianne to Sin. And then he burst out laughing. "Lord," he said once he caught his breath. "There's something I never would have expected." His eyelids lowered. "Although I've trained her up nicely for you, haven't I, Staunton?"

The duke's body jolted, and Marianne grabbed his hand and pulled, her forearm flexing until it hurt.

Dominic raised his pistol and came close, until the tip of the gun rested on Sin's forehead. "You'd better heed her, Staunton." He looked at their joined hands. He clucked his tongue and smirked. "Talk about inappropriate choices, my dear duke."

Sin turned to Marianne. "On the contrary, I've never met a more appropriate woman in my life."

Marianne blinked rapidly and looked down, unable to hold back her tears.

"Oh, this is touching," Dominic said. "But I wasn't talking about you, Staunton. I was talking about her."

Marianne's head whipped up.

"Is it worth asking what you are nattering about?" Sin asked.

"I'm *nattering* about a royal princess, my dear Staunton. It is rare for one to marry a mere duke—at least not a royal one." Dominic grinned at their stunned faces and turned to Marianne, dropping a low, court bow. "I haven't greeted you properly yet. It's a pleasure to see you again . . . Your Royal Highness."

Chapter 31

Marianne just stared at Dominic.

Dominic's brow furrowed, and then his eyes began to widen. "No!" He turned a look of genuine shock on Barnabas. "Bloody hell! You never told her, did you? You brought her all the way here—ignorant, like an innocent lamb to the slaughter."

Barnabas looked ill and at least a decade older, his jaws flexing.

Sonia, Marianne absently noticed, looked as confused as Marianne felt.

Personally, Marianne wanted to punch Dominic in the face so badly she could taste it.

For once, she restrained her temper. "Leave him alone, Dominic. Why don't you let them all go? It was the money and me that you wanted."

"How handsome of you to be so self-sacrificing," he mocked. "But I think I'll hold on to all of you for a while, if you don't mind."

"I anticipated this eventuality, Strickland," the duke said coolly. "And I left instructions to deny all ransom requests."

"And—as you're well aware—my family has no money to ransom me," Guy said, all traces of the genial man that Marianne knew, gone.

Cecile cut Dominic a look of pure loathing. "My pig of a cousin has money—*my* money—but he would probably pay you to kill me."

Dominic gave a hearty and very false laugh. "Why must you all assume the worst of me?"

Guy snorted, earning a frown.

"I only meant that I would detain you until I complete the deal I've made," Dominic said. "Once Marianne is safely on her way, I'll release all of you—you have my word on it."

Guy wasn't the only one who laughed then.

Dominic scowled. "Get them ready to go," he snapped at his men. "And shoot anyone who gives you any trouble."

Marianne rode Reggie beside Dominic while the others were bound and split up among the caravans.

"Sorry about the ropes," Dominic said as he led Reggie by the reins. "But I recall you were far too handy with your fives to leave at liberty."

"I thought you enjoyed a good mill," she said. "Oh wait," she added with a look of exaggerated comprehension. "You only like them when they are fixed in your favor."

He chuckled. "Oh, Marianne. You have no idea how much I've missed you."

She ignored him.

"Aren't you going to ask me who your mother and father are? I know you must be perishing of curiosity."

"I'm sure you'll tell me when you're ready."

Dominic gave her look that appeared to be genuine respect. Of course, there was very little, if anything, genuine about him. "You've matured a great deal in barely a year. Tell me, are you and Lord Flawless lovers?"

It was slight, but Marianne heard it—the edge in his voice when he asked the question. It wasn't her that he was jealous of, it was the duke. Dominic didn't just hate Sin, he was consumed with jealousy.

"How it must have eaten away at you to grow up around such a man," she said in a pleasant tone.

His jaw tightened.

"Wealthy, attractive, honorable—admired and respected by the entire—"

"If you think I envy a dried-up stick like Staunton, you're not nearly as clever as I thought you were."

She chuckled.

"What?"

"Oh . . . nothing." She smirked to herself at his visible irritation.

They rode in blessed silence for a few minutes, but anger, jealousy, and spite were boiling off him.

"I never did apologize for that little trick I played on you."

It pleased her that she didn't even experience a twinge at a subject that had once left her blind with humiliation and fury.

"It was my fault as well."

His lips parted in shock. "I'm sorry?"

"Yes, I should have expected that Sonia was a double-crossing snake and guessed she was in your pocket," she said, purposely misunderstanding the *trick* he was talking about.

He scowled. "I wasn't talking about that."

"Then what? Oh—" She gave him a condescending smile. "You meant when you hired an actor to pretend to be a vicar and marry us?"

"Yes," he said, eyeing her sharply. "That's what I meant."

"No apology necessary. In fact, I should be thanking you."

"*What?*"

"The notoriety was good for my career. Before you, I was just another novelty act. As the Boxing Baroness, I always take top billing. So, your *trick*—as you call it—has made me a great deal of money, Dominic."

He eyed her shrewdly for a few moments. "You are much more interesting than you were before you met me; you *should* be thanking me."

It was Marianne's turn to throw back her head and laugh.

Dominic didn't like that. "You were just another green girl—pitifully grateful for any attention from a man of my status."

It was easy to smirk at his puffed-up assessment of their past.

Especially when one considered the *status* he was referring to—that of pariah.

When she failed to take the bait, he went on. "What happened between us has given you . . . texture. And you're much more confident—it looks good on you."

"And all thanks to you," she said.

"I'd like to think I had my share in shaping you."

"So you actually did me a favor?"

"You could say that. If nothing else, I've brought you to the notice of a man like Staunton. Now that he's taken you as his mistress, I've elevated you beyond your dreams."

"So, you're something of a humanitarian, then?"

Dominic grinned. "You could call me that."

"I could also call you a traitor and a murderer."

His good humor vaporized like a drop of water on a hot stove. "Be careful with that clever mouth, darling. I need to deliver you alive to the man who wants you. But your *friends* are another matter, entirely."

The sun rose and fell twice before they finally reached their destination.

From Sin's position tied up on the floor of the caravan it was only possible to see the sky out the small window. He had no idea what direction they'd headed. The only thing he knew for sure was that they'd been increasing in elevation almost the entire time.

The days had been long, but at least Dominic had periodically sent a man to feed him and let him take care of his private business. But the hours had dragged, filled with nothing but his own unpleasant thoughts.

His fear for Marianne threatened to eat him alive. Not just what Dominic had planned for her, but how Sin was responsible for her present situation. It was, without a doubt, his fault that she was in her current predicament.

But if he was to be any help to her, he had to guard against Dominic and his incessant poking and prodding and game playing.

The other man would goad him—just as he'd always done—but now would be a terrible time to give in to his manipulation.

As for Dominic's lies about Ben, well, Sin had felt sick at his disclosure, but he'd scarcely been surprised. Deep down, he'd never really allowed himself to hope that his brother was still alive. Although he'd found the ring and letters compelling enough evidence, it had been Sin's unwillingness to believe that Dominic could make up such a horrifying lie that had really persuaded him to make this journey. He'd simply not been able to accept that the other man could have sunk so low.

And now Marianne would pay for his foolishness.

The door opened and the young man who'd brought him food last night stood in the opening. "We're here," he said, aiming his musket at Sin. "Come out and don't try anything."

As if he could. His arms had gone numb ages ago and sitting on the floor tied up for so long had made him so stiff that he could barely get up and stumble from the caravan.

He squinted into the brightness of midday, his gaze immediately drawn by the smallest castle he'd ever seen. It was built on an escarpment that overlooked a valley. Calling it a castle wasn't quite accurate; it was more like a large house with a single turret. The most impressive part of it was the stone bridge they'd just crossed, the only point of access to the castle from the rest of the mountain.

It was charming and reminded him of a dollhouse he'd bought for one of his nieces a few years back—tiny and perfect. All it was missing was a moat and drawbridge. Although the drop of at least five hundred feet was probably protection enough against invasion.

Marianne stiffly climbed down from the caravan she'd been sharing with Cecile. He only had time to exchange a quick glance, ensuring himself she was unharmed, before Dominic strode to the front of their small group.

"Welcome to Himmelhause—which translates to heavenly home." He dropped a mocking bow and turned toward the castle entrance just as a slender man in a heavily decorated military-style coat strode toward them. "For the time being you are the guests of His Royal Highness Gustav IV Adolph, true King of Sweden and ruler of Finland."

Sin wondered if he was still inside the caravan, dreaming.

The man who approached them wore kingly raiment, but a less regal king Sin could not imagine. He wasn't just slender, but gaunt in the extreme. He had a nervous tic and his arms and legs constantly shifted.

"Welcome," he said in accented English, his gaze flitting over the small group and landing on Marianne. A stillness settled over him as he stared at her, his face hardening.

Sin took a step toward her, but the two guards grabbed him.

The king did not appear to notice the slight scuffle. Instead, he walked up to Marianne with an entranced expression.

"She looks like him," he said, seemingly unable to pull his gaze away from her.

Dominic stepped up beside him, smiling, his eyes on Sin rather than Marianne. "She does, indeed. Same lips, mouth, same arrogant set to her jaw."

The king stared, riveted.

"She doesn't know," Dominic said, a gleeful smile twisting his mouth.

Sin's hands clenched.

Gustav's pale brown eyebrows shot up his forehead. "You don't know who your father is?" His lips stretched into a petulant sneer. "Who your whore of a mother is?"

Marianne must have given King Gustav the same look she'd frequently given Sin in the beginning—the one that threatened physical violence—because Gustav stepped back.

"Come, let's not have this discussion out here," Dominic said, still smiling.

The king shook himself. "No, of course not. My housekeeper has made preparations." His eyes skipped over the gathering. "Although I'm afraid I do not have rooms for so many."

"I don't think we shall need all those rooms," Dominic said, chuckling. "I think it would be best if we put several of our guests in, er, alternate accommodations."

The dungeon, like the rest of the miniature castle, was tiny. In fact, it looked as if it had once been a single cell that had been divided in half.

There was only one window, a square hole in the brick without bars or glass. It didn't need bars or glass because there was a horrifying drop waiting for anyone foolish enough to climb out of it.

Marianne couldn't help smiling. It was like something from a gothic novel: imprisoned in an evil lord's—or king's, in this case—impregnable castle.

"What are you so happy about?" Guy demanded crossly from the adjacent cell, where he was crammed in beside Barnabas on the single bench.

"I feel like I'm in one of those novels from the Minerva Press," Marianne said, her gaze flickering to Sin, who sat on the other end of the bench, with Barnabas book-ended between him and Guy.

Sin didn't smile, but his green eyes glinted with humor.

Cecile snorted and glared at the heavy wooden door that stood between them and their guards. "Minerva Press? Don't they print those books you like to read, Barnabas?"

Marianne's erstwhile uncle turned beet red.

"If we are in a book, what is the title?" Guy asked, a smile pulling at his lips.

"Something with the words *evil*, *king*, or *baron* in the title," Marianne suggested.

Everyone smiled, even though it wasn't really very funny.

Cecile leaned forward until she was touching the bars that divided her and Marianne from the three men. Sonia had not been locked with them, and was presumably free to roam the castle.

"Where were the guns?" she asked, voicing the question that had been burning a hole through Marianne's mind for hours.

"I have no idea," Guy said. He looked at Sin. "Did you plan something with Elliot that I didn't know about?"

Sin shook his head. "It wasn't I who removed the guns. And, as far as I know, it wasn't Elliot, either. He never would have done such a thing without—"

There was a flapping nose outside the window and claws scrabbled on stone as a huge black bird landed on the sill.

"Holy hell," Guy said. "Is that—"

The bird dropped a tiny knife onto the floor at Marianne's feet and then launched itself out the window.

"I can't bloody believe this," Guy muttered.

Marianne picked up the knife; it was so small it fit in the palm of her hand.

"Is that *all* she could bother to send?" Guy demanded loudly. "It's the size of a bloody toothpick, and that damned bird is big enough to carry a saber."

All four of them shushed him, but it was too late, keys rattled outside the door.

Marianne lifted her hip and slid the knife beneath her.

The guard took several moments to fumble with the lock—she suspected they were the first prisoners the king had kept in some time—and flung open the door with an irritable shove.

He pointed at Marianne. "You, come with us."

"Me?" she repeated, sliding her bottom close enough to Cecile that their hips touched.

The guard pointed at Sin. "And you, too."

Marianne hastily shoved the knife beneath Cecile as the guard waved for someone outside the cell. One of Dominic's men wedged himself into the narrow doorway, carrying a musket.

"He'll shoot one of the others if you try anything," the first guard said, having to perform contortions to get to the lock on their cell.

"Hands up," he ordered once they'd both left their cells. "Walk this way—slowly."

"Tell Strickland to send food," Guy called after them.

"And a chamber pot," Cecile added drily.

The guards marched them up the same narrow stairs they'd descended only a short time earlier.

"Where are you taking us?" the duke asked.

The two men spoke at once:

"To the—"

"No questions!"

Marianne turned to Sin. "They can perform comedic skits if the kidnapping business doesn't work out for them."

"No talking!" they both snapped.

Sin winked at her.

They kept going up when they reached the main level.

They stopped on the third floor and the guards led them down a narrow hall that had four doors off it.

"You go in here." The guard flung open the first door and pointed to Marianne.

She hesitated, but then stepped into a tiny bedroom. Before she could turn around, the door snapped shut and she heard the tumbler click.

Her new cell was, like the rest of the castle, so small it couldn't be anything but adorable. It had a narrow bed with a canopy, fine tapestries on the walls, two armoires and a large window—this one with glass, although the drop was every bit as breathtaking as the one from the dungeon.

She'd inspected most of the small space when she heard a rattle of keys and the door swung open.

An older woman dressed in the clothing of a housekeeper ushered in two men Marianne recognized as guards, now unarmed and bearing a gorgeous enameled hip bath. Behind them came four servants dressed in the garb of stable lads, each bearing a steaming bucket.

"I am Frau Meyer," the woman said after the water had been deposited and the door relocked from the outside. "I am to dress you for dinner."

"I don't have a dress with me," Marianne said. "My baggage is still down in my caravan."

The woman strode across to the armoires and opened first one and then the other, exposing a variety of garments.

Marianne leaned close, fingering a rich red velvet sleeve. "Why, these are beautiful." She took the gown from the armoire, her eyes widening. It was a style that had not been in fashion for hundreds of years. "How is it that they are so undamaged—they look almost new?"

"His Royal Highness likes to put on plays." Her pained expression told Marianne what she thought of such a frivolous pastime. "These are some of the costumes. Come," she said, "we've not been given much time. Strip and I will bathe and prepare you."

"Prepare me for what?"

"That is a question you will need to ask the king."

Chapter 32

After he'd bathed and dressed Sin was escorted down to the dining room by the same young guards.

And what a dining room it was. Thus far it was the largest room he'd seen in the small castle. But that wasn't what was unusual. It had a ceiling that went up at least twenty feet, and he could see a balcony of sorts ringing the room—a mezzanine. But there were no stairs to reach the higher level.

He wasn't surprised to find Dominic and the deposed King of Sweden already there. Both men were enjoying a glass of something, standing off to one end of the long dining table, warming themselves in front of a roaring fire.

Dominic looked up. "Ah, Staunton—looking more like yourself, I see."

Sin had, out of caution, had his valet pack one outfit of fine clothing. He had found it, along with his toiletries, waiting in the room where he'd been taken. For the first time in weeks a servant had shaved and dressed him. He felt strangely naked without his beard.

"Drink?" Dominic offered.

"Please," Sin said. As much as he wanted to beat the other man bloody, there was nothing to be gained at this point by behaving uncivilly.

Sin turned to Gustav while Dominic poured him a glass.

"Good evening, Your Highness," Sin said, dropping a court bow.

The king's gaze slid nervously to Dominic, as if he couldn't quite believe Sin's greeting was genuine.

It wasn't, of course, but again, why insult his host?

"This is quite an unusual room," Sin said, rather than asking what he really wanted to know: *Just what the hell do you want with Marianne?*

"It used to be a ballroom," Gustav said. "That area above was a minstrel's gallery. I have no need for a ballroom, so I turned it into a dining room." The king hesitated, and then added, "I must apologize for locking up you and your companions."

"Most of my companions are still locked up," Sin pointed out.

Dominic handed him a glass. "We shall let them out—once we've spoken with both you and dear Marianne and have guaranteed your cooperation. Also, Marianne will likely wish to have this conversation in private." He cocked his head and smirked. "She might even wish to send *you* away."

"If that is what she prefers, I will abide by her wishes."

Dominic laughed. "I must admit I never saw this coming—you and her," he clarified, as if Sin hadn't already guessed. "Good luck getting her to see reason and allow you to set her up somewhere in London. Lord knows I tried for long enough."

Fury boiled in his belly, and it required a herculean effort not to give in to it. But then that was what Dominic craved: conflict.

Instead, Sin said, "Marianne preferred taking a weekly beating on stage to becoming your mistress? How singular." He raised his glass and took a sip of some rather fine brandy.

Dominic's smug smile turned unpleasant. "Your tendency toward superiority is rather out of place in this situation, isn't it?"

Sin ignored the question and asked one of his own. "Were you involved in ransoming the other men—the three soldiers?"

"Not that it is any of your concern, but *no*, I was not."

"Obviously you know them," Sin said.

"We are acquainted," Dominic admitted. "If you think to get any information from me about them, you are sorely mistaken."

"Ah, honor among thieves."

"Honor is for fools, my dear Staunton. It is self-preservation that motivates me."

Before Sin could respond, the door opened and Marianne entered.

All three men stood.

Sin didn't know what the other two looked like, but he knew that his own mouth was hanging open.

She wore a red velvet gown that would have been in fashion in the fifteenth century. The bodice laced up the front with thick gold cord and the dagged sleeves were long enough that the points almost reached the floor. Her hair, which had grown out during their trip without his realizing it, was a riot of short, loose ringlets, with a gold circlet nestled among the curls. She looked as if she'd just walked out of a Renaissance painting.

She was breathtaking.

"Welcome, Miss, er, Simpson," Gustav said, the first of them to gather his wits.

She made her way into the room, her gaze on Sin. Whatever she saw on his face made her lips curl up in a mocking smile. She stopped in front of the king and dropped a graceful curtsy.

"Your Royal Highness," she murmured, and then turned to Sin. "Your Grace." She ignored Strickland entirely.

The baron laughed. "Very nice, Marianne."

Sin and Marianne locked eyes. "You look lovely," Sin said, amused when her cheeks darkened.

"You look . . . perfect, as usual," she said, her smile turning into a smirk.

"Yes, well, now that you've both engaged in mutual admiration"— Strickland yanked the servant bell and then strode back to the table— "perhaps we might all be seated. His Royal Highness is accustomed to *ladies* taking more time with their toilet, so he pushed dinner back a half hour. Now that you're here, they can serve."

Sin bristled at the other man's sarcastic emphasis on *ladies* but

Marianne didn't appear to notice. He suspected she was better at ignoring barbs than he was.

The table was large enough for sixteen, but only four places had been set at one end. Sin seated Marianne and then took the chair beside her. Strickland sat across from them, and the king, naturally, at the head of the table.

"Wine?" Strickland offered, holding up the decanter. Both Marianne and Sin nodded. It was an odd arrangement for a guest to serve other guests, but then the castle did not seem to have a great many indoor servants.

The door opened while Strickland was pouring and an older woman and two maids, rather than liveried servants, entered, each bearing platters. While the first three were busy arranging the dishes, two more servants came in, one a very old man and one very young.

"As we have so much to discuss tonight, we can serve ourselves, without interruption," Strickland said, reading Sin's perplexed expression correctly.

"What the baron is trying to say—politely—is that my modest *allowance* does not stretch far enough to cover food, shelter, *and* an adequate number of servants," Gustav said, bristling with hostility.

"Your Royal Highness has been treated most unkindly," Strickland agreed, using the soothing tone a person would employ with an unruly child. He gave Gustav a look of pure loathing when the king turned to the dishes arrayed before him and began heaping food on his plate.

So, that's how matters stood between the two men. Once again, the baron had found somebody to use to his advantage.

Sin fixed plates for both himself and Marianne, while the other two seemed to be engaging in some sort of competition for the platter containing the roast lamb. It was easy to see that the men barely tolerated each other.

The cavernous dining room was filled with the sound of cutlery and crockery clinking for several moments. Sin looked toward their host, hoping he would explain himself once he'd filled his plate, but the king was busy eating—diligently and quickly, as if afraid that the food might suddenly disappear.

Sin exchanged a look with Marianne, and she gave a slight shrug and picked up her fork.

So, they ate.

What a bizarre night and a what a fantastical place.

Marianne had not been speaking in jest when she'd said their situation felt like something from a gothic novel.

There was the castle itself, the servants—most of whom seemed very young or quite old, including Dominic's seven or eight guards—the deposed King of Sweden, a man who had all the charisma of a tree stump, and Dominic, who oozed desperation from his pores in the tradition of a bad melodrama.

But at least the food was good—simple, hearty fare, not what a royal probably expected, but good.

And at least Sin was with her.

Marianne decided that putting on the ridiculous gown and allowing the housekeeper to fuss with her hair was worth the duke's stunned expression.

She had to admit the style suited her far better than the current fashion for high waists. She lacked the bosom to look good in that sort of dress, but the structured bodice of the Renaissance gown flattered her shoulders and narrow waist and she felt strangely regal with the magnificent sleeves, which almost skimmed the floor when she walked.

Somewhere between the bath and getting dressed, the butterflies that had been flitting around her stomach for days settled.

It had turned out that seeing Dominic again hadn't been the traumatic event she'd been fearing. She felt nothing for him—other than annoyance. And she no longer felt ashamed for ever having fallen into his web. He was a very charming man, until you'd realized the truth of him, and then it was ludicrously easy to see his true character.

He had exerted himself to get to know her, and Barnabas had

encouraged her to accept his suit—after all, what else did she have in her future except a life of boxing? Only a fool would have refused an offer from a baron, even one as disgraced as Dominic.

Cecile had warned her about Dominic, but then Cecile hadn't liked any of the men who'd shown either of them attention—not even the ones she had ended up taking as lovers.

"Men are good for one thing," she'd often said. "And most of the time they are not even good for that. Don't trust a man and you will never be hurt."

Marianne had been so stunned when Dominic had offered marriage, rather than the expected carte blanche, that she'd done the unthinkable and trusted him enough to agree to spend the rest of her life with him.

She had been devastated when she'd learned the truth of their *marriage*. But her anger had been more for herself than him. And it hadn't taken much time for her to realize that she was actually far better off the way things turned out. Being married to him would have been a disaster.

Dominic was as different from St. John as two men could be.

Any woman fortunate enough to marry Sin would never want for love or support or loyalty.

If Dominic was a gothic villain, then Sin was the stuff that storybook heroes were made of: honorable, strong, and beautiful.

Marianne had seen him in his evening blacks before, of course, but that had been before she'd fallen in love with him.

He'd been achingly handsome then. Now he was heartbreaking.

He felt her gaze and smiled at her—not one of his barely there smiles, but a full-blown grin, complete with dimple.

She dropped her hand to her lap and laid it on his leg, giving his muscular thigh a hard squeeze.

His eyes darkened and his smile shifted into something hungry and—

"*A-hem*." Dominic exaggeratedly cleared his throat.

Marianne and Sin exchanged an amused glance; the duke cared as little about Dominic's opinion of them as she did.

The king's brow furrowed as he looked back and forth between them, visibly confused.

"Perhaps you might enlighten Miss Simpson now, Your Royal Highness," Dominic suggested, making it sound more like a command.

Gustav flushed and nodded vigorously, his weak chin an excellent indicator of his character.

"You have heard of me, I am sure," he said with an arrogance that grated.

It wasn't a question, which was just as well because the only thing she'd heard about Gustav was that he'd been overthrown by his own officers after a disastrous campaign in Finland.

"When the traitors in the Riksdag had the effrontery to seize my crown and give it to the usurper, they were repaid by his rapid demise. But what did they do then? Why, they gave the Swedish crown to a pawn of Bonaparte!" he ranted, no longer pale and feeble, but overwrought and unhinged.

Dominic had leaned back in his chair, watching the king with the indulgent smirk of a man who'd heard everything the king had to say many, many times.

"The Prince of Pontecorvo," Gustav spat. His gaze sharpened on Marianne. "A man too busy doing the Corsican's bidding to even bother to visit the country that offered him a crown." He ground his teeth. "And then there is his *wife*! A Catholic whore who remains in Paris, even now, no doubt spreading her legs in celebration of her former lover's return." He was breathing heavily. "A whore who is, in fact, *your* mother, Marianne *Simpson*."

Marianne blinked, unable to scrape together a single word.

"I would remind you that you are in the presence of a lady, Your Royal Highness." Sin's voice was like a blast of frigid air.

The king gave a hysterical laugh. "A lady! That is true, but only by unholy means. The spawn of an unfaithful wife and the scourge of Europe."

"Are you actually saying that Miss Simpson's mother is married to the Prince of Pontecorvo?" Sin demanded in disbelief.

"That is exactly what I am saying!" Gustav was clutching his fork and eyeing Marianne as if he were going to leap across the table and stab her with it. "And she and her husband now style themselves the Crown Prince and Princess of Sweden."

Dominic chuckled in a way that made Marianne want to break his jaw. "Perhaps I might elucidate, Your Royal Highness?"

The king gave an abrupt, savage nod.

Dominic turned to them. "Through a serendipitous series of events, King Gustav is privy to an interesting bit of information. Ever since Désirée, the crown princess, abandoned her son and the prince and moved back to Paris, there have been a number of—well, there is no pleasant way to say this—spies in her household. Some report to her husband, some to the Riksdag, and some . . . let's just say some of the little ears listening are entrepreneurs willing to sell information to the highest bidder. His Royal Highness and I were just beginning to despair that neither of us would ever find a way out of this delightful little backwater when we learned that Désirée had been a very naughty princess twenty-one years ago." He grinned. "Not until I was in Paris last year and saw a rendering of the crown princess in the newspaper did I realize just how serendipitous my newfound knowledge was. Because, lo and behold! I recalled exactly where I'd seen that face before: in a locket I once found in a Whitechapel theater. You can imagine my chagrin when I realized just whose portrait that was."

"I'm surprised you didn't steal the locket," Marianne spat.

Rather than be offended, he grinned. "I did give it some thought, but I knew your uncle—er, Barnabas—would have made a stink about such a theft. And I was in no position to deal with Barney's wrath on the issue . . . at the time." He shrugged. "But no matter, the idea had been planted, and eight months ago I was finally able to do something about it, so I paid the crown princess a visit. It was not difficult to find her . . . Even though she is supposedly living incognita, everyone knows of her."

"Why in the world would she agree to see *you*?" Marianne asked.

He took a sip of wine, unruffled by her scathing tone. "The reason she agreed to see me is because I mentioned having seen two rather fascinating miniatures in a lovely locket."

"*Two*," she repeated, rising from her chair. "You *did* steal from Barnabas. You thieving—"

The king lifted a pistol from beneath the table and aimed it in her direction, his shaking hand revealing that he wasn't entirely comfortable handling a firearm.

Dominic carefully reached over and laid his hand over the king's. The two men stared at each other for a long moment before Gustav scowled and released the pistol.

Dominic set it down beside his wineglass and turned to Marianne. "Please sit."

Sin's hand landed on her arm. "Marianne," he murmured softly.

"Yes, do listen to him, dear," Dominic advised.

Marianne sat. "You stole that other miniature."

"I did not," he said, his expression one of wounded virtue. "No, my dear, that miniature was in Barney's possession until only a few nights ago—when I took his precious satchel from him."

Still grinning like a maniac, he reached inside his coat and took out a small fabric-wrapped package. "Would you like to see it, Marianne?"

Marianne's temples pounded as he slid the miniature across the table. She picked it up, stared at it, and gave a sharp bark of laughter. "You are mad!"

"No, my dear, I'm afraid it's true."

"May I?" Sin asked.

She handed him the miniature without speaking.

"Good God." His head whipped up. "What sort of idiocy—"

Dominic raised a hand. "If you listen, I will tell you a story."

He paused long enough for Marianne to jerk out a nod.

"Not quite a year after Bonaparte married Joséphine, he was on campaign when he received a letter informing him of his beloved wife's infidelity with a French officer. He crossed hundreds and hundreds of miles like a madman to return to Paris. His confrontation with Joséphine was . . . explosive. Never again would he worship the wife to whom he'd once penned pages and pages of love letters. While he was in Paris, he went to see a woman he'd once loved—a woman he'd treated shabbily. He had been engaged to Désirée but had done the unthinkable and broken off the engagement. In spite of that, the two remained close friends, and, on that occasion—became lovers. Both Désirée and Bonaparte were married to other people, of course. Nine months later Désirée found herself in a rather delicate position. You see, she had not seen her own husband for almost a year, as he was also on campaign, and so she had a difficult decision to make. That was you—my dear Marianne, you were the decision."

She looked down at the miniature again, as if it would tell her something. The man in the portrait had an infamous face—she'd seen countless renderings in newspapers, but never an actual painting. Yes, his nose, perhaps his jaw, and most especially his mouth, resembled her own, but many people looked like somebody else. It happened all the time.

She looked up. "It could be a coincidence."

"Perhaps. But the letter, that is no coinci—"

"Barnabas told me about the letter from Sandrine—"

"No, my dear—not that letter," Dominic said. "The one from your real mother."

Her chest hurt, as if she'd been punched. "My mother? But—I don't—" She broke off and glared at Dominic. "Even if this is true—what does it mean to you?" She turned to the king. "Or to you? Do you really believe you'll be able to blackmail money out of a royal?"

"Think about it for a moment, you fool!" Gustav snapped. "If the Crown Princess of Sweden gave birth to Bonaparte's child *while* married to the crown prince—how eager do you think my people will be to go through with a coronation? Who is to say that their son—their only child as far as my country knows—isn't Bonaparte's, as well? Already there is unhappiness about Désirée and the fact that she refuses to live in the country that has chosen to take her as its queen. But to take Napoleon's whore as its queen?" He gave an ugly laugh. "Impossible!"

"You really believe that my existence will be enough to force the crown prince to step aside?" It was her turn to laugh. "Who is the fool?"

Gustav shouted something in his own language. Marianne suspected it was less than flattering.

"We shall use you however we see fit!" the king snapped, his hand curving around his table knife so tightly his knuckles were white. "You can either come along quietly—and politely—or we can tie you up and put you in a crate."

"Come along *where*?"

"To Sweden, of course."

Marianne gave a choked laugh, looking from the king's furious face to Dominic's smirking one. The baron shrugged slightly, his mocking expression telling her that he had no faith in the scheme and was only humoring the demented ex-monarch. Probably for money.

Why was she even a little surprised? It was pure Dominic—using somebody as a tool to reach his own ends.

"And what do you get out of this?" she demanded.

"The satisfaction of knowing that I have done the right and honorable thing," Dominic said. His pious expression melted into a familiar wicked grin. "Oh, and a great deal of money from your mother."

Her mind was reeling so wildly it was hard to assemble any words. "If you think that two miniatures and my presence will convince anyone of your wild story, you are both delusional. Even *I* don't believe you."

"You are forgetting the letter," Dominic said, reaching into his coat pocket again.

"Something else of mine you stole?" she retorted.

"Think of it this way, my dear, if it had been up to Barnabas, you would never have learned the truth. He will insist that he kept you in ignorance of your birth because your mother requested his confidence, but I think we both know the real reason he kept his mouth shut was because of the money." He smiled unpleasantly. "If not for me, you might have lived your entire life in ignorance. So, you should be thanking me."

She snorted and reached out for the letter.

"Why are you giving that to her?" Gustav demanded petulantly.

"What harm can it do?" Dominic asked.

The king scowled. "And we are just to sit here and wait on her?"

"We are in no great hurry and the meal is not yet finished, Your Royal Highness." Dominic cut an irritable glance at the table, which was still laden with the remains of their cooling dinner. "Where are the servants? Why haven't they cleared the table? Is there no dessert tonight?"

"Ring the bell again," the king ordered. "Frau Meyer said there was to be streusel."

Marianne gave the two men a glare of loathing, blocked out their babbling, and unfolded the letter.

My Dearest Marianne:

I am writing this now, when you are only one month old, so that you may read it on your twenty-first birthday and know that your mother loves you.

It is my hope that you are a happy English girl who has grown to womanhood under the care of Sandrine Simpson, a woman who has always been as close to me as my own sister Julie.

Where to begin this story?

I suppose at the beginning.

I was born Désirée Clary.

Your father—who now goes by the name Napoleon Bonaparte—and I have known and loved one another for years. The love remained constant on my side but waned on his.

It was Napoleon who broke our engagement to marry another woman—she was called Rose, then, but he never cared for the

name and preferred to call her Joséphine. That is your father in
a nutshell, Marianne: bold and fearless, but, I'm afraid, often
insensitive and selfish.

I could see that he was truly in love with her in a way he'd
never been with me—a passionate and consuming love.

Because my sister Julie—your aunt—married his brother
Joseph, I was kept close to the family and moved with them to
Paris.

Was I angry and hurt? My pride, I think, more than my
heart.

Your father felt guilty for what he'd done to me and wished to
see me married—to assuage his conscience. Because of him I was
introduced to eligible men and encouraged to marry.

And so I married one of your father's generals, a fine, noble
man, although I cannot say that we have ever loved one another.

The story of how you came about is, in some ways, known
by most of the world. Your father discovered Josephine had taken a
lover. The letter he wrote her was passionate and filled with pain.
The British captured the courier with the letter and the subject was
used to humiliate him all over Europe.

There is one part of the story that only a few know. When
your father returned to Paris, it was not his wife he went to first. It
was me.

Am I ashamed that I received him?

I find that I cannot be.

My husband has his mistress.

Joséphine has her lover.

And Napoleon has numerous women.

What I did is not, for our sort, unusual.

But to have a child when my husband was obviously not the
father?

No, I could not allow that to be known. It would have
destroyed too many lives.

I have deprived you of much you should have had as my legal
daughter. Why did I do so? I cannot lie that a great part of my

reason was to avoid the shame and scandal. I knew you would always bear the stigma of your birth. Life at court is a shallow, pointless existence and I despise it. I wanted better for you.

But it is also true that I feared for your life, Marianne. To be the child of Napoleon is not a safe or comfortable burden. The attempts on his life have been legion. No. I wanted you somewhere safe and secure.

Do you hate me for what I have done to you? Do you hate me for keeping you in ignorance of your birth until now? Can you forgive me? Although I can never acknowledge you as my daughter, I like to think that perhaps one day . . .

But that is a foolish desire, and I shall put it aside.

As I look down at you now, lying beside my desk in your cradle, I think of all I will miss—but I pray you will live a freer, more joy-filled life than I could ever give you here.

My love to you always,

Your mother, Désirée"

The writing wavered on the page, and Marianne stared at the parchment, her mind whirling as she tried to absorb what she had just read.

She didn't want to look up—to be pulled into a discussion about desserts and lazy servants. She wanted to creep out to the caravan and lock herself inside and pull the blankets over her head.

"Just what the devil is going on!"

Dominic's angry voice jerked her head up and she turned to where he was staring.

An old woman stood in the doorway, hunched over and dressed in the clothing of a laundry woman or kitchen servant.

"Who the hell are you? Where is Frau Meyer?" Dominic demanded.

"I am Gerta—I work in the kitchen." Her voice was shaky, as was her person.

"What are you doing up here?"

"Men came—men with guns—and all the others ran off."

"What men?" Dominic screeched as he shoved back his chair hard enough to send it clattering to the floor. In his hand was the pistol that had been on the table; he pointed it at the old woman.

The king, Sin, and Marianne all got to their feet.

"Put down the gun, Strickland," Sin said.

Dominic took a step back, moving the gun from the woman to Sin. "I think it would be a good idea if you sat back down, Your Grace. *Now*," he ordered when Sin hesitated.

The duke sat.

When Marianne began to lower herself back in her seat, Dominic shook his head. "No. You come over here, right next to me. If there are strange men with guns in the castle, I'm guessing it has something to do with you. They won't shoot me if you are beside me."

Sin laid a staying hand on her forearm. "The way you're waving that gun around, Strickland, somebody will get hurt."

"And it could very easily be *you*, Staunton," Dominic snarled. "Now get over here!" he ordered Marianne.

Marianne squeezed Sin's hand before going to stand where Dominic was pointing.

"There's a smart girl. Now," he said, turning back toward the woman.

Instead of standing by the door, the servant was barely ten feet away.

"Here then," Dominic said, frowning. "Get back. What are you—"

The old woman moved so quickly her hand blurred. Something silver flashed across the room.

Dominic screamed, dropped the gun, and grabbed his bleeding hand.

"That's not a good idea, Your Royal Highness. Miss Tremblay never misses."

Marianne jolted and whipped around at the familiar voice, which sounded as if it had come from the heavens.

It was Guy, and he was up on the mezzanine level. Beside him was Cecile, leaning low over a rifle that was pointed at Gustav.

The king had backed up to the fireplace when everyone's attention was elsewhere and was reaching for a pistol on the mantel.

"Hands up," Guy ordered.

Gustav complied.

"It's good to see you both," Sin called up to his friend.

"Did you save any food for us?" Guy asked.

"You . . . *bitch*."

Marianne turned at the sound of Dominic's voice. His face was puckered in pain and he was squeezing his arm, glaring at the old woman, who was—

"Blade!" Marianne blurted.

Jo gave her one of her sleepy smiles. "Hello, Marianne."

"You just about cut off my bloody arm," Dominic whined.

"Does it hurt, Dom?" Marianne asked.

"What the hell do you thi—"

Marianne knew it would hurt, but she didn't care.

Her hand exploded when it struck Dominic's jaw, but watching him hit the floor was well worth any broken bones.

"You were right about keeping my hands tied up, Dominic," Marianne said, shaking out her hand.

"I can personally vouch that she has an excellent right cross," Elliot called out as he strode into the room, followed closely by Barnabas and Sonia.

"It's good to see your face, old man," Sin said.

Elliot gave one of his rare grins. "It's good to be seen. I'll admit it was touch-and-go for a while, thanks to our friend Dominic, here."

Dominic pushed himself up until he was sitting on the floor, still cradling his bleeding arm. "How in the name of all that is unholy did you get away from Broussard? The man has thirty-five armed men!"

"I had some excellent help." Elliot cut a look at Blade, who was stripping off the big white mob cap and heavy clothing she'd been wearing, exposing a pair of battered breeches, old coat, and boots.

"One bloody woman?" Dominic scoffed.

"She took you down quickly enough," Elliot pointed out, smirking.

Dominic glared up at him and struggled to his feet, clutching his arm. "I don't suppose you'll—"

"You lying, cheating son of a whore!" Barnabas shoved past Jo and Elliot and barreled right into Dominic, flinging him to the floor for the third time in less than ten minutes. He straddled the other man's much larger body, grabbed his lapels, and banged his head on the floor. "We had a bargain—I helped you plan your *death* and got you out of Britain and you were supposed to leave that goddamned book. You always—"

Elliot and Jo marched up on either side of Barnabas and slid hands under his arms, lifting the squirming, thrashing older man off Dominic's body and setting him on his feet.

Dominic struggled to his feet, glaring at Barnabas with loathing. "How dare you lay hands on me, you—" He lunged at Barnabas, as if he were going to strike him, but at the last moment he slid an arm around his neck, the elbow of his bleeding arm locking tight, clutching a knife—probably the one Blade had thrown at his arm—in his undamaged hand.

"Get back!" Dominic snarled at Jo and Elliot, dragging Barnabas along with him as he backed up to the fireplace, where the king stood gawking.

"Now," he said when he'd reached the wall. "I want all of you out of this room—and I want His Royal Highness's post chaise harnessed, with Staunton's trunk full of money in it."

"Or what?" Guy shouted from up on the balcony.

"Or I'll kill Barnabas." He gave an ugly laugh. "He's not much of a hostage, I'll admit—but I know there aren't any murderers among you beacons of morality willing to—"

"I'm sorry for everything, Marianne," Barnabas said, his voice strangely calm as his hand slid into his opposite sleeve and he pulled out a knife.

"Uncle—no!" She lunged toward him as he drove the knife into Dominic's side.

And then three things happened at once: Dominic plunged the blade into Barnabas's throat, an ear-shattering bang filled the room, and Dominic's head exploded, showering the room in bone, blood, and brain matter.

"Nooooo!" Sonia screamed, her agonized cry drowned out by Gustav's far louder shriek.

Marianne pulled away from Sin's grasp and ran to her uncle, dropping to the floor where he'd fallen. She took one look at the huge wound in his throat and knew there was no hope.

Barnabas fumbled for her hand, his lips moving, but no sound emerged as his life blood pumped from him.

Sonia fell to her knees on Barnabas's other side, weeping loudly while she tried to close the gaping slash in his neck.

Marianne squeezed his hand. "I love you, Uncle."

She would never know if he'd heard her. Barnabas was there one second, and gone the next, leaving an empty shell in place of the man she'd always believed to be her only living relative.

Chapter 33

"Staunton?"

Sin looked up at the sharpness in Guy's voice. Both he and Cecile had come down from the minstrel's gallery, whose staircase must be somewhere outside the dining room.

They hovered by the door, where Gustav was attempting to sidle past them.

Sin strode over to the king, who looked pitifully small between Guy and Cecile, who was still cradling her Baker rifle.

"Where are you going, Your Royal Highness?" he asked.

Gustav's guilty gaze flickered to the table before jumping away. Sin turned to see what he'd been staring at, and then swung back when he realized what was missing.

"That letter is not yours." He held out a hand.

"I don't need it—I can tell the truth without it." Gustav's face was a canvas of impotent rage.

"You could," Sin agreed. "But who would listen? Besides, you must know that even with this letter, your cause is hopeless at best and dangerous at worst."

"Those fools in the Riksdag should know what they are getting!" he shouted, the veins pulsing beneath the thin skin of his temples.

"Give me the letter."

Gustav scowled but reached into his coat and slapped the letter into Sin's palm. "There, *Your Grace*. Now all of you can get out of my home."

"Not quite. The miniature, too, please."

The king cut loose with a stream of angry Swedish.

"I never got a chance to ask Strickland," Sin said, "but how is it that you and he came to be working together?"

Gustav clenched his jaw and Sin thought he might tell him to go to hell. Instead, he said, "I met him at a country house not far from here—he'd come to play cards." His eyes narrowed as he looked across the room, to what was left of Dominic. "I didn't know it then, but he'd gotten on Beauvais's bad side somehow. I daresay he tried to take more than his share." He shrugged. "He needed money and was willing to do anything to get it. He wasn't much to work with, but he was all I had." He glared from Sin, to Guy, and then took a step back at the cold, empty expression on Cecile's face. "As for *you*. At least one of you has committed murder in my house," he accused, jabbing a finger at her. "If you know what is—"

Guy stepped between them, glowering. "Watch your tone, *Your Royal Highness*."

Gustav recoiled. "Where are my servants? Did you kill them, too?"

"Most of them are down in the kitchen—I told them it was a holiday and to indulge themselves. The last time I saw them, they were in your wine cellar," Guy said. "But your men—those who were armed, are in your dungeon." He smiled unpleasantly. "Since there are nine of them, they're a bit cramped."

Jo came to stand beside the king, moving in the eerily silent way she had. "They can stay in the cell until tomorrow, after we leave." She gestured toward the open doorway, where a small cluster of scruffy men stood in the corridor. "Take His Royal Highness to his chambers and make sure he doesn't leave them until after we're gone."

Gustav sputtered as an unsavory looking fellow in greasy leathers, hefting a wicked cudgel, pushed into the room and seized him by the arm. The newcomer grinned down at the king, the expression more than a little terrifying. "I always wanted to see how the other half lived."

"Now wait just a—"

Gustav's captor slapped a hand over the king's mouth and dragged the scuffling ex-monarch from the room.

Once they'd gone, Guy said, "We're going to the kitchen to find something to eat." He cut a quick but significant glance at Cecile, who was staring in horror at Strickland's body, which had slid down the wall but was still mostly upright, half his head missing.

"Of course," Sin said.

Guy carefully pried Cecile's fingers from the rifle and handed it to one of Jo's men before escorting the stunned woman from the room.

Jo marched over to one of the windows, grabbed the velvet drape, and gave it a yank that pulled down the rod, both drapes, and sizeable chunks of plaster.

She motioned to her remaining henchmen—and, Sin noticed, two henchwomen—and gestured to the two bodies. "You can use these to wrap them up. Take them out into the courtyard. The old man in the stables will know who in the village to summon to bury them."

The men and women got to work without delay.

"You might have just rung for some old sheets instead of destroying the place," Elliot said mildly.

Jo ignored him and jerked her chin to where Sonia still knelt beside Barnabas. "What about her?" she asked, her opal gaze cold as it flickered over the sobbing woman.

"That's up to Marianne," Sin said.

He saw a flash of pity on Marianne's face as she looked at the older woman. "She's a traitor and a spy, but I don't have the desire to drag her back and see her punished. Barnabas loved her. He may have been a liar, a cheat, and a spy, but he did his best by me. I don't care what she does—as long as she never returns to England."

Sonia cut her a look that wasn't nearly as grateful as it should have been as she followed the men who carried the velvet-wrapped bundles from the room.

Jo strolled over to the table, sat down in the king's vacated chair, and began eating the remains of his dinner.

Sin snorted and turned to Elliot, who grinned. "She does whatever she wants, whenever she wants," Elliot said, sounding almost . . . proud. He then dropped into Dominic's chair, shoved away the plate of food, and dragged the platter of roasted fowl toward him "I hope neither of you mind? I'm afraid we've been a little too busy to eat."

"Help yourself," Sin said. He pulled out a chair for Marianne and then sat beside her. "Tell us what has been going on since we last spoke."

"Well, Strickland had spies watching us from the moment we stepped off the packet in Calais," Elliot said in between bites.

"Why didn't you tell me that?" Sin asked, exasperated.

"Because I didn't know." Elliot jerked his chin toward Jo. "She's the one who told me."

"Why didn't *you* tell us?" he asked Blade.

She didn't appear to hear him and kept eating.

"Jo?" Marianne said.

Elliot chuckled when she didn't look up. "If she doesn't want to hear you, she really won't hear you." He continued his story. "Strickland revealed my identity to that same band who caused such problems in Lille, the Red Cats, and they grabbed me just as I was headed into Charleville. They roughed me up a bit, but before they could turn me over to the authorities and claim the reward for me—"

"What?"

Elliot ignored his outburst as effectively as Blade had done.

"—Miss Brown and the fellows you just met showed up."

The woman in question was refilling her wineglass.

"Miss Brown has been one step ahead of us—and Strickland—ever since we arrived in France," Elliot continued. "She suspected either Barnabas or Sonia, or both, were colluding with Strickland, so she didn't want to make herself known to any of us."

"You took the guns from the caravan?" Sin asked.

"Yes—sorry I didn't tell you. But Miss Brown didn't want to apprehend Strickland before he led you all back to his lair. She wanted to make sure she had access to any information he was planning to use to extort Marianne. So we followed you here." He cut Marianne a quick look. "Your locket and the pretty enamel box are both safe, by the way."

"Thank you."

"How did you get past the guards?" Sin asked. "I know they weren't exactly threatening, but they had guns."

"Yes, and that's why Miss Brown came in first. She managed to distract them all just long enough to prevent an exchange of gunfire. Cecile and Guy used the knife Angus brought to pick the locks on their cells. And they were free and waiting when we arrived."

"Distract them how?" Sin asked.

"Arlette, Monique—the two ladies you just saw with the other gentlemen—and Miss Brown dressed up like, er—"

"Prostitutes," Jo said, pushing away the plate and glancing around for a napkin. When she didn't see one, she wiped her hands on the sleeves of her filthy coat.

"Who *are* you?" Marianne asked her. "And why did you do all this?"

Jo threw back the contents of the king's wineglass and then fixed her flat gray stare on Marianne. "Who I am doesn't matter. As for why: I was paid to keep you safe and get to the bottom of Strickland's scheme. I was also paid to bring you to Reims."

"Reims," the duke snapped before Marianne could say anything. "That would be madness."

It was only the second time she'd heard Staunton raise his voice.

"Yes, Reims," Jo repeated calmly.

"And what is in Reims?" Sin demanded.

"I was paid to keep that information to myself," Jo said. As usual, she had a knife in her hand and was spinning it, looking sleepy and bored. "But it was the same person who paid me to look out for Marianne on this journey."

Marianne set a hand on the duke's arm when he looked as if he'd argue. "I assume this is somebody who can answer my questions?"

"I'm not paid to know that."

Sin gave a snort of annoyance.

"I'll go," Marianne said, giving Sin's arm a gentle squeeze.

"Only Marianne needs to come," Jo said. "I'll escort her home afterward. The rest of you are free to leave whenever you want." She cut Elliot a wry look. "That includes you, Mr. Wingate."

"I'm going where Marianne goes," Sin retorted before Elliot could respond. "I hope that won't be a problem." His tone said he didn't care if it was.

Jo gave her knife one last spin and then shoved it into the top of her boot. "It makes no difference to me what you do."

"I'm going, too."

Cecile's voice came from the doorway, where she stood with Guy, both bearing platters of food. She glared at Jo. "I see you've already fed yourself. And you—" She turned her glare on Marianne. "Don't try to talk me out of coming with you."

"I'll be grateful for your company," Marianne said honestly.

Guy sighed. "Well, then I guess I might tag along. Elliot, will you be joining us?"

"I've nothing else pressing."

Jo gave him a long, cool look. "We'll leave first thing in the morning." She rose from her chair and strode to the door. "I'll make sure the men ready the caravans."

"I'll help you," Elliot said, not two steps behind her.

Cecile put the platter down with a loud clunk and then dropped into a chair with a disgruntled sigh. "Why do I even bother?"

"Don't worry, darling, I'll eat it all," Guy soothed.

"Marianne—these are yours," Sin said. He held the letter and miniature in his palm.

She smiled. "I feel like you're always giving me letters, Your Grace." She met his concerned green gaze. "Would you like to read it?"

"Are you sure?"

"I'm sure," she said. It hurt to add the next few words, but she knew the piece of paper was too incriminating to keep, even if it was the only letter she'd ever received from one of her parents. "I want you to read it before I burn it."

Later that same evening

Marianne collapsed on Sin's chest, winded.

"You're losing your stamina," Sin murmured beneath her.

She laughed. "I wouldn't talk if I were you, old man—you sound a bit breathless yourself."

"Old man?" he repeated menacingly, rolling her over so swiftly her head spun, until he was looking down at her, their bodies still joined. "Do I feel old to you?" he asked, flexing his shaft.

"Pax!" she whimpered when his pulsing hips ground against her already overstimulated flesh. "I didn't mean it."

His nostrils flared, his barely there smirk triumphant. They both hissed when he withdrew and rolled to his side, propping himself on his elbow and staring down at her with a hungry, adoring look that never grew old, his fingers stroking the damp hair back from her temple.

"Marry me."

Marianne's heart, which had just begun to slow, thundered in her ears. "Sin—"

"Why not?"

"Because . . . you can't."

"There is no law forbidding it." He gave her the same haughty look she'd seen on his face that first morning. But now she knew the man behind it—a man who gave his heart rarely and loved deeply when he did.

She laughed weakly. "I am flattered—no, no, no," she said, when he opened his mouth to argue. "Let me finish."

He scowled.

"I'm beyond flattered. But can you honestly say that marrying the Boxing Baroness won't jeopardize your standing in Parliament—

and among your peers? All the causes you've worked so long and hard to promote?"

"It might matter to a few people, but—"

"Marrying me would destroy everything you've sacrificed for and worked so hard to build. The people of Staunton and—"

"What are you talking about?" He pushed himself up, until he was looming over her. "What sacrifices? And what do you know about Staunton?"

"You gave up so much for your people—you gave up the love of your life, so that—"

"Stop." His pale green eyes were frostier than they'd been in weeks. "I can only imagine that Guy has been talking to you?"

Marianne chewed her lower lip.

He said something vulgar and then winced. "I'm sorry, darling—that was uncalled for."

"Please don't yell at Guy."

"I'm not going to yell at him, I'm going to go seven rounds with him—or as long as it takes for me to beat him senseless." He snorted. "Although I should probably aim for sense-*ful* in his case."

"He only meant to—"

"What rubbish did he tell you and when?" His eyes narrowed. "Oh!" he shouted before she could answer. "That—that—meddling, interfering—" he sputtered.

She laughed at his crazed expression. "I've never imagined this side of you even existed."

"When somebody meddles with the woman I love, I tend to get a bit starchy." He glared down at her open-mouthed face. "Yes, you heard that right. I love you, Marianne. I don't care what twaddle Guy poured into your ears—in Lille?" he guessed. She nodded. "I knew it. That's why you didn't come to me?" She nodded again. Sin looked like he was chewing the inside of his cheek to ribbons to keep from cursing.

"Tell me again," Marianne said softly.

His gaze sharpened as he came back from wherever he'd gone—

likely to some future where he was pummeling his friend. "I love you, Marianne," he said without hesitation, kissing her savagely to punctuate his words. "Guy told you about Jenny, didn't he?"

"Yes, and—"

"*You* are the love of my life."

"But—"

"I loved Jenny—I always will. But she was the love of my boyhood, Marianne. I was seventeen when I gave her up. I was unhappy about it—make no mistake—but I came to terms with myself before I offered for Vanessa. And I was honest with her. I told her I wasn't in love with her, but that I'd commit my life to her. And I would have. I came to care for her deeply." He caressed her face, his magnificent eyes consuming her. "But *you*—you are the love of my life. Shh, what's this?" he murmured, wiping away the tears she'd not known were falling.

"It would wreck your life, Sin. You would be shunned—"

He laid a finger across her lips. "All will be fine. There will be scandal—the sort the *ton* adores. John Lade married—"

"Lade is a degenerate baron, *not* Lord Flawless."

He frowned at the title he hated. "This won't be the first time a duke has married—"

"You are going to say the Gunning sisters. But they were the daughters of a viscount, not—"

"Not the daughter of the Queen of Sweden and the Emperor of France?"

"Good Lord, St. John! That would only make matters a hundred times worse."

"Say that again."

"I said that would only make—"

"Not that—my name."

Marianne growled. "How can you jest about this?"

"I never jest about my name."

"If the truth about my lineage were ever to see the light of day, you would be ruined."

"With that letter gone, there is no proof, Marianne. Nobody

would ever believe such a thing. Hell, I hardly believe it and I *know* it's true. Now," he said, lifting his body over hers and pushing her thighs wide. "I have better things to do than argue with my betrothed."

Marianne stared helplessly as he settled between her legs and proceeded to wipe thoughts of any kind from her mind.

There would be only two caravans on the trip to Reims, as Marianne had given Barnabas's caravan to Sonia.

Sin had no idea what, if anything, Marianne had said to Sonia. He just knew the other woman would not, thankfully, be joining them on their journey.

As they were loading up to leave, Marianne marched up to the caravan Sin shared with Guy and Elliot and tossed her valise into the wagon.

"I'm going with you," she said, crossing her arms.

Guy, who'd been about to put his own bags back in the caravan, stared at Marianne, puzzled. "But—"

Cecile, who was leaning against the women's caravan, sighed and said, "Pick up your bags, my lord."

Guy obeyed without hesitation, and then looked disgruntled when he realized what he'd done. Cecile grabbed his arm and marched him toward the other caravan.

When Sin turned back to Marianne, her confident expression had turned pensive. "You don't mind?"

"Mind?" he asked haughtily. "I was going to *command* you to stay with me."

She laughed, as he'd hoped, and began to climb inside.

He laid a hand on her arm. "Wait—don't we need to drive?"

"No. Elliot will drive one and Jo the other."

"Hmm," he murmured. "That's convenient."

Sin found out just *how* convenient over the next six days.

They made love all the way to Reims—a journey that sped by far too quickly—only seeing Cecile and Guy when they made camp at night and met for breakfast in the mornings.

Where Jo and Elliot stayed, neither of them knew.

"Do you think they are, er—"

"Lovers?" Sin suggested.

They were wrapped up in each other's arms, naked and sweaty, so the fact that she was blushing seemed oddly charming.

It was their last night on the road together and there was a certain tension between them. He was glad to talk of somebody else rather than the unanswered questions between them.

"Jo doesn't seem to notice he's alive," he said.

Marianne smirked. "No, but Elliot has certainly noticed *her*."

"She is actually very pretty, once you get past all the knives," Sin said.

"And her bird."

They laughed.

"Yes, getting accustomed to Angus would be . . . challenging," Sin agreed.

"Does Elliot have a mistress in London?" she asked.

Sin frowned at the question. "I don't know. He is a man who keeps such matters very private."

"Hmm." She twisted her finger in the hairs on his chest.

Sin winced and laid a staying hand over hers. "What is wrong? You have become full of fidgets suddenly."

"Do you keep a mistress in London?" She swallowed. "Or a lover?"

"Not at the moment," he said, his mind flickering back to his last, very unpleasant, conversation with Alanna.

"But you have in the past."

"Yes, in the past."

"How long in the past?"

Sin took her chin and tilted her face to his. "I think this is not a very productive subject."

"Don't you wonder about me and Dominic?"

"I try not to think about it."

"But you *have* thought about it."

Sin sighed. "What is this really about, Marianne?"

"I was just wondering."

"Yes?"

"When you marry—"

"You mean when *we* marry," he corrected.

She didn't argue, but neither did she agree. That was fine. Sin still had plenty of time to convince her.

"What did you want to ask," he prodded.

"When you marry will you keep a mistress?"

He pushed up onto his elbows. "Don't you know me well enough to answer that?"

She winced at his sharp tone.

"I'm sorry," he apologized. "I should not have been short with you. But I am . . . offended."

She pulled him back down. He resisted for only a moment, before lying beside her again. She laid her head on his chest. "I'm horridly jealous," she admitted, the confession surprising him.

"Well, I hope I never give you any reason to be jealous." He smoothed a hand over her hair and held her tight to his chest. "I am like one of those birds who mate for life."

"You mean a vulture?"

He barked a laugh. "You little beast." He pushed his hand below the blankets and pinched her bum, making her squeal. "I was thinking of some more regal bird."

"Like a goose?"

He rolled his eyes. "Yes, Marianne—just like a goose."

Her body shook with laughter.

Sin felt a silly smile spread across his face; was there anything more intimate than laughing with one's lover after making love? If so, he couldn't think of it.

A moment later, she shattered his warm contentment.

"I know you are nothing like Dominic, but I never would have believed that he would have done to me what he did, either. So, I guess . . ."

"You don't trust your own judgment?"

She nodded, her silky hair tickling his chest.

Sin had hoped to leave this particular story buried forever, but he suspected it was still too close to the surface for Marianne to forget it.

"Why don't you tell me what happened, love."

She wanted to quit picking at the subject—an abhorrent one to her—but something drove her to keep at it, even after Sin made it clear he didn't want to know. She couldn't blame him—she didn't want to know about his lovers either. Not how many there were, how beautiful they were, or any other details.

But . . .

"Why don't you tell me what happened, love."

She squeezed her eyes shut, as if she could keep the feeling swelling in her, trapped inside. She loved him *so much*. But for a time, she had felt almost as obsessed with Dominic. He, too, had said he loved her. He'd charmed her, courted her, and made her feel like the only woman for him.

She told herself she'd been more naïve, just out of school. Barnabas, for all his faults, had kept her away from Dominic until after she'd begun to box, and then he'd suddenly encouraged her to eat dinner with Dominic.

"He courted me—he could be very charming and came across as the perfect gentleman. He never behaved inappropriately with me, always insisting on a chaperone. It was . . ."

"Intoxicating? Overwhelming? Flattering?"

"Yes, all of those things."

"I saw Dominic when he put himself out to please, Marianne. I was taken in by his charm in other ways time and time again. He used us all. You were not alone in being fooled. He was blessed with many talents, and one of them was the ability to entrance people. At least for a time."

"Well, he entranced me long enough to lure me into a ceremony."

Sin had heard of the sort of ceremony she meant.

"Almost as soon as we moved to his house in Chatham he began to change. At first it was little things—like staying out all night. But then he began to bring people to the house."

He heard her swallow.

"I grew up in a circus—I should have been . . . hardened against debauchery. But you spent time with us. You know how strict Barnabas was."

"I know," Sin said. "I'll admit I was surprised when I saw how little occurred in the way of—"

"*Vice*, I think was the word you used."

Sin smiled wryly. "You are correct. I was very wrong lumping the Fayre in with those others."

She kissed his chest and continued. "I was appalled by what Dominic made people do. And everyone who worked for him was so desperate and beaten down. He held parties every night, and life became more sordid daily. And then I caught him in one of the guest chambers in bed with two women."

Sin squeezed her tight but remained silent.

"I didn't know what to do, Sin. I believed we were married and that I was trapped. It was . . . horrible. And then there was that announcement in the paper and I discovered that Dominic had already *been* married for almost a year." She snorted. "I now suspect that he was behind the sudden, mysterious announcement—it was a perfect way to get rid of me without having to tell me the truth himself." She pushed up onto her elbows, until she was looking down at him. "He knew who my father was by then—he'd seen the letter and locket. I'm guessing he'd had his escape from England planned for some time, and I believe he'd thought to use me when he went to France. I think he hoped I would be a feather in his cap when he entered French society. But then—"

"But then your father began to lose the war and being the son-in-law of Bonaparte would not be such a good move."

She nodded. "I know this will sound like I'm trying to make excuses for being a silly fool, but I would swear on my life that the ceremony between us was real, Sin. I was so . . . shattered when I discovered the truth."

"Dominic was a master of lies and deception, Marianne." He smoothed his hand over the taut muscles of her stomach. "You have ample reason to be suspicious of men, but I swear to you I will always put your life, safety, and happiness before mine."

She cupped his cheek, her expression more tender than any he'd ever seen. "I know. I never meant to impugn—"

"Hush," he said, pulling her back down beside him. "Get some rest, darling," he said, turning onto his side and tucking her against his chest.

"Tomorrow we get to Reims," she said, and then yawned." Who do you think will be waiting to see me, Sin?"

"I don't know, darling." But he hoped to God that whatever awaited her did not break her heart.

Chapter 34

Like every town they'd passed through—no matter the size—Reims was mobilizing for war.

Marianne had wanted to ride Reggie, but it had been Jo who'd—very quietly—suggested that she wear a dress when they'd all met at breakfast that morning.

"You are beautiful," Sin murmured when Marianne nervously smoothed the elegant skirt of the gown she'd borrowed from Cecile.

Sin had shaved, but he still wore the clear spectacles and modest clothing.

They sat on the bench in the caravan and watched the bustling streets of Reims roll past their window.

Every newspaper along the way had lauded Bonaparte, repeatedly printing his already famous words from Grenoble when he'd stepped in front of royalist troops, ripped open his coat, and proclaimed, "If any of you will shoot his Emperor, here I am."

Instead of shooting him, the troops had flocked to him like hens to corn.

He'd been in Paris for weeks now, dismantling France's government and preparing for war while the allied coalition appeared to be dragging its feet.

Sin didn't want to think of what the rest of this year—and probably the next few—would yield if Bonaparte wasn't stopped before he could rouse the rest of the giant country to his defense.

Marianne pointed to the magnificent cathedral looming just ahead. "Notre-Dame de Reims," she murmured. "It's hard to imagine that its more famous namesake in Paris could be any grander, isn't it?"

The Cathedral at Reims, as the English called it, was truly awe-inspiring, and their caravan seemed to be headed directly toward it.

Indeed, that was exactly where Jo pulled up.

Blithely ignoring the shouts of outraged French drivers, Jo hopped down from the bench—with Angus on her shoulder—and came around to open the door.

"Here is where you will get out, Marianne." She reached into the satchel she kept slung across her body. "I meant to give you this earlier." She pulled out a lacy black head covering, somewhat the worse for wear. "Put this on and sit in the back of the church—on the right-hand side, the last pew. Wait there, and someone will meet you."

"How the devil can somebody meet her?" Sin demanded. "We only just rolled into town minutes ago."

Jo's opal gaze slid to the duke, and her lips curved into a faint smile. "Don't worry, Your Grace. Marianne is expected."

The irate Frenchman whose wagon was trapped behind them had had enough. He hopped down and stormed toward them, shouting all the way.

As Jo turned to face her aggressor, Sin pulled Marianne close and kissed her hard. "No matter what happens, or what you hear, know that I love you with all my heart."

Marianne's eyes prickled and she bit her lip, too afraid that she'd sob like a child if she opened her mouth.

Instead, she hopped out and stepped around Jo.

The blond woman had crossed her arms and was leaning against the back of the caravan, smirking at the screaming carter, who was arguing with Angus.

The bird was excitedly bobbing up and down on Jo's shoulder

and hurling insults—in French—its voice eerily like Jo's. As Marianne waited for a gap in the steady stream of oncoming traffic, she couldn't help laughing at one particularly crude and anatomically impossible instruction the bird tossed at the now raging Frenchman.

She left the argument behind and hurried toward the cathedral, pausing as she approached to admire the ancient church.

After five or six minutes of gawking, she tore her gaze from the magnificent rose window, myriad carvings, friezes, and gargoyles and forced her feet to resume their journey.

The sense of entering God's house was almost overpowering as she passed through the narthex and into the nave, where she again paused to stare in awe at a vaulted ceiling that soared impossibly high overhead.

She had never been in a Catholic church before. Although there was no mass in progress—indeed, there were only a scattering of people in the massive nave—there were subtle differences in the structure itself.

"*Excusez-moi,*" a woman murmured behind her, making Marianne realize that she'd stopped right in the middle of the aisle. She glanced over at the right rear pew: It was empty.

She could gawk just as well sitting down.

Marianne was admiring the breathtaking stained-glass windows, crowded with crowned men and winged angels, when she felt movement beside her.

The woman who'd sat next to her was so heavily veiled that Marianne could see nothing of her face. She was garbed in the manner of a housekeeper or upper servant.

"You will please to accompany me, mademoiselle?" she said in heavily accented English.

Marianne nodded and stood, her heart pounding in her ears.

The woman proceeded to lead her on a Byzantine journey into the bowels of the massive building.

Marianne quickly lost track of the number of turns and doors and corridors. Finally, after what felt like years, her guide stopped in front of an elaborately carved door and knocked softly.

A voice inside called out, "*Entrez!*"

The servant, if that's what she was, opened the door and gestured Marianne into a lavishly appointed, book-filled room that was obviously some important person's study.

A slender dark-haired woman of middling years came toward Marianne, her hands outstretched, her brown eyes wide with wonder.

Marianne hesitantly held out her hands and her mother clenched them hard enough to hurt. "*Mon Dieu*," she said, tears glazing her eyes. "But you are so like him."

She gazed into Marianne's eyes for so long that she began to squirm.

"Oh!" the Crown Princess of Sweden said, a flush darkening her cheeks. "But what am I doing making you stand here? Come—" She gestured to the chair she'd just vacated. "Sit with me. Lavigne has gone to fetch tea for us. Please, sit."

Marianne was grateful to sit; her knees felt as if they were made of water.

They stared at each other.

Désirée spoke first. "I'm sorry—I know I must be making you uncomfortable. Mademoiselle Brown told me you did not know of me until just recently."

"Yes, just a few weeks ago. Although I didn't learn of my f-father until less than a week ago."

"I'm afraid those were my instructions to Sandrine. I wanted to wait to tell you the truth until you were of age." Her lips pulled down at the corners and her chin wobbled slightly. And then she leaned forward and clutched Marianne's hands, her own as slender and fine-boned as Angus's claws. "Did you suffer? Please tell me I did not make a mistake sending you with Sandrine? She was so happy to have you—she could not have children herself." She swallowed noisily. "She sent me letters four times a year. Even right before she died she sent one last message suggesting a cousin of hers, Sonia, and her husband Barnabas."

Marianne's head was pounding, and it was difficult to gather her wits.

"I'm sorry, I'm babbling—asking too many—"

Marianne squeezed the hand that was still entangled with hers. "Please, er, Your Royal Highness, you are—"

The queen shook her head vigorously. "No, no, no! Don't call me that. If you cannot call me *maman*—" She hesitated, no doubt seeing Marianne's reluctance on her face. "You must call me Désirée."

Marianne nodded. "Thank you . . . Désirée."

"But go on. I interrupted."

"I just wanted to say that I am . . . well, a bit stunned, by all of this."

"Naturally you are."

"But to answer your first question—no, I didn't suffer. Barnabas—the man who raised me—took me in almost immediately after my m-mother died. My life with him has been unconventional, but not unhappy," she said truthfully.

"And you were never hungry? Or in want?"

"No."

"That is a great weight off my mind." She cut Marianne an uncomfortable look. "You must wonder how all this happened. You must think I am a terrible woman."

"I don't think that," Marianne said honestly.

There was a knock on the door and the maid, Lavigne, entered bearing a tray. By the time the lavish tea and pastries had been set out, Désirée's anxious expression had faded somewhat.

"I will serve, Lavigne," she said, dismissing the woman.

Once they were both settled with cups and pastries that neither of them wanted, she began to talk.

"My sister—Julie, is her name—she is married to Joseph Bonaparte."

Marianne nodded.

"It was she who introduced me to his brother." Her lips curved into a fond, nostalgic smile. "Your father was . . . well, when he entered a room, there was nobody else who mattered. He was only a junior officer then, but we all knew he was bound for greater things. How great, of course, none of us guessed." She laughed breathily.

"When he went off to Paris, things changed quickly. I later learned that many women pursued him." She gave Marianne an almost proud look.

"And he was unfaithful to you?"

She shrugged, taking a sip of tea. "That, I don't know. But he did sever our engagement. He was . . . besotted with her. With Joséphine."

"I'm sorry," Marianne murmured.

"Oh, don't be. It was so long ago. And—to be honest—it did not break my heart. I came to Paris to be with my sister and also because Napoleon's family wanted me there." She pulled a face. "They hated Joséphine. Oh, the things they called her." She chuckled. "But I could not hate her." She cocked her head at Marianne. "You know I carried her veil at the coronation."

"No, I didn't know that."

She laughed again, the sound infectious. "People looked at me oddly, but then they always have and still do." She gave Marianne an impish smile and then sighed. "Napoleon felt guilty about what he'd done and was eager to marry me off. I was engaged again, but my betrothed died. Napoleon did not give up, and not long after I married Charles." She pursed her lips. "But of course he was only plain Jean Baptiste Jules Bernadotte back then."

She gestured to the teapot, but Marianne shook her head; her cup was almost untouched.

"Bernadotte is another like your father."

Marianne's stomach tensed every time this woman referred to a man who was yet again upending the world.

"What do you mean?" she asked.

"Charles is a man who was bound to make his own future. So ambitious for grander things." She sighed. "I . . . let me just say that court life does not agree with me." She shrugged. "But we were married, and it was good for me—although at the time . . ." She stopped and chewed her lip—a habit Marianne had, herself. "Charles's family and the Bonapartes were . . . Well, let me just say that things did not run smoothly between them. It was a rough time.

There were attempts on your father's life—the friendship between him and my husband became strained. For a year or more I did not see Bernadotte while he was on campaign. I did not see your father, either. Until late in 1795, when he came back to Paris—very unexpected it was. He had received word about Joséphine's relationship with a young officer."

"You mentioned that in the letter," Marianne murmured, her face heating.

"Oh yes, that is right." She clucked her tongue. "The letters he wrote to Joséphine had been very passionate until then."

"She let you *read* them?"

Désirée smiled indulgently. "She let her maid read them, and soon word of his love was well-known. That is life at court—not so different from a small village, where everyone is into everyone else's business. In any case, he was full of passion—something he never felt for me. But she was cold to him—not at first, I think. But, er—" She cut Marianne a shy look.

"He was not faithful to her?" she guessed.

"Yes. The first time with one of her ladies-in-waiting. And after that?" She shrugged. "Who knows. But she could not forgive him for it. And when he was away, she saw her chance for revenge. He was in a rage when he found out—some people thought he would divorce her. He was angry and hurt when he came to me. He said—" Her cheeks pinkened. "He said foolish things. I think, for that one night, that he believed he had truly made a mistake when he ended our engagement."

She chewed her lip, fiddling with the tea strainer. "We became lovers—" She looked up and met Marianne's gaze. "It was the first and only time. Afterward—well, he left Paris without any word to me."

She took a sip of tea that had surely gone cold and then looked up at Marianne with a sweet smile. "And then nine months later, you came."

"And your husband—he was—"

Désirée clucked her tongue. "Yes, that was not good timing.

Bernadotte was still away from home. There would have been no way to explain."

"You must have been frightened."

"I was terrified. But Sandrine—she had been with me since I was a girl. It was her idea to say I was convalescing in the country." Her eyes were vague with memories. "After you came, I wanted to keep you near, but I had promised Sandrine that she could claim you as her own. And everyone knew she was barren. Her husband had left her—abandoned her when she could not give him children. So, she took you away to start a new life. I knew it was for the best."

"And my . . . f-father, does he know about me?"

"Of course, I told him. In fact, he is the one who gave you your name."

Something strange—not unpleasant—twisted inside her at that information. "He did?"

"Yes." Désirée smiled. "Marianne is the heroine of the Revolution—of course you know that. A strong and noble name."

They sat in silence for a moment.

It was Désirée who broke it. "Brown told me that a duke travels with you?"

"Yes, that is true," she said, not especially wishing to talk about Sin with a stranger. "As for the king, er, ex-king, it is possible he still might tell your husband—or the Swedish government—about my existence," she felt compelled to warn her.

Désirée chuckled. "He has no letter or miniatures?"

"The letter is gone and I have the miniatures."

"Then he has nothing and nobody will believe anything he says."

"But your husband might think—"

"Charles already knows about you."

Marianne goggled. "He does?"

"Oh, yes." She gave a girlish gurgle of laughter. "You have no idea of the foolish intrigue that goes on in court circles—it is dreadful. Why do you think I delay my return to Sweden?"

Marianne *had* wondered about that but hadn't wanted to ask.

"Even in Paris there are spies in my house. That is how Charles learned about you—long ago. And, of course, he has people keeping an eye on Gustav. As pitiful as he is, he was once the King of Sweden and this current political environment is ripe for his sort of mischief. It was Charles who saw to the hiring of your Miss Brown, and it was she who discovered the link between Gustav and that baron."

Jo, again!

"Who *is* she?" Marianne asked.

"I don't know, dear." She smiled nervously. "At first, when I spoke to her, Miss Brown offered to, er, *eliminate* Gustav and Strickland. That was the word she used."

Marianne's jaw sagged and the older woman nodded.

"When I said that I did not feel comfortable with such a thing, she suggested that she go to London to investigate. She said that plan was probably better as it was the only way to—how did she put it? Oh yes, *remove the weed and all the roots.*"

Marianne shivered.

Désirée nodded. "Yes, she is a formidable woman, that one. She came highly recommended, so we let her guide our decisions and allowed the matter to unfold." Her lips flexed into a rueful smile. "Things would have gone more smoothly if your father hadn't come back from Elba, of course. I was horrified that we'd allowed you to wander into such a dangerous situation. The only thing keeping me sane was the knowledge that Brown was with you."

Jo and Angus, her guardian angels.

"Now," Désirée said, her manner that of a woman wanting to get down to business. "I don't have much time. I will have to get back home before too long. Things are—well, I'm sure you can imagine Paris right now."

"Are you in danger?"

"Oh, no. I have managed to keep friends on both sides, if you can believe it. Louis has been kind to me." Her lips puckered. "Although not kind enough to let me bring my dear sister and her husband to Paris."

Marianne almost laughed at that. Considering that her brother-in-law—Marianne's uncle!—was Napoleon's brother, the King of France's reluctance to invite him to live in the capital was understandable.

"Before I leave, I wish to speak of this duke Brown mentioned."

Marianne's face heated under her intense, knowing gaze.

"Ah," Désirée said, nodding as if she'd actually spoken. "You are in love."

Marianne opened her mouth to deny it, but then realized this was her one and only chance to speak honestly with the woman who'd given birth to her. "Yes."

"He is the one the papers call *Lord Flawless*?"

Marianne winced at the nickname Sin disliked so much. "Yes."

"You have agreed to a carte blanche?"

"No!" she said, nettled the other woman should make such an assumption.

Désirée chuckled tolerantly. "That was not meant to be an insult—I am proud of you for capturing the attention of such a man."

"He asked me to marry him," Marianne blurted, and then wished she'd held her tongue. What was wrong with her? Boasting of such a thing.

"*Mon Dieu*! He must love you very much."

"Yes. And I love him. Which is why I cannot accept his offer."

"But why?" Désirée demanded, visibly irked. "Is it because of what Brown says—that you suffered a humiliation at the hands of that"—her lips twisted into a vicious sneer and for one startling moment Marianne thought the woman might actually spit—"that swine Strickland?"

"That's part of it. But do you know what I do in my uncle's circus?"

"Brown said you are his"—she snapped her fingers, searching for the word in English—"*compatable*?"

Of all the things Jo had shared, why had she lied about what Marianne did for a living?

She sighed. "No. I do not manage his ledgers. I am one of the acts; I am a pugilist."

Désirée's eyes widened in shock. "You are a . . . *boxeur?*"

"Actually, I think it would be *boxeuse.*" When the other woman failed to smile at her jest, Marianne felt compelled to say, "Now you see why I can't accept the duke's offer."

"It is certainly an . . . obstacle." She seemed to shake herself. "But you say you love him?"

"Yes."

"Well, he must perhaps marry elsewhere, but you can still be with him."

"He would never do such a thing."

"Why not?"

"Because he is a good and decent man," Marianne said firmly. "Besides, I would never accept such an offer."

Désirée looked like she had more to say on the subject of aristocrats who remained faithful, but prudently kept it to herself. "What will you do?"

"Operate Barnabas's business."

"I don't understand—is the money not enough? I can send more—"

"The five hundred pounds was more than gene—"

"Five hundred pounds? But my man of business sends fifteen hundred English pounds every year—on your birthday—to an English bank."

"You send money every year?" Marianne repeated stupidly.

"You never received this?"

"No."

"Surely somebody has?"

Marianne now understood why Sonia had been so careful to collect Barnabas's bag before she departed. She'd foolishly believed it was sentiment on the other woman's part. Doubtless there was information about this bank account.

"I don't know—this is the first I'm hearing about the account or money."

Désirée laid a hand on Marianne's, which had clenched into a fist. "Do not fret," she soothed, misinterpreting Marianne's anger. "I will see that there is a new account—this one only for you to draw on. I should have done that long ago—when you were old enough to know about it."

"That's very kind," Marianne said. "But you don't have—"

"I *want* to. And there is the money your father put aside for you, of course."

"He did?"

"Yes. It was only right and just. He did the same for—" She broke off.

"For the other children he fathered outside of wedlock?" Marianne guessed. "Do I have many half-brothers and -sisters?" All people she'd never be able to meet.

"A few," she admitted. "And of course there is my Oskar."

"You have only one child?"

"No, I have a daughter, too."

Marianne was about to ask her name when she saw the twinkle in her mother's brown gaze.

"Ah," she said.

"You are my daughter, Marianne. Had the timing of your birth been different, you would have been a princess."

"But I'm not," Marianne reminded her.

"No, unfortunately, you are not." Her sadness dissipated and she smiled broadly enough to display dimples. "But perhaps you might be a duchess."

Marianne did not bother to disagree with her. The sort of life her mother led was so far from her own existence, there wasn't any hope in explaining just how impossible such a union would be.

So she let Désirée continue to think pleasant thoughts.

At least one of them could enjoy Marianne's future.

Chapter 35

Sin was standing on the deck, looking out over the same body of water he'd crossed mere weeks earlier. It felt like a lifetime ago.

Of course, the four days since they'd left Reims also seemed like a lifetime ago.

It had been the last night he'd spent with Marianne.

"This must end before we return home," she'd told him in the early hours of the morning—after she'd shared the conversation with her mother, cried a little, and then made love to him with a ferocity that left him both sated and restless.

He should have guessed what she was about to say.

She'd not been mourning—at least not entirely—the loss of the mother she had met and then lost so quickly. She'd been saying goodbye to him. To any chance for them.

Sin had looked into her eyes and seen the truth: She would not be badgered—or even begged, which he was not too proud to do—into accepting him.

But he'd opened his mouth to try both.

In the end, nothing that he'd said had moved her.

"You feel this way, now," she'd said. "But you would come to resent me over time—no, you would," she'd insisted when he'd tried to argue. "A marriage so unequal would only end in anguish for us both."

"I believe you are wrong, Marianne."

"Then we are destined to disagree." She'd given a shaky sigh, her eyes glassy with unshed tears. "You gave me your word when we started this that it would end before we returned home. Are you really going to break your promise to me now?"

What a cunning, punishing jab that had been.

And so, after a long, miserable moment, he had nodded. "It will be as you wish."

Surprise had flashed in her beloved hazel eyes, and for an instant he'd wondered if he had made a mistake giving up so quickly—if she might have capitulated? But the moment, if it had ever existed, had been lost.

The drive from Reims to Calais was nothing like that from Himmelhause to Reims.

Elliot, Sin, and Guy shared a caravan, while the three women stayed in the other. Conversation, when it happened between the two groups, was brief and stilted.

He wasn't the only one who'd been given his marching papers it seemed.

Guy dropped his arms on the rail beside Sin. "So . . ." he said, and then waited.

Sin had been avoiding his best friend for days. It hadn't been easy—especially considering they had only the one caravan among the three of them.

"So . . ." Guy said again, as if Sin could have possibly missed it the first time.

"You will not stop, will you?" Sin asked.

"No. Did she give you the boot?" Guy asked.

"Did *you* get the boot?" Sin countered.

"Yes," he answered promptly, clearly more interested in discussing his own situation than prying into Sin's. "I think the two of them must have bolstered each other up in Reims."

Sin disagreed but kept that to himself.

"I suppose it is for the best." Guy sighed.

Sin *definitely* disagreed with that, but he had no intention of baring his shredded soul for inspection, not even to his oldest friend.

"Still, you'd have thought I was offering her a dead badger by the way she reacted to my offer."

Sin raised his eyebrows. "A carte blanche?"

"Of course." Guy's forehead furrowed. "What else could there be?"

Sin stared.

Guy's eyes widened until there was white all around the irises. "You didn't."

Sin turned back toward the horizon.

"Are you *mad*?"

Why did people keep asking him that? He was one of the sanest people he knew.

"Is who mad?" Elliot asked, coming up on Sin's other side.

"Sin asked Marianne to marry him."

Elliot's mouth opened and his eyebrows shot up. He took one look at Sin's face and closed his mouth. "Hmm."

"That's all you have to say?" Guy demanded.

Elliot ignored him.

"And what about you and, er, Brown, Elliot?" Guy prodded. "Did you ask *her* to marry you?" He chortled. "Did you need to ask Angus's permission, first?"

Elliot was as expressive as a granite carving.

Guy flung up his hands. "What? I am only jesting. What has gotten into you two? How did you *think* this would all end? Am I the only one with any sense left at all?"

"Not if the word *sense* means what I think it does."

All three of them turned at the sound of Cecile's mocking voice.

Cecile and Jo—and Angus—had just come up on deck, and the Frenchwoman smirked at Guy, arching one black eyebrow, as if daring him to speak.

Wisely, Guy kept his mouth shut.

"How is Marianne feeling?" Sin asked.

"She will live," Cecile said, coming to rest against the railing. "But seasickness makes one wish one would die."

"Please, let us not say the *S* word." Elliot shuddered.

"That's right," Guy said. "On the way over you were the one bent over the rail and, er, never mind," he said at Elliot's murderous look.

Cecile turned to Sin, purposely ignoring her erstwhile lover. "What will you do when you reach London, Your Grace?"

"I'm not going to London," Sin said, assuming Cecile was on a mission from Marianne to determine the best way to avoid any awkward meeting once they disembarked. "I shall go home—to Wortham." He didn't know how long he'd stay. It had been his plan, if he'd brought Ben with him, to remain at Wortham until the end of the year, continuing with the deception that he'd gone to America.

Now, however . . . Well, with war on the table, he'd need to go to town sooner than later. When people asked about his sudden return, he'd have to fabricate something.

"I'm going to London," Guy offered when Cecile pointedly did not ask.

"And you?" she asked Elliot.

"I shall be returning to work. I daresay I'll be quite busy." He cut a quick glance at Jo, but she seemed unaware of their conversation, scratching Angus's head while the raven purred exactly like a cat.

"Indeed," Elliot added more loudly. "I'm sure they'll have desperate need of me—perhaps they will even be hiring more employees with certain, er, talents."

Jo strolled away from them, walking toward the bow.

Guy looked from the rapidly disappearing woman to Elliot. "Are you saying what I think you're saying?"

"Blade already has an occupation," Cecile said, addressing this comment to Elliot before her gaze, hard and unpleasant, slid to Guy.

"The three of us will have our hands full operating the theater. We shall be busy *working*."

Guy cleared his throat and inched away from her venomous look.

Cecile turned back to Sin. "I have convinced Marianne that she will need to focus all her attention on business matters. She will no longer be fighting."

Sin already knew that. It was the only promise he'd extracted from her after she'd told him her plans to continue operating the Fayre. He had to admit the promise had relieved him of his worries for her health.

Unfortunately, that reassurance did little to fill the hollow void inside him.

Although Marianne didn't know it then, the summer of 1815 would be unlike any other summer in her life.

As miserable as she was after stepping off the packet in Dover, she was somewhat distracted by the heavy, expectant atmosphere that colored the weeks of May and early June—weeks that felt like months.

The collective national horror at the slaughter and death that took place over those few days in June made the rest of the summer feel like a post-nightmare fugue.

The mood of the allies after Waterloo was determined: Napoleon Bonaparte would not escape punishment for his actions.

For several weeks Marianne wondered, along with the rest of the world, whether her father would be executed in a spectacle in Paris, escape to America, or—as he seemed to hope—yet again rouse France to his defense.

As it happened, he surrendered without any fanfare on July 15, 1815, one day after Bastille Day, Marianne's twenty-first birthday.

It was the same day she received a letter from a French lawyer informing her of an account in her name, bearing the princely—or princess-ly—sum of five thousand pounds and the assurance of an annual amount of fifteen hundred.

Another letter came, as well, this one sent by a woman named Marie Dupont. Marianne had smiled at the name, pleased that her mother had found a way to write to her.

The mood in Paris is a somber one, she wrote. *Twice in as many years this magnificent city has been brought low. With the restoration of the Bourbons have come repeated entreaties for me to assume my own duties in the Frozen North.* Those last two words had been underlined multiple times. *I am holding firm against the pressure, but I cannot be sure how long I will last.*

I spoke with your father shortly before he left Paris and made his pilgrimage to his beloved's grave.

Marianne knew she meant Malmaison, which had been Joséphine's last home, near the small town where she was buried.

I spoke of you. You should know that was the first and last smile on his face—when he learned how his daughter had once earned her way. "She is her father's daughter," he said. "A fighter until the end."

Had Marianne cried when she'd read that?

Well, maybe a little.

But she'd been as relieved as the rest of the world when, on July twenty-third, her father had boarded the *Bellerophon*, the ship that took him halfway across the world to his new prison, the island of Saint Helena.

Sin's name was often mentioned in the political section of the nation's newspapers that summer and fall. But not until winter, and what was called the Little Season, did she begin to see him mentioned in the society columns. The crack in her heart grew a little each time his name was linked with that of some young, eligible, and likely beautiful woman.

His betrothal announcement was inevitable, she knew that. After all, the Duke of Staunton had long been a marital prize, rivaled only by Lord Carlisle.

By the end of 1815, with people both rich and poor wanting to put the tumultuous year far, far behind them, the speculation in the society columns had begun to run wild.

Eighteen-sixteen, the gossips predicted, would be the year when both Staunton and Carlisle took wives and settled down.

Marianne stopped reading the newspapers entirely at the beginning of the New Year.

Chapter 36

The first few months after Sin's return, he was far too busy with the mess Marianne's father was causing on the Continent to wallow in self-pity.

Indeed, his duties in Parliament kept him busy through the fall and into the winter of 1815.

But after Christmas—which he had foolishly decided to spend in London, in case *anyone* should change her stubborn mind and come looking for him—he gave up hope that Marianne would see reason.

She had rejected him and would not relent.

On Christmas Day he received a message from his aunt Julia; his mother had died in her sleep at the age of fifty-six.

Preparations for a small, intimate funeral consumed the month of January.

Just when he'd prepared to return to London, he received a second courier-delivered message, this one from Guy.

Unlike Sin's mother, whom most people believed had died years ago, the Duke of Fairhurst, Guy's grandfather, had been well-liked, and his funeral had drawn hundreds.

Death comes in threes, was his aunt Julia's ghoulish prognostication when she accompanied him to London—the first time she would take part in a Season since her own, many decades before.

She had only come that year because they would, as a house in mourning, have only intimate entertainments. Although his aunt was not as self-conscious about her scars as many who'd been afflicted, she was by nature retiring.

As Sin mounted the steps to Staunton House after a long day, he thought, yet again, how grateful he was that he had his aunt to come home to—even though he often didn't manage to get home until late, like tonight.

In the past, living alone had not bothered him. But since returning from Europe . . . well, his house felt even larger and emptier.

As usual, Buffle was waiting at the door and opened it before Sin even reached the top step.

"Good evening, Your Grace," Buffle said, and then turned to dismiss a hovering footman before taking Sin's hat. "I was just going to send one of the footmen with a message for you," he added.

Sin paused in the act of stripping off a glove, his stomach clenching. "Is something wrong with Lady Julia?"

"Oh, nothing like that, Your Grace. It is Mr. Wingate—he is in the library. He said he was happy to wait for your return, but I thought you would like to know."

"You thought right," Sin said, glancing at his watch; it was after eleven. He wondered why Elliot hadn't just met him at the club, where he'd been having dinner with Guy. "My aunt?" he asked.

"She went up to her rooms an hour ago, Your Grace. Can I send something up for you, sir?'

"No, thank you, Buffle—not unless Mr. Wingate asked for anything." He knew his butler well enough to know he'd offered.

"He did not, sir."

"Then take yourself off to bed."

"Thank you, Your Grace."

Elliot was beside the fire, reading one of the newspapers Sin had delivered each day. "It is good to see you, Staunton," he said, smiling and putting aside the paper.

"You, as well. I thought you were going to be in Paris for another week."

"No, I drew the long straw and was allowed to come back early."

Sin gave him a wry look. "That bad, is it?" Elliot had accepted a special appointment last year and had been out of the country more often than not.

"Bad enough." He sighed. "But I'm home for the duration."

Sin poured himself a drink and lifted the decanter.

"I'm still fine," Elliot said, gesturing to his glass. "Buffle fussed over me as if I were a long-lost grandchild. He said I've lost weight and threatened to wake up the kitchen to feed me."

Sin cocked his head and gave him an appraising look. "You do look a bit on the scrawny side."

Elliot chuckled.

"So," Sin said, taking the chair across from his friend. "What brings you here at this time of night?" He ran his gaze over Elliot's travel-stained person. "And without even stopping at your house first."

"Yes, I apologize for that."

Sin waved his words away. "Nonsense. You know what I mean."

Elliot bent to the leather bag beside his chair. "I have something that might be . . . very important." He pulled out an official-looking letter and handed it to Sin.

"What's this?"

"It's better if you read it yourself."

Sin studied the seal and his eyes widened. He quickly glanced up. "Are you sure I should—"

"No, actually. I'm breaking several dozen laws and no small number of international agreements by giving you that. I'm only partly jesting," he said at Sin's startled look. "Just open it and . . . don't tell me anything."

Intrigued, Sin cracked the heavy wax seal and unfolded a document that made even him—a man long accustomed to the sight of royal decrees and missives—raise his eyebrows.

It wasn't long, but it was written in flowery, almost illegible script. When he came to the pertinent section—and a very familiar name—his head whipped up.

Elliot was already grinning.

"You *devil*," Sin whispered. "How did you—"

"I had nothing to do with it. In fact, there seems to be a considerable amount of confusion as to how or who was behind it. Although scuttlebutt would indicate it came from *outside* the country."

Sin carefully refolded the document—which both of them had broken the law by opening—and handed it back to Elliot.

"No. I don't want it."

"What?"

"I thought you might like to deliver it."

Sin opened his mouth to argue, but then stopped, his mind racing. When he looked up, his friend—always a step ahead of him, it seemed—was nodding knowingly.

For the first time in weeks—hell, in months—Sin felt a genuine smile crease his face.

"Indeed, I would like to deliver it very much."

Marianne had heard the phrase *tear one's hair out* more than once. Since taking over her uncle's circus, she truly knew what it meant.

Francine, her magician, was holding her prize rabbit, Henry, and shooting accusing glares at Jo. Or at Angus, rather, who was sitting on Jo's shoulder. "I know he took it."

The *it* in question was Henry's toy, a crudely wrought wooden carrot that one of the stagehands had whittled. Until meeting Francine and Henry, Marianne hadn't even known a rabbit would want a toy. But she had to admit that she'd seen Henry chewing on the carrot more than once.

And now it was gone.

Jo, who was dressed to go on stage after Francine's interlude— if there was an interlude, which wasn't certain just then—pulled a knife from one of the many reinforced pockets sewn into the black leather breeches she wore. She spun the knife with a bored expression on her face, and Angus looked like butter wouldn't melt in his beak.

Marianne sighed. She'd believed when she'd begun this job that it would be so much easier than taking punches to the face. She now had infinitely more respect for Barnabas, and more than once she'd asked forgiveness of the man, wherever he happened to be spending eternity.

"Jo." Marianne spoke sharply, as one needed to do when Jo had slipped into one of her dreamy fugues.

Her eyes slid slowly from whatever she'd been staring at to Marianne. "Hmm?"

"Does Angus have Henry's carrot?"

"Carrot?" she repeated, as if she didn't recognize the word.

That blank stare was an evasion tactic Marianne had noticed the other woman used often. It always worked on Cecile, who'd get so emotionally worked up that she'd forget the original issue.

Marianne was made of sterner, less distractible—stuff. "Henry's wooden carrot. Did Angus take it?"

"No," she answered without hesitation.

"I *saw* him with it," Francine insisted.

"You need to get ready to go on," Marianne told Francine. "We'll find the carrot later." She gave Jo a pointed look that went completely unnoticed.

"Henry is *distraught* without it," Francine insisted. "He won't be able to perform."

Marianne looked at the rabbit, whose nose was twitching the way it always did, and then looked at Francine. She liked the magician, but the woman had tested Marianne's patience in ways she never would have dared with Barnabas. Marianne had encountered such testing behavior often and wasn't sure if it was because of her gender or her age. Either way, she was getting tired of it after almost a year.

She turned to Jo. "Go look for the carrot," she snapped.

Jo left without any theatrics.

She turned to Francine. "If Henry wants more *real* carrots, then you had better get him out on that stage in"—she looked at the watch pinned to her bodice—"six minutes."

Francine blinked her huge blue eyes—a maneuver that might have worked on Barnabas but was less than effective with Marianne. "I'm sorry, Marianne. You know how much I hate to be a bother." She paused and waited for an agreement that would never come. "I'll go get ready," she hastily said.

Marianne waited until Francine and her rabbit had disappeared in the direction of the wings before returning to the small room that Barnabas had used as an office.

She slumped into her chair and propped her head on her hand; she was exhausted. Wooden carrots and manipulative employees were the least of what she had to deal with. There were hundreds of things Barnabas had managed without her even guessing they existed. The number of bribes, alone, was staggering.

Most days Marianne came into the theater at six or seven in the morning and didn't leave until after midnight. At first, she'd worried that she'd need to take over Nora and Lucy's training, in addition to all the other duties, but Jack had hired two more employees at his boxing parlor.

"That leaves me free to keep an eye on you, ducks," he'd explained.

Marianne had almost wept; just having Jack's sturdy presence had made those first terrifying months of managing the Fayre bearable.

Still, there was only one person who could manage employee disputes and difficulties—like stolen pet toys—and that was *her*.

Marianne sighed, took a deep breath, and turned back to her spot in the ledger.

Less than a minute later, the door flew open.

"A closed door means *do not enter*," she said flatly without looking up.

"You will never guess who is in the audience tonight!" Cecile demanded.

Marianne's heart leapt into her throat. "Who?"

A curly brown head pushed between Cecile and the doorframe.

Marianne held out her hand and Neddy set a stack of messages in her palm. "Thank you, Neddy."

He grinned. "I'm rich as a lord tonight, Marianne."

"Yes, well, see that you save some of that meg for a rainy day."

He ran off, heedless of her advice. He was loving the new method of dealing with lovelorn swains—he could take all the money and notes offered, and all he had to do was deliver the notes to Marianne. If they did not contain anything illegal, she passed them along to their intended recipients.

Already the system had led to her discharging four stagehands— men who'd had a flourishing crime enterprise operating under her nose.

"Aren't you going to guess?" Cecile demanded once Neddy had gone.

Marianne opened the first note. "Prinny?" she said, setting aside the cologne-soaked missive from the young Viscount Foley to Cordelia Black, her Harlequin—the third message from the man this week alone.

Cecile made a scandalized squawk. "If you aren't even going to be serious, then I won't tell you."

"This one is for you," Marianne said, handing her a message that was on expensive paper with a very familiar crest.

As she'd done with the other letters that Guy had sent, Cecile crumpled it up without looking at it and threw it in the rubbish bin. "There is no joy left in you," she accused.

Marianne sighed and steeled herself for another of Cecile's rants as she opened the next message

> *Five minutes. That is all I request of you. Surely what we had is worth that? Sin*

Marianne read it again, and then again.

"Fine," Cecile said, flinging up her hands. "I'll tell you who it is—"

"Go fetch Neddy," Marianne ordered.

Cecile stamped her foot and uttered a few choice words in French that no lady should even know. "Don't you even—"

"You can tell Neddy to show His Grace of Staunton back here."

The startled look on the other woman's face—not to mention the sudden silence—was priceless.

Of course, it couldn't last.

"You need to go and change into a dress. And your hair—ah! It is a mess and—"

"Cecile. Go. Now."

Cecile made a noise like a tormented kitten but flounced out of her tiny office.

Marianne couldn't help smiling—even though her heart was threatening to pound out of her chest. She'd used the tone the duke had employed on more than one occasion. A person could not use it too often, but when wielded judiciously, it was astoundingly successful.

She shut the door Cecile had left open and looked at herself in the small mirror she'd hung by the door after she had once spent half the day walking around with a giant smudge of ink across her face.

No ink now, but she looked the way a person looked after more than twelve hours of work, which was to say *frazzled*.

Her hair, which she no longer kept short now that she didn't fight, had grown like a weed. In fact, it *looked* like a weed. A brown weed.

She put it up in a bun each morning, but it usually came down long before now.

Marianne briefly considered trying to put it back up, but her hands were shaking so badly she decided it would be a disaster. Instead, she removed the few remaining pins and shook her head.

She looked at the result.

"Ugh." She turned away from the mirror and sat on the chair in front of the desk. But then she moved to one of the three chairs she'd arranged for meetings with her employees.

She was just rearranging the chairs to no purpose when the door flew open. Again without a knock.

Cecile stood in the doorway, blocking Sin's entrance with her body. "His Grace of Staunton is here to see you. Do you wish to—"

"Cecile."

Cecile ignored Marianne's chiding tone. "Shall I bring tea?" she offered brightly.

"Just let him in and shut the door," Marianne said through clenched teeth.

"Marianne will see you now, Your Grace," Cecile said to Sin, as if he'd not been standing right behind her.

He didn't appear to hear her—or maybe not even see her—his eyes were flickering over Marianne's face and person.

As were hers over him.

He looked glorious.

Magnificent.

Godlike.

He was dressed in black and white evening garb; the only thing she'd seen that suited him more was nothing at all.

He was thinner, and she'd forgotten just how fair his hair was naturally.

His eyes, however, were exactly the same, and they cut right through her.

"Thank you for seeing me," he said, hovering in the doorway.

"Of course. Have a seat. What can I do for you?" she asked once he was seated on a rickety chair in her shabby little room, as conspicuous as a diamond on a dung heap.

"How have you been?" he asked. She could tell by the look in his eyes that the question was not the same one that thousands of people asked each other every day in Britain. She knew he meant: *Isn't this awful? When will it stop hurting? Have you missed me? Do you think of me at least five times an hour?*

At least those were the questions she would have asked.

"I have been well," she lied. "And you?"

"I have been miserable."

Marianne groaned. "Why are you here, Your Grace? Why?"

He reached into his elegantly cut, perfectly fitting evening coat and pulled out a rather large envelope. "This is for you." He handed it to her. When she didn't take it, he said, "I really hope you'll take it. My valet will be most displeased if I show up at home with it distorting the cut of my coat."

She snorted. "Well, we wouldn't want that, would we?" She snatched the missive from his hand, glanced at the front, and her head whipped up. "This is addressed to *me*."

He gave her a sheepish look. "Is it?"

She turned it over. "And the seal has been broken."

"Has it?"

Her hands shook. "What is this?" she asked weakly, too afraid to open it. "Did something happen to my—my mother?" She swallowed several times and then grimaced. "My father?"

"No, they are both fine, as far as I know. Open it."

She unfolded the heavy paper and her eyes immediately lowered to the bottom of the page and she gasped.

"The Prince of Wales has sent me a letter!"

"I'm afraid he didn't really write it, darling. If he had, you'd not be able to read it. His handwriting is execrable." An anxious look passed over his face. "Did you read it?"

She started at the top of the page this time.

She was three paragraphs in when her head shot up. "A *viscountess*!"

"I thought it was rather paltry, myself. Lord knows you'd look lovely in strawberry leaves. But perhaps I can do something about that."

"What—who—how—"

He smiled—one of those rare, once-in-a-blue-moon smiles she'd been privileged to see. "I believe your mother is behind it. According to Elliot—he is the one who broke a dozen laws by giving me the document, in case you want to have us both jailed—this came through channels so circuitous it put the Byzantine Empire to shame."

Marianne thought back to her conversation with her mother in Reims and smiled. "I should have guessed. She asked about you."

"Did she? You never told me that."

"No, it—well, at the time it just seemed pointless to mention it."

He nodded; that last night had been bittersweet agony.

"How did she even know of my existence?"

"Jo told her about us." Her face heated. "Everything."

"Ah."

Marianne was pleased to see she wasn't the only one blushing.

"Was she shocked?" he asked.

"No, she was rather, er, proud, I think."

His eyebrows shot up.

"Not proud that you and I were—er, well, you know—but proud that I had attracted such a significant prize."

"A prize, am I?"

Marianne gave a bark of laughter. "As if you didn't already know that." She hesitated, and then added, "I stopped reading the newspapers because of you."

The amusement slid from his face and he leaned toward her, taking the hand that wasn't currently holding the key to her happiness. "I hope you didn't believe everything you read?"

"I don't know what I believed." She glanced down at their joined hands, not quite believing he was really *there*, holding her hand, sitting right in front of her. She looked up. "I could hardly expect you to remain a bachelor all your days."

"I would have. And I will do. If you won't marry me." His beautiful green eyes were warm and hopeful—a suggestion of spring after what had been the longest winter of her life. "Let me remind you that your chief concern was our unequal status. That is no longer an issue."

"This—" She held up the letter that turned her into a peeress with the stroke of a quill. "This will be a thin shield against the barbs you will suffer if you marry me," she warned him, her voice shaky with poorly suppressed hope. "Are you quite *sure* that you won't eventually resent me, Sin? Because I could not go through with this if I believed that—"

He moved like a blur, catching her in his arms and crushing her mouth with his.

Nothing of any sense happened for at least five minutes.

"Where's one of those fussy settees when you need them?" he muttered, coming up for air reluctantly.

She laid her head on his chest, thrilling at the familiar masculine scent of him and the strong beat of his heart.

"It will have to be a small ceremony—my mother died Christmas Day."

She looked up, "Oh, Sin! I'm so sorry."

"She died years ago for me and my sisters. This was a happy release. For both my mother and my aunt Julia." His kiss-bruised lips curved. "You will like my aunt. And she will be delighted with you." He stopped and cocked his head. "But I am taking your answer for granted."

She burrowed her face into his coat, probably ruining it. "You know it is *yes*," she said, her voice muffled.

"Good." He kissed the top of her head. "I came prepared with a large sack and manacles in case you needed persuasion." He tilted her face up to him and kissed her, a gentle reacquainting kiss this time. "I never want another year like this last one, my love."

"I'm sorry," she said. "I know it was—"

"Shh." He kissed her lightly. "You did what you thought was best for me. I was furious with you every single hour of every day, but I knew your heart was in the right place."

"So," she said. "A small wedding?"

"Unless you want to wait until the end of my mourning period?"

"Absolutely not."

"Good. Or, again, I would have employed the sack and chains to convince you. A small wedding, *soon*. And then afterward a long tour of the Continent so I can have you to myself."

"You mean a *tour* tour?"

His eyes widened in mock horror. "If we take a caravan, it will only be one. And we will have a coachman. And a chef. And perhaps a few well-armed guards, and—"

Marianne laughed. "My, what a lot of maintenance a duke requires."

His eyes darkened and the hungry look on his face stole her breath away. "Oh, darling, you have no idea of the sort of maintenance I'll need from you. Starting tonight, I think."

Several long, strenuous hours later in a small house on Brune Street . . .

Marianne heaved a gusty sigh of contentment.

Sin emerged from beneath the blanket and smiled down at her. "I could get accustomed to the sound of that."

"Mmmm," she murmured. "So could I." One eye popped open and her hand slid down his torso, coming to rest on the only part of him that was truly awake at three o'clock in the morning. "What's this?"

"It's a betrothal gift, sweetheart."

Her eyes opened wide. "*Another* one? Impressive. What a generous husband I will have."

"Hmm, well, it might not be as impressive as the last three," he warned her.

She chuckled and placed him at the entrance to her body.

Sin sheathed himself in one long thrust and they both groaned. As late as it was, and as exhausted as they both were, they held each other's gaze as he moved inside her.

He took her slowly, giving her every inch with each thrust. They'd made love three times that night already, but he was afraid to let her go. Afraid he'd wake up in his bed alone with only the memory of her.

As if sensing his need, she wrapped her legs around his hips, pulling him tighter. "I love you, St. John Powell—both man and duke." She ran her strong hands up his flanks, her eyes saying what mere words weren't enough to express.

He thrust twice more, deeply, before hilting himself. "My Marianne," he murmured as his bliss claimed him.

Sin awoke with a jerk, a familiar and precious body trapped beneath him, strong hands caressing his back and bottom.

He raised himself up onto his elbows and smiled down at her. "I fell asleep," he said foolishly.

"I know. I took advantage while you were defenseless." She dug her fingers into the dense muscles of his buttocks.

He groaned. "Feel free to continue." He shifted off her and to the side, so that only his leg and arm were weighing on her.

She continued to stroke and massage with her magical hands. "Sin?"

"Hmm." He lowered his mouth and sucked one of her pert nipples between his lips.

She groaned. "I wanted to ask you a question."

He took her nipple between his teeth and tugged.

"*Sin*. Quit trying to distract me."

He reluctantly released her and heaved a sigh. "Ask away, darling."

"I'm just wondering about where we will live."

"We can live wherever you like," he said, leaning forward to drop a quick kiss on her nose. "Well, perhaps not on your new property."

"What property?" she blurted.

"You didn't get to that part of the letter, did you?" He clucked his tongue. "So hasty—so eager to get me into bed and—"

"I have a property? What sort of property?"

"I wouldn't get too excited; it's just a rocky patch on one of the Channel Islands, love."

She gave him a haughty look. "But it's *my* rocky patch. Perhaps I shall want to live there."

"You might like it."

She brightened. "Really?"

"If you had gills. I'm afraid it's likely under water for a good part of each day."

"Oh."

"Don't worry," he said, sliding his arm around her and pulling her on top of him. "I'll find a little corner for you at Wortham."

She chuckled and straddled his hips before wrapping a hand around his shaft. "So generous."

He purred and began to pulse his hips. "I can be—with the proper motivation."

"I thought you were sleepy?" she taunted.

"You came along and woke me up."

Marianne met his serious gaze and understood what his words really meant. Her teasing expression dissolved. "Oh, St. John."

"It's true. Until I met you, I was just existing."

"When you say things like that—you knock the wind right out of me."

"You'd better get accustomed to it, darling." He pulled her down into his arms and kissed her soundly. "Because I intend to keep delivering loving levelers every day for the rest of our lives."

Epilogue

"Are you ready?" Sin asked his wife, eyeing her pallor with concern. She was three months with child and this journey—which had taken almost two months—had been difficult for her, even though the ship they'd traveled on was one of the newest and finest in His Majesty's Royal Navy.

Marianne looked up at him and smiled—it was a determinedly brave expression, though her lips quivered slightly. "I am ready."

As they approached the inhospitable looking prison that had contained Napoleon Bonaparte for the last five years, Sin couldn't help being appalled. His journey here was the result of a Parliamentary commission charged with investigating allegations of abuse of the exiled emperor.

Sin had found the evidence he'd seen in England less than persuasive, but looking at this island, he realized that the harsh conditions would be their own form of torture for a man who'd been less than hearty to begin with.

"Oh, Sin," Marianne murmured behind her hand as eight sailors rowed them toward the small stone pier. "It is so . . . brutal."

He could only nod.

A meager delegation stood ready to greet them. Sin recognized Hudson Lowe, Bonaparte's custodian and the governor of the island. There was another civilian, whom he took to be either the former emperor's private physician, Barry O'Meara, or Count Emmanuel de Las Cases, who had remained with Bonaparte for some time, teaching him English, along with providing much-needed companionship. The third man wore a uniform and would be part of the garrison stationed on the island.

Lowe hurried to greet them when they stepped from the small boat. "Your Graces." He bowed low, his face shining with pleasure—no doubt more because they were visitors, than because of their status. Few people, Sin knew, made the journey to Saint Helena—and even fewer were permitted on the island.

Although the exiled emperor was allowed a small entourage, his social life was closely monitored and extremely limited.

When they reached a vehicle that was more cart than carriage, Lowe hesitated. "Perhaps the duchess might wish to remain in Jamestown while you—"

"She will accompany me," Sin said, using what Marianne still called his dukely manner.

"Oh, of course, of course. It is a bit of a trek, and the conditions . . ." He stopped when he realized to whom he was speaking—the man his government had sent to investigate said conditions. "Wilkins," he barked at the soldier. "Help the duch—"

Sin slid his hands around his wife's waist and lifted her up to the running board.

The governor kept up a constant chatter as the wagon rattled through the small village of Jamestown and then began to climb.

Marianne held Sin's hand tightly, her gaze desolate as she took in the inhospitable terrain.

It was hot at this time of year and they both wore summer clothing. Even so, the weather was stifling.

Sin answered the governor's many and pointed questions. He knew the man was wondering what a duke was doing on such an errand—and why he would have brought his spouse on such a long, arduous journey. It wasn't the first time he'd been regarded strangely.

In truth, the trip was too dangerous for his wife, but he could not deny her this chance to meet the man who'd fathered her.

It had taken Sin three years of careful maneuvering to gain this position. They could have come for a visit without the excuse, but it would have raised uncomfortable questions, and Marianne had rejected that option, both for Sin and for their son, Richard—who at four years of age had been far too young to make such a journey. Instead of accompanying them, he was likely running wild under his great aunt Julia's lenient supervision at Wortham.

They crested the rise and Sin had his first look at Longwood House, where the emperor had been confined since shortly after his arrival. It had originally been built as a storage barn and although it had been converted into a residence before Bonaparte's arrival, it was, at best, an exceedingly humble residence—especially for a man who had once owned thirty-nine palaces.

"The General does not come out on most days—not until later in the evening," Lowe said as they pulled up in front of the shuttered building.

There was a guard tower built right beside the structure and sentries were patrolling the pretty, but overgrown gardens.

Sin hopped off the cart and helped Marianne down.

Lowe climbed down slowly and then paused in front of them, rubbing his hands together in a nervous gesture. "Of course, you understand that you are not to address him as Emperor?"

Sin and Marianne nodded; they'd already been instructed by protocol experts before leaving London, who'd made a point of reminding them that Bonaparte was no longer emperor of France, and that he should be called *General*.

"I feel that I must warn you that the General has been, mmm, fractious since we confiscated his fowling piece."

"He had a *gun*?" Marianne blurted.

"Yes, he enjoys hunting."

"Then why did you take it?" she asked.

"He began shooting hens that roamed the property—even though we discouraged such actions. Then two weeks ago he shot General Bertrand's goat when he caught it eating flowers in his garden. And he shot at one of the sentries when they tried to take the gun away from him. He has not felt well enough for hunting lately, so it is not so much of a deprivation. We do allow him to use it in the evenings, of course."

"In the evenings?" Marianne frowned. "But . . . why?"

"For—well, you will see after dinner." He smiled uneasily. "But come, he has been most excited to meet you."

Sin and Marianne exchanged a look. Her father knew who she was, of course—Désirée had told him. They'd learned all the details when they'd visited her in Paris last year where she was still living, refusing to return to her husband or her new country. The main reason for the journey to France had been to bring Richard to meet his grandmother, although they would not tell their son the truth about either of his grandparents until he was older.

"Are you ready, my love?" Sin asked his wife.

She nodded. "I'm ready."

They turned toward the clapboard house.

Napoleon Bonaparte was expecting them.

Marianne struggled to conceal her shock at the man before her. It wasn't just that he looked ill—he did—or that he appeared frail and old beyond his years—he did—it was that she could look him in the eyes.

At five feet and seven-and-a-half inches she was accustomed to being taller than more than a few men. But she had expected the man who'd shaken the world for almost two decades to be a giant. She had always assumed the British newspapers had depicted him as short to ridicule him. Although the man standing before her wasn't tiny, he was no taller than Marianne.

It was Sin, the consummate gentleman and aristocrat, who recovered from his shock first.

He bowed low. "General Bonaparte, thank you for receiving us."

Marianne's father visibly wrenched his gaze from her face. He inclined his head to Sin and gave him a piercing examination.

Marianne flattered herself that he was looking at her husband the way a father would survey a son-in-law.

But it was more likely that he was just scrutinizing an English lord, a class of men he was well-known to dislike.

He seemed to gather his wits and nodded to the hovering Lowe and the servant who'd shown them in. He smiled and the expression was charismatic, for all that his teeth were off-color, which her mother said came from years of eating black licorice.

"The coffee on Saint Helena is superlative," her father said in heavily accented English. "Or perhaps you would prefer *le thé*?" He directed the question to Marianne.

"Coffee sounds lovely," she answered in French.

His smile grew and she could see that her facility with the language pleased him.

"Thank you for escorting us safely here," Sin said, giving Lowe a pointed look.

"Er, yes—yes, of course. If you will excuse me, I've got a few important matters to see to. I will leave you to have your discussion— and collect you after dinner."

Sin nodded and the governor left, taking his soldier with him.

"Please, sit," her father said. He actually appeared *less* at ease now that Lowe had left, almost as if he found it easier to perform a part before his enemy than face his daughter.

Well, she could hardly blame him. She was so nervous there should be a new word for it.

She sat on a settee, surprised when her father sat beside her. Sin gave her a quick look, as if to see whether she was comfortable, and she smiled slightly.

"You take after me," Napoleon said, gripping her hands with both of his, which were swollen and strangely cold for such a hot day. "Same mouth—profile—we get that from my own father," he confided.

He looked so pleased by their resemblance that she couldn't help but smile.

He reached out and touched the bump on the bridge of her nose, startling her.

"So, what Désirée says is true—you were a fighter, eh?"

Her face heated at the unexpected admiration in his eyes. "Yes, for a little while. Before I married."

"Like your father!" He laughed, but it quickly turned into a wet, wracking cough, which persisted.

Marianne stood, thinking to summon a servant, but he shook his head and waved her back down to her seat.

This close to him, she could see that his skin was waxy in appearance. His color was poor and he was corpulent, she presumed from a combination of poor health and inactivity.

The official reason for this visit was the allegation his personal physician had sent to London—that Lowe was cruel and inhumane to him.

"My apologies," he said, once he'd caught his breath. "I find this weather does not agree with me." He gave a sharp, bitter laugh. "What do you think of my home, Marianne?"

The sound of her name in French always surprised her—it was so musical. In English, it was simple and plain, recalling rosy-cheeked milkmaids.

"It is beautiful here," she said carefully. "But perhaps a little . . . harsh."

"It is relentless," he said, the adjective strangely fitting. His jaw tightened and anger livened his tired eyes. "The wind blows every day, all day. It is always damp, and the rot—" He stopped abruptly and flashed a forced smile. "But we will not speak of that." His posture relaxed and he shifted on the settee, stifling a grimace of discomfort as he tried to find a position that suited him.

He turned to Sin, seemingly finished with their conversation.

"You are here because of O'Meara, eh? He is convinced I am being tormented. Ha! I am—but then so are we all who live here.

I am deprived of civilized company, bored out of my wits, and fed with food unfit for hogs." He shrugged. "But other than that, all is well."

Sin asked him about particulars, encouraging him to speak French so that he might explain more fully. As her father chatted with her husband about his conditions, Marianne studied him closely, searching for signs of herself in this stranger.

She'd had almost six years to accustom herself to the fact that she—Marianne Simpson, raised in a circus—was the daughter of Napoleon Bonaparte.

And here she was, actually sitting beside him—Boney, the Nightmare of Europe, the Devil's Favorite, the Corsican Fiend and a hundred other names the world had invented to ridicule and hide their own fear of one average-sized man.

He was charming, but oddly stilted. And the deep lines around his mouth and eyes told her he was often in pain—perhaps even constantly. There had been crude jokes about his inability to sit his horse at Waterloo, and it was common knowledge that he was a victim of severe piles. He was not an old man, and yet he seemed worn, like a once-sharp blade that had been honed too often on a whetstone.

When he released her hand, he immediately settled it on his stomach, his fingers pressing and massaging his abdomen in such a way that stories of his gastric pain had not been exaggerated.

More than all those physical discomforts, however, Marianne suspected that it was his diminished circumstances that chafed him most cruelly. The weight of his failure was an oppressive fog in the room. He had been the first Emperor of France in a millennium; now he was a prisoner reduced to shooting his neighbor's goats and chickens.

And even that was denied him.

They shared excellent coffee and lackluster pastries and sandwiches, talking of the news of the outside world, which came slowly to the island.

Watching her husband and father talk to each other, perhaps

even come to respect one another a little, touched her more deeply than she ever would have expected.

It was painfully clear that the general was much more comfortable with men—not unusual given the trajectory of his life. In spite of his frequent love affairs, she did not think he was a lothario. She doubted he chased women; rather they would have been drawn to him because of his power.

The time she'd spent with her mother last summer had been enlightening, and not always happily so.

Désirée had known of this upcoming journey and had taken pains to make sure Marianne was aware how little respect her father had for women in general, how he'd once been heard to denounce all females as nothing more than "machines for producing babies."

"It was the way he was raised," she'd said, her gaze apologetic.

It was not an unusual viewpoint among men, powerful or otherwise, but it was disheartening.

It also made her realize how fortunate she was in her choice of husband. Her daughters, if she were to be blessed with any, would grow up with a man who valued them for more than their ability to expand their family's dynastic reach.

By the time they finished their coffee, Marianne could see the older man was fatigued.

She was trying to think of a politic way to suggest he rest before dinner, when Sin came to her rescue.

"Would you mind terribly if I took a walk with Marianne? We saw a lovely overlook on the drive up here and she expressed an interest in seeing it closer."

"Of course, of course! Yes, you must see our views." He gave a short bark of unamused laughter. "That is one thing of which there is no shortage." He patted his stomach lightly. "I will leave you to explore at your leisure, if you don't mind." He took Marianne's hand and kissed the back of it. "That way I will be fresh for dinner."

He rang for a servant to show them out, and his eyes were already heavy lidded before they left the room.

"Did you really see a place you wanted to go?" she asked as Sin led her out of the gloomy, dismal house.

"No. But I thought you could use a little time away and some fresh air. I did see a bench situated with a few of those odd trees beside it. We can sit for a while there."

"The house is rather—"

"Dreadful?" he supplied. "Yes, it is. But I daresay most of the others are not much better. The damp, as he mentioned, is quite pervasive. And the house is necessarily dark to combat the oppressive heat."

"I saw a rat beside the leg of the chaise longue."

He winced. "I was hoping you hadn't noticed. Lowe whispered to me that we should leave soon after dinner. It appears the evening entertainment is to gather the servants and dogs in the dining room after the dishes have been cleared and hunt for vermin."

They'd reached the bench and she turned to stare, wide-eyed. "You are jesting, surely!"

"Unfortunately, I am not. That is why they give him back his gun in the evenings."

"Good Lord!"

"I noticed that more than a few of the servants had visible bite marks on their hands."

Marianne shivered. She wasn't a coward when it came to mice, but rats . . . well, she had no desire to shut herself in a room and engage in mortal combat with vermin.

"So," he said.

"So."

"Is he what you thought he'd be?"

She snorted softly. "He has been larger than life for decades. Nobody could live up to that reputation."

Sin looked relieved.

"Did you think I would be disappointed?" she asked.

"I worried you might be. Are you?"

She inhaled deeply and then sighed. "I don't know. I suspect it will take years before I can sort through this day." She cut him an amused look. "You have to admit the two of them—my mother and father—make quite a pair."

His lips curved into that almost smile that never failed to cause a flutter in her belly. "Yes, they are certainly unusual."

She chuckled at his understatement.

Sin kissed her lightly, lingeringly. "But the one thing they did right was produce a delightful daughter."

After spending a month with her mother the previous summer, she had realized the woman was only loosely tethered to reality. She loved her mother, but she couldn't help being grateful that it was practical, caring Sandrine Simpson who'd raised her those first years.

"Perhaps being raised in a circus, by Barnabas, was more of a blessing than I thought."

He laughed, the rich sound warming her. "Perhaps." He slid his arm around her. "Well, are you ready to go back?"

She took his face in her hands. "I'm ready to go anywhere with you." She kissed him.

He cocked an eyebrow at her. "Even if there are rats?"

They laughed and then stood and went to face dinner with her father together.

But perhaps not the rats . . .

Author's Note

Yes! There really was a woman called the Boxing Baroness, although she was neither an actual boxer nor a baroness.

Her name was Mary Anne Pearce and she was briefly the mistress of the Earl of Barrymore, better known as Hellgate, the Rake of Rakes, whom the character of Dominic is loosely based on. Barrymore set Pearce aside as a mistress when he eloped with a more suitable bride.

There is little known about Pearce herself, and many of the stories about her time with Barrymore and afterward are apocryphal. Did Barrymore teach her to box? Did she have actual matches with other women while they were together? Did she fight Hellgate himself in the boxing ring?

Pearce left no record and Hellgate, who died at the age of twenty-three, was not a diarist, which is where most of the historical information about women in traditionally male roles can be found. (See *Following the drum: British women in the Peninsular War* by Sheila Simonson).

What we do know about Pearce is that she ended her days living on the streets, a gin addict who was called the Boxing Baroness for her habit of "boxing the watch." *The watch* was early law enforcement, and it was considered a good time for young bucks (and some ladies, apparently) to get liquored up and fight them when they tried to impose the law.

I like to think of this book as a happy ending for poor Mary Anne—and also an homage to all those women who've been neglected by history and likely received very little fame, acclaim, or money while they competed in a man's world.

There really were women boxers, and if you'd like to read a far grittier depiction of female boxing, I highly recommend Anna Freeman's book *The Fair Fight*, which chronicles the life and times of a fictious female boxer during the Georgian era.

Yes, Gustav IV really was overthrown by his own officers. His wife left him and took the children with her, and he died alone, in obscurity, in Germany.

No, he didn't attempt to regain his kingdom (at least not as far as I know), but I like to think he entertained such grandiose plans in his lonely exile.

The details about Désirée and Napoleon—their engagement and family connections—are true enough, although I've meddled with the chronology a little bit.

Désirée Clary was, to say the least, a character.

She managed to avoid living in the frigid north for many, many years—going so far as to abandon her husband and son so that she could continue to live in Paris, where she was often ridiculed by the French elite for her eccentricities.

Much of the correspondence between her and the man who would become Charles XIV John, King of Sweden and Norway, has been lost.

Just like Mary Ann Pearce, there is so much unknown about Désirée's life. Chiefly, why did she stay away from Sweden and her son for so long? There are all sorts of opinions.

Some say it was because she feared sea travel. Some that she despised life at court and preferred a simpler existence.

Another rumor was that Peter of Russia wanted Charles to divorce Désirée and marry his sister to strengthen the bond between the two countries. Désirée was quoted as fearing divorce if she returned to Sweden.

But, return she did, for her only son's wedding in 1823. Afterward, she never left Sweden again.

There is no castle Himmelhaus; it's a conflation of several delightful German castles. As for traveling circuses—at least the way modern Americans think of a circus, with animals—I've jumped the gun by quite a few years for the "golden age" of circuses. However, there is evidence in the record of many touring groups traveling

Europe from the early 1500s. Most offered plays or harlequinades, but some offered a variety of other entertainments like magicians, tumblers, and the like.

I've also used some (mildly) anachronistic terminology. The first documented use of the term 'pug' for pugilist isn't until a bit later in the century. However, it is commonly accepted that words are around a lot earlier in their spoken form than in print, so I'm happy with the liberties I've taken.

Please keep in mind this story is first and foremost a romance novel. Although a great deal of the story is factual, an even greater part is the product of my imagination. If you wish to learn more about Désirée, Napoleon, or any of the other real historical figures, there are plenty of academic works to slake your curiosity.

Oh, and yes, there really was such a thing as the Secret Office.

Please read on for an excerpt from *The Dueling Duchess,*
the next novel in Minerva Spencer's
Wild Women of Whitechapel series.

Prologue

"Manon Cecile Tremblay Blanchet!" Michel Blanchet hissed.

Cecile always knew she was in trouble when her father used her entire name.

"I'm hurrying, Papa," she protested.

"You must hurry *faster!*" he whispered, his grip on Cecile's arm painful as he pulled her along.

Cecile knew better than to complain or argue. It had been months since either she or her father had gone out on the streets of Paris in broad daylight. Not since her father's patron—the Duc de la Fontaine—had gone to meet a man about smuggling them all out of France but never returned.

Her father had heard nothing about the duke's fate until yesterday, when he discovered the aged aristocrat had been arrested and thrown into the infamous La Force Prison.

As much as Cecile loved the duke—he was like a grandfather to her—she wished that her father could have found some other way to see the old man.

"He is dying, Cecile," her father said when she'd asked why they needed to go to the terrifying prison. "He kept us alive all these years—going to him when he asks for me is the least I can do. We will be safe; Joubert paid the guards well to allow us and the priest to visit. We will be under the protection of God."

Cecile was only fourteen, but even she knew that God had forsaken both the church and its priests—at least in France. Only a few weeks ago she'd read about the slaughter of unarmed priests and nuns by state-sanctioned killers.

But even the minions of the state were no longer safe in France—the beast was eating itself; only last month the loathed and feared Robespierre had himself gone to Madame Guillotine. The duke had said more than once that France had gone mad. He'd promised Cecile and her father that he would get them to England, where blood didn't flow in the streets of the capitol.

Cecile couldn't bring herself to believe that. It felt as if all she'd ever known was violence and death. Could there really be a country where it was safe to walk down the street without fearing arrest?

"Cecile! *Mon Dieu!*"

She realized that she'd almost walked into three gendarmes while she'd been gathering wool.

"I'm sorry, Papa," she whispered, peering from beneath her lashes to see if her behavior had drawn unwanted attention. But the three men had merely continued on their way, laughing raucously at something and paying no attention to the crowds of people who skulked in the shadows and cringed away from them.

La Force Prison loomed up before them like a monster sprouted from the ground itself. If walking down a street in daylight was frightening, then entering the most infamous prison in France—now that the Bastille was nothing but a tumble of stones—was even more terrifying.

"Keep your eyes down, daughter," her father murmured. "And remember that you cannot speak."

She nodded sharply and schooled her features into a slack expression, twitching her shoulders under the ugly lump her father had attached to her shoulder with sticking plaster. It had been their neighbor, Madame Dubois, who'd taught Michel to apply theatrical face paint and disguises. The two of them had worked on Cecile until she didn't even recognize herself.

They'd even changed her hair, rubbing so much charcoal dust into her almost black curls that the glossy locks had turned a dry and brittle gray-brown.

She looked like an old, hunched-over woman, and when she allowed her jaw to hang open, the teeth that Madame Dubois had blackened made her look even older and witless.

Cecile shuffled beside her father as he went through layer after layer of prison authorities, the dull clink of coins occurring with each transaction. New France might have scoured away the exploitative presence of the aristocracy and church, but new levels of bureaucracy had sprung up like rampant weeds to take their place.

Finally, they made it through to the prison itself.

Just as Cecile was about to follow her father and their escort into one of the cell corridors, yet another guard grabbed her arm. "The old lady stays here."

Cecile felt as if her heart had blocked her throat, allowing only a whimper to escape.

"I paid for her, too."

"Not me, you didn't."

Cecile didn't look up, but she could hear the smug leer in his voice.

Her father sighed and reached a shaking hand into the pocket of his ragged coat. He had to dig around before he located a coin. "This is the last of what I have," he said as he handed it over.

The guard grunted.

"What about her?"

"She is simple. I give her no money."

The guard looked disgusted. "Well, get on with you—a quarter of an hour is all, mind."

Her father grabbed her shoulder and Cecile didn't hesitate to follow.

They walked past several open rooms where dozens of prisoners were all shoved together. People called out to them, begging for food, asking them to bear messages, the voices quickly drowning each other out.

They tried to walk faster, to escape the din, but the man escorting them seemed deaf to the agony around him and moved at the pace of a snail.

Cecile had to grit her teeth to keep from screaming. By the time this oaf delivered them to the duke, it would be time to turn back again!

Eons passed before the man stopped and dug around beneath the heavy gray wool coat all the jailors wore, the clatter of many keys filling the dank silence. He fumbled with the lock for another eternity and then shoved opened the door, the shriek of metal on metal making both Cecile and her father jump.

"Ten minutes," the man growled. "And tell the priest he will have to leave then, as well."

They plunged into the darkness of the cell, the only light a weak candle in the corner, on the floor.

When the door slammed behind them Cecile let out a startled squeak.

"Michel?" The weak reedy voice came from near the candle. Cecile realized that the priest was kneeling in front of the duke, their two figures making one large gray shape in the near-darkness of the cell.

"I'm here, er—Citizen."

Cecile cringed as her father almost slipped up and used the duke's honorific. Although it felt like they were alone, they'd learned the hard way that even bricks and mortar had ears.

"He doesn't have long," the priest said. The man struggled to his feet and turned to them. He didn't wear the collar of a priest, but he carried a plain rosary in one hand. The candlelight flickered across his pinched features and she saw him look at her. "And I'm not sure how I feel about this. The girl is so young—and there can be no consum—"

Her father cleared his throat, interrupting the man. It was rude and unlike him. What had the priest been about to say? What about her? Why was—

"You know the reasons we are doing this," her father whispered in a heated voice. "You agreed already. And now—after I've spent every sou I have, you are changing your mind? Do you realize—"

The priest raised his hands in a placating gesture. "I will not go back on my word. I just wanted to make sure she is aware of what will happen here today."

Cecile looked from one man to the other, perplexed. "Father? What—"

"Shh." He pulled her past the priest, toward where the duke was lying on a low cot, covered in a filthy, ragged blanket. He was so thin and pale she hardly recognized him.

Her father bowed his head and sank clumsily to his knees beside the cot, pulling her down with him.

"Your Grace," he whispered and then leaned forward and took the old man's frail hand, kissing the place where his seigneurial ring had sat for so long that there was a permanent indentation in the flesh. "I'm honored that you called upon me in your time of need."

The duke's heavy-lidded gaze was on Cecile, not her father. "Have you told Manon the truth, Michel?"

Cecile wanted to remind all three men that she was right *there*. She also wanted to remind the duke that she went by *Cecile* now, not her hateful first name. But her father would be mortified, so she remained silent.

Michel Tremblay opened his mouth, hesitated, and then turned to Cecile. "The priest is here to marry you to His Grace."

Cecile thought her jaw would come unhinged. She tried to form words, but nothing would come.

A low, raspy chuckle filled the dank chamber. "I cannot blame you for looking so horrified, Manon."

Shame flared in her; she'd insulted a dying man—a man who'd taken care of them like family over the past few years. "I'm sorry, Your Grace. I didn't—"

"Hush, child. I can hardly expect you to be joyous about marrying a corpse." His faded blue gaze flickered to the priest and back. "I'm afraid we have little time. I am the last of my line, Manon. When I go, what I have will go to the jackals who've harried me for years. It is likely a will might be invalidated, but a spouse has rights that cannot be gainsaid, even by the godless rabble who've seized our great country by the throat. This—this *nightmare* will not last forever. And when it is over, you, Manon, will have all that remains to my name."

CPSIA information can be obtained
at www.ICGtesting.com
Printed in the USA
LVHW091759100622
720633LV00001BA/1